Alice's Farm

A RABBIT'S TALE

Maryrose Wood

With illustrations by Christopher Denise

FEIWEL AND FRIENDS

NEW YORK

A Feiwel and Friends Book
An Imprint of Macmillan Publishing Group, LLC
120 Broadway, New York, NY 10271

Library of Congress Control Number: 2019940841

ISBN 978-1-250-22455-2 (hardcover) / ISBN 978-1-250-22456-9 (ebook)
Book design by Mallory Grigg

Feiwel and Friends logo designed by Filomena Tuosto

First Edition, 2020

10 9 8 7 6 5 4 3 2 1

mackids.com

To the real-life Harveys, the truest of friends.

And to Lil, the noblest of Shibas.

The moment of twilight is simply beautiful.

—John Glenn, American astronaut (1921–2016)

CHAPTER ONE

A first spring birthday brings a surprise.

The trouble between rabbits and farmers goes way back, no doubt to the first garden that ever was.

This isn't to say that farmers are bad, or rabbits are bad. Under the right circumstances, a rabbit and a farmer might be tickled to discover the basis of a real friendship between them, if they could ever sit down and put their feet up for a spell, share a glass of lemonade and a fistful of fresh spring clover, and talk things through.

As long as the topic didn't stray to vegetables, they'd probably get along just fine.

Vegetables! See, that's the problem right there. When it comes to vegetables, farmers and rabbits have a serious impediment. It's what you might call a clash of priorities.

Here's the trouble, in case you didn't know: Farmers love to grow, and rabbits love to eat.

Maybe that's putting it too gently. Farmers *have* to grow; it's how they put dinner on their tables and everybody else's tables, too. And no self-respecting rabbit can resist the mouth-watering menu offered by your average vegetable garden. Why, it's practically a rabbit's sworn duty to find the loose board in the wooden fence, the damp earth beneath the chicken wire that's just right for tunneling through, the spare tires foolishly stacked too near the garden gate, like an engraved invitation to climb on up and hop right in.

Once that happens, it's good night, vegetables. Rabbits eat like it's a race to the finish. Two half-grown cottontails loose in a garden can wipe out a whole springtime of effort in a single early morning raid.

You can see why this would trouble the farmer, can't you? And how that farmer might easily start thinking of rabbits as the enemy, and vice versa?

It's hard to know whose side to be on, in this type of situation.

After all, everybody's got to eat.

⁂

The farm across the meadow from where Alice and her littermates lived had been empty for years. Two years, to be precise.

To a grown-up human, two years flits by quick as a sparrow, in a "my, they grow up so fast!" kind of way. To a human child, two years is a long stretch of time indeed. It's the difference between being a third grader and a fifth grader, a little kid or a big one. It's the endless wait to grow tall enough to ride the bumper cars at the fair.

To an eastern cottontail, genus *Sylvilagus*, species *floridanus*, two years is a whole rabbit lifetime, full of joys and sorrows, adventure and friendship, and great-great-great-grandbunnies, too. To a young cottontail like Alice, a farm that had been without a farmer for two years might as well have never had a farmer at all.

Lester was the oldest cottontail in Alice's warren, and even he only dimly remembered the stooped, gray-bearded fellow in overalls who used to live in the big red house. That didn't stop Lester from telling stories about the old man, though.

"He was a deadly one, that farmer!" he'd say to the kits (young bunnies are called kittens, or kits for short). The old showboat of a rabbit would flatten his long ears against his head and make his whiskers quake. "A real villain. With his devious traps and his razor-wire fences, sharp as an owl's beak! All to keep us rabbitfolk out of his garden."

Lester would freeze like a statue and let his eyes go dead and glassy until every kit within earshot whimpered in delicious fear. Then he'd blink himself back to life and stand up tall on his hind legs, batting his front paws like a fighter. "As if rabbitfolk can be kept out of a garden with good eats inside! Not we, not we."

"Not we, not we," the kits would repeat, and ruffle their fur in brave defiance.

Alice would ruffle her fur, too, and flare her nostrils. She'd never laid eyes on a farmer, but she knew full well that farmers and rabbits were sworn enemies, always had been and always would be. All rabbits knew that, from the day they left the nest.

⁂

It was the morning of Alice's first spring birthday. Rabbits have four birthdays a year, one for each season, so the kits of her litter were three months old in human time. There'd been six kittens born and four had made it this far, two does and two bucks, not bad at all. For any winter-born kit to see springtime was a happy occasion. These kits were celebrating in the usual way, by making their first foray past the thicket of shrubs and laurel bushes at the wood's edge into the great wide meadow beyond.

Lester had gone with them, and they were glad about it. That silver-muzzled know-it-all loved to scare the young 'uns with his old rabbits' tales, but there wasn't a cottontail in the valley more skillful in the ways of being out in the open than Lester. The weather was just fine, and the morning sun sparkled on the dewdrops.

Alice was having a grand old time. A meadow seen from the shady edge of the forest is one thing, but when you're tearing back and forth in the bright sunny middle of it, leaping high and slapping your hind feet together from the sheer pleasure of being young and alive, that's a different experience altogether.

The grass spread wide in every direction, and the sky above spread even wider. She play-fought with her brother Thistle, the sweet, undersized runt of their litter, and ran circles through the tender spring greens, stopping now and then for a nibble with Berry, the other buck, a big, impulsive fellow. She touched noses with strong-willed Marigold and then jumped back as if stung with a wild half-twist in the air, to make her sister laugh.

When that wore her out, she flopped onto her side and stretched so long you'd think she was made of taffy. She rolled belly-up and kicked her back feet like she was trying to jump off the sky. She'd never yet felt so open to the world, so small and so big at the same time. If this was what growing up felt like, it was all right.

"Hop on up here, youngster!" Lester commanded.

Alice hopped once, twice, three times—it's a rabbit's inborn wisdom to zigzag when going from place to place, for safety's sake—and landed on a low, wide tree stump the fabled former farmer had never bothered to drill out. She pressed her body close to Lester's. She wasn't scared, exactly, but being out in the open had a strange, floaty quality about it. It was nice to have something warm and familiar to lean against.

"You're missing the view," Lester said. "Why don't you sit up and look?"

Alice rose halfway, until she could see over the tallest grass. So that's what the big red farmhouse looked like! She'd heard the place talked about so many times she'd thought she had a pretty good notion of it, but to a young rabbit with no experience in such matters, big and red was the broken wheelbarrow some human-person had dumped in a forest clearing and left to rust.

The real-life farmhouse was nothing like a wheelbarrow. It was tall as a good-sized tree and scarlet as a holly berry, with white-painted trim around the windows and doors and along the roof's edge. It gave the words *big* and *red* a whole new meaning, and Alice realized how off the mark her imaginings had been.

For instance, she'd never imagined the farmhouse would have a giant, square-cornered truck sitting in the driveway, with its back wide open and people swarming in and out. They were man-people with thick arms, and they moved furniture and boxes off the truck and through the front door of the house. Back and forth they went, with purpose, the way ants carry crumbs back to the anthill.

It was Alice's first glimpse of a human.

"Lester," she said, whiskers aquiver. "I thought you said the farmhouse was empty."

"I know what I said, youngster." He thumped his back feet, a sign of irritation. "When I said it was empty, that's because it was empty. Now it's got people crawling all over it." Lester didn't sound happy about this, but he didn't bolt, either, so Alice knew not to be alarmed. If the sight of people was an emergency, he'd either freeze or bolt. That's what rabbits did when danger was near.

And Lester was a bona fide expert about people, as he'd once nibbled and shredded his way through a box full of mail-order catalogs and yellowed paperbacks that had been left by the roadside. It was a real treasure trove of information, judging from the things the old rabbit knew, or claimed to.

The other kits sensed a change in Lester's mood and gathered close to the stump. Thistle was too small and scared to jump up next to Alice, but Berry and Marigold weren't. They hopped up and huddled against one another to watch the goings-on down by the farm.

At the back of the truck, three men struggled with an item that was bigger than they were. They grunted and groaned as they finally got it out of the truck and onto a wheeled dolly, which they pushed into the house.

"That, my young friends, is what is known as an armoire." Lester flicked his ears forward twice, for emphasis. "Arm. Waahr."

"Arm Waahr," Alice repeated, learning it. "What's it do?"

Lester flipped his ears to one side. "An armoire is a thing to put other things in. People do love their things."

After a while, the men returned, pushing the empty dolly. One shoved a hand in his pocket and offered what he found there to the others. They each took a piece, put it in their mouths, and began to chew.

Alice's nose twitched as she tried not to sneeze. Even half a meadow away, the harsh, minty smell was stronger and sweeter than any mint she'd ever nibbled, and she'd nibbled plenty in the weeks since the snows had melted and the early-greening plants had peeped through the soil.

The men chewed and chewed, but didn't seem to swallow. Probably something to sharpen their teeth, she thought.

Soon the man-people went back to work. Boxes, lamps, dressers, more boxes. Lester's ears flipped to the other side. "Look. There's a bed. That's what people use for a sleeping burrow."

Alice stood up all the way, to see this bed-burrow. "That's big enough for ten people, at least," she exclaimed.

"You'd think. But people are funny. They mostly sleep in ones and twos, even in winter. Now *that* bed is big enough for two."

The movers were having a hard time squeezing a king-sized mattress through the doorway. But they got it in.

"How many farmers does that make?" Thistle asked from the ground, too nervous to keep count.

"Three, so far," Lester said. "Looks like we're in for a real infestation."

Something less big, with bars on all four sides, came out of the truck.

"Is it a trap?" Berry blurted. Marigold and Thistle squeaked with dismay, and no wonder. Most animals will flinch at anything that looks remotely like a cage.

Lester's tail twitched, but his voice stayed calm. "No, not a trap. There's a word for it, let me think . . . crib! That's it. It's a sleeping cage for a baby people."

The kits took this in with a collective shiver. Baby rabbits slept all together in shallow nests dug by their mothers, lined with grass and leaves and soft fur plucked from the mothers' own bellies. But perhaps baby people were dangerous in some way, and needed to be kept apart.

They all pondered this, until Marigold piped up. "Baby people are so . . ."

"Ugly!" All four kits said it at the same time, and laughed. You wouldn't have been able to hear them, of course. No human ear could. Even a belly laugh from a rabbit in the throes of utter hilarity is quiet as the whisper of wind in the trees.

Still, it's a well-known fact that rabbits have terrific senses of humor.

Less well-known is that their favorite thing to joke about is baby people. It's not nice, but can you blame them? Even the cutest baby people are nowhere near as cute as the least cute baby bunny rabbits, and every rabbit knows it. They're conceited about it, to be honest.

Alice laughed along with the others, but she wasn't sure how to feel about this turn of events. Farmers in the big red house! Baby people in sleeping cages! It was a lot to take in.

Lester hopped off the stump, and the others followed. Caution had overtaken them all since seeing that crib, and their zigzags back across the meadow were somber and silent. They didn't stop until they reached the place where the shade of the treetops cooled the grass beneath their feet. They'd be harder to see here in the shadows, and closer to good hiding places, too, and that's all pretty important to a rabbit.

Alice blinked and hunkered down into a loaf shape. "Lester, will it be good or bad to have farmers in the house again?" she asked.

Lester didn't answer right away. When he did, he sounded wise as the Great Rabbit himself.

"Life's been quiet for a spell," he said. "That was bound to change, sooner or later. Looks like today's the day."

"But aren't farmers dangerous?" Thistle chirped.

"There's danger and rewards, young 'un. The danger is great, and so are the rewards. It's been long time since I tasted broccoli," he added, sounding dreamy. "And brussels sprouts. And Swiss chard, oh, my! A long time indeed." He flicked his ears, thinking. "Remember, we're rabbitfolk. A rabbit is way more clever than a farmer."

"Really?"

"Are we?"

"Are you sure?" All the kits wanted to know.

"There's no doubt about it." Lester paused for effect. "Anyway, it's not the farmers you have to worry about. It's their dang dogs."

"Dogs!" The kits' eyes went blank and their bodies froze midbreath. Their mottled brown fur blended perfectly with the muted tones of dirt, dead leaves, and the rugged bark of the trees. That's called camouflage, and it means that a rabbit holding stock-still at the wood's edge is as invisible as a visible thing can be. Anyone watching would swear the four little rabbits and one big one had vanished in a blink.

Alice was first to move again, tipping her muzzle upward to sniff. Her wriggling nose cataloged the grassy perfume of the meadow, the salty tang of man-people at work, and that stinging odor of mint.

She wasn't sure what a dog smelled like, but she didn't think it was any of those. Even so, her rabbit nerves tingled, and every muscle begged to race into the shadowed safety of the woodland, back to the cozy underground burrow that she and the others called home.

Lester sniffed, too, and said nothing.

"Do *these* farmers have a dang dog?" Thistle asked, taking one tiny hop closer to the wood's edge.

"We'll soon find out. Until we do, it's one hop at a time, young 'un." As if to prove the point, Lester jumped sideways into the sun where any hawk could have spotted him, and nibbled the fresh grass, too. "Yes sir! I expect we'll find out soon enough."

CHAPTER TWO

Carl's whole life is wrecked.

"Sit, Foxy! Make Foxy sit, would you, champ? I can't see out the back."

"Sit, girl," Carl mumbled.

Foxy kept staring out the car window, panting right in Carl's face. Her front paws dug into the tops of his thighs. That dog was being a real pain.

That was one way of looking at it, anyway. The other was that Carl's dad was the one being a pain. Carl was inclined toward this second interpretation. His main grievance was that they'd been driving for three hours and his dad had only stopped the car once, even though they'd passed approximately one million drive-thrus. Grinning buckets of crackle-coated fried chicken! Triple-decker meat burgers! Curly fries dripping with gloopy, cheesy mystery sauce! This was fine dining, in Carl's opinion.

His parents felt differently. It had been quite a few months since Brad and Sally Harvey, the reigning adults of the Harvey household, jointly decided they were henceforth going to cook everything from scratch. "Henceforth, we will eat like royalty," Brad had proclaimed in a kingly voice, as Sally nodded and smiled. A pair of cardboard crowns from a burger drive-thru would have made it comical, but they weren't kidding. "That means whole foods only, prepared at home."

"But what if I only want half?" Carl had objected, which led to a long explanation that defied the laws of math and common sense. An entire Frosted Toasty-Tart with cherry-flavored filling and candy sprinkles was not a whole food, but half an apple was?

The boy was confused, but soon enough he discovered the awful truth: What the Harveys' royal decree really meant was that, henceforth, Carl couldn't get within ten feet of a decent French fry, a supersized cola, or any foods that were of the type that some nice young person in a uniform packed up in a paper bag and handed you through a window. It was just one unhappy meal after another.

On a day like this, you'd think his parents would make an exception, but nope. Sally had been so unreasonable as to pack a cooler for the trip, full of carrots and hummus sandwiches on whole-grain sourdough bread she'd baked herself, a fact she mentioned far too often, in Carl's opinion. Also, he still wasn't clear where hummus came from. Did anybody know? It was so beige and smooshy. *Highly* suspicious.

"Champ? The dog? Please?" his dad said, less nicely this time.

"Almost there, honey," Sally added.

Carl wasn't a big fan of champ, but he really did not like being called honey. This was a relatively new and strongly held opinion that had taken hold of him since he'd turned ten. Double digits have a way of changing a person's outlook on such matters. He hadn't worked up the nerve to tell his mom yet, but that day was coming, and soon.

Not that his name was such a masterpiece. He was named after Carlsbad Caverns, a park full of caves that his parents had liked to visit before he was born. It was hard for him to imagine Brad and Sally exploring caves. He'd seen them carry a stroller down the subway steps lots of times, though.

"Carlsbad!"

"Okay, Dad! Come on, girl, *sit*." Carl pushed Foxy's rump down onto the seat and rubbed her belly to keep her occupied. Naming your first-born child after a cave was bad, but calling a dog Foxy was just inaccurate. A dog is a dog; a fox is a fox. Case closed, as his dad liked to say.

Nope, nope, nope. Picking names was not a thing his parents were good at.

Neither, it seemed, was picking places to live.

"Prune Street?" he blurted as the car turned down an even narrower and less inhabited road than the one they'd been on. "You're kidding, right?"

"Not kidding." His dad sounded weary, like he needed a supersized cola to perk him up. "Eleven Prune Street is where we're going."

"Is that our new address?"

"Yes."

"Prunes are very tasty," Sally added.

"Your statement is false," Carl said in his robot voice. Prunes were what happened when plums were left out to go bad. Carl had known this ever since Sally became obsessed with her dehydrator. The dehydrator was a thing that took perfectly good fruit and made it rubbery and hard to eat. Sally had paid actual money for this contraption and loved it like a sister, or so it seemed. When the holidays came, she filled approximately one billion glass jars with ruined fruit and gave them as gifts. It was a wonder anyone was still speaking to her.

Eleven Prune Street! Carl slumped as far as the seat belt would let him. Their old address was normal: 1260 Oxford Street, Apartment 5F,

Brooklyn, New York. It was one block from the subway that could take you anywhere, even to the beach, plus the bus stopped right on the avenue if you didn't feel like taking the train.

School was a ten-minute walk from home, and the big park with the lake and the carousel was a twelve-minute walk. Most of his friends lived nearby, and Frank's Market was right downstairs. It was so close that he used to be allowed to go there by himself to buy his favorite treat. Captain Skeeter's Crunch Nuggets! Now, *there* was a candy bar.

Of course, that was before the dehydrator arrived and the henceforth rule went into effect. No more Crunch Nuggets for Carl. Now his mom just gave him dried-out rubbery fruit when he wanted something sweet. Or carrot sticks. Carrot sticks! The indignity!

Sally peeked into the back seat. "Imagine how much Foxy is going to like living in the country!" she said, much too cheerfully. "Maybe she'll learn to chase rabbits."

His dad snorted. "That dog wouldn't know what to do with a live rabbit if she saw one."

"Woof," Foxy said, not bothering to open her eyes.

"Don't make fun of Foxy," Carl said rudely. He'd just realized the nearest bar of Captain Skeeter's Crunch Nuggets was three hours away, in Brooklyn, and he wasn't going back there anytime soon. "She didn't ask to move. You're forcing her."

That made his parents settle down. But Carl felt bad that they didn't scold him about being rude. That's how he knew that moving to the country was a real catastrophe: from the way his parents had almost completely stopped scolding him, even when he was angling for it.

It wasn't one hundred percent fair to blame them, either, since the move was fifty percent his fault. Here's how he figured it: Last summer he'd gone to sleepaway camp for the first time. He'd begged and begged, because his best friend, Emmanuel, was going and had done a powerful sales job about how fun the place was, all pocketknives and swimming holes and secret handshakes. The camp was upstate, in a woodsy kind of place that looked a lot like the last hour of the drive to Prune Street.

After doing their "due diligence," which was a mysterious ceremony the Harvey parents always performed before making a decision, they said yes. Carl was thrilled. He'd driven up with Emmanuel's family, who seemed to handle the change of scenery just fine. But when Brad and Sally arrived at the end of two weeks to pick up the boys, they took one look at the trees and, blammo. It was like they'd been hypnotized. They couldn't stop talking about how *beautiful* it was, how lovely to be in *nature*, how nice it was to be away from the *city*, which was so dirty and smelly and crowded.

What a tragic mistake he'd made, and all because he wanted to learn to shoot a bow and arrow! If Carl had never gone to camp, his parents wouldn't have ever noticed how dirty and smelly the city was.

Carl had stopped rubbing Foxy's belly somewhere along the way. Now she was up again, panting like a racehorse and fogging up the window with her breath. She looked excited and happy, but that's dogs for you. Life is all chew toys and belly rubs as far as a dog's concerned, even in the midst of disaster.

"You dumb dog," Carl whispered, right into the dog's neck, so no one could hear. "Our whole life is wrecked, and you don't even know it."

Foxy grinned like she'd just won a prize.

Carl made his most unhappy expression: He pushed out his lower lip; his mouth scrunched upward and his eyebrows glowered down, as if all his features were trying to reach the middle of his face. He would have liked it if just one living creature would admit what a horrible situation they were in.

His sister, Marie, snored in her car seat next to him. Marie was named after a famous scientist his parents admired. She'd recently turned one, and Carl still didn't quite see the point of her. All she did was eat applesauce, mess her diaper, and prattle in baby talk that no reasonable person could understand, although Brad and Sally always pretended that they could.

"Looks like the moving truck beat us here." Brad turned the steering wheel all the way to the right and pulled over on the side of the road, since the driveway was occupied.

Sally unbuckled her seat belt and twisted around to face Carl with a goofy smile on her face. "That's it, honey. The big red house!"

Carl craned his neck to see past the moving truck.

"That's our house? All of it?" he asked, disbelieving. You could fit four whole apartments into a house that size.

"It's not just a house. It's a farm." Brad unlocked the car doors, *ka-chunk,* and let out a long, satisfied breath. "Come on, champ! The place is amazing. Wait until you see it."

CHAPTER THREE

The cottontails gather and decide.

The warren held a meeting that very night; Lester made sure of it—but only Lester, Alice, and her siblings knew what it was going to be about.

The last warren meeting had been a few days after Alice was born, and its purpose was deciding how to share a patch of wild winter crocus that had been discovered on the far side of the creek. Being a tiny, hairless, and helpless thing at the time, as all newborn rabbits are, she'd had to send her regrets.

There hadn't been a meeting since, but that's cottontails for you. Some types of rabbits live in busy underground towns with lots of rules about who's in charge and who isn't, who gives the orders and who does what they're told. That's natural for those rabbits, but it's not the cottontail way.

Cottontails are more like Quakers, if you know anything about Quakers. They're peaceable by nature, hold a wide range of opinions, and mind their own business as much as seems prudent. There isn't any one rabbit or group of rabbits in charge. If there's something to decide or discuss, they gather together and sit, quietly, to think about whatever the problem is.

Being still and quiet takes practice, as rabbits are skittish by nature and ready to bolt over the slightest thing. However, if most of the warren manages to stay calm enough and quiet enough long enough, sooner or later, the right thing to do becomes clear to everyone.

It's a slow-paced system, no question, but it works for cottontails. Most creatures could probably do with less talk and tussle about who's right and what's wrong, and more time spent in quiet, companionable rumination. That's just an opinion, of course, and as any wise old rabbit could tell you: Opinions are common as chickweed, but not nearly so easy to yank up by the roots.

It took time for the cottontails to gather. All that fresh spring grass after a winter diet of twigs and tree bark made them want to stay out and graze until it was good and dark. Cottontails are crepuscular feeders, which means they prefer to eat at twilight, in the half-lit hours near sunrise and sunset. For that dim little while, when the day predators are changing shifts with the night predators, the world is as safe as it gets, for a rabbit.

Soon enough the sun was down and the stars were peeping through the purple sky. Once the owls woke up and started to *whoo-whoo* back and forth with breakfast invitations, the cottontails had had enough, and they scurried underground for the meeting.

They called their home Burrow, since that's what it was: an abandoned groundhog's burrow the rabbits had taken over. Groundhogs are powerful diggers and much larger than cottontails, so the tunnels of Burrow were spacious. The two longest tunnels led to a large den, big enough for a whole fluffle of rabbits to gather. It was pitch-dark down there, but smell and hearing are more important than sight to a rabbit anyway.

The cottontails arrived in ones and twos, and the den began to fill. Alice and her littermates huddled together, teeth chattering with excitement.

"What a discovery we made today!" Thistle said quietly, to Alice. "What do you suppose will happen when Lester tells everybody about the—you-know-whats?"

"We'll find out soon enough. I just hope . . ." What did she hope? She thought for a minute. "I hope we get to a chance see them."

Thistle's body tensed, for he'd learned his lessons well. "*See* them? But what if they're deadly, like the other one was? He was a real villain!"

"From a distance, I mean," said Alice, to calm him. Not all rabbits are curious, but after one trip to the meadow, Alice was discovering that she was.

Marigold tipped her nose up and sniffed. "I think our mother's here," she said. This fact was of only mild interest to the kits. Their mother was with the other does. She'd recently had another litter, but they were still in the nest. Cottontail mothers don't trouble themselves about babysitters. They just cover the nest with leaves and grass and go about their business, stopping by twice a day to feed whatever little ones remain. This might sound neglectful, but baby cottontails only stay in the nest for two weeks anyway. After that they're on their own.

Lester was there, too, of course, and an older doe named Violet who was nearly as old as Lester. She was missing an ear tip due to a long-ago run-in with a trap. That she'd survived it at all lent her a battle-scarred air that commanded respect. When Violet spoke, everyone listened.

The press of warm bodies underground grew until the den could hold no more. One rabbit thumped a hind foot, as a way of saying, "Let's get started!" Others did the same, and the vibration of all those thumping feet rumbled through the earth. It made Alice's belly tighten and her ears tingle. Something important was about to happen.

Lester combed his whiskers three times with his front paws and gave his ears a shaking out. Then he spoke.

"There are farmers again," he said. "Farmers in the big red house."

It was big news, no doubt about it. Muzzles twitched and fast-beating hearts beat faster, as the rabbits took it in.

"Same farmer?" asked Violet.

"New ones," Lester replied.

"Did you see them?"

"Nope. We saw their things, though, going into the house. Judging from what I saw, I'd say it's a breeding pair, plus a kit or two. Maybe a small litter. Ha ha!"

All those pressed-together bunny bodies shook with silent laughter. A litter of baby farmers! That was about the ugliest, most hilarious thing any of them could imagine.

"Any cats?" someone asked when the laughter faded.

Cats were no friends to rabbits, but most house cats were overfed to the point of never being hungry at all. They'd chase rabbits for fun but without ambition, and would give up as soon as they grew bored, or were summoned by the mesmerizing whir of a can opener. The real danger posed by cats was their hypnotic, predatory stare. Humans will sometimes say "I nearly died of fright" as a way of being dramatic, but rabbits truly can die of fright, and plenty have been known to expire just from staring too long at a cat.

"Cat status, unknown," Lester replied.

"Dogs?" Violet asked, as calmly as any rabbit could.

"Unknown at this time. That's my report." Lester drew back, satisfied. Now it was time to stay quiet and think.

"Dang dogs," one of the bucks remarked, interrupting the silence. The very notion of dogs was enough to put the whole warren on edge. Soon, more rabbits broke the quiet.

"Burrow is too close to the farmhouse," one rabbit said.

"Too close, yes! Too close!" others repeated.

"We could leave, maybe?" another rabbit suggested.

"Leave!" Lester flattened his ears. "Because of farmers? This is not bad news, friends. Why, it's a golden opportunity."

"To get caught in a trap, you mean," young Berry exclaimed. Very likely he was still thinking of that crib, but to cry "trap" in a crowded burrow was poor manners. A few older rabbits growled at the kit, to teach him a lesson. The one nearest to him swiped him with a paw.

"Rabbitfolk don't live long," Violet said sternly, beginning a familiar saying.

"But we can still be careful," Berry finished, contrite. All two-week-old kits were taught that old chestnut on the day they left the nest. "Sorry, everyone," he added.

"Apology accepted, youngster. You're not thinking straight, but that's because you've never feasted on a garden full of broccoli. Why, it's dee-lectable!" Lester often talked like the magazine advertisements he'd once eaten. "You kits don't know what you're missing. I bet you don't know the difference between cauliflower and clover."

"We've lived without a garden to raid for two springtimes already, two summers, two harvests," one of the does observed. "What difference does broccoli make now?"

Lester's whiskers quivered in outrage. "Have you no cottontail pride? These young 'uns have never so much as tasted a radish! Where's the meaning in a life so deprived? And Swiss chard! Oh my!"

"I like my life just fine so far, even without radishes," Marigold primly declared.

"Tsk, tsk." Lester shook his head. "A cottontail with no love for vegetables." But he didn't go on about it. There was no need. He'd made his point, and the others had made theirs. Now it was time to think.

"Let's be quiet," Violet said, a gentle reminder. The rabbits settled down, jaws grinding like tiny motors to help them concentrate. The grinding went on for a long time. At the end of it, Violet spoke again.

"Here's what the ground tells me. Some of us long for radishes, and some of us are content without. But even those who don't care about vegetables care about a dang dog. On this we all agree," she concluded. "A dang dog will be trouble for all of us."

"No doubt, no doubt."

The warm thrum of agreement ran through the rabbits' pressed-together bodies, flank to flank. A dog on the farm would be a problem indeed.

"If there *is* a dang dog, the radishes won't matter," one cottontail said, after a bit. "We'd never be able to raid the garden anyway."

"Cowards," Lester muttered, not unkindly.

Others chimed in with suggestions:

"If there *is* a dang dog, we shouldn't let the kits out of the woods."

"If there *is* a dang dog, none of us should set a paw in the meadow, ever again!"

"If there *is* a dang dog, we ought to move away from the farmhouse altogether."

Alice was young, and it was her first warren meeting, but she knew she had as much right to speak as anyone. She'd been listening hard—listening with both ears, as the rabbitfolk say. Now she decided to speak.

"It seems to me," she said, in a clear, high voice, "that we ought to find out if there's a dog at all, before making rules and jumping to conclusions and so forth."

"I agree!" Thistle chimed in, to no one's surprise. Thistle idolized his sister, who'd always been kind to him, despite him being half the size of the rest of his litter. Most runts wouldn't have made it to three months, but Alice had kept an eye on him, making sure he got his chance to graze and teaching him how to zigzag properly, even though his hops were so much shorter than the others'.

"I'm with Alice, too. Good thinking from the youngster," Lester said firmly.

"Quiet," Violet repeated, but she hardly had to say it. The rabbits fell silent again, brains whirring, jaws grinding.

"On this we all agree," Violet said at last. "Someone should go find out if there's a dang dog or not."

But she didn't say how it should be done, or who should be the one to do it. Cottontails would never presume in that way.

Alice felt the quiet, quick breathing all around her, the hum of rabbit bodies with their tiny hearts beating fast. It was dark down here in Burrow, cozy and safe, with so many of her own kind close by. There was barely enough room to turn around.

But the memory of the morning's adventure in the meadow was fresh in her nose and whiskers, too, the grassy, sun-bright, wide-open joy of it. And that was only the meadow's middle! What would it be like to go all the way across?

Crossing would be dangerous, but being a rabbit was dangerous. Everything about rabbits was designed with constant peril in mind: their keen ears and nervous noses; their big eyes, which were placed so far back on the sides of their heads they could practically see behind them; their powerful hind legs for running away—even their talent for making new kits year-round, to replace the ones who had been lost. Life at the bottom of the food chain was no picnic, and only a foolish bunny would pretend otherwise.

Then again, thought Alice, whose ears and nose were as sharp as any of her kind, and who could bolt like the wind, too—it's not easy to sneak up on a rabbit.

"I'll go." Alice stretched her back legs, one after another. "I'd like to get a look at the farm. And the farmers. And I wouldn't mind tasting a radish someday, too."

"We all agree," Violet said, after a moment. "Alice will go."

"I'll go, too," said little Thistle. "With Alice."

Thistle's small size made him extra vulnerable, even for a kit. But everyone knew how inclined he was to follow his sister around. "Alice's other tail," the older kits liked to tease. If he wanted to go, that was his choice.

Lester stroked his whiskers. "I won't go with you. I'm slower than I was, and getting slower by the day. But I'll tell you all I remember about the farmhouse and the yard, and about farmers, too. And their dang dogs."

"Thank you," said Alice. "That will be a great help. Thistle and I will go tomorrow morning, after the breakfast graze."

The meeting was over. No other rabbit volunteered, but two rabbits were enough. Enough to find out if there was a dang dog or not, with a fifty-fifty chance of one of them making it back to Burrow with the news.

It would be nice if both kits made it home, of course. But if not, there were plenty of young kits getting ready to leave the nest, and plenty of new litters on the way. The warren wouldn't be running out of rabbits any time soon.

Still, before they left the meeting den, each of the rabbits of Burrow came up to Alice and Thistle. One after another, they touched noses and said,

"Use your ears. Use your nose."

"Use your ears. Use your nose."

"Use your ears. Use your nose."

It was a cottontail's way of saying "be careful," but rabbits are always careful and don't need to be reminded. What they were really saying was "good luck and farewell, it's been nice to know you," in case it turned out that there was a dang dog out there, or a farmer's trap, or a lean-flanked fox waiting in the shadows, or an owl or hawk swooping down from above—well, you get the idea.

Alice understood what they meant. So did Thistle. It didn't bother the two young'uns, or make them sad, or even particularly afraid. Cottontails aren't sentimental about all the ways they're likely to get eaten. That's just the way life is, for a rabbit.

CHAPTER FOUR

First night in a new house.

You may remember how young Carlsbad Harvey, once a proud city dweller with a collection of expired subway passes to prove it, now a reluctant resident of 11 Prune Street, had taken half the blame for his family's move upon his own bug-spray-scented, summer-camp-loving self.

Lots of kids blame themselves for stuff that has nothing to do with them. Often, it's because the grown-ups on duty won't spill the beans about the real reasons for a big change. Brad and Sally were better than most in that respect, and they'd done their best to explain, but Carl's math was still way off.

Their trip upstate to retrieve Carl and Emmanuel from Camp Kids in the Woods was a factor, true. The landscape was magnificent, home to straight-trunked hemlocks and sugar maple trees that grew there long before Brooklyn had a bridge. Brad and Sally made cartoon googly eyes at each other as they swiped real estate brochures from near the cash register at the diner where the gang stopped for breakfast on the way home.

But that was only ten percent of it.

Another ten percent came a few months later, at Thanksgiving, when a supersized New York City street rat scared Sally half to death by crashing into the front wheels of Marie's stroller. They were on a last-minute excursion to Frank's Market to get cranberries, which Brad and Sally always forgot to buy in advance. The Thanksgiving Day cranberry run was an annual holiday ritual that usually had an air of comedy about it.

Not this year. *SQUEAK!* went the rat, thudding into the wheels so hard it had to stop and shake it off before skittering away. Sally screamed like an actor in a horror movie, and Marie yelled mysterious baby words, which sounded something like "Baahhhmowww!" Bad mouse, maybe?

Sally quickly regrouped, at least on the outside. She managed to buy the cranberries and get her racing heart and a gleefully *bahhhmowwwing* Marie back to the apartment, where arriving holiday guests were already kicking off their shoes in the hall. On the inside, something had snapped. By the time appetizers were served, she'd stolen to the bathroom with her phone to quietly plug her email address into a half-dozen websites with names like "Your Country Dream House," "Back to Nature Real Estate," "Elite Rural Properties" and so on.

So the rat was to blame as well. But ten percent for summer camp and ten percent for the rat still left eighty percent of the blame unaccounted for. All of it belonged to the parachute.

This was no ordinary parachute. It was a golden parachute that had been given as a gift to Brad Harvey by his job, months before the drive to summer camp and the terrifying Thanksgiving of the Rat.

It was a funny kind of present, since the golden parachute was also a way of saying Brad didn't have to go to work anymore. That's how Brad and Sally had explained it to Carl. You'd think an object of that size and so prone to glittering would be tough to keep hidden, but Carl never could manage to find it, even after looking under all the beds and conducting a sneaky search of his parents' dresser drawers and closets.

Meanwhile, Brad, who used to get up at dawn, put on a suit, and kiss his sleeping family goodbye with a smooth-shaved chin and skin that smelled like pine, now slept late in the mornings and didn't shave at all.

He grew his hair long and tried different kinds of beards. For a while he was a drummer in a band. Then he was a bike mechanic. He became obsessed with beekeeping, even though there was no place to keep bees in the apartment, but he read a stack of books about it and bought himself a real beekeeper's suit. To Carl it looked like a space suit from the old science fiction movies, the black-and-white ones that predicted that by the far-off year 1995, the Planet Earth would be a garbage dump and humans would live on Mars.

Brad and Sally used to watch TV in the late evenings after Carl went to bed. Once the golden parachute arrived, they spent their nights talking. Voices were kept low, but phrases like "the money won't last forever" and "just pick something!" and "but what about school?" would find their way to Carl's half-asleep, half-awake ears.

The next thing that happened was that Brad started spending a lot of time on his computer.

"Are you looking for a new job?" Carl asked one night after dinner, when he saw his dad gazing intently at the laptop, writing down phone numbers.

"More than a job, champ. A new life. One that means something. Check this out."

There it was, in rows of tiny photographs scrolling across the screen. A big red house tucked into a grassy slope, with white trim around the windows and no other houses in sight. It had a front porch with a swing seat and a barn out back.

Inside the house were way more rooms than Carl was used to. Even in the bedrooms, the windows looked out at trees, not buildings.

"You like it?" His dad had smiled expectantly, like the answer really had to be yes.

"It's nice," Carl admitted, never dreaming he'd be waking up in that house before long.

⁂

Carl took a cautious spoonful of the oatmeal his mother had glopped into his bowl from a big pot on the stove. Without even asking, she'd sprinkled it with chopped-up fruit that had already given the best of itself to the dehydrator.

Taste-wise it was no Fruity Pebbles, and the oatmeal was so thick his spoon just might be able to stand up on its own. Carl proceeded to investigate.

"Did you sleep okay, honey?"

"I guess." He always found it odd that if you couldn't remember how you slept, it meant you slept well. For a first night in a new house, it hadn't been bad. Everything from his room in Brooklyn had survived the trip in the mover's truck: his bed with the deep drawers underneath and the race-car comforter on top, the blue-painted dresser for his clothes, the shelves for his books and bins of small toys.

Carl had been most concerned about Big Robot, but the big guy seemed okay. The toy blinked and made noise when it had fresh batteries in it and stood there keeping an eye on things when it didn't, which was most of the time. Still, the robot was a friendly presence, an old friend who still meant a lot to Carl. When Grandma and Grandpa Harvey had sent it as a gift, years earlier, boy and robot were the exact same height. Now Big Robot barely came up to Carl's waist.

"It's nice to see you up so early," Sally said, chopping away at something on the counter. "This is my favorite time of day."

"I couldn't help it," Carl groused. "All those windows! It was like someone turned on the lights."

Brad and Sally had unpacked Carl's room first, so he'd feel "right at home," as his dad had said, and he wasn't even kidding. But Carl's new room was way bigger than his old room. It made his bed seemed tiny, like a little kid's bed. Big Robot looked small and lost, like a dumb old toy.

And that sun! His room in Brooklyn had one window that didn't get any sun until the afternoon because the apartment building next door was in the way. His new room had windows on three sides and the sunbeams poured right in. The light had woken him up gently but firmly. "If I've got to be up, then so do you, my fine young fellow!" That's what it felt like the sun was saying, anyway.

He could have stayed in bed on principle, but the breakfast smells rising from the kitchen were hard to ignore. He'd gotten dressed and headed downstairs. He fully intended to still be crabby about moving, but now he was curious, too. And hungry. He'd been dreaming about pancakes, but a Frosted Toasty-Tart would have done just fine.

Instead, oatmeal with rubber fruit. Carl decided to keep an open mind. He took another taste. The fruit was chewy, dark and sweet. Could it be prunes? That would be an awful joke, if so.

"Isn't it nice to hear the birds?" his mom said, still at the stove. From the smell of things, she'd moved on to making applesauce. No surprise there. Marie was pretty much made of applesauce. The baby was already up, buckled into her high chair, happily kicking her feet in mismatched socks. Foxy was curled up in her new dog bed, which Carl had picked out for her before the move. It looked like a miniature fancy sofa, with throw pillows and everything.

"Honey, did you hear what I said about the birds?"

"What birds?" Carl's concentration was on the spoon. He'd shored it up by heaping oatmeal around the base and adding a foundation of prune bits, but it still tipped to one side.

"The birds outside. Listen."

He listened.

There were no car engines spluttering, no garbage trucks rumbling, no faint sounds of the TV coming from the apartment next door.

But there were birds, lots of them, singing prettily in all different ways, high and low, fast and slow. It was nothing like the city-bird sound of pigeons cooing and clumsily flapping their wings. Pigeon wings never seemed to work right anyway. If Carl ever grew wings, he'd make sure he learned how to operate them, that's for sure.

"Wait," he said, staring at the spoon, nudging it right, then left, then right again. "Does this mean we're farmers now? Are we going to have cows and stuff?"

Sally brought a bowl of fresh applesauce to Marie and pulled up a chair for herself next to the high chair.

"Farmer can mean a lot of different things," she said.

"I just want to know if I'm going to have to milk a cow."

"Moooo!" Marie was learning the animal noises. She banged her plastic spoon on her tray and the applesauce splattered all over. "Moooo! Da da!"

Brad strode into the kitchen. He wore a checked shirt and jeans and boots, and he looked as happy as Carl had ever seen him.

"Good morning, all! What a beautiful family! What a beautiful day!" The man was practically singing.

Carl let the spoon fall. "Dad, are we farmers now?"

"We sure are." He grabbed a corner of Marie's bib and wiped the goo off her face. "Gross!" he said cheerfully, and kissed the baby's head.

"Mooo!" she yelled. "Moo moo, faam!"

He poured coffee for himself and straddled a chair at the table. "We don't have a cow yet, Marie, but who knows? Maybe someday we will."

"Don't promise things, Brad," Sally warned, but her eyes were smiling.

"I'm talking one cow, not a thundering herd. Although a flock of goats might be fun. Goat milk and goat cheese, yum. And chickens! Hey, champ, that oatmeal smells good! What a great cook your mom is."

"I like it when we have pancakes," Carl replied philosophically. "What other kinds of animals are we getting? I don't want horses," he added. He'd seen police officers riding horses in the park. Those animals were large.

Brad sat back in his chair. "We'll figure it out soon enough."

"When?"

"Let's circle back on that one, champ." Circle back meant his dad didn't know the answer. It was also a joke about his former job that Carl didn't get, but when his dad said "circle back," his mother usually chuckled. Not today, though. She was looking, not tense exactly, or unhappy, but like her brain was full of thoughts.

Brad poured sugar into his coffee and drank it with closed eyes, like it was the best thing he'd ever had in his life. "Man, oh man. Everything tastes better in the country. Hey, Carlsbad, are you gonna eat that oatmeal, or play with it, or what?"

Carl brought one small spoonful to his mouth and made a tragic face. Brad waited until Sally's back was turned and poured a ton of sugar right into the bowl. Then he winked, which looked so weird it made Carl laugh.

"Eat up, champ. You'll need the energy. We've got a lot of work to do today. Farm work!" He said it like he was announcing a trip to the circus.

Carl considered the implications. "Are there, whatchamacallits? Plants?"

"You mean crops. There will be, once we plant some."

"Will I get to ride a tractor?"

"Maybe."

He grew quiet, imagining it. Riding in a tractor would be all right. He just wished Emmanuel and his other friends from Brooklyn would be around to see it.

Foxy stirred in her dog bed.

"A tractor, honestly, Brad. Hey, did anyone take the dog out?" Sally asked.

"Carl can do it." Brad turned to him. "Take the dog out, champ."

"Do I still have to pick up her poop?"

"Poopy!" Marie yelled, and squealed until she turned red.

"Yes, you have to pick it up," Sally said.

"No," Brad said at the same time. "Farmers love to step in poop. In fact, you don't even have to keep her on the leash. Let Foxy loose! She's a country dog now."

Carl frowned. "What if she runs away?"

"Dogs are smart. She knows where her food bowl is."

"She's not that smart." There was a worried tone in Sally's voice. "I don't think it's a good idea to let the dog loose, Brad. It's a strange place, after all . . ."

"Poop! Poop!" Marie yelled.

Precisely two seconds later it became clear to everyone present that Marie wasn't kidding. Brad leapt up to handle the diaper change. Sally finally started laughing.

"C'mere, Foxy," Carl called, pushing back his chair. "C'mon, girl! Let's go outside."

CHAPTER FIVE

Off the leash, at last.

Alice and Thistle finished their breakfast right around the same time Carl Harvey started his. They opted for a quick graze of clover and wild bluegrass, as they didn't want their bellies overfull for the adventure that lay ahead.

The kits were almost too jumpy to eat. Their nervous systems were on high alert in the usual rabbit way, with a heaping spoonful of adventure mixed in. What they felt was neither fear nor the lack of fear, but a useful kind of excitement. It would keep their ears sharp and their legs quick.

As promised, Lester escorted the two young 'uns to the meadow's edge. They stood together on a flat granite outcropping behind a thicket of laurel bushes. The cottontails called it Split Rock. It was a good landmark and a good hiding place, too.

"Now, listen with both ears, you two," he began. "Cross the meadow separately, it'll draw less attention. Alice, you take the far side, by the hedgerow. You, little one—Thorn? Thistle, that's right—go down the middle.

There's less cover, but it's the shortest way back to the trees if you have to bolt."

That Lester couldn't recall Thistle's name didn't offend the young kit. Cottontails can't afford to be fussy about names, given how many baby rabbits are born, season after season, year after year, most of them named after familiar plants. It would take a whole rabbit encyclopedia to keep count of all the Ragweeds and Clovers and Bluebells and Daisies hopping about the valley between the hills. Alice was short for alyssum, a pretty little plant with white flowers that country folk call Sweet Alice, because of how sweet those flowers smell.

Even Lester was named after a plant. He'd chosen the name himself. It was a type of heirloom tomato called "Lester's Perfected," listed in *The Field and Garden Vegetables of America, 2nd edition,* a guide whose yellowed pages were in the box whose contents had long ago served as a feast for the very young, very curious rabbit he'd once been. The young 'un had liked the sound of "Lester's Perfected" a great deal, almost as much as he liked the mushroomy taste of the old pages. He'd gone by the name Lester ever since. (Remarkably, *The Field and Garden Vegetables of America, 2nd edition* had listed thirteen different kinds of Swiss chard, and this had made a big impression on Lester as well.)

Lester ground his teeth for a moment, to gather his thoughts. "Both of you, aim for the near corner of the barn. You can meet there. Sneak along the shady side, toward the back of the farmhouse. That's where the old farmer used to tie up his dog, to a post sunk into the ground with a metal ring screwed into it. I expect the new farmers will do the same."

"If there is a dog," Thistle interjected. "That's what we're going to find out."

"Farmers and dogs go together like moss and the backside of a rock, and you'd best be prepared for the worst. If there is a dog," Lester went on, "and the dog's tied up, that's good news. When the dog gets wind of you, it'll bark like mad and race to the full length of its rope, but that's as far as it can go. No need to bolt, and don't let the noise bother you. Just keep your distance."

"A tied-up dog is good. Don't freeze, don't bolt," Alice said, imagining it.

"That's right, young 'un. You know what else is good? A dog that's locked in the house."

"Inside, you mean? Like the farmers?" Thistle gave a shiver of horror. "How awful. Imagine being locked indoors!"

"Don't waste your sympathy on the dog," Lester said with a silent chuckle. "He won't waste any on you. A dog in the house can't hurt you. But any mutt worth its tail will smell that you're close by and bark at the door, and it'd be just like a farmer to open that door, too. So keep your wits about you."

"Should we look inside the house, too, just to be sure?" asked Alice, as if breaking into farmers' houses was a thing wild rabbits did every day. Truthfully, her curiosity was growing by the minute. The Arm Waahr, the crib, the countless boxes—where were they now? And was a baby people really as ugly as everyone said?

Lester gave her a look. "I wouldn't attempt it, personally. But if you can peek in a window, feel free. Knowing what manner of dog we're dealing with could be useful."

"I thought all dogs are bad," Thistle said.

"These things have nuances, youngster! A little dog that makes a big noise is less bad than a big dog that makes a little noise. You might as well find out as much as you can. If you even make it that far," the old rabbit pointed out.

"Tied-up dog is good, dog in the house is good but keep our wits about us, peek in a window if we can—and what if there's a dog that's loose?" asked Alice, who was determined to make the most of this adventure.

"I'm getting to that." Lester paused to rub his chin on the warm rock. "If the dog's loose, run! Show it the flash of your tail! Whatever you do, don't let yourself get cornered, and don't freeze. Once the dang dog's got your scent, holding still can't save you."

"Loose dog. Don't freeze. Bolt," Thistle repeated, memorizing it. "Wait. What does a dog even smell like?"

Lester bared his teeth in disgust. "You'll know it when you smell it, believe me. Almost as bad as a fox. And don't be fooled. Sometimes people give dogs bubble baths and they come out smelling like flowers. Doesn't matter. It's still a dog."

"What about traps?" Alice asked. "And what about the farmers?"

"They won't set traps until they've planted a garden. That'll take a while. A farmer can't run for beans, so even if one of them sees you, you're all right. Unless it has a shotgun."

Alice and Thistle started to speak at the same time. Lester double-thumped his back feet for silence.

"I know you don't know what it is; that's why I'm telling you! A shotgun looks like a stick and smells like hot metal—like when the sun beats down on that old wheelbarrow in the woods. It's not dangerous unless the farmer lifts it up and points it at you." Lester sounded matter-of-fact. "If that happens, same rules as a loose dog. Run like the wind, and make extra sure to zigzag. Keep running even if you think you're safe. The farmer won't chase you, but the shotgun can still reach out and grab you, with not a lick of warning."

"Like a hawk?" Alice asked, with hope. Hawks were known to be sure, silent killers that could dive to the earth and snap a rabbit's neck before the victim even knew what happened. "May a hawk take you, in good time!" was a common rabbit expression of goodwill. A quick and painless death after enough of life has been enjoyed is what most living creatures prefer, after all.

"Not quick and quiet like a hawk, no. I should have said so. It'll make a big noise to scare you, the loudest bang you've ever heard, but don't freeze. Just keep running."

The kits' ears drooped to hear this.

"Shotguns are the darndest things. I'd rather deal with a dog, myself," Lester went on, nonchalant. "When a dog's chasing you, at least you can tell if you've got a chance of getting away or not."

"Were *you* ever chased by a dog, Lester? What happened?" Thistle asked, eyes wide.

The old rabbit flattened his ears. "If I ever was, I must have got away, now, mustn't I? That's all I've got to tell you. Any questions?"

Thistle shook his head, but there was one more thing on Alice's mind.

"Last night, during the meeting, you said a life without radishes is hardly worth living." She hadn't stopped thinking about it since. "Is that really true, Lester?"

"It's a matter of opinion. I've got mine. You'll make up your own mind, that's why you've got one." He paused. "What's good for the rabbitfolk is good for the rabbit. You're doing a fine, brave thing, both of you. Now, off you go."

"Use your ears, use your nose," said Thistle earnestly.

"Use your brain, young 'un! That's your best hope. I'll wait here for you as long as I can. But don't come back until it's safe."

⁂

"Come on, girl, run!" Carl slipped the leash from Foxy's neck, but the dog just stood there. "Why won't she run, Dad?"

"She's not used to it, champ. Try throwing a stick."

"I don't have a stick."

Carl and Brad stood where the backyard opened to the meadow beyond. There were plenty of sticks on the ground, as it turned out. They gathered a few, and Carl tried again.

"Fetch, Foxy! Fetch!" He threw the stick a short distance, maybe a dozen feet.

Foxy sat her tail end down on the grass and lifted one paw, to shake.

"She doesn't like sticks." Carl turned to his dad. "Should I go inside and get one of her toys?"

"Give her a chance," Brad advised. "Throw a few more."

Carl squatted next to the dog. "Hey, Foxy! You know how you like to watch me play video games? And when the zombie dinosaur skeleton comes on the screen, you always bark?" He waved a stick in front of her. "This might look like a stick, but it's really a dinosaur leg bone. Don't you want to chase it now?" Most video games had gone the way of fast-food drive-thrus in the Harvey household, but Carl's parents and a few of their like-minded friends had decided that *Attack of the Zombie Dinosaur Skeletons* was just educational enough to let the kids play on weekends. It wasn't a great game, or even a good one, but the lack of alternatives had made it pretty popular among Carl's old crowd.

Carl pretended to gnaw on the stick, to get the dog excited. "Ooh, dinosaur leg bone, yum-yum! I'm gonna throw it, and you run get it, okay? And bring it back! That's playing fetch."

Foxy yawned. But she stood up again, at least.

Carl threw the stick and cheered. First he pretended to run, to show Foxy what to do. Then he ran for real but in slow motion, calling "Come on, girl, come on!" in an overexcited voice. The beleaguered dog finally trotted after him. Carl had to pick up the stick himself and urge her repeatedly to follow him back, but they made it.

"Good girl, Foxy! That was awesome!" From the way Carl praised her, you'd think she'd solved world peace. Her tail didn't wag, exactly, but it did curl up a bit, which was usually a good sign.

"Throw it farther," Brad suggested. "And show her a treat first. For motivation."

Carl did. At once Foxy looked more interested. Together, she and Carl went to get the stick. This time Foxy was the one to carry it back, though she dropped it twice and Carl had to help her pick it up again.

They did it again, and again. Each time the stick went a little farther. Foxy seemed to be getting the hang of it. After a few more tries she finally went by herself. She made it all the way back to Carl and dropped the stick at his feet.

"Foxy!" Carl hugged her around the neck. "You fetched!"

Brad grinned. "See, she's not going to run away. Don't worry, champ. Just give it a good throw. That lazy dog could use the exercise."

"I'm not worried anymore," Carl said, elated. His dad was right. Foxy was a good dog, a smart dog. Of course she'd come back! And it was fun playing fetch with her outside in their own enormous yard. Living on a farm was like having a private park. Maybe they could even put in a carousel!

"Woof!" Foxy barked at him, bright-eyed, ready to play.

Carl drew his arm back and gave the stick a mighty throw into the meadow. This time it went so far he couldn't even see where it landed. Impressively, Foxy broke into a run.

"Go get it, girl!" he yelled.

⁂

Alice took the long route to the barn along the meadow's southern edge, just as Lester had advised. She was liking this adventure so far. Grazing and making pellets got dull after a while, and she wasn't yet old enough to have a litter. There had to be more to a rabbit's life than that, didn't there?

That's why Lester's talk about radishes had gotten under her fur. Maybe radishes were what she was missing. "Radishes and Swiss chard, oh my!" She said the words aloud, trying out the idea.

Thistle burst through the grass, terror in his eyes.

"Thistle, what happened? You're supposed to be in the middle of the meadow—"

"It's raining sticks!" he said, gasping.

"Sticks? Are you sure?"

"Yes! They keep falling from the sky. That's not good, is it? Didn't Lester say that shotguns look like sticks?"

"Yes. But he didn't say they fell from the sky."

"Go get it, girl!"

The two rabbits stared at each other, then looked up.

THWACK!

The stick landed right in front of Alice. Both kits bolted at top cottontail speed, covering fifteen yards in a single second. Then they turned and hopped warily back. They regarded the stick in wonder.

"See?" Thistle yelped.

Alice pushed the stick with her nose. She gnawed the bark, to be sure. "It's just a stick," she said, far more calmly than she felt. "It can't eat us. I don't think there's anything to worry about . . ."

But her very next inhale delivered a pungent smell that was half drooling carnivore, half lavender-scented pet shampoo. The rhythmic footfalls of whatever was galloping toward them shook the ground beneath their sensitive feet.

"Loose dog, bolt, don't freeze!" cried Thistle.

It was too late. An orange-furred face with a wet black nose and two dark button eyes loomed over them. The panting creature talked to itself in a kind of cheerful self-narration. "Go go go, look at me go! Running, running—wait, what's this?"

Alice couldn't help it. She froze. Thistle froze. The animal froze, too, but just for a moment.

"I believe that's my stick," the creature said. "Carl thinks it's a dinosaur bone. He's a nice kid, but gullible. How do you do?"

"You look like a fox," Alice blurted. "But you're not. Are you?" No fox would smell like lavender, she was fairly certain. Foxes were notorious for their stink.

"Pish-posh! Hardly. But I have an attractive resemblance to a fox, so I'm told. That's why my name is Foxy. I'm a Shiba Inu." Foxy said it with great pride. "A purebred Japanese Shiba. We're a rather popular breed at the moment. But what on earth are you?" The dog sniffed. "Not a pigeon, that's obvious. Not a cat? Not a squirrel? Not a rat? No offense!"

"We're cottontails," said Alice, mimicking Foxy's proud tone. "It's a rather popular kind of rabbit." It wasn't her nature to boast, but if they were about to get eaten, at least they could go out with some dignity.

Foxy grinned. "Oh, rabbits! I should have guessed, I've seen pictures. Carl has several books about your kind. There's a faint whiff of rodent about you, I hope you don't mind my saying so, but I knew right away you weren't rats. You're much too cute. Well, how do you do, rabbits! It's a pleasure to meet you."

Foxy held out her paw to shake. Alice jumped back. Thistle trembled but touched his tiny nose to the paw.

"How do you do?" the little rabbit said. Then he laughed. "A Shiba Inu, what a relief! We thought you might be a dog!"

Like all Shibas, Foxy had triangular ears that stood up on her head like the ears of a teddy bear. Now those ears wilted in disdain. "*Inu* is the Japanese word for dog, you provincial creature. Shiba Inu means Shiba dog."

The rabbits stared, uncomprehending. Foxy tried again. "A Shiba is a kind of dog. Like a cottontail is a kind of rabbit, I suppose. Oh dear, now what's the matter?"

Both rabbits had gone frozen and glassy-eyed. Foxy nudged them with her cold, wet nose, to wake them up.

"Hello!" Alice cried, the first to come to. "Are you going to kill us?"

"I beg your pardon! Why would I do that?"

"To eat us," Thistle squeaked.

"Don't be ridiculous." Foxy let her eyes close halfway, which only increased her regal air of mystery. "If you must know, I'm on a prescription diet from Dr. Yang, my veterinarian. Perhaps you've heard of him? He's well known in Park Slope, very well known. I get low-carb canned food in the morning, kibble for sensitive stomachs at night, and one Spearmint-Flavored GlitterTooth Chew-Bone every day, to freshen my breath." The dog licked her lips with a tongue that was pink as a rosebud. "Sometimes they give me a biscuit!"

"So, you don't eat rabbits?" Alice said, not trusting her senses quite yet. "We thought all dogs ate rabbits."

"'All dogs' is a great many dogs, my quivering friend! We're not all the same, as you rabbits seem to think."

"Foxeeeee!"

"Foxeeeee!"

"That's Carl. One of my humans. He's calling my name." Unperturbed, the dog yawned, sat on the grass, and scratched her right shoulder with her back right foot.

"Foxeeeeeee!"

"Foxeeeeeee!"

"That's Brad." Foxy repeated the scratching exercise on the other side.

"Foxeeeeeee!" Now both voices called in unison. There was desperation in the sound.

"What do they want?" Alice asked.

"I wish I knew! They call my name a lot. I think they just like saying it." The dog's head tilted adorably to one side. "Would you like to see my new house? I have a new dog bed, too, it's luxurious. New bowls. New toys. A new box of biscuits! I don't know what I did, but it must have been very good."

Neither of the young rabbits knew for sure if this was a wise idea, but if the dang dog wasn't going to eat them, and the farmer hadn't set any traps, why not? It would make a great story back at Burrow. Even Lester would be impressed. And Alice was still deeply curious about the Arm Waahr and the baby who lived in a cage. This might be her only chance to see these things.

"All right," Alice said, speaking for them both.

"Delightful! I'm so pleased. Do me a favor, though, would you, dear rabbits? Brad, whom I mentioned, he's Carl's father—he thinks I'm lazy. If he sees us together, can I chase you, just a little bit? I won't catch you, I promise," she added eagerly. "I just hate it when he makes fun of me like that. It's terribly embarrassing." Her ears drooped and her tail unfurled, and all at once she was the picture of abject canine misery.

"You can chase me," offered Thistle. "That'll be fun."

Foxy's ears and tail popped up again like someone pressed the happy dog ON button. "Marvelous, that's a good lad! Let's go."

CHAPTER SIX

The welcome wagon arrives.

If anyone had noticed those two young rabbits and a dog who looked like a fox crossing the meadow together like old friends, they'd have scratched their heads over it for sure.

Foxy trotted along straight as the crow flies, her curled-up tail bouncing proudly on her back, but the rabbits couldn't help acting like rabbits. No straight lines for them. They tacked back and forth like sailboats in a headwind and dashed for cover every ten yards, so it was a ragtag parade and took quite a while.

The closer they got to the farmhouse, the bigger and redder it grew. It smelled like oats and apples and cinnamon, which was unexpected and pleased the rabbits a great deal. There was no one outside. Foxy offered to bark at the kitchen door to let her humans know that company had arrived, but Alice and Thistle felt compelled to check the place out first, as any sensible cottontail would. Alice thought of Lester's advice, and asked if they could peek in a window.

"A brilliant suggestion!" Foxy replied. Like all dogs, she'd spent countless hours looking out windows, and she liked the idea of looking in for a change. All they had to do was find a window low enough for a small dog and two pipsqueak rabbits to peep through.

Luckily, the farmhouse was built into a slope. The kitchen door opened to a small porch with three wooden steps that led down to the backyard, while the window on the opposite wall, above the kitchen sink, was only a foot aboveground. From there, Foxy could see in easily, and the rabbits stood up with their paws and fuzzy little chins resting on the sill. Now all three animals had a clear view of the kitchen.

Carl was at the table, crying. Brad sat next to him, stroking the boy's head and saying consoling things, although you can imagine how terrible he must have felt about Foxy running off.

Sally carried Marie on one hip as she talked into the old-fashioned landline phone. This phone was a real antique, with a long, curly cord that tethered the handset to a receiver mounted on the wall. Sally could walk only as far as the cord could stretch before having to change directions.

"Yes, the dog's microchipped," she was saying, "but we've just moved, and our new address isn't on file. It's Eleven Prune Street. Her tags have my cell phone number on them and the signal here is terrible, so I want to give you our new landline number, too, in case she turns up. Yes, I'm calling from the landline now."

Sally listened and wrote things down on a pad. Marie sucked on her fist and looked around until she saw the animals at the window above the sink. Her wide baby eyes grew wider still.

"Will you look at that," Foxy remarked. "They took the leash off me and put one on Sally. Poor thing. I wonder what she did wrong?"

Marie stared and burst out laughing.

"Hi, Marie!" Foxy wagged her tail and grinned. "Marie's the baby," she explained to the rabbits.

A baby-people! Alice and Thistle looked hard.

"She's not ugly at all," Alice said, amazed.

"She's all right," Thistle agreed. "But she's not ready to leave the nest yet, that's for sure."

Foxy's tail waggled faster. "Marie's fun. She can understand pretty much everything we say."

"The others can't?" Alice asked, even more impressed.

"No, they're too old. Hey, Marie! Tell them to open the door. I'm bringing some friends over." To the rabbits, she said, "Do you like carrots?"

"Sure, probably," Thistle said. They'd never tried them, of course.

Alice was tempted to ask if they might have radishes instead, but she didn't want to be rude. This adventure was already far beyond her expectations. Imagine two cottontails being received as guests among farmers, with a friendly dog as their host!

Foxy's breath was already fogging the window from the outside. "I don't think Sally's had time to go shopping yet, but she always has carrot sticks somewhere. Marie, tell them to put out some crudités. Now, follow me, dear bunnies!"

The rabbits did as they were told.

⁂

The baby clapped. "Doggo!" she said. "Bun bun! Veggie!"

"Sorry, I can't hear you, the baby's yelling." Sally propped the phone on her shoulder. "Can you take her, Brad? I'm still on the phone with Animal Control."

Brad held out his arms. "Sure. How about a nap, punkin?"

Marie hurled her sippy cup to the floor. It rolled right up against the kitchen door.

"Doggo, doggo, *doggo*!" she screeched, long and loud.

Carl jumped to his feet. "Dad, look! It's Foxy!" The dog's shadow was visible through the curtained storm door. Still sniffing back tears, Carl ran to open it. There sat Foxy on the mat, her spiraled tail flopping back and forth like an overjoyed doughnut.

Carl threw his arms around the dog and pressed his face against her fur. "Foxy, I thought you ran away!"

"Carlsbad, my boy, I fear you've overreacted," the dog replied, though all Carl heard was a series of sharp, happy barks. "Why throw a stick if you don't want me to chase it? I'm only canine, after all. Anyway, I'm back. And I've brought some friends over for you to meet. Get this: They're bunnies!"

"Bun bun!" yelled Marie. "Veggie!"

But Carl had already dragged Foxy inside by the collar and shut the door. He squeezed the dog so hard she yelped. "Did you have fun, girl? Did you? I'll get you a biscuit, wait."

"See, champ? I told you she'd come back," Brad said, sinking into a chair. He looked like he needed a nap himself.

"Bun bun!" Marie kicked, and squirmed in her father's lap. "Bun bun! Veggie!"

"False alarm, yes, I guess it was! I do appreciate your help." Sally hung up the phone and took Marie back from Brad. "Bun bun? That's a new word, sweet girl. I wonder what it means. You want veggies, really? After all that applesauce? All right, if you say so . . ."

Carl returned with the dog biscuit and offered it to Foxy. "Here, girl! Here's a treat for you. Don't you want it?"

Foxy didn't seem to hear him. She quivered with alertness, her whole being fixed on something outside, in the backyard. A growl started in the back of her throat and rolled into a fierce, protective bark.

"Grrrrrr, woof!" she said.

A second later there was a knock at the kitchen door.

"Now what?" Brad hauled himself up from his chair. "Carl, hold the dog, please."

A woman stood outside, beaming. She had a swirl of bright red hair piled on her head like the top of a soft serve ice cream cone, and she wore a skirt and blouse like you'd wear to an office. Her shoes were knee-high rubber boots that were spattered with mud.

Cradled in her arms was an enormous fruit basket wrapped in clear cellophane, with a sizeable bow of red ribbon tied at the top.

"Good morning! Are you Mr. Harvey?" she said brightly.

"I'm Brad Harvey, yes." Brad kept his hand on the doorknob. "Can I help you?"

She hoisted the basket to one side and tilted her head to the other, to talk past the bow. "*So* nice to meet you! I'm Ruth Shirley, of Ruth Shirley Realty. Maybe you've seen my billboard? On Route Two-Twelve, when you get off the Thruway? Well, on behalf of the community and everyone at Ruth Shirley Realty, I just wanted to deliver a little welcome wagon present to you and your family. We're all *so* glad to have you as a neighbor!"

She stood there smiling, her head tipped to the side, until Brad finally took the basket from her and let her in. "Well, thanks, that's awfully nice," he said, putting the basket on the kitchen table. Carl examined it at once. It was packed with fresh fruit, cheese, nuts, jams, even chocolate. He pitied the fruit, since he knew what was going to happen to it. The rest looked pretty tasty.

Sally slid Marie into her bouncy seat and wiped her hands on a kitchen towel. "How lovely! Please, Ms. Shirley, come in. I'm Sally Harvey. Would you like coffee? I was just about to make some."

"I'd love some coffee, how'd you guess? I'll just take off my wellies, if you don't mind. I hate to track mud into a clean kitchen." Still on the doormat, Ruth Shirley started pulling off her boots. "You can call me Ruth Shirley. Everyone does, friends and strangers alike. Comes from having a billboard with your name on it, I guess."

"I bet it does," said Sally. "And what about you—Mr. Shirley, I presume?"

Behind Ruth Shirley was a man. He wore a white button-down shirt with a suit jacket but no tie, and shiny dark shoes. He carried an overcoat folded over one arm. To Carl's deep fascination, his head was completely bald and smooth as an egg.

Ruth Shirley prattled as she struggled with her boots. "Oh, *this* isn't Mr. Shirley! Phil, my husband, he's at work. He sells farm equipment, all kinds. I bet you'll be hearing from him soon, if I know Phil Shirley! *This* gentleman is Tom Rowes. He's a well-known figure locally. Tom serves on the school board and sponsors our Little League and the Elks Club and, well, I can't tell you all the good things he does for our community. He couldn't wait one more day to meet the new owners of Prune Street Farm, so of course I invited him to join me on the old Ruth Shirley Realty welcome wagon! Tom's a big fan of this farm, aren't you, Tom?"

Tom Rowes was already inside, looking around. He hadn't bothered to take off his shoes. "What Ruth means is, I want to buy it from you. Is this a good time to talk?"

"You've got quite a sense of humor, Mr. Rowes," Brad said, after a moment. "How do you take your coffee?"

"I'm not joking. I've had my eye on this property for a long time."

Mr. Rowes tossed his overcoat over the back of a kitchen chair like it was all his already. "I'll pay you double what you paid for it. Cash deal. My lawyer will get the paperwork started Monday. Congratulations, folks! You just won the lottery."

"I don't understand," Sally said, cool but polite. "The house was empty for two years before we bought it. Why didn't you make an offer when it was on the market?"

"I did. Several times. That thick-headed old fool—"

"He means the former owner, Mr. Crenshaw," Ruth Shirley explained, hopping on one foot as she yanked off the second boot. "Such a character! He used to be a real fixture in our little town."

"Old Man Crenshaw! Stubborn as a stone wall," Mr. Rowes said. "But I'm sure you found that out for yourselves."

"We never spoke to Mr. Crenshaw directly." Sally pronounced the mister with extra care. "His daughter in Florida handled everything to do with the sale."

"He's down there now, too, I hear," Mr. Rowes said. "I bet he's thrilled. Who wouldn't be? Sunshine, golf, no income tax, and all the early-bird specials an old man can eat. Out of curiosity: Did Crenshaw's daughter ever ask you if you were farmers?"

"She didn't have to ask," Brad replied. "That's why we bought this place. To farm it. We told her that straightaway."

"Wait, how come I missed all this?" Carl was still holding Foxy. Now he let go of the dog's collar and hopped in front of his dad, waving his arms. "Where was I when all this was happening? Why did you keep it a secret?"

"Sit down, champ. We'll talk about it later." Brad used his powerful dad gaze to get Carl quiet and in a chair, then turned back to Mr. Rowes. "Sorry, I'm not sure I heard you right. You say you'd offer double . . . ?"

"Double. Times two. In cash. And I know exactly what you paid for this place, to the penny. It's a matter of public record. This is the easiest money you'll ever make in your life." Mr. Rowes paused. "Can I get a woo-hoo, at least? This is fantastic news, in case you were wondering."

Carl's parents exchanged a look, but neither said a word, as rabbits aren't the only creatures who can freeze up from sheer surprise.

Mr. Rowes seemed to take their silence as negotiation. "All right, I'll sweeten the deal. I'll pay twice what you paid, plus I'll cover the cost of moving you to a new place. Ruth here is the hardest-working real estate agent in the county. She'll find you the home of your dreams, not a creaky fixer-upper like this old wreck, and you'll have money in the bank left over."

"Why, Tom, aren't you kind to say so." In her stocking feet at last, Ruth Shirley stepped daintily inside. "What a charming, old-fashioned kitchen! And look at that cute baby!"

Marie burped with feeling. Ruth Shirley smiled even more brightly. "Brad, Sally: Tom's offer is totally legitimate, I assure you. And I've got some lovely properties available; wait until you see." She reached into her purse. "Here's my card. That's my number right there, at Ruth Shirley Realty. We're open seven days."

"Why, thank you, Ms. Shirley—Ruth Shirley, I mean." Sally took the card between two fingers. "We'll be sure to give you a call, if we're interested."

Mr. Rowes laughed. "Come on, now. Do you really need to think about it?"

Brad held up a hand. "It's a generous offer, Mr. Rowes. Just give us time to talk it over."

"Are you nuts?" Carl said, leaping to his feet. "The answer is nope! Nope, nope, nope!"

"Decisive young man you've got there." Mr. Rowes reached into his pocket. "Here, Brad, take my card, too. I'll write my lawyer's number on the back. We'll sort it all out on Monday."

"No, you won't!" Carl didn't mean to sound angry, but it sure came out that way. It'd been a tough morning, what with waking up early in a strange room, the prunes on his oatmeal, Foxy running away. It'd been a tough couple of days, too, a tough couple of weeks, even months, if you counted back to the day his parents had told him they'd sold the apartment, the only home he'd ever known—sold! gone forever!—and he should start thinking about which of his possessions he wanted to keep and which he wanted to get rid of. What kind of a nutty question was that?

All of Carl's feelings about moving, packing up his stuff, leaving his friends and his school and his neighborhood far behind—all of it tumbled out right there and then, in front of Ruth Shirley and Mr. Rowes, whose shiny head caught the light like a cue ball. "You won't talk it over and you won't sort it out on Monday," he wailed, his face hot. "We're staying right here."

Marie's face crumpled like she was going to start wailing, too. Sally swooped in to rescue her from the bouncy seat while saying, "Carl, don't yell—"

"But we just got here!" he yelled, turning to his dad. "There's birds and stuff. Mom hasn't even unpacked her stupid dehydrator yet! Sorry I said *stupid*," he added, not sounding sorry at all.

Foxy barked, a low woof of warning. Brad spoke in a low voice, too. "Champ, why don't you go to your room for a few minutes and settle down?"

There was nothing Carl would have liked better than settling down, but he was worked up beyond his own control. If he were a rabbit, he'd have bolted a hundred yards by now. "You said this was our new home. Eleven Prune Street. You said I would like it and I would make new friends. So how am I supposed to make friends if I don't even get to meet them?" He looked wildly from one parent to the other. "It's not like I can go back to my old friends. Because somebody else already lives in our *real* home, in Brooklyn, right? We can't go back there even if we wanted to."

His words put a strange, about-to-cry look on Sally's face, which was so awful it just made Carl want to get madder so he didn't catch the sad feeling himself. "Anyway, you promised Mr. Crenshaw we'd live here and be farmers." He pointed at Mr. Rowes. "The bald guy said so himself. Mr. Crenshaw didn't want *him* to have it. He wanted *us* to have it."

Carl stopped. He was out of breath and all the grown-ups were staring at him. The red-haired lady had a fake smile on her face. The bald guy looked almost amused.

Brad stepped behind Carl and put his hands firmly on the boy's heaving shoulders. "Mr. Rowes, I apologize for my son's outburst. He's been through a big change, as we all have, and tempers are short." He glanced at Sally. "But he raises a good question. Why wouldn't Mr. Crenshaw sell this property to you?"

Mr. Rowes shrugged. "It's no secret. Your boy's right. Crenshaw didn't want me to have it because I'm not a farmer and don't intend to become one. And I already have a house. A much nicer house than this one, frankly. I only want the land."

"You mean, you'd tear the house down?" Like the flick of a switch it was Brad's old voice talking, the cool, clipped work voice that he used to use on the phone, in the days before the golden parachute arrived.

"Well, I'd have to tear it down, Brad, so I could build something of real value."

"And what exactly would that be?"

"That's a strategic, market-driven decision, best kept between me and my business partners." Mr. Rowes tugged at the cuffs of his shirtsleeves until they were perfectly even. "It'll be something useful, I assure you. And profitable."

"Do you mean, some kind of shopping mall?" Sally asked, dumbfounded. "A multiplex? A mini storage facility?"

He smiled. "Those are all good ideas, Sally. You ought to go into real estate! You've got the knack."

The look that passed between Carl's parents was quick as the flash of a cottontail's rump.

"Your offer is very generous, Mr. Rowes," Sally sounded polite, but firm. "However—"

"We don't need any time to think about it," Brad finished. "Case closed. The answer is no."

"The answer is nope!" Carl crowed in joy. "Nope, nope, nope!"

"Nope, thank you," Sally corrected him.

"Naaa!" yelled Marie. "Naaa, naaa!"

"Woof!" said Foxy.

Mr. Rowes stood there and rubbed his smooth head. He beckoned Brad to step closer and slung an arm around his shoulders, as if they were buddies. "Let me ask you a question, Brad. Have you ever farmed before?"

"Can't say I have, Tom." Brad threw the name back in the same chummy tone. "We've got a lot to learn. That's the fun of it."

"Spoken like a man who's worked indoors all his life. Look, no hard feelings. I've met other folks like you—folks from the city—who fall in love with the idea. Buy a farm, plant a garden, pull a few weeds, and call it a day." He dropped his arm and faced Brad. "Trust me. You have no idea how much work it takes to make a small farm break even, never mind turn a profit. I'm giving you a friendly warning: This place is a money pit. You're gonna rue the day."

"What's a money pit?" Carl asked. "What's rue the day?"

"I'll tell you later," his mom said, her voice tight.

Mr. Rowes folded his arms against his puffed-out chest. With his shiny bald head and crossed arms, he looked like the man on the ammonia bottles. "I'll tell you right now what it means. A money pit is a money-losing proposition, and rue the day means your folks are gonna kick themselves when harvesttime comes and they're broke and exhausted and wishing they'd said yes to me right here, right now." He turned to Brad and Sally. "If you even make it to harvest time, that is. I wouldn't be surprised if you bail out long before then."

Ruth Shirley was at the door, frantically pulling her rubber boots back on. "Oh my *gosh*, I've lost track of the time! We have another appointment, Tom, I totally forgot! *So* sorry we can't stay for coffee, Sally! We'll have to do it—ugh!—another day."

Mr. Rowes kept his eyes on Brad and Sally. "My offer stands, but I can't promise for how long. I need to find a property that suits my business plan. I like this one. I like it enough that I was willing to wait out the old man and deal with someone more reasonable. I assumed whoever bought this place would jump at my offer. But if you won't seize this golden, once-in-a-lifetime opportunity, I'll look elsewhere. Sooner or later I'll find what I need. Could be tomorrow, next week, next month." He shrugged. "Until then, if you change your mind, call me."

"It's been *such* a pleasure to meet you all," Ruth Shirley sang out. "So long, now! Bye-bye!" She gave a special bye-bye wave to Marie, who burped again, loudly.

"Thank you *so* much for coming by," Sally replied, an icy smile on her face. Brad held the door open while the real estate agent waved and cooed.

"Oh, look," Ruth Shirley said as she stepped outside. "Rabbits! Two little ones, hiding under the steps. How cute!"

"Where?" Carl dashed forward to look. "I don't see them."

"They were right here. I must have scared them coming out. They just ran away."

"Rabbits on a farm, oh boy! Good luck with that." Mr. Rowes chuckled as he picked up his coat. "Better set some traps before you plant anything, Brad. If you don't . . ."

Brad's eyes narrowed. "I'll rue the day. Got it."

Foxy had been staring at Mr. Rowes this whole time. Now she growled fiercely, with her lips pulled back over her gums until all her teeth showed.

"Cute dog," Mr. Rowes said. "Looks just like a fox. I hope nobody shoots it by mistake."

As if all that wasn't ill-mannered enough, Mr. Rowes grabbed an apple out of the fruit basket and bit it on his way out.

CHAPTER SEVEN

The worst thing there is.

"Hold on one minute there, young 'uns!" One of Lester's long ears stood up straight, and the other one cocked to the side. Lester hadn't been at Split Rock when the two adventurers got back, but they found him easily enough among the trees, keeping a watchful eye over a new litter of kits who were fresh out of the nest. "You mean to tell me you made *friends* with that diabolical tail-wagger? That murderous, drool-encrusted barker? That howling hound? That canine killer?"

"She's a Shiba Inu," Alice explained. "It's a special kind of dog."

"She was nice," Thistle added. "She wanted to chase me, but she said it was only pretend."

"She even asked the farmers to give us carrots," Alice said earnestly. "I wish they had! But then more people came, and we had to hide." Alice and Thistle had huddled there together under the wooden steps, willing themselves not to die of fright when those two heavy-footed humans stomped right over their heads. They didn't unfreeze until Ruth Shirley stepped outside again, and that's when they finally bolted.

Meanwhile, they'd heard every word spoken in the kitchen, between Ruth Shirley and Mr. Rowes and the Harvey clan. They hadn't understood it all but were confident that Lester would, and had zigzagged so fast across the meadow and back to the wood's edge that there wasn't time to be afraid.

"Carrots!" Lester sounded outraged, but he was drooling, too. "So you met the dog *and* the farmers! My, my. Start talking, you two. No, wait. I'd like Violet to hear this." He turned to the newly independent litter of baby bunnies. "Lesson over! You're on your own now, pipsqueaks. Remember what I told you! Rabbitfolk don't live long—"

"But we can still be careful," the kittens answered, in tiny voices.

"That's right. Good luck to you all, it's been a pleasure," Lester said, and the three of them went in search in Violet.

They found her in Burrow, napping, but rabbits are light sleepers. Their approach was enough to wake the wise old cottontail, and they gathered beneath the big tree whose tough web of roots encircled and protected their underground home.

"It's good you made it back alive," Violet said to Alice and Thistle. "Now, tell me everything. Four farmers, you say?"

"We saw four. I think that's all there are," Alice said. "The smartest one is Marie. She's still in the nest and screeches like an owl, but she's no danger to us. From the smell of her, she only eats apples."

"Intelligent. I like apples, too," Lester remarked.

"These had a different scent mixed in. It was like tree bark, but spicy," Thistle explained, for of course he'd never smelled cinnamon before. "But Alice, don't leave out the dog."

"Oh, the dog, sorry! We already told Lester but I'll tell it again." When Alice related how Foxy asked to chase Thistle and offered them carrots, Violet blinked.

"It sounds like a trap," she said flatly.

"I thought a trap was a box that closes and won't open again?" Alice asked.

"Or a metal mouth that bites you and won't let go? Oops, sorry!" Thistle said, remembering about Violet's ear.

Violet thumped her back feet. "Pretending to be a friend when you're not a friend is a trap, too."

"It's a sneaky kind of trap," Lester agreed. "It's an odious bit of trickery, if you ask me."

"What's odious?" Thistle asked.

"It means it stinks, young 'un. Like the breath of an owl who just ate skunk for dinner."

Alice's nose twitched at the thought. "Maybe it does. But I don't think Foxy is the one who smells. It was those two other humans, the ones who walked over our heads while we were hiding. They pretended to be friends to the new farmers, but they weren't." She looked at Lester. "Do humans set traps for other humans?"

The old cottontail chuckled. "I wouldn't be surprised. But human problems are not rabbit problems, oh lucky we!"

"What if they are, though?" Alice persisted. "What if the new farmers are about to get caught in a trap?"

"What are you talking about, kit?" Violet asked intently. "Start at the beginning."

Alice and Thistle proceeded to tell the two older rabbits all they had seen and heard: that a man with a head like a giant egg wanted to take the farm away from the new farmers. That a woman with plumage like the crest of a cardinal was helping him, and that she even brought food as bait. That the more the egg-head man talked, the more the new farmers smelled like fear. All rabbits know that smell.

"The egg-head man said they didn't know how to run a farm and should let him have it instead. Otherwise it would make them 'rue the day,'" Alice said. "That's the part that sounded like a trap. Though I don't think it's the kind that bites—well, *you* know."

Violet was listening hard, her damaged ear cocked just so. "Indeed I do," she said. "Go on."

"Whatever kind of trap it is," Alice finished, "if the farmers get caught in it, the farm gets caught, too."

"The egg-head man said something about tearing it all down," Thistle added.

"Tearing it down! Tearing it down!" Violet's eyes grew glassy as death. "This is terrible news. Terrible! Lester, do you think so, too?"

Lester groaned with anxiety. "The Mauler!" he finally said.

Alice and Thistle nearly collapsed. The Mauler was the worst thing there was. It was worse than a monster under the bed would be to a human child. It was worse than the scariest supervillain in one of Carl's comic books, worse than all the zombies in all the zombie horror movies put together.

The Mauler was even worse than a bear, and a bear was the biggest, most frightening animal in the valley. A bear could rip its way through a thorn-filled hedge and tear branches from a tree to get what it wanted. But a bear was just trying to eat and stay alive, which made it no different from a rabbit, or any other animal, for that matter.

The Mauler was something else. It would appear early one morning, yellow as a buttercup, to knock down trees and heave up the ground with its great mechanical jaws. It roared like a hurricane and spewed exhaust, and left vast muddy pits in the earth from which squat, square buildings rose. Or else it turned meadows into strange, hard-surfaced lakes, black as scorched wood. In time, the people's cars would swarm on these lakes, gathered close and still, and then leave again all at once, like migrating birds.

The Mauler sometimes traveled in a pack, wreaking havoc with others of its kind. It had something to do with humans, and never arrived without one of them riding on its neck. But whether the Mauler served the people or the people were enslaved by the Mauler was never quite clear to the animals of the valley between the hills. It might not have been perfectly clear to the people, either. But the rabbits knew nothing about that.

"I didn't believe the Mauler was real," Thistle whined. "I thought it was just a story, to scare us!"

"The Mauler is real," Lester said, whiskers aquiver. "All too real. I've seen one. I know."

Alice's heart thumped fast in her chest. She, too, had thought of the Mauler as an old rabbits' tale. That it was real was almost too terrible to comprehend.

"The Mauler eats the ground. Eats it right up," Violet added. Her voice was thick with defeat. "If the Mauler's coming, we're all doomed."

Even as the four rabbits crouched there, a rumbling throbbed in the earth. They felt it first in their feet. Then they heard the mechanical roar and the slow turn of wheels, and a rhythmic *bang! bang! bang!* as exhaust combusted through a pipe.

The noise grew closer and louder, until the rabbits' thin ears trembled.

"Is it here?" Thistle squeaked. "Is it the Mauler?"

But it wasn't the Mauler, this time. Just the roar of a tractor lumbering along Prune Street, making its slow way to the farmhouse the Harveys now called home.

⁂

The tractor groaned and clambered up the hill like a tired green elephant. The sight of it out his bedroom window brightened Carl's spirits considerably, and though it wasn't quite lunchtime, he decided it was worth going outside to inspect.

He'd been hiding in his room—well, he'd been sent there, as punishment for his rudeness to the bald man, but it felt like hiding—for hours, reading comic books aloud to Foxy and Big Robot while his parents talked heatedly in the kitchen. In Brooklyn it would have been easy for Carl to eavesdrop, but this house was too big for that. The Harvey parents were rooms away and down a flight of stairs, barely audible. Carl couldn't even tell how much of the conversation was about him and how much was about what Mr. Rowes had said.

With no way to track the substance or progress of the debate, he'd decided he wouldn't come out of his room until he got hungry. By then, his parents would have had time to cool off. But the arrival of the tractor was too appealing to resist.

Foxy was stretched out in Carl's bed, snoring. No dogs allowed in people beds was a serious Harvey household rule, but she looked so cute with her little fox-orange head on his pillow, he decided to leave her there. He closed the bedroom door behind him, so the dog wouldn't get caught, and tippy-toed downstairs and out the front door, where he broke into a run.

"Wow!" he said, racing to greet the new arrival and its driver. "Is that a real tractor? Why is it green? Can I touch it? Who are you?"

"Sure it's real. It's green because it's a John Deere, the finest farm machinery money can buy. You can touch it if your hands are cleaner than the tractor. Lucky for you it's pretty dirty. I'm your neighbor, Janis. Gimme a handshake, kid. Firm, that's right! Show me what you've got."

The woman wore overalls, a neckerchief and work boots, and a wide-brimmed canvas hat. Her shirtsleeves were rolled up, revealing a prominent tattoo on her forearm.

Carl did his best with the handshake. "What's that?" he said, pointing.

"What, my arm? What, my sleeve? Oh, that! That's a tattoo. Want one? I'm getting pretty good at them. I'm very artistic, as you can probably tell from my demeanor. Nah, you're too young."

She was teasing him, he knew that. Normally he didn't like being teased, especially by grown-ups, but when it was a grown-up with a tractor he didn't mind so much.

"I know it's a tattoo, but what *is* it?" He peered close. "It looks like writing. It says Farmer at the end."

"It's in German. It says, 'Ich bin ein Farmer.' I am a Farmer."

"We're farmers, too," Carl said with newfound pride, now that he knew it was the kind of thing people got tattoos about. "We didn't used to be, but now we are."

Farmer Janis gave him an appraising look. "Well, congratulations. You do have a pretty nice farm here, kid. You don't mind if I call you kid, do you? I name all my chickens and I never forget any, but when it comes to people, I only learn the names I have to."

"My name's Carlsbad," he explained.

"Is it really?" Farmer Janis whistled. "I'm definitely gonna call you kid."

"And I have a baby sister named Marie."

"That's all right. I'll call her kid, too." She looked around. "So. You and your sister do all the farming around here?"

Carl laughed. "Noooooo! We're just kids!"

"In that case," she said, slipping the keys to the tractor into one of her many pockets, "take me to your leader, kid."

⁂

Farmer Janis looked right at home at the kitchen table with Kid Marie perched on one knee. She'd been there nearly an hour already, drinking coffee, listening and nodding while Sally and Brad told her the whole story, starting with Brad's golden parachute and ending with the morning's unsettling visit from Mr. Rowes.

"So that's where we stand," said Brad, leaning back in his chair. "We're serious about making this place succeed. We're ready to work hard. We're good learners. But this freaked us out, to put it bluntly. I think we could use some guidance."

"We need help, desperately," Sally said with feeling. "I don't want to see that Mr. Rowes's face again—or that awful redheaded woman, either!"

Janis burst out laughing. "Ruth Shirley! Aw, Ruth's all right. You'll get used to her. You'll have to. She runs half the organizations in town, and her husband sells all the farm equipment. Ruth's just trying to make a buck like everyone else. But Rowes . . . well, he's bad news, and that's a fact. Here, take this kid off me, would you? That's a bumper crop of saliva right there."

Brad retrieved the drooling baby, and Janis wiped her hands on her overalls. "Look, I'm not going to lie," she said. "Maybe you guys did bite off more than you can chew. So what?"

As if to demonstrate, she chose a piece of dried fruit from the snack plate Sally had put out and chomped away on it. She chewed, and chewed, and chewed. Finally, she swallowed. "Did you make this?" she said to Sally, who nodded.

"Pretty good." Janis helped herself to another piece. "Hey, that's pretty darn good."

Carl squirmed. "But why take perfectly good fruit—"

"Kid, hold your questions. I'm trying to relate to your parents here, farmer to farmer." Janis chewed a bit more, then spoke. "You want this farm to make money, right? Here's my advice. Get some sheep."

"Sheep?" Brad and Sally said it together.

Janis nodded. "People like sheep. They find them scenic. Of course, that's because they never got kicked in the ribs while shearing one, or had to force a dose of medicine down a sick ewe's throat, or chase a ram down the street because the thick-headed bully got loose."

As he listened, Carl found himself reaching for a piece of the dreaded fruit. Maybe if he pretended it was a gummy bear . . .

"I thought you didn't like it," his mother said, not missing a trick.

"It's not so bad," he quickly mumbled. He didn't want to miss a word of Janis's fascinating information. The gummy bear self-hypnosis was working, though.

"Janis, you were saying, sheep?" Brad asked, a touch of strain in his voice.

Janis took another piece of dried fruit. "I'm serious," she went on, chewing with abandon. "Get yourself some sheep. Leave a couple grazing out front, where folks will see 'em. Put a sign on the lawn: 'Come pet our sheep!' It'll attract visitors, and then you'll have customers to sell your wares to. Sheep are good workers, too. Best lawn mower in the world is a hungry sheep. You know about planting cover crops?"

Marie was fussing in Brad's arms. He handed her off to Sally, who shoved a pacifier in the baby's mouth and strapped her into her bouncy seat.

"No, but I hope you're going to teach me," Brad said, wiping the spit off his shoulder. "Are sheep hard to take care of?"

"No more than any other animal. You have to feed them and keep them fenced in and call the vet when they're sick. Sheep are stubborn. They need to be bossed around. A cow's obedient, but with a sheep, you have to get physical."

Sally looked appalled. "Physical, in what way?"

"You whack it on the nose. Hard." Janis demonstrated by delivering a brutal blow to the top of her own thigh. "Ow," she said.

"No!" Marie yelled from her bouncy seat. "No hit!"

"You'll do great in preschool someday, kid." Janis turned to Sally. "Did you ever watch two rams butt heads? Check it out on YouTube sometime. A sheep's skull is thick. It takes real muscle to get their attention."

Both women looked at Brad as if evaluating his ability to swing a club. Carl thought of the strong man in the old cartoons who swung a mallet so hard it blew the bell off the top of the scale. Could his dad do that, he wondered?

Brad flexed his arms like Popeye. "I've never pictured myself going mano a mano with a sheep," he said, with a nervous laugh.

Janis didn't seem amused. "You learn something new every day on a farm, trust me. As for cash flow, sheep are versatile. You can shear 'em for the wool and sell it. If you dye the wool and spin yarn, you can sell that, too. You could get into the cheese-making business, or supply sheep's milk to a cheese maker. I know a few; I can introduce you. And when it comes time to slaughter the lambs, don't worry. There's a fellow in the next town who'll do it for you, cheap."

"Slaughter the lambs?" Carl was on his feet. "You mean, kill them?"

Farmer Janis looked at him kindly. "Where do you think lamb chops come from, kid?"

That gave him pause. "I don't even like lamb chops," he said.

"How about Ronald MacDoodlemeat's Extra-Strength Cheeseburgers, then? Or Uncle Cholesterol's Deeply Fried Chicken Fingers?" Janis added ruthlessly. "You know chickens don't really have fingers, right?"

"Buck buck buck," Marie gurgled, and wiggled her chubby digits. "Buck buck buck!"

Nobody spoke. Janis pushed her chair back. "Well, I'm no gambler, but I'd bet a bag of good hayseed that this farm is not going to be in the butchering business any time soon."

Sally put her hands on Carl's shoulders just firmly enough to send a calm-down message. "We see ourselves more as plant-based farmers," she said.

The expression on Farmer Janis's face was inscrutable. "Plant-based, sure. If it's gardening you're after, my advice is to be creative. A gimmick helps. Specialize! One more roadside stand of zucchini is not going to pay the oil bill around here, or the taxes. Grow something special. Something nobody else has."

"Magic beans?" Carl suggested. He was being sarcastic now, but Janis nodded and patted him on the knee.

"That's the spirit. And think about what you'll do in the winter. You don't have a greenhouse, do you?"

Brad and Sally shook their heads.

"You can't grow plants in the winter unless you have a greenhouse." Farmer Janis spoke gently, as one does when talking to the woefully uninformed. "Winter's a challenge on the farm. I hope your barn's in good shape. Art Crenshaw was a good farmer and a good friend, but everybody gets old sooner or later. Things slip through the cracks. If you want, we can take a walk out there and inspect it. Chop all the wood you can, when you can! There's a trick to stacking it so it stays dry. I'll show you how another day. Right now, I gotta go home and feed my chickens." She stood up, stretched, and looked at Carl. "Wanna come help me out? Feeding chickens is a real farmer thing to do."

But the thought of all the chicken fingers he'd eaten in his young life weighed heavily on Carl's conscience. How many had there been? Hundreds? Thousands? Could he ever wash the stain of all that BBQ sauce off his guilty, sticky hands?

He shook his head, nope.

Farmer Janis seemed to understand. "Not today, huh? No worries. You'll get plenty of chances. Those birds have to be fed every day, rain or shine, summer and winter, whether you're in the mood or not. It forms a real bond. They get to be like family."

"Buck buck buck!" said Marie. She was the only Harvey still smiling. "Buck buck buck!"

CHAPTER EIGHT

Alice has a remarkable idea.

Bad news spreads quickly among the nervous, and rabbits are nothing if not that. The mere whisper of the word *Mauler* started rumors that multiplied quicker than cottontails in springtime. They spread through the warren like the tendrils of a fast-growing vine.

Most of the younger rabbits had held the same mistaken idea as Alice and Thistle. They thought of the Mauler as a made-up monster, an outlandish fiction designed to frighten and thrill. But now the facts were out. Who would have guessed that somewhere on the far end of the food chain, that blessedly unsentimental system that turns sunlight into grass, grass into bunnies, and bunnies into nourishing food for every small, medium, and large carnivore in the valley between the hills, there was some kind of mechanical monster that fed on the very earth itself?

"Rabbitfolk don't live long," the cottontails remarked somberly to each other upon hearing the awful news, and "May a hawk take you, in good time." Then they went about their business. For if the Mauler was real, and the Mauler was coming, then that was a thing that couldn't be helped.

Certainly, Burrow wouldn't survive it. A few of them might escape, if they managed not to die of terror on the spot, but who could say how far the destruction would reach?

What mattered was that rabbits—not these particular rabbits, perhaps, but rabbits in general—would carry on, somewhere. Far away, perhaps, but somewhere. That's how the cottontails of Burrow felt, anyway. Once they got over the shock, there wasn't much else to say or do. Life would continue until it didn't anymore.

Still, Alice couldn't stop thinking about it. That evening at dusk, she and Thistle took dinner side by side, in their usual, crepuscular way.

Lester was nearby, teaching the newest batch of kits how to graze—nibble-nibble-nibble, pause and check for danger with an ear swivel ("Use your ears!") and some rapid-fire sniffing ("Use your nose!"), then back to the tasty grass.

"You remember the story of how Violet lost her ear tip, don't you?" Alice asked her brother, seemingly out of the blue.

"Yes, of course! I'm so embarrassed, I shouldn't have brought it up in front of her. It was in one of the old farmer's traps, wasn't it? She got caught, and struggled, and she got away somehow, but she had to leave a piece of her ear behind." Thistle paused and did his own well-practiced nibble-nibble-nibble, ear swivel, *sniff-sniff-sniff* before going on. "That was long before we were born. Why do you ask?"

Alice also paused to use her ears, use her nose. "I was thinking about the Mauler," she said.

"Can we not talk about it anymore?" Thistle pleaded. "At least, not during dinner?"

In answer, she hopped in front of him, right on the grass he was trying to nibble-nibble-nibble. "Thistle, hear me out. If the new farmers get caught in the egg-head man's trap, I don't think they'll be able to get away, no matter how they struggle."

"Because they have no ear tips to leave behind?" Thistle said, quite seriously. To rabbits, it was a wonder humans could hear themselves think, with those absurdly tiny ears of theirs.

"Yes," said Alice. "Then they'll rue the day, and the Mauler will come. And that will be the end of Burrow." Her own ears flattened despairingly against her head. "I don't want to that happen. We have to stop it."

"But we can't stop the Mauler," Thistle said. "Nothing can! It's bad! It's—"

"The worst thing there is, I know. But what if we stopped the farmers from getting trapped in the first place?"

She pressed close to her brother. Together they watched Lester lead the babies in practicing the nibble-nibble-nibble, ear swivel, *sniff-sniff-sniff* routine, over and over again, until it became second nature. "See those kits?" she said. "They're true-born rabbits, but they still have to be taught how to do things properly. What if the new farmers are the same?"

Thistle snorted. "They're not farmers; that's the whole trouble. The egg-head man said they don't know the first thing about vegetables."

"But *we* do." Alice's nose quivered in excitement. "We're rabbitfolk, after all. And rabbits are way more clever than farmers. Why can't *we* run the farm? Perhaps the new farmers can learn from us."

"You're joking, I think," Thistle said, after a moment. To be fair, the silent-laughter issue meant it wasn't easy to tell when a cottontail was kidding. Good manners dictated a quick tail shimmy accompany any attempt to be funny, and a longer tail shimmy from the listeners to show laughter, if they were amused. Alice's tail hadn't budged. Instead, her whiskers flared with excitement as the idea took shape in her mind.

"I'm not joking," she insisted. "If we rabbits can sneak into a garden to steal vegetables, surely we could sneak in to *grow* vegetables. Then the farmers won't rue the day, the egg-head man will leave, the Mauler won't come, and life here in Burrow and the valley between the hills will go on and on, season after season, just like it does now."

Thistle was naturally inclined to think his sister was more clever than a crow, but now he did a wild double flip of joy, jumping straight up and kicking his feet together in the air.

"Alice! You're a genius!" he cried.

"Stop all that cavorting, young 'un! You'll wake the owls for sure, and there's a litter of babies just behind you that don't yet know a zig from a zag." Old Lester's hops were getting shorter by the day. Sometimes he didn't even bother, and walked in a shuffling waddle. That's how he approached them now.

"Pish-posh, Lester!" Thistle sounded like Foxy when he said it. "It's not dark yet. The owls are still asleep. Listen to Alice! She's going to save the valley, the hills, Burrow, everything!"

"She is, eh?" Lester looked dubious, and Alice told the old rabbit her plan. When she was done, he growled, and his yellow teeth chattered with disbelief.

"Of all the rodent-brained ideas!" he exclaimed. ("Rodent-brained" is a very rude insult among rabbits and quite unfair to rodents, who have perfectly good brains. Rats are known to be especially sharp-witted, although not always sharp enough to avoid colliding with the wheels of an expensive Italian-made stroller when crossing a Brooklyn sidewalk.) "Rabbits can't be farmers! Why, that's colluding with the enemy. Where's the cottontail pride in that?"

"Same place it's always been," said Alice, with growing enthusiasm.

"Being clever and crafty! Tricky and hard to catch! Think of it this way, Lester: Once you brave the meadow, dodge the dog, outwit the farmer, and tunnel beneath the garden fence, what difference does it make what you do once you're inside?"

"No fence can stop a one of us, and no trap can catch us all," Thistle piped up. This was an old cottontail proverb that he'd most likely learned from Lester.

"No fence can stop us; no, sir . . . you're right about that, young 'un . . ." Lester grew quiet, for Alice's words had touched his very core. What self-respecting rabbit *wouldn't* hop at the chance to be tricky and hard to catch, zigzagging with merry confidence through a world full of predators and peril? This particular adventure may have come too late for a weary-legged, gray-whiskered flop-ears like Lester—but it wasn't too late for a young 'un to graze on glory, and hop on high for all that a rabbit stood for, no, sir!

Alice could tell the old rabbit was coming around by the way his back feet began to twitch. "And they'll never know it's us doing the farming! *You* can still sneak into a garden, can't you, Lester?" she teased.

The old bunny's chest puffed with pride. "You bet I can! At least, in my 'salad days,' I could." He paused and shimmied his tail to show he'd made a joke. "Sneaking in and sneaking out, hmm? Outwitting the farmers, eh? I like the way you think, young 'un." For a moment it looked like Lester was close to a celebratory hop himself.

"She's clever, isn't she, Lester?" Thistle said, wriggling with excitement.

"She's a cottontail! We're all clever, it can't be helped. Some are more clever than others, maybe," Lester added, a grudging compliment. His tail shimmied once more, to indicate a chuckle. "Boy, oh boy! What a change of outlook this will be! Rabbits being farmers! Rabbits growing vegetables! Of all the crazy, unnatural things."

"Can we steal a *few* vegetables, though?" Thistle begged. "A radish top? A single baby carrot?"

"No." Alice was firm. "We have to think like the farmers do. We want the vegetables to grow so the farmer-people can . . ." She paused. "Lester, what do farmers do with vegetables, anyway?"

"They sell them," he replied. "They bring them to market and turn them into money."

Here he had to pause to explain what money was, as Alice and Thistle had never heard of such a thing. Lester's own understanding was far from complete, but he did know two things about it: first, that money consisted of small circles of metal and rectangles of dry, tough paper, very hard to chew; and second, that money was the whole point of nearly everything people did.

"Turning perfectly good food into money squeezes all the juice out of it, in my opinion," he concluded. "I'd rather have a nice bushel of spinach, myself."

"Then we'll grow you some," Alice said, full of the confidence that comes of contemplating a great adventure that hasn't yet begun. "But you'll have to pay us money for it. Because we're going to be farmers now, too!"

⁂

"Look at me, Marie! I've got a golden parachute! I've got a golden parachute!" The dog ran back and forth in long semicircles, showing off the new bright yellow reflective doggy vest that Brad had purchased for her at the big hardware store in town.

The vest had been Sally's idea. She wouldn't let the dog set one paw outdoors without it, after what Mr. Rowes had said about hunters mistaking Foxy for a fox. It was the day after their rude encounter with Tom

Rowes. All that new information had had a powerful effect on the Harvey parents, but it wasn't the same effect: Sally was much more worried now than she'd been previously, while Brad had grown less so. If anything, he was feeling cocksure and ready for a fight.

This led to some misunderstandings between them. For example, she'd wanted him to get yellow vests for Carl and Marie, too, but Brad said she was making way too much of that whole unpleasant encounter with Mr. Rowes. The man was rude, no question, but he was in the business of making money first and foremost. Brad had known many such characters at his old job—he called them "clients"—and understood that people like that tended to bulldoze over the social niceties.

Sally was not one bit comforted by this and had offered two observations in return: Number one, good manners were not the only thing that awful man wanted to bulldoze. Number two, maybe they should have thought more carefully about the fact that they had no clue how to run a farm, as was made painfully clear by that illuminating visit from Farmer Janis.

Well, that was a whole other conversation, Brad replied, which they should certainly have at a later time, when Sally wasn't so busy overreacting. But overreacting was a poor word choice on Brad's part, as it made Sally doubly convinced that Brad wasn't seeing the seriousness of their predicament *at all*. The rest of Brad's day would be spent digging himself out of that particular hole—after he got back from the hardware store with the dog-sized yellow vest, of course.

Dogs have much better hearing than humans, and Foxy had gotten the gist of the previous day's events despite being locked in Carl's room for most of it. She wasn't angry at Carl about the accidental imprisonment. The boy had simply run out to chase a tractor. Frankly, she was proud of him, as Foxy approved of chasing vehicles in principle, though she'd never had the chance to do it herself.

Now she was tied with a long swivel-leash to a post in the backyard, in partial view of the kitchen. The Harveys couldn't have known that Old Man Crenshaw used to tie up his dog here, too, but a sturdy backyard post with a metal ring conveniently screwed on top spoke for itself. "Tie a dog to me," it said, and so Brad Harvey threatened to, sternly, when he discovered what Foxy had done to Carl's room while she'd been locked in and forgotten. She'd gouged deep claw marks on the door and chewed a hole in a pillow that sent feathers flying everywhere. *Buck-buck, buck-buck, buck-buck*—soon the whole family was saying it, as they cleaned up the downy mess.

But first the dog needed a yellow vest, Sally insisted, and that's how that got started.

As always, Foxy was deeply touched by how sweet her humans were, and how much they'd enjoyed the amusing feather-gathering game she'd provided. Look how nicely they'd thanked her! They'd put her outside, with her own new yellow cape to show just how special she was. It was the closest thing to a golden parachute around, and Foxy was the one who got to wear it, which was just as it should be. She wouldn't have minded a Spearmint-Flavored GlitterTooth Chew-Bone, either, but perhaps she'd get one later.

Marie was outside, too, buckled in her swing seat, chortling at the dog's antics. Carl slouched in a canvas camping chair next to the swing seat. He was supposed to be watching his sister and Foxy while his mom finished up a project in the kitchen, but since both baby and dog were tethered, the job didn't require much of his attention.

Instead, he played on a handheld game console of a type so prehistoric they didn't make it anymore. His dad had found it in the barn during the inspection that Janis had urged, buried in a pile of old tools and broken metal things. Brad had cleaned it up and put fresh batteries in it. Miraculously, it worked. Had Old Man Crenshaw played it? Carl couldn't imagine such a thing. Maybe the old guy had a great-great-great-grandchild who'd visited now and then.

"Wheeeee!" Foxy cried, zooming back and forth to the full length of the leash in a wide arc. "My parachute is a streak of purest gold, pulsing through the firmament!"

"Stop barking, Foxy," Carl said absently.

Marie shoved her fists into her eyes, she was laughing so hard.

"Chute!" she yelled. "Fa ma mint!!"

"You said it, Marie! I haven't felt this fancy since Carlsbad put me in that bumblebee costume last Halloween!" Foxy galloped one more truncated lap, then slammed on the brakes. She arched her back in a play bow and snarled at the sky just for fun, then sat in front of Marie and scratched beneath the yellow vest with her hind leg. "This front strap itches, I must say. The price one pays for being stylish!"

"Me, me." Marie kicked her feet in Foxy's direction.

"Aren't you a sweet little dumpling to offer! But those mushy toes of yours are of no use; my fur is much too thick and luxurious for them to penetrate. A job like this calls for—*ahhhhhh*—claws." Foxy tipped her head to the side and closed her eyes in bliss as she found the spot with her back foot. "*Ahhhhhh!* I believe the other side could use some attention, too. Thank goodness I'm flexible . . ."

Carl looked up, bored. His dad had called the console "eight-bit," but the game was just dumb. He'd already tried texting Emmanuel, but there was no signal. That Crenshaw guy must have been pretty eight-bit himself. He hadn't rigged the place with any modern conveniences—no cable, no internet of any kind, not even a rooftop antenna for regular TV. What did that old farmer do all day long, anyway?

"Chute!" Marie yelled, in a warning tone. Foxy's energetic scratching had managed to undo the front strap of the yellow vest. It was short work for the dog to wriggle out of it completely. She gnawed a few holes in the vest, for fun. She gave herself a happy shake that undulated from her wet black nose to the tip of her curled-up tail.

"*Au naturel* is best after all, come to think of it," Foxy said, fluffing herself. "Much more comfortable. Anyway, a coat this attractive ought not to be concealed. The thickness! The softness! And this glorious Shiba color, ooh la la! Some call it orange, but I think it's more of a burnt umber. Either way I'm a work of art, don't you agree?"

"Mom!" Carl bellowed, without getting up. "Foxy took off her yellow thing!"

Sally couldn't hear him, as she had the blender running. Unbeknownst to Marie, Sally was planning to mix pureed, home-cooked organic vegetables into the dinner applesauce. It was a secret plan, and it's why she'd sent the kids out of the kitchen for a few minutes.

Foxy seized the torn yellow vest in her mouth and ran with it, waving it like a flag. "Who wants a golden parachute?" she said, though her woofs were muffled. Marie was in stitches. "Who wants a golden parachute?"

"Me, me!" the baby said, spreading her arms.

Tik tik tik tik tik!

It was a whistling, high-pitched call, coming from the sky.

Marie and Foxy looked up. Even Carl looked up. High above, a bird circled. It was not your everyday bird. It was enormous, for one thing, although it was hard to tell exactly how big it was from the ground. It hardly moved its wings at all, just floated in the air like one of those balsa wood glider planes Carl had built from a kit once. With each lazy circle, the bird descended.

The lower it got, the bigger it looked.

"*Tik tik tik tik tik!*" the bird whistled again. It landed on the post and unfolded its wings. Carl literally fell out of his chair as he scrambled to get away, dragging Marie's bouncy seat with him.

From wingtip to outstretched wingtip was easily seven feet. The bird's body and wing feathers were blackish brown, but its head and neck were snowy white, and so was its blunt-edged tail. Its feet were as yellow as the torn vest dangling from Foxy's mouth, with black, curved claws that were each the length of Carl's whole hand.

Its beak was yellow, too, with a hooked tip that looked needle sharp. Its human-sized eyes were golden. Around one ankle, it wore a bracelet of white plastic, pulled very snug.

It was the most terrifying animal Carl had ever seen outside of a zoo. Yet there was something familiar about it. Maybe he'd seen one of its kind before somewhere, maybe in a book, or at the Natural History Museum. But what was it?

Then he figured it out.

"Mom!" he yelled. He grabbed Marie and ran for the house, the baby kicking in his arms. "There's a pterodactyl in the backyard! It's going to eat Foxy! Help, help!"

⁂

Foxy and the newcomer watched the humans disappear into the house.

"I apologize for the behavior of my boy," Foxy said, gazing up at the winged visitor. "You'd think he'd never seen a bird before, although you're quite a grand bird, if I may say so. He's more used to pigeons. Why, I bet you eat a dozen pigeons a day, for snacks!"

"I prefer fish, actually. I'm John," the bird said. "John Glenn. American bald eagle, genus *Haliaeetus*, species *leucocephalus*. It's an unusual name for a bird, I know. But I've had an unusual life. I was named after a famous human."

"Pish-posh! I think it's a fine name. I'm Foxy, named after a fox. Not a famous fox. Just a fox in general, due to the attractive resemblance." Foxy grinned and wagged her tail, as it always pleased her to think of how fox-like she was. "Do you resemble your famous human?"

"I don't think so. I've only seen pictures. He was bald, but I'm not; that's a misnomer." The eagle tipped his great white head downward, to show Foxy. "I have plenty of white feathers on my head. See?"

"I see that, yes. Abundantly feathered; quite thick." Foxy panted with friendliness. "Well, aren't we a pair, John Glenn! A bald eagle who's not bald, and a dog named after a fox."

"You're tied up," John Glenn said. "Would you like to run free?"

The dog's tail rocked back and forth twice before she stilled it. "I would adore nothing better, but at the moment, my leash is firmly attached to this post." She shook herself and tugged, but the collar held fast. "Funny; being on a leash never bothered me much before, but just yesterday I had a brief taste of the alternative. I must say, I rather liked it."

"I, too, have been tied up," John Glenn said darkly. "It saddens me to see you suffer the same fate. May I be of assistance?"

"You mean, unbuckle my collar? With those claws? No, thank you, I fear that's far too much trouble . . ." Making friends with the giant bird was one thing, yet Foxy had no desire for that terrifying beak or those curved, brutal claws to get anywhere near her throat.

But there was no time to object. Pushing off with his strong legs, his great wings half open, John Glenn floated off the post and landed smoothly on the ground right next to Foxy, who couldn't help but shrink back in fear. The bird was easily twice Foxy's height.

"Hold still, now," John Glenn commanded. He stretched out his thick neck and drew the razor tip of his beak across the dog's collar. One stroke was enough. The collar fell to the ground, sliced cleanly in two.

"My word, that *is* sharp!" Foxy exclaimed. "Thank heavens your aim is true."

"We eagles," John Glenn said modestly, "are known for our keen eyesight."

"I'm not surprised." Foxy trotted in a circle, amazed. "And look, I'm completely unfettered! No more vest or leash or collar, no more ceaseless jingle-jangle of those annoying metal tags. How marvelous! John Glenn, I can't thank you enough. If I can ever be of service to you, please don't hesitate to ask."

The eagle lifted onto his toes. His wings began to unfurl.

"I won't," said John Glenn. "I hope you enjoy being loose. Let freedom ring! That's what my scientists always say to me, when they set me loose."

The powerful wings spread wide and threw their shadow across the ground where Foxy stood.

"Your scientists? What on earth does that mean?" Foxy's tail drooped in confusion. "Wait, friend bird! Scientists—does that mean you're a robot? It's all right if you are; Carl has one in his room already and we get along fine. John Glenn! John Glenn!"

But the eagle had already returned to the sky.

CHAPTER NINE

The evidence is examined.

Farmer Thistle and Farmer Alice, as they immediately took to calling each other, zigzagged around the forest's edge until it was dark. They did it again the next morning during the breakfast graze, announcing their new venture to every cottontail they met.

Nearly all made the same reply that Lester had, at first: "Rabbits helping farmers! Rabbits *becoming* farmers? Are you out of your cottontail minds? Don't you know that farmers and rabbits aren't friends, have never been friends, and never will be friends?"

But the two kits wouldn't let their long ears hear no for an answer. Anything was better than the Mauler, they argued. Anyway, the new farmers were their neighbors, geographically speaking, and you don't have to see perfectly eye to eye with your neighbors to act neighborly toward them. That was just plain common sense in the valley between the hills. Matters relating to the food chain and who-eats-whom aside, what was good for one species was generally good for all. "One flood washes away all burrows," as the old rabbit proverb goes, "and one sun dries all the rain."

Alice and Thistle had to do a great deal of patient explaining to hop over all those nopes, can'ts, and nevers, but they had faith in the common sense of cottontails and didn't give up. Before the morning sun had risen past the treetops, they'd managed to get not all, but a good portion of the warren to agree that this farmer-rabbit business was maybe worth a try.

"Good luck, then," the other cottontails would remark as they turned back to their grazing, napping, cavorting, pellet-passing, and litter-making. "Let us know how it all turns out!" Which was their way of saying they'd gladly mind their own business about Alice and Thistle tending the farm, as long as they didn't have to get their own paws dirty with the actual doing of it.

This rankled Thistle, but Alice would simply reply, "Thanks, and we surely will, but there's just one more thing"—at which point she'd ask each rabbit to solemnly swear not to raid the garden that she and Thistle would work so hard to grow. This promise wasn't hard to obtain, since by this time everyone had heard that a drool-encrusted, tail-waggling menace of a dog now prowled those fertile premises! All the radishes in the world wouldn't tempt them to get within snapping distance of those vicious, rabbit-hungry jaws.

Now, Foxy was undeniably prone to tail-waggling, but if anyone at Prune Street Farm was drool-encrusted, it was Marie. Still, Alice and Thistle saw no need to correct the other rabbits' misapprehensions about Foxy. It seemed that even the idea of a dog on the farm could prove useful, once there was a vegetable garden to protect.

Isn't that something? Already the two young 'uns were starting to think like farmers, and they hadn't yet planted a seed.

⁂

Speaking of seeds: Getting hold of good seeds is the first order of business for any farmer. Cottontails don't gather or save seeds like some other animals do, so Alice and Thistle had to ask around. Who in the valley might have seeds to spare?

The squirrels loved to hoard food and would have been willing to help, but by spring they'd already eaten their winter stores. Even if they hadn't, acorns weren't the right kind of seeds for a vegetable garden. Acorns have one job and one job only, and that's to sprout into oak trees; no amount of tender care would persuade them to do otherwise.

"We need radish seeds, spinach seeds, and carrot seeds, to start," Alice explained to a blue jay. Most birds were seed eaters and experts on the subject, but they ate what they found and didn't save any. However, telling a blue jay was the quickest way to spread any kind of news in the valley. All the small animals gossiped among themselves, but once the blue jays knew something, everyone knew, for no bird loves to chatter more than a jay.

"And Swiss chard!" Thistle added. Lester had made them promise to find some.

"I'll do what I can, *caw!*" said the jay, and flew off.

It wasn't long before a small diplomatic envoy of chipmunks appeared at Split Rock, asking for Alice. Chipmunks are known for being great seed savers, so Alice and Thistle dropped what they were doing (which was napping, as they'd had a very busy morning already) and went to meet their visitors.

There were five of them lined up in a row, very formal looking, with their neatly striped flanks and wee front paws held up entreatingly near their mouths.

"It has come to our attention," said the chipmunk leader, "that you need seeds."

"That's right, we do," Alice said, flattening herself to the ground. The little fellow was barely the size of her head. "Do you have any?"

"Of *course* we have seeds," he retorted, his high voice full of scorn. "What do you think we are? Rabbits?"

"Apologies," Alice said quickly. "I didn't mean to offend."

"They're *our* seeds!" another chipmunk said, his plump cheeks atremble.

"If you need seeds now, you should have gathered and saved them in autumn, before winter came," the leader scolded. All five chipmunks wrung their paws in agreement.

Alice was flummoxed, but Thistle was nearer the chipmunks' size and better understood the impulse of the tiny to act bigger than they are. "We didn't gather any seeds in autumn," he explained gently, "because we weren't born yet."

The chipmunks laughed, a combination of high-pitched chirps and low-pitched chucks. "*Chip-chuck, chip-chuck!*" the leader chortled. "Since when do rabbits eat seeds, anyway? And in springtime, too! You've plenty of good grass and clover now."

"These are not eating seeds. They're planting seeds. We're farmer-rabbits now, and we intend to plant a vegetable garden down by the farmhouse." Alice did her best to sound nonchalant, as if rabbits did such things every day. "We don't need many seeds. Just enough to plant our first crops. Might you have just a few, to share?"

"We *eats* our seeds! We *needs* our seeds," the other chipmunks chimed in, breaking ranks and speaking over one another. "No sharing!"

"*Ch-ch-ch!*" the head chipmunk scolded, before turning back to Alice. "Our seeds are our business. We heard about your deal with the other rabbits, and we came to ask you this: Does this mean that we too will be expected to leave your 'garden' alone?"

"Even in autumn?" asked one chipmunk.

"Even the *seeds?*" asked another, nearly frantic.

They all looked gravely concerned. Chipmunks work to the point of obsession to fill their underground pantries in autumn. The seeds and nuts they save are what keep them alive during the cold, snow-blanketed days of winter, so you can see why the little striped creatures were so anxious about the idea of any seeds being off-limits.

"Actually, we were hoping you wouldn't leave the garden *completely* alone," Alice said, for their worried faces had given her an idea. "By harvest-time, we'll have so many seeds we'll need help gathering them all up! And no one's better at seed gathering than chipmunks." The local sparrows might have argued otherwise, as they were great seed gatherers, too, but Alice hoped to flatter her stylish little visitors. "Of course, you can keep what you gather."

Ten inflatable chipmunk cheeks puffed greedily at the thought.

"That we can surely help you with," the leader said.

"The thing is," Alice went on, "we would need just a few of your saved seeds now, to get the garden started. Otherwise there won't be a harvest-time. Assuming you've got the right kinds of seeds, of course."

She threw Thistle a meaningful look.

"Oh, naturally! They have to be the right kinds of seeds, or the deal's off," he said, full of bravado. "You don't happen to have any vegetable seeds, do you?"

The chipmunks consulted among themselves, for they were proud of being organized, and their storehouse was as well-ordered as a library. One of them finally spoke. "We have carrots, lettuce, basil, zucchini, spinach, three kinds of tomatoes, string beans, green peas, bell peppers, garlic chives, and radishes. And pumpkin."

"Wow! Where'd you get all those?" Thistle asked, impressed.

They all laughed, *chip-chuck, chip-chuck.* "The lady-human with the green tractor plants a vegetable garden every year," the chipmunk leader said. "She plants it twice, I mean! We dig it all up the first time." He paused. "We can still raid *her* garden, can't we?"

"I don't see why not. Her garden is no concern of ours," Alice said (and she was mistaken in this, but she was new to farming and still had a lot to learn). "Those seeds will do. Bring us enough to plant our garden and, come fall, you'll get back ten times as many seeds in return."

"A hundred times as many!" exclaimed Thistle, for rabbits are good at multiplying. The chipmunks looked confused.

"It'll be as much as your cheeks can carry," Alice assured them.

That was all the chipmunks needed to hear. After promising to deliver the seeds to the garden that very evening after dark, they bowed their neatly striped bodies all at once—they really were quite dapper looking—and took their leave.

Alice couldn't have been more pleased, and Thistle was already counting radishes in his mind. What tricky, clever farmer-rabbits they were, convincing those hotheaded little rodents to go into business with them! Tonight they'd make their first trip to the garden to plant the seeds the chipmunks brought. With a little bit of sun, rain, and time, the garden would be as good as grown.

Wouldn't the farmer-people be surprised!

⁂

"We'll get to the bottom of this, kid, don't worry." Farmer Janis sounded like one of those detectives on TV who talk fast and never smile. "I'll need a pair of chopsticks."

That Foxy had run off for a second time would have been more of an annoyance than a catastrophe, if not for the terrible evidence found at the site of the dog's disappearance. Carl had burst into the kitchen yelling about pterodactyls and wouldn't stop until Sally shut off the blender and agreed to come outside and see for herself. In Carl's mind the bird monster had grown to Godzilla-like proportions, and it got bigger and meaner each time he described it.

"It wasn't a pterodactyl, honey. It couldn't have been."

"But it had claws! *Huge* claws! Bigger than Marie's head!"

From Sally's hip, Marie let out a wail of displeasure.

"It's all right, cutie." Sally switched the baby to the other side as she walked. "Anyway, dinosaurs are extinct, Carl."

"Your statement is false," Carl retorted. They were nearly at the scene of the crime. "What about the living dinosaurs that are birds? That's what they said in the movie."

"Do you mean the movie at the Natural History Museum?"

"Yes. But don't start talking about what's-her-name, *please*."

The Natural History Museum's movie about how birds were living dinosaurs was narrated by an actor named Meryl Streep, who happened to be Sally's favorite—so much so that Sally had gushed about how great Meryl Streep was every single time Carl had seen the film. He'd seen it a lot, thanks to family outings, the school field trips Sally chaperoned, and the many visiting friends and relatives they'd taken to the museum over the years. Poor Carl had already heard more about the genius what's-her-name than was strictly normal for a boy his age. Alas, it was about to happen again.

"When Meryl Streep said that birds were living dinosaurs, she meant that today's birds are descended from dinosaurs." Sally spoke as calmly yet expressively as Meryl Streep would have. "She didn't mean that pterodactyls are going to land in the backyard and steal your dog."

That's when Carl spotted the torn yellow dog vest lying on the ground. "Where's Foxy?" he cried.

Sally reached the post and looked around. "Wasn't she tied up?"

The ruined collar with its useless tags lay at their feet.

"Big bah, bye-bye!" said Marie.

Indeed, the big bird had gone bye-bye. So, it appeared, had Foxy.

Brad wasn't home, and with such spotty cell service, there was no knowing when he'd get Sally's panicked message. In need of backup, Sally had called Janis, who'd pedaled right over on her Schwinn, as Tin Can (that's what she called her tractor) was in sore need of new spark plugs. The vintage bike was painted John Deere green and sported a yellow wicker basket and rainbow streamers.

Now they were all in the kitchen with Exhibit A, the vest, and Exhibit B, the collar, displayed on the table before them.

Using the chopsticks Sally solemnly provided, Janis lifted each item in turn and gave it the once-over. "Evidence of foul play? Maybe. Maybe not."

"Why chopsticks?" Carl asked. "Do you think there are fingerprints?"

"Nah, I just need the practice. I have dinner plans this weekend at a restaurant that doesn't use forks. I don't want to embarrass myself."

There was a scuffling noise outside, and a *thump*.

"Someone's at the door!" Carl said, running to see. "Maybe it's Foxy!"

But it was only Brad, his arms laden with books and magazines he'd had to drop on the mat so he could rummage for his key. He'd been at the regional Farm Bureau office when he'd gotten Sally's message that the dog had disappeared. To be completely honest, he hadn't rushed home as quickly as he might have. The comings and goings of a dog on a farm didn't merit this level of scrutiny, in his newly ruralized opinion. He'd even stopped at the diner and treated himself to a coffee and doughnut on the way home, sitting at the counter with the local paper and feeling like a lucky man indeed.

"Hey, honey! I got your text, finally." He kissed Sally on the cheek and Marie on the head. "Howdy, son o' mine. Howdy, Janis. So, the dog ran off again, huh?" He began to dump his armload of reading materials on the table.

Carl stopped him. "Not there, Dad! We're examining the evidence."

Obediently, Brad regathered his books. "She'll come back when she's hungry, champ, like she did the other day. She's a country dog now. She'll play outside during the day and come home for dinner—what's that?"

Janis held two chopsticks in front of Brad's face. The torn yellow vest dangled from one, and the sliced dog collar hung from the other. "Doesn't look good, Brad," she said. "The dog is gone, and this is all that's left. The kid says a bird took it."

Brad put his books on a chair. "That's weird," he conceded.

Carl leaned on the table. "Not a bird. A pterodactyl. With claws."

"Big bah," Marie agreed.

Brad gave his wife a look before answering, "Okay, but it wasn't a pterodactyl, champ."

"But what about Meryl Streep?" Carl looked imploringly at his mom, who busied herself spooning green-tinged applesauce into a bowl. "Dad, I *saw* it. Marie saw it, too! You have to believe me!"

Brad spoke in an extra-reasonable tone. "I believe you, Carl. You saw something big, maybe a bird, with claws that made you think of a pterodactyl. What kind of animal could that be?"

"Book!" Marie yelled, grabbing with her sticky hands.

"Careful, peanut, I have to return that . . ." Brad rescued the book she was reaching for. It was *An Illustrated History of the Tractor.*

Janis's eyes lit up. "Nice! Where'd you get that?"

Brad handed it to her. "The Farm Bureau lending library. I was doing research. Orchard management, cover crops. You know." He sounded pleased with himself, slinging around farmer talk like an old hand.

Janis leafed through the pages. "Eagle Tractor, will you look at that. Started building tractors in 1906, in Appleton, Wisconsin. One of the first manufacturers to use a six-cylinder engine. Their 1929 Model E was tough enough to take down a house." She paused and dabbed at her eyes with the edge of her neckerchief. "Sorry, I'm a real tractor nerd. They're such beautiful machines."

"Big bahhhhhhhh," Marie said, long and loud, banging on the page with her fist.

"That's it! That's the pterodactyl!" Carl grabbed the book. The page Janis had open showed a vintage advertisement for Eagle Tractor, with a picture of the namesake bird right up top.

Sally put down her mixing spoon and came to look. "Eagle Tractor. That's the bird you saw? Did it have a white head?"

Carl tried to remember. "Maybe. I think it did."

"Well, why didn't you say so? There's only one kind of bird with a white head like that!" Sally sounded exasperated, but one could easily imagine her relief: Meryl Streep got it wrong for once, and ravenous living dinosaurs did not prowl the skies above the Country Dream House in which her children slept.

"Who cares about the color of its head?" Carl retorted. "It was big! With a beak! And claws!"

Janis put an understanding hand on his shoulder. "It was the life-threatening details that caught your attention, kid, and that's perfectly natural. It means your fight-or-flight reflex is working, and you're a brave boy for not freezing up in terror and leaving your sister out there alone. You saved the baby from Godzilla, and I bet she'll thank you for it one day."

"Big bah, ja glaaa!" Marie squealed. "Fah ma mint." By which she meant that the big bird named John Glenn was no silly lizard monster from a low-budget horror movie, but a national icon who had flown back to the glorious firmament of the sky, where he belonged.

"Bath time is later, punkin; be patient," Brad cooed in answer. "Janis, are bald eagles common around here?"

Janis shook her head. "I've never seen one. They were gone for a long time. Now they've come back. They're mostly fish eaters. They hunt up and down the river, thataways." She waved a hand to indicate where thataways was.

Carl struggled to understand. "What do you mean, they've come back? From where?"

"From nearly going extinct." Janis made a throat-cutting gesture. "Lights out! This whole beautiful valley was their habitat, until people messed up the water. You want more details, talk to a bird scientist."

"Bird scientists are called ornithologists," Sally said knowingly, in her Meryl Streep voice.

"I wonder what drew it away from the river. They can see for miles, though—maybe something unusual caught its eye." Janis turned to Carl. "What were you kids doing when this highly symbolic bird arrived?"

Carl thought. "I was sitting, Marie was sitting, and Foxy was tied to the post, running back and forth."

"Wearing this. Interesting." Janis waved the yellow vest back and forth in a semicircle. "Like a golden arch. Plenty of folks will pull right off the interstate when they see one of those in the distance. Maybe our bird's no different."

Brad was still fingering the collar. "Janis, is it possible that an eagle—*took*—the dog?"

"Carried it away and ate it, you mean?"

"Don't say that!" Carl objected.

"Two words for you, kid: Chicken. Fingers. The bird's gotta eat, no different from you and me." Janis scratched her chin. "How much does the dog weigh?"

Brad looked at Sally, who made a thinking face. "Maybe fourteen pounds?" she guessed.

"That seems like a lot for a bird to carry. But I'm no expert."

"I think Foxy is fine," Carl declared, with sudden forced optimism. "The eagle scared her and she got loose somehow and ran off to play. She'll be back."

"Let's hope." Janis turned to Sally. "Out of curiosity: What was the point of the vest?"

Sally looked embarrassed. "Well, you've seen her. She looks like a fox. We were afraid of hunters."

"It was something Tom Rowes said," Brad explained. "He said that the local hunters might get—confused."

"Well, he's not wrong about that. If it looks like a fox it'll get treated like a fox. But hunting season's not until fall. Rowes was just being what my drooling friend here would call a poopy. I wouldn't worry about it. Much."

Brad turned the dog collar over and examined the severed edge. "That's a clean cut. Could have been a knife. But who'd do a thing like that?"

"I know who." Carl ran both hands over his head, to indicate complete and utter baldness.

Janis looked dubious. "That's awfully low to stoop. Anyway, why not just unbuckle the collar?" She tapped her fingers on the table, thinking. "It was definitely an eagle you saw? And you were only gone a few minutes?"

Carl nodded, his optimism already fading.

"It's a mystery, kid." Janis stood to go. "But I like mysteries. I'll keep an eagle eye out for your dog. Eagle eye, get it? You wanna come feed my chickens? Nope? Still feeling bad about those fingers, huh?"

"*Veggie!*" Marie roared. She splayed her own fingers in displeasure and pushed the new green applesauce out of her mouth with her tongue. It was like something out of a horror movie called *Attack of the Disgusting Baby*, and Brad and Sally both leapt into action to clean her up.

Janis leaned over to Carl. "Sounds like your sister wants to know if you plan to become a vegetarian. Thoughts?"

Carl couldn't bring himself to answer. "I'm gonna sit outside and wait for Foxy," he said, and that's what he did.

CHAPTER TEN

Foxy makes a friend.

Where, oh where, was Foxy? And how would she possibly manage with no ID tags, no reflective yellow vest, and no reliable smell map of where she was? Her go-to landmark aromas that showed the way home—the tempting meat sizzle from the hot dog stand at the entrance to the park; the school playground that smelled like gym socks, sunscreen, and peanut butter; the front steps to their old building on Oxford Street, where every dog in the neighborhood liked to spritz a little "hello, there" on the ironwork railing—were all a hundred and fifty miles away.

The Harveys were worried and longed for Foxy to come back, but they may have been underestimating their little Shiba.

In the first place, the supersized Smell-O-Vision that comes as standard dog equipment is nothing short of a superpower, as impressive as the eyes of an eagle. Foxy may have gone soft from being a house pet, but a dog is a dog is a dog. Her nose worked just fine, and all her animal instincts were still there, if rusty. A few hours of running in the woods would sort that right out. She hadn't been outdoors without a collar on in her whole life, and although she felt a wee bit naked, she also felt thrillingly, dizzyingly wild.

She wanted to run everywhere and sniff everything, to nourish her primal dogness with the smells of this new place, which were so unlike the smells she'd known before. Brooklyn was all stony concrete pavement, asphalt streets, and car exhaust, with top notes of pizza and the occasional, irresistible stink of a hydrant.

And the Goldfish crackers! That smell was all over Brooklyn, especially in the park. All the Marie-sized people were always eating them and dropping them. The kids smelled like Goldfish crackers, and so did the parents' coat pockets, the strollers and diaper bags, too. Foxy had seen a real goldfish when Carl briefly kept one in a bowl in his room (the boy's interest in the new pet didn't last long, and the goldfish didn't, either), and she could not figure out how one of those small, shiny swimmers could be multiplied into such a vast quantity of cheesy-flavored treats.

That was all behind her now. Thanks to John Glenn, she was Foxy the Free, and the perfumed air currents were blowing in from miles around. She planned to follow her nose and see where it led. Maybe she'd try to find that noble, sharp-beaked bird again, to thank him, and then look for those friendly rabbits who'd had to leave so abruptly, but the smells of nature were numerous and subtle, and her own soapy lavender fragrance was getting in the way. The first order of business was to get rid of it.

She followed the cool metallic scent of water to the crooked stream that ran through the back of the property, behind the orchards. After a few exploratory paw dips, she plunged all the way in. The water ran fast and cold, as springtime streams do, and she stayed in until she shivered.

The stream bath removed most, but not all, of her floral shampoo smell, so she rolled on her back on the streambank and wriggled in the mud. Soon she was plastered with odorous muck.

"Much better!" she thought, giving herself a splattering shake. "I would so love to see my reflection in the water and admire it, the way I used to do in the pond in the park, but this stream is too fast-moving for that. I must look like a true creature of the wild, all matted and muddy! The very picture of untamed ferocity and canine pride! Now all I need is a pack to lead and a few starlit nights baying at the moon. I've always been adorable, but in my current ungroomed state, I do believe I've acquired some gravitas . . ."

She thought all this as she clambered up the bank to flatter, drier ground—and gazed upon her reflection. There she was, right in front herself.

She tipped her head to the side, puzzled.

Her reflection did the same.

She swiveled her ears forward, in a gesture of keen alertness.

So did her reflection.

She pulled back her lips to show her teeth. When her reflection followed suit, she startled. "Oh no!" she exclaimed. "Those Spearmint-Flavored GlitterTooth Chew-Bones are not working as advertised. Look at all that tooth gunk!"

"I beg your pardon," the reflection said, "but I've only just eaten. Once I take a drink from the stream, my mouth will be much cleaner."

Foxy wasn't sure how to react, so she did what any reasonably friendly dog would do when meeting her double: She panted through a half smile and wagged her curled-up tail in hope.

"You poor thing," the creature said. "What happened to your tail?" It raised its own tail, which was long and bushy and straight.

Foxy waggled her doughnut-shaped tail faster. "Well, this is unexpected! Look at us: same color, same size, same pointed snout and stand-up ears. Only our tails tell us apart. I'd bet my favorite chew toy that you're a fox. Am I right?"

"Of course I'm a fox," the fox said. "But I'm not sure what you are. A strange-smelling fox with a broken tail, perhaps? My condolences if so. Were you caught in a trap?"

Foxy's lips pulled back in displeasure. "I beg your pardon, but my tail is flawless. A tightly curled tail is a great point of pride among my kind." Still, hers drooped in dismay. "I'm a dog, if you must know. But in what way am I strange-smelling?"

"You smell like flowers that shouldn't be in bloom for months yet, mixed with . . . let me think." The fox sniffed. "Goose poop! You must have rolled in the mud by the stream."

"I thought it would cover the dog shampoo," Foxy admitted.

The fox wrinkled his nose. "It's too much. My advice is to wash it off. The stronger your scent, the harder it is to sneak up on your prey."

"Sneak up on my prey? How thrilling." Foxy trotted back to the stream and plunged in once more. "Brrrr! It's not so cold!" she yapped, shivering. After climbing out she shook herself again, thoroughly. "Now, be frank, friend fox. Do I smell any better?"

The fox had followed her to the stream's edge to lap water. He lifted his head, muzzle dripping. "Much better. If you dry off by rolling in the meadow grass it'll help a lot. Smelling like grass is good cover. I'd say let's go hunting, but I've just eaten." Now that his teeth had been rinsed, he smiled with confidence. "What's your name?"

Foxy hesitated, but she was a truthful creature at heart. She summoned as much dignity as a wet dog could.

"My name," she said, "is Foxy. What's yours?"

The fox looked at her in amazement.

"You're not going to believe this," he said, "but my parents named me Doggo."

Now, foxes are known for their quick wits, and after a moment's surprise Foxy realized the fox must be joking. Doggo! The irony! But he insisted he wasn't, and that she must call him Doggo, as it was his true name and he was used to it.

They exchanged more pleasantries as Foxy rolled in the sweet grass and shook herself again in the sun. Soon she felt dry enough to continue adventuring.

"I imagine you know this area well, Doggo," she said. "I'm looking for some friends of mine. Perhaps you might tell me where to find them?"

"More dogs?" he asked, sounding cautious. "You seem nice, but I wouldn't like to be outnumbered by a pack. Nothing personal. We foxes live solitary lives, and we're not terribly trusting, as a rule."

Foxy chuckled. "Oh, no, not dogs! All my dog friends are in the dog run in Brooklyn. No, these friends must live nearby; they're too small to travel far. They're rabbits."

"Rabbits?" Doggo repeated, with a strange tenderness in his voice.

"Yes, and rather young. Do you know where the rabbits around here live?"

Doggo licked his muzzle. "I believe I do. I could tell you how to get there, but I'd much rather show you. Would you like that?"

Foxy, who'd never in her life eaten any meat that didn't come out of a can, was delighted at the fox's kind offer of an escort, and off they went.

⁂

Once Alice and Thistle finished congratulating themselves about their clever deal with the chipmunks, they'd gone right to work. First, they consulted with Lester about the various vegetables—which ones liked to spread out and which liked to climb, which loved the sun and which tended to wilt in the heat—and between Lester's own youthful garden-raiding experience and his vast intake of seed catalogs, farming magazines, and so on, they'd come up with a fine plan for their garden.

There was only one problem left: How would they travel back and forth every night to care for their new, tender green responsibilities? Two small rabbits crossing the meadow after dark were easy pickings for the night predators, and though they knew that rabbitfolk don't live long, these two particular rabbitfolk had a job to do. Being careful was no guarantee they'd make it to harvesttime to finish what they'd started, and finish they must. They hadn't forgotten about the Mauler for a second.

"I wish I had an answer for you, but there's many who prefer to dine by starlight. Especially the owls," Lester said. They were talking it over at Split Rock while enjoying the warmth of the sun-warmed stone. "May the luck of the Great Rabbit be with you!"

"We were hoping for a more practical solution," Alice said, watching a family of lizards sunning themselves. They nested in the cool damp earth beneath the rock and spent the day sunbathing on the stone, a near-perfect match to their mottled gray skin. "What if we disguised ourselves as something predators don't eat?"

"If it's alive, they'll eat it. That's what predator means." Lester thumped the rock and sent the lizards scattering. "And two hopping rocks zigzagging through the meadow wouldn't fool anyone. Bleh! That's a foul stench in the air all at once." Lester's tail flashed, ready to bolt. "Smells like we're about to have company."

Alice and Thistle smelled it, too. It was the stink of carnivore, and the cottontails' feet vibrated with the rapid approach.

"Friend rabbits, friend rabbits!" a joyful voice cried, getting closer. "How delightful to find you once more."

"Run!" Lester yelled, already bolting. But Alice and Thistle stayed put. Seconds later, a furry orange face loomed before them.

Alice didn't move, except for her quivering whiskers. "You smell different," she said.

"I've been swimming in the stream, that's all. It's quite muddy. And those geese! They're everywhere."

Thistle hopped forward, delighted. "Hello, friend dog! You found us! Do you want to chase me now?"

Those thin lips spread into smile. "Well, all right, since you ask! How about I give you a head start? You go, and I'll count to three before I follow."

Thistle thumped his feet in pleasure, as all young rabbits love to play chase. "Wonderful! Okay, here I go!"

With a mighty push of his strong back legs, Thistle bounded into the meadow.

"One." The animal gazed at Alice with amber eyes. "Two."

"Hey," Alice said, her fur bristling. "You're not Foxy, are you?"

"Oh, but I am," the creature said. "I am as foxy as foxy can be. Three!" It tore off into the meadow after Thistle.

"Thistle, come back!" Alice cried, but a rabbit's voice is not a loud one. "Thistle! *Thistle!*"

The real Foxy had spent nearly as many hours watching Carl play *Attack of the Zombie Dinosaur Skeletons* as Carl had spent playing it, which meant that, despite her excellent diet, she was not in the best of shape. Heavy-footed and panting with exertion, the exhausted dog finally came galumphing through the grass.

"Alice, is that you?" she said, her tail rocking back and forth in weary victory. "I nearly gave up, but now I'm glad I didn't. My friend Doggo offered to help me find you, but he's so quick! I couldn't keep up. And he can climb trees, too! It's practically catlike. I was very impressed."

"Doggo?" Alice repeated. She too was winded, from calling for Thistle. "He's your friend and looks like you?"

"Almost exactly like, yes. Have you seen him?"

Alice's heart slowed with relief. Another dog like Foxy was probably fine. "Yes, he's here. He's playing chase with Thistle."

"Chase! Do you think that's wise?" Foxy's regal expression grew suddenly fierce.

"Well, all dogs are not as bad as we rabbits think," Alice replied, now confused. "You said so yourself."

"On a case-by-case basis, that is surely true . . . but Doggo is no dog."

Alice's paws clenched. "What is he, then?"

"He's—oh dear!" Foxy exclaimed, and raced off into the meadow herself.

Alice hopped on Split Rock, stood tall, and yelled as loud as she could. "Thistle! *Thistle!*"

"What?" Thistle was back, breathless and thrilled. "Well, I've never run so fast in my life! Zigging and zagging! I tell you, Alice, it's a whole different experience to run when someone's *really* chasing you. You find speed you didn't know you had! But now my legs are absolutely limp." The happy kit rolled onto his side, spent.

Doggo trotted up right behind him, panting hard.

"Well, friend rabbit—quick friend, quick rabbit!—that was a marvelous adventure! Lucky for you I've eaten recently. A big meal makes a slow fox, as my mother always said, and a wise vixen she was, too."

Moments later Foxy appeared, her fur so stiffly bristled with outrage it flared around her neck and shoulders like the mane of a miniature lion.

"Doggo, how could you! It seems you've had some fun at the expense of my friends. I am not pleased about it, not one bit! Why can't you learn to chase a ball, for heaven's sake? Thistle, poor fellow, are you all right?"

But at the sight of both dog and fox Thistle finally realized the truth of things; now he was fear-frozen and on his way to worse. "A big meal makes a slow . . . slow . . . oh!" he stammered. Then he fainted.

⁂

He hadn't gone dark, but he'd come close. Foxy scolded Doggo roundly as Alice huddled with her brother, nuzzling him back to life. After a few minutes Thistle was fine, and the rabbits weren't nearly as upset about the incident as Foxy was. Rabbits are used to fear, and they don't think of it as a bad thing. As Thistle himself said, it puts a bit of extra kick into the legs when needed.

And fear doesn't stick to rabbits. Even if a cottontail's been frightened half to death, when the danger's gone, the fear goes with it. Once Thistle awoke and realized he was still alive, with Alice right there and Foxy, too, while a guilt-ridden Doggo stood nearby, wearing the most hangdog expression ever yet seen on a fox—why, he thought it was all quite hilarious.

"And I thought Doggo was Foxy, and . . . well, all I can say is, if I live to be as old as Lester and tell an old rabbits' tale like this one, the kits won't believe it for a minute! 'Hey, young 'uns! Did I ever tell you about the time I asked a fox to chase me?' 'Why'd you do that, Old Thistle?' 'Because I thought it was a dog!' Oh, my! Can you imagine?" His little body shook with silent laughter.

"All right, I heard my name mentioned—and I'll thank you not to make fun of me," Lester said, slowly hopping toward them. His attempt at bolting hadn't gotten the old trickster too far, and he'd quickly found the courage to come back, which was no small thing. "And here I thought we'd lost you two young 'uns." Bravely, he looked Foxy and Doggo in their near-identical eyes (Doggo's were more amber-colored, and Foxy's were brown). "All right, tell me: Which one of you is the good dog?"

"I'm a good dog, I'm a good dog!" Foxy blurted, out of habit. Then she regained her composure. "That is, I am Foxy, resident dog of the farm across the meadow. You have nothing to fear from me, as I'm on a special rabbit-free diet. And this is my"—*friend* seemed too intimate a word, given Doggo's recent behavior—"fellow canine, Doggo." Her ears swiveled forward, signaling full alertness. "Full disclosure: Doggo is a fox, and not entirely in control of his impulses."

"I'm just wild," Doggo explained. "Not tame, like Foxy."

"I would not describe myself as tame," Foxy said haughtily. "However, I am domesticated, and proudly so. Good manners are a virtue."

Doggo sneered. "Well, I'm neither. I'll do my best, but no guarantees, rabbits! A fox has to eat, just as you do. I see no reason to change my ways."

Lester took another hop, right up to the fox's pointed snout. "Understood, fox. It's the way of things. Even so, I'd appreciate it if you'd pick on the older rabbits first. A young fellow like Thistle here deserves a little more time in the meadow, if you get my drift."

Doggo seemed unmoved by this argument. "And which do *you* prefer, old rabbit?" he retorted. "The tough bark of winter, or the tender green grass of spring?"

"Speaking of tender greens," Alice interrupted, for she felt no good could come of Lester and Doggo arguing about which rabbits to eat and in what order, "Thistle and I intend to visit the farm tonight after dark, to plant the garden. Foxy, could you travel with us, to make sure we don't get taken by owls on the way?"

"I'd be delighted," Foxy said. "But I won't be able to bring you back again. Once the Harveys find me, I'll likely be tied up again for a good, long time. But perhaps our wild friend here could help? As a way of making amends for today's poor choices?"

All eyes turned to Doggo. The fox gaped at them, disbelieving.

"Do you honestly expect me to escort *rabbits*?" he exclaimed. "At night? Those are my prime hunting hours! I'll be hungry by then, too."

"My dear Doggo," Foxy said, "it's the least you could do, after frightening poor Thistle half to death. However, I am prepared to offer a further incentive." The dog's manner softened, and her eyes grew bright. "Have you ever tasted a Spearmint-Flavored GlitterTooth Chew-Bone?"

"No," Doggo said, wary. "Should I have?"

"Oh, friend fox! You have no idea." Foxy closed her eyes and waggled her tail in bliss. "Absolutely the *most* delicious thing in the world. And I will be blunt, for what is a friend, if not someone who will tell you the uncomfortable truth? You need them."

"Why?"

"To make your teeth white and your breath smell nice."

"But I don't care about that."

"Well, you should. Didn't you tell me that having a strong smell was bad for hunting?"

"All foxes stink," Lester said, full of scorn. "They're almost as bad as skunks."

Doggo's pupils narrowed into slits as he stared at Lester. A thin strand of drool dripped from his mouth.

Dainty as a dancer, Foxy stepped between them. "I realize personal hygiene is a sensitive subject! Even so, Doggo, you will not be sorry to taste these GlitterTooth treats! You'll love them, I promise. But in exchange, *you* must promise to escort the rabbits safely to and from the farm, whenever they need you. Do you solemnly swear?"

Now, as he himself had admitted, Doggo was a wild creature driven by his appetites, and unused to negotiations at this sophisticated level. And Foxy was charming in a way this country bumpkin of a fox had never seen before. He found himself being persuaded in spite of himself.

"Are there any traps?" he asked, quite practically.

"Traps? Heavens, no! My humans are not the trap-setting kind."

"Maybe I'll do it, then," the fox said, beginning to yield. "When can I have one of the treats?"

"Very soon! I've trained Carl to fetch them on demand. As soon as I get home I'll start begging for them, and I'll put some aside for you."

"We'll need to visit the garden most nights," Alice said quickly. "From now until the autumn harvest. That's a lot of treats. Do you promise?"

"Autumn harvest!" Doggo objected. "It's barely springtime now."

Foxy came so close to Doggo, their noses nearly touched. "Time flies, dear fox! It's a modest and dare I say noble commitment, to protect these sweet bunnies for a few short months! All in exchange for that rarest of pleasures, the finest of treats, the best of the GlitterTooth product line. It will take all my willpower to part with them, Doggo! Those spearmint Chew-Bones are—ahhh! Words cannot begin to describe."

Then Foxy drew back her lips, and the light glinted off her smile. Her once-perfumed fur now reeked of dirty, wet dog, but her breath was minty fresh, and her teeth glowed like a moonlit bone.

Doggo not only found himself agreeing to this absurd schedule of rabbit-escort duties, but feeling deeply pleased with the new arrangement without even knowing why.

You might say he'd been outfoxed.

CHAPTER ELEVEN

The night of the great planting.

Carl sat on the back steps, waiting. There were two things on his mind which at first seemed unrelated, but the longer he sat, the more he suspected that maybe they had something to do with each other after all.

One was his missing dog. The other was Janis's chickens.

That's what sitting in quiet rumination will get you. For the first time in his young life, Carl suddenly found it strange that he should care so deeply about the well-being of one particular animal, while shamelessly dipping batter-fried parts of others in barbecue sauce and chomping away.

Dogs were more lovable than chickens, of course—or were they? Maybe he only felt that way because he didn't have a pet chicken, while he did have a pet dog. He used to, anyway. At the moment, he didn't know whether he'd ever see Foxy again.

And why would Farmer Janis name her chickens in the first place? Didn't that just make things worse, in the end?

Every now and then, one of his parents would come outside to check on him. They'd offer snacks and glasses of lemonade. He'd refuse. If

Foxy hadn't yet come home to eat, he wasn't going to eat anything, either. Inevitably, they'd suggest he wait inside, where it was warmer.

"Not yet," he said, hunkering down. "I'm waiting for Foxy."

His stomach was sure feeling empty, though. Finally, Brad ventured out with a jacket on, all premeditated, and sat down next to Carl. There was a bag of pretzels in Brad's coat pocket but he didn't make a fuss about it; he just put it there on the steps between them and matter-of-factly tore it open.

"I'm not coming in," Carl said, stubborn as a post.

"I know. I'm just keeping you company." Brad thoughtfully removed a pretzel from the bag and stuck it in his mouth. "I thought maybe we could talk about school. Spring break's almost over. All the local kids will be going back next week."

"I'm not going to a new school," Carl said.

"Champ, I thought you were on board with this—"

"I changed my mind."

"Well, you can't go back to your old school," his dad replied, quite reasonably.

"That is correct," Carl said in his robot voice.

Sally opened the door. "Hey, men," she said, with false cheer. "Anybody interested in dinner?"

Carl leaned back on his hands and talked straight up. "Mom. I'm not going to a new school."

"That's a big statement right out of the blue—"

"I'm the one that brought it up," Brad began, like a man confessing to a crime, but Carl interrupted.

"Dad just asked me about it. I changed my mind. I'm not going."

"I see." Sally looked at Brad with lifted eyebrows. "Maybe this is not the best time to talk about it?"

"CORRECT." Carl's robot voice settled the matter.

Sally pursed her lips until they looked like they'd been through the dehydrator twice. Then she dropped whatever she'd been thinking and spoke, pleasant as can be. "Well, Marie's napping. I only wanted to know if I should start dinner."

As ever, Carl marveled at how hard it was for grown-ups to stay on one subject. "I just want Foxy to come home," he muttered.

"We all do. But you must be hungry, honey. At least let me bring you a snack."

"I already brought him snacks. See?" Brad crinkled the pretzel bag, as if to demonstrate that he'd gotten something right.

"Snacks! That's a great idea." Carl jumped to his feet, inspired. "Mom! Can I have some treats?"

Sally frowned. "Do you mean Goldfish crackers? I stopped buying those, you know that."

"No, Foxy's treats. Those minty Chew-Bones that she loves. I need a whole box."

Brad nodded. "Interesting, champ. What do you plan to do with them?"

Carl helped himself to a pretzel. "You'll see."

⁂

Hunger was a curious sensation for Foxy, who'd been bountifully fed all her life. It seemed to sharpen her senses, which was interesting. The strong rabbit aroma surrounding Burrow became ever more pleasing to her, although she certainly didn't plan to do anything about it. It was along the lines of how bacon sizzling in the pan is universally delicious-smelling, even to a stalwart vegetarian.

Foxy envied the casual ease of the rabbits' dining habits. They just nibbled on the grass whenever they chose, no can opener required. Soon she began wondering about this "hunting for prey" activity that Doggo had mentioned, and how that experience might compare to the satisfying but monotonous nutrition offered by her daily prescription diet from Dr. Yang, can after identical can.

She would have liked to ask Doggo more about it, but he'd already left to spend the rest of the day in his foxhole, alone. Resisting temptation takes effort, and the poor fox had quickly grown exhausted from it. Foxy didn't mind; in fact she'd encouraged him to go have a nap. "Make sure you eat something, too!" she called, sounding like Sally. She wanted the fox well-rested and well-fed before he saw Alice and Thistle again.

The afternoon sun was low in the sky. It would be hours yet before she could bring the rabbits across the meadow. The chipmunks wouldn't arrive until after dark with the seeds, and the farmer-rabbits would have to work at night, after the Harveys were indoors for the evening.

So Foxy napped, or tried to, a little ways off from Burrow so as not to frighten anyone, empty belly rumbling, smell and sight and ears razor keen, the rabbit scent making her drool, as if Brad had thrown a steak on the grill.

She wouldn't have minded a biscuit, and the minty-fresh quality of her breath was already starting to fade. Let freedom ring! That's what John Glenn had said. But it would be good to go home, she decided. For now, she would just have to wait.

⁂

It was nearly an hour past sunset when Alice declared it was time to go. The moon hadn't yet risen, but rabbits see better in the dark than people can, and dogs have even better night vision than rabbits. For creatures who go largely by sound and smell, traveling in the dark was not a problem.

Zigzagging, however, was. As soon as they entered the meadow, the two cottontails kept angling off in different directions. Foxy tried to reason with them. "Rabbits, listen," she said. "There's only one of me, which means I can only protect one of you unless you stay close. Can you at least zigzag together?"

They tried, but thousands of years of rabbit-brain instinct wasn't easily overruled. Finally, Thistle agreed to climb on Foxy—the kit weighed barely more than a pound, not much of a burden—and ride on the dog's back, while Alice moderated her back-and-forth impulse by reminding herself that she didn't *need* to evade predators as long as her bodyguard—her body-dog? her Foxy-guard?—was on duty. This cut the evasive maneuvers by half and saved a lot of time. Thistle held on and squeaked with glee as Foxy's prancing gait bounced them across the starlit meadow, toward the waiting farm.

The chipmunks were already there, about a dozen this time. Chipmunks are punctual to a fault, as planning ahead is at the core of their nut-hoarding, winter-is-always-around-the-corner way of life. They carried the promised seeds in their cheek pockets, which made them comically full in the face.

At the sight of the approaching rabbits, their eyes grew nearly as round as their cheeks. One rabbit loped along in a nearly straight line, just as a predator would, and the other was riding on the back of a—

"Fox!" one of the chipmunks cried, spraying zucchini seeds everywhere.

Thistle placed his front paws on top of Foxy's head and sat upright as he rode. "Relax, you scaredy-munks!" he cried, full of good cheer. "The dog works for us. No harm will come to you!"

But the chipmunks had already launched a high-pitched verbal assault, squealing insults at Foxy in their needle-sharp voices. It was hard to make out the exact words, as they all shrieked at once, but the phrases "chipmunk-killer, stink-paws, munk-monster" were among them.

Alice feared they'd wake up the farmer-people. There was no time for explanations. "Foxy," she said with authority, "growl!"

Foxy bowed low so Thistle could slide off. Earlier, Alice had explained that, despite their sincere admiration for Foxy's peaceful nature, it was the fear of dogs that would keep the other animals from raiding the garden. There would be times when Foxy would have to put on a show of ferocity, even if she had no intention of acting upon it.

This appealed to Foxy's proud sense of duty, which every dog has, no matter how people dress them up like dolls and take undignified photos for their own amusement. A dog needs a job to feel truly happy, and now, at last, Foxy had one.

"Grrrr," she growled at the chipmunks, unconvincingly.

"Flea-house, slobber-mouth, skunk-breath!" the chipmunks screamed.

"That is just needlessly rude." Foxy's tone was menacing, but her drooped ears showed that they'd hurt her feelings.

"Hush, chipmunks!" Alice scolded. "Do you honestly think we would travel with such a dangerous, bloodthirsty dog if we couldn't control her? Now, be quiet! Your screeching is enough to attract every owl in the valley."

That stopped the awful noise, but now the chipmunks were desperate to get as far away from the slobber-mouth as possible. They spit out their seeds in turn, babbling information about what kind they were and how they grew best. Alice was especially excited about the radish seeds, which were tiny but held great promise. The chipmunks had brought some extras, too—herb seeds, green beans, and a few withered peas.

"And, behold," their leader said with a sweep of his tiny arm, as a terrified chipmunk came forward to spit out the seeds on command. "Swiss chard!"

"Lester will be pleased about that." Thistle's tail twitched with glee.

"Yes, it's quite tasty. Can we go now?" the leader begged, his striped flanks trembling.

"Of course," Alice said. "Thank you for being as good as your word, and so punctual, too."

"Chipmunks always are!" he cried as they began to back away, eyes locked on the fur-tongued, puddle-drooling farm demon!

"And we'll keep to our end of the bargain, too, come harvest time." It was such a momentous occasion, Alice felt she ought to say a few words. "May these seeds sprout and grow! May the garden prosper! See you in autumn, when the days grow short! Farewell, chipmunks, and—thanks?"

But the dapper little rodents had disappeared into the night.

"All right," said Thistle, who was excited and nervous, too. "Let's go be farmers!"

The rabbits began hopping toward the garden, but Foxy stayed where she was, eyes half closed, nose in the air. She'd become distracted by the powerful smell of Spearmint-Flavored GlitterTooth Chew-Bones, which seemed to permeate the whole yard.

"Foxy?" Alice called, once she realized the dog hadn't followed. "Is it safe to begin?"

Foxy chalked up the minty hallucination to hunger and resolved to ignore it. There would be real Chew-Bones soon enough. "Not quite yet," she replied, trotting after the rabbits. "See? The lights in the house are on. It means my humans are still awake. They usually don't wander outdoors at night, but I've been gone all day. I wouldn't be one bit surprised if they came outside to look for me." Foxy paused, to savor the deep emotional satisfaction of it. "Sweet, sweet humans! I miss them so, but think how happy they'll be to see me again."

"How long do we have to wait?" Alice asked.

"Until the lights change. It won't be long."

Sure enough, within the hour the yellow lights downstairs went off, and a flickering, blue-toned light shone through Carl's window. Minutes later, a similar blue light came on in Brad and Sally's bedroom.

"That's it. They won't come out now. Carl's playing his zombie dinosaur video game, and Sally and Brad are watching something on the television."

"What's television?" asked Thistle.

"Aren't you a country bunny! Imagine not knowing what television is." Foxy nuzzled the little rabbit, of whom she now felt extra fond since he'd ridden on her back. "It's a like a small version of the world inside a frame. You watch it to see how things turn out."

Alice thought about this. "How *do* things turn out?" she asked.

Foxy waggled her tail, pleased to be the expert. "It depends which channel you watch. On one, people are always cooking. That's Sally's favorite. Things always go well there, and everyone eats at the end. Brad's favorite is very odd; it's just the heads of unhappy people who argue with each other. I feel sorry for them. It must be dreadful to only have a head. Brad calls it 'news.' Carl doesn't have a channel, just the zombie dinosaur game."

Ever curious, the rabbits started peppering her with questions. "What are channels? What are zombies? What are dinosaurs?"

"One at a time, dear bunnies! Channels; well, I don't know how it works, but they're all different and everyone prefers their own. Dinosaurs are animals, but extinct, which means you won't be meeting one anytime soon. Zombies are hard to describe. They look alive but they're not. They're quite terrifying and everyone is always running away from them."

"You mean, like the Mauler?" Thistle asked with a shiver.

Foxy didn't know what the Mauler was, so now it was the rabbits' turn to explain. When they finished, Foxy flattened her ears. "It sounds like it might be a machine, but there's one sure way to tell. Does it eat?"

"Yes," Alice said gravely. "It eats the ground."

Foxy's tail unfurled in dismay. "Not a machine, then. How awful! It'll probably have its own channel soon. And here I thought zombies were only pretend!"

"We'd better get to work," said Alice, flexing her paws. The Mauler was the whole reason they were there, after all.

⁂

The vegetable garden was modest by family farm standards, about an acre. It hadn't been planted in a few years and needed a good digging to loosen things up and get rid of the weeds. Thus, the farmer-rabbits' first job was to till the soil.

Farmer Crenshaw used to do this by hand with a spading fork when he was young and his back was up to it; in later years he used a gas-powered garden tiller that had been sold to him by an eager young farm equipment salesman by the name of Phil Shirley. Alice and Thistle had eight paws between them; these would have to be tools enough. Foxy offered to help, but a dog's way of digging is nothing compared to a rabbit's, and it was more important that she stand guard anyway. The owls could come at any time.

Luckily, the cottontails' earnest efforts woke a family of voles who'd been sleeping underground, not far from the garden gate. Voles spend most of their lives beneath the earth. Digging is their specialty and there's nothing they like to do better. This particular vole family had lived in the abandoned garden for months, but as soon as the new farmer-people had arrived they'd arranged to move, as a garden full of traps was no place to raise a family.

Their new burrow was safely away from the farmhouse and on higher ground, too. It was mostly dug and ready to move into, and they'd come back this one last time for nostalgia's sake, for a final nap and to pick up their cherished trinkets: special twigs and pebbles and so on that they'd grown attached to. Voles are sentimental that way. They don't see very well (eyesight's not much use when you live in the dark) and so their inner life tends to loom large.

Being rousted by rabbits put an end to their lingering. It was time to go. But once Alice and Thistle explained what they were doing and why, the voles offered to help out a bit before making their exit. It was awfully nice of them, but it wasn't often that voles got to show off their digging skills to rabbits, either, and even voles have their pride. In a few hours, every square inch of the garden soil had been turned over until it was fluffy as the seed head of a dandelion. No gas-powered tiller could have done the job better.

Impressed and grateful, Alice offered the voles a share of the harvest as payment, as seemed only fair—but only if they promised not to raid the garden, just as the rabbits and chipmunks had agreed. Her tone was sweet as clover, but Foxy was her ace in the vole, so to speak. The threatening stink of a meat-eater was unmistakable, and the voles said "Yes, yes, of course!" before scurrying to their new residence.

Alice and Thistle touched noses for good luck. It was time to plant the seeds. This wasn't difficult now that the soil was so well prepared, but it still took time to do right. By the time they buried that last shriveled pea, a warm glow brightened the eastern sky, promising a new day ahead.

It was an hour before sunrise, and the farmer-rabbits were done.

They'd worn their claws to the nailbeds with digging and had never been so tired in all their short lives, but they were rightly proud of what they'd accomplished.

Foxy was just as proud. Her empty belly and sense of duty had summoned a spirit of steadfast alertness she didn't know she had. All night long she'd stayed vigilant. She'd resisted that minty Chew-Bone smell by imagining the bold spirit of Shibas of antiquity rising within her, those agile, fearless dogs who hunted alongside the samurai of long-ago Japan!

Now, as the dawn approached, she had one more duty to perform. It was time to call Doggo to take the rabbits home.

"Dog-ohhhhhhh!" Foxy howled. "Dog-ohhhhhhhhh!"

Although they use it rarely, Shibas have a distinctive, piercing howl, and even a quarter of a mile away in his snug fox den, Doggo got the message.

So did the roosters at Farmer Janis's place, who were up and crowing a full half hour earlier than they otherwise would have been.

Carl was asleep and didn't budge, as he was bone-tired from crying half the night over his missing dog, but in the big room where his parents slept, Sally stirred and rolled over, dreaming. She was a pioneer woman in the old west, churning butter and fending off outlaws as coyotes howled in the distance, tending her sourdough starter with one hand and branding cattle with the other. It was a hardworking dream, but Sally liked it, and there was a contented look on her sleeping face as she made little O lips—*dog-oh, dog-oh,* the coyotes in her dream howled!—and sank deeper into her pillow.

Brad was dreaming of branding, too, the kind he used to do at his old job, not for cattle, but for clients, and the dream was all too familiar . . . the clients were waiting but his slide presentation refused to work! And he was in his underwear! He hated this dream so much. He used to have it every night in the old days, more rarely since the golden parachute landed. But it still came back in times of stress.

In the smallest bedroom Marie lay in her crib, wide awake, playing with her endlessly fascinating toes. She chortled when she heard the haunting Shiba howl.

"Dog-ohhhhhh!" she sang, so softly even the baby monitor didn't hear it. "Doggo, hooooooome!"

CHAPTER TWELVE

The prettiest little garden you ever did see.

"Mom, Dad, look! She's home! Foxy's home!"

All the Harveys, but especially Carl, were filled with emotion to find their long-lost dog curled tail to nose in a perfectly foxlike circle, snoring on the mat outside the kitchen door. Carl's emotion was joy. His parents had different but equally strong feelings. Little did they know the pup had been on the property all night.

Foxy was so deep in an exhausted sleep she didn't hear her boy coming until it was too late. Carl seized her and held her so tightly she yelped. "Did you smell the GlitterTooth Chew-Bones, girl? Did you?" he said, arms locked around her neck. "Is that how you found your way home? I knew it would work, I knew it!"

Foxy really deserved a lot of credit. Even with the yard booby-trapped, nothing could deter her from her watchdog duties, not until her rabbits (she thought of them as hers now, just as she thought of the Harveys as hers) were safely turned over to Doggo and on their zigzag journey home.

After they left was a different story. Bleary-eyed with fatigue but also obsessed, she'd followed her madly twitching nose around the yard. By the dawn's early light she found one, then another. When she realized what her boy had done—and she knew it was Carl who'd done it, as the scent of his unhappy tears was prominently mixed in—she was deeply moved. What heart-tugging proof of her value to the household! And what largesse on Carl's part, to scatter such a wasteful quantity of the precious treats willy-nilly, outdoors, all for her!

She was too tired to do a proper count, so she divided the pile roughly in two. Half she buried for Doggo. The rest she gobbled up. She hadn't intended to eat so many, but it had been a long, hungry day and night, awash in the tantalizing scent of small prey animals. By this point her appetite was tugging the leash, as it were, and there was no reason to hold back.

Soon her belly was stuffed and her breath was so minty fresh she could have passed for a dental hygienist, if she'd been human. She was filthy and exhausted and as happy as she'd ever been.

"How lucky I am, to have been born a Shiba!" she thought, yawning widely, with a spearmint-flavored burp. She briefly considered scratching at the kitchen door so she could enjoy the comfort of her fancy dog bed, but it was too early to wake her humans. Anyway, the idea of spending the sunrise hours outside after a whole night out-of-doors appealed to her, as she'd never done that before. Once the Harveys got hold of her, she suspected she might not get the chance to do it again.

The doormat was flat and rough, but it didn't matter. She spun around three times before lying down, as was her custom, and fell asleep at once, cushioned and warmed by her own luxurious fur. She would have slept there for hours, dreaming of samurai adventures, but forty-five minutes later Carl came stumbling outside in his pajamas and woke her with his cries of joy and too-tight hugs. Within moments Brad appeared with a brand-new collar, buckled her up, and dragged her inside the house.

They tempted her with a freshly opened can of her prescription food from Dr. Yang, and Carl waved still more GlitterTooth treats in front of her overwhelmed nose, but she couldn't force herself to eat another bite.

Carl wanted his parents to call a vet right away. Brad promised they would certainly do so if Foxy hadn't regained her appetite by dinnertime. After that it took exactly five minutes for Sally to take the lavender-scented shampoo out of the cupboard and place it menacingly near the sink.

"That dog," she said, wrinkling her nose, "needs a bath."

⁂

The voles told the squirrels, the squirrels told the jays, and soon every animal in the valley had heard some version of the unbelievable tale: a young rabbit named Alice and her runt-sized brother had attacked the farm on the far side of the meadow and taken it back from the farmers. They commanded an army of chipmunks and had a pair of trained foxes working for them, too!

Ordinary rabbits could never do such things, the other cottontails said, so Alice and her brother must not be ordinary rabbits. On that they all agreed. Some thought a warren meeting should be called to discuss the wisdom of having these otherworldly creatures living among them. No prey animal wants to draw attention to itself, after all. Only bad things could come of being noticed.

Violet pooh-poohed the question, and her opinion carried enough force to end the debate, or at least postpone it for a while. It had only been a week since the warren meeting where Alice volunteered to go to the farm. Then, Violet had taken Alice for an eager young kit, too curious for her own good, perhaps, and too oblivious to danger, but the young were often like that.

Now she wondered if there wasn't something unusual about Alice after all. An army of chipmunks was a ridiculous notion, but anyone with a nose could smell that a fox and something very like a dog had been shockingly near Burrow—yet not a rabbit had been taken. It was strange, to say the least, and Violet intended to do some quiet rumination about it herself, before speaking her mind to anyone.

Rabbits don't believe in magic as a rule. They feel no need for it, as the natural world has wonders aplenty. But there are scores of old rabbits' tales about rabbits with special powers. These stories have been told so often and for so long that some of them have snuck into the stories told by humans. Do you know the rabbits in East Asian myths who live on the moon, cooking up tasty snacks? That's a rabbit's tale. Or the African stories about Kalulu, the trickster hare? Those are rabbits' tales, although who knows how the fellow got turned into a hare. Hares might look like rabbits, but they're a whole different species, as different as a fox and a Shiba Inu.

And what about the four hundred drunken rabbit gods of the Aztecs? Or Nanabozho, whose stories are still told by the Anishinaabe people of the Great Lakes? They say Nanabozho helped create the world and named all the plants and animals. To Alice and her fellow cottontails that was the most important rabbit's tale of them all, for those achievements belonged to the Great Rabbit and none other.

Marigold and Berry heard the strange stories going around, and they came looking for their siblings right away. Marigold especially was always one to speak her mind.

"We've known each other from our blind days in the nest, dear sister! But now we don't know what to believe. As your littermates, we feel we deserve an explanation," she said. All four rabbits nibbled, ear-swiveled, and *sniff-sniff-sniffed* as they talked. It was the sunset feeding, the day after the Night of the Great Planting, as the story-loving cottontails of Burrow had already taken to calling it. Alice and Thistle had slept most of the day and missed all the gossip, but now they were getting an earful. "Trained foxes standing guard? Honestly! Everyone keeps asking us if it's true. What are we supposed to tell them?"

Berry pressed close to Marigold. His tone was less sharp, but just as concerned. "Alice, we know you're a clever cottontail, maybe cleverer than most. But you should hear what the others say about you. It's like you're a character from an old rabbits' tale! What will you do next? Fly to the moon and bake clover cakes for us all?"

"Don't be silly, Berry; all rabbits are full of tricks," Alice said jokingly, but her ears prickled with embarrassment. "There's nothing special about me. If I could fly to the moon that would be something, though!"

Her siblings' snow-white tails shimmied with amusement. "Anyway," said Thistle, when their tails had stilled, "only one of the guards is a fox. The other one's a—"

"What Thistle means," Alice interrupted, "is that we've been lucky to get help from all kinds of animals who see the purpose in what we're doing. If some of them are foxes, or look like foxes—well, we're grateful for any help we can get."

"You mean, there *is* a fox standing guard?" Berry said, trembling.

Marigold's ears flattened in annoyance. "If there is, he'll be having a feast of rabbit soon enough! Alice, listen to me. Do you really think that this *farming* of yours"—she said *farming* the way you'd say something shameful—"can really stop the Mauler? Personally, I think it can't be stopped. It's much bigger than we are, and we oughtn't to indulge in false hope. Anyway, we don't know for sure if the Mauler's coming, or when. Shouldn't we just enjoy our days in the meadow, and be grateful for the nice life we have now?"

They were hard words to hear, for Alice herself was grappling with how much work farming had already proven to be. Poor Thistle's front paws were still bleeding from all that digging; she'd licked the wounds clean herself.

"Marigold and Berry, your words make sense," she began. "But it seems to me that all hope is false until what you hope for comes true. A patch of grass to eat, a quick escape from a hungry owl, enough time in the meadow to bear a few litters . . . every rabbit hopes for those things. I do, too."

Marigold looked at her with impatience, and Berry seemed full of doubt, but Thistle gazed at her with pure admiration, and she took courage from it. "And I also hope that our litters—and our litters' litters—will have a valley to live in, a burrow to sleep in, a green meadow to nest in, a forest's edge to run to when danger is near. The Mauler could take all that away, and none of us can imagine what life would be like afterward. If there is an afterward."

Alice shivered, for she had spooked herself with imagining the worst. "If we can at least *try* to stop it—surely it's worth a try," she finished.

"I agree with Alice," Thistle said. "It's worth a try."

Marigold fluffed herself from head to toe. "Well, sister. It sounds like you have the situation between your teeth, and nothing we say will change it." ("Between your teeth" was a cottontail's way of saying "you've already made up your mind.") "But remember: Rabbitfolk don't live long! You might as well enjoy your life, and not take things so seriously."

"I agree with Marigold. Use your ears—use your nose!" Berry could barely bring himself to say it, as the revelation that his own littermates conversed with foxes had made him woozy, and his hind legs were twitching to get away.

"Use your ears, use your nose," each kit repeated, as they all touched noses farewell, and "may a hawk take you, in good time!" Then Marigold and Berry went to graze elsewhere.

"They don't think we'll make it to the harvest," Thistle observed, nibbling contentedly.

"Perhaps they're right." The idea didn't trouble Alice—it's not a thought that troubles rabbits in general—but who would tend the farm if she and Thistle couldn't see things through to the end? Rabbits don't plan for the future much, for obvious reasons. Now that she was a farmer-rabbit, that, too, had changed. But she kept this particular worry to herself. One hop at a time, she thought. One hop at a time.

At least Thistle's exuberant sense of possibility was undimmed—riding on a dog's back will do that to a bunny. "Never mind them," he said, play-fighting with her. "We did it, we did it! We planted the seeds, and now we just have to watch them grow."

"Planting seeds is only the beginning," she said, sounding weary. "I'm no magic rabbit, Thistle, and neither are you. Farming is going to be hard work. It might be harder than we thought."

"Keep your tail up, sister!" He stopped play-fighting and nuzzled her ear instead. "Rabbits are way more clever than farmers. If farmers can do farming, we certainly can."

That cheered her somewhat, and with full tummies they headed to Burrow to sleep some more. There, her spirits were fully restored by Lester's reaction to the news about the Swiss chard.

"Rabbitfolk don't live long," he crowed in joy, when Thistle told him they'd been able to plant some after all. "But I'd sure like to be hopping around the meadow long enough to taste that Swiss chard!"

⁂

The seeds sprouted the way so many things do: slowly at first, then all at once. All it took was rain and sunshine, the well-prepared soil, and some luck. Being new to farming, the rabbits hadn't anticipated this, but their chipmunk delivery team had moistened the seeds by carrying them in their mouths. That moisture had worked through the outer husks and softened them, so that the seeds sprouted in half the usual time. The radishes came up first; most of the other seedlings poked through the soil within a week or so.

Brad Harvey made the big discovery himself when he went out to remeasure the garden. It wasn't so much that he thought it had changed size in the preceding days, but now that the time had come to actually farm, rather than just dream about it, he found himself curiously reluctant to begin. Each morning, he'd sit at the kitchen table with his seed catalogs laid out in front of him and a calculator beside his coffee mug, sharpening his pencil more often than he needed to as he drew one graph-paper diagram after another, trying different layouts and plant combinations.

In one version, the pea vines climbed up bamboo stakes in the garden's center. Another had them trailing on metal hoops around the edges. A different design featured a swooping double helix of marigolds planted around and between the heirloom tomatoes, to discourage a kind of tiny worm called nematodes from eating the roots of the tomato plants. Using marigolds to protect tomatoes was called "companion planting." According to Brad's research, people held mixed opinions about this practice—some thought it worked, some didn't—but Brad figured, why not? Everyone likes a companion, and the marigolds would look pretty, at least.

Best to measure everything one more time, he'd decided. It was raining lightly and Carl, bored, had followed his dad outside to try out his new work boots. They walked the garden perimeter twice. Brad fiddled with the tape measure and calculator, the hood of his rain slicker enveloping his head like blinders on a horse. Carl walked with his face turned up to the pale sky, catching raindrops on his tongue, until they reached the garden.

"It's growing already," Carl observed. "Cool."

"What is?" Brad said absently. He was busy making notes in his garden journal—*light rain since midnight, temp 52 deg @ 11 AM.*

"The garden, Dad. Look."

Brad looked.

He tugged his hood away from his face to see better, then pushed the hood all the way down. He rubbed his eyes, in case the mist had impaired his vision. It hadn't.

Neat rows of seedlings had sprouted through the soil. They weren't in straight rows, like in Brad's graph-paper drawings, but complex zigzag patterns. It was as if some genius gardener had carefully thought out how to get the most production from every square inch of earth.

"Zigzags," Brad mumbled, amazed. "Why didn't I think of that?"

Back in the house, he sheepishly told Sally that the garden had miraculously come up on its own.

"When you say miraculously," Sally said, without a break in her stirring, "do you mean, in a supernatural sense?"

Brad looked at Carl. They both shrugged.

Sally laughed and suggested that the rain had simply made weeds sprout all at once, and that's what you get for spending so much time planning your garden on graph paper and no time at all laying weed barrier fabric on the actual dirt, as had been advised by the nice man at the hardware store.

Brad begged to differ. Not only were the seedlings growing in neat, efficient patterns, but he'd spent a lot of time looking at seed catalogs, and these tender leaflets looked awfully familiar. "There were radishes, carrots, cucumbers. I swear I saw some zucchini. Lettuce, too, I'm not sure what kind. Sal, I'm not kidding. Come see for yourself."

Sally reluctantly put on her boots, stuck the baby monitor walkie-talkie in her coat pocket, and came outside, despite it being a waste of a perfectly good naptime. Then she looked.

There was no way it could be weeds. The patterns were too perfect, the seedlings too carefully grouped and arranged.

There was nothing to do but ask Janis. She was busy with her own chores but promised to pop in at lunchtime. So they waited. When she arrived, an air of normalcy was carefully observed. Sally fixed coffee and served it leisurely, and the Harveys all held their tongues about the miracle garden, in order to get Janis's pure, unvarnished interpretation of what she was about to see.

By then it had stopped raining, but only just. The sun caught the raindrops that clung to every newly unfurled leaflet and made a sparkling rhinestone display of all those zigzags. The efficient and tidy pattern was unmissable, and all the more striking.

Farmer Janis scratched her chin.

"Well, that's just about the prettiest-planted little vegetable garden I've ever seen." She cocked her head. "A zigzag pattern! Clever, Brad. Where'd you get the idea to do it that way?"

Brad explained that the garden had sprouted that way on its own, and what he really hoped Janis might provide was some explanation of how that might be. He also wanted to know if these seedlings were what he thought they were.

Frowning, Janis strolled through again, careful not to step on any of the newborn plants. Following the trail of seedlings forced her to walk in a zigzag pattern herself. If she'd been hopping instead of walking, she'd have looked like a human-sized cottontail in overalls.

Brad was right about the seedlings, Janis confirmed. She grew pretty much the exact same vegetables in her own garden and knew these seedlings like old friends. There was no mistake about it, although it did seem like a strange coincidence.

"Zigzags!" she said, shaking her head. "Who'd have thunk. I'll try mine that way, too, when I replant. Which might be soon. I've never had such a problem with chipmunks! They're everywhere this spring, aren't they?"

Brad confessed that he hadn't noticed any chipmunks in the vicinity.

Meanwhile, Carl thought of a documentary film he'd seen at his old school about the ancient Mayans, and remembered that they liked zigzag patterns and gardens and had even invented a kind of building called a zigzag-orama. Or so he told Janis. She laughed.

"It's ziggurat. And you're thinking of Mesopotamia. The Mayans were in Peru."

"Where's Peru?"

"Where's Peru, he says! South America. Hey, kid, when are you going to school?"

It was a sensitive subject, as Carl was still being stubborn. Brad put his hands on the boy's shoulders.

"Soon, right, champ? Meanwhile—I don't mean to suggest something magical about the garden just coming up like this, but it does seem odd. I mean, what do you make of it, Janis?"

Janis gave Carl the fish-eye. "First, I think the kid could use a few geography lessons. Second, I planted my vegetable garden two Wednesdays ago and the first radishes are just breaking through the ground. You're a week ahead of me. Clearly you know a lot more about farming than you let on, Farmer Brad! I hope I haven't embarrassed myself, giving advice you don't need. I wish you'd tell me your secret."

Brad flung his arms wide. "We didn't do anything, really. I'm as puzzled as you are."

"That's awfully humble of you to say. Congratulations, Harveys! You've got yourself an excellent little vegetable garden here." Janis reached down, scooped up a handful of the rich black earth, and gave it a squeeze. "Look at that soil. Fluffy as a feather pillow. It's been well tilled"—she held it to her nose and sniffed—"and well fertilized, too."

"Fertilized with what?" Sally asked, bewildered.

Janis closed her eyes and gave another *sniff-sniff-sniff*. "If I had to guess? Rabbit poo."

For, of course, the farmer-rabbits had thought of that, too.

CHAPTER THIRTEEN

Alice makes one more deal.

Now there were two types of farmers at the old Crenshaw place on Prune Street: those with two legs and those with four.

Only the four-legged ones knew that, of course. They did their work in secret, by moonlight and starlight. In daylight, the two-legged farmers scratched their heads. Something strange was going on down in the vegetable garden, no question.

Luckily for the rabbits, the Harveys didn't have the experience to know just how strange. They'd have been way more curious if they had known. As it was, there were plenty of other chores that required their full, furrowed-brow attention. Dreaming about being farmers had given way to actually being farmers, and it was a revelation. All the online beekeeping courses and kitchen table seed catalog browsing in the world didn't prepare a person for the dirt on your hands that never fully scrubbed off, the blistered palms from pruning an orchard's worth of neglected fruit trees, the sunburn on the nape of your neck and the tops of your ears from long days spent outdoors.

There was always more work than daylight, and if the vegetable garden seemed to carry on independently, why, that was just a welcome bit of good fortune, wasn't it? Something to be thankful for, and the Harveys were thankful, when they remembered to be. Most of the time they were too dang busy to give it much thought.

Farmer Janis was a different story. She kept an eye on that pretty little garden. She knew it wasn't farming itself, and she didn't like being taken for a fool, either. She liked to drop by unannounced to see if she could catch the Harveys in the act of caring for it, but she never did. Still, there was only one conclusion that made sense: Brad and Sally knew way more about farming than they let on, and that "we're just a wide-eyed family from the city" routine was nothing but a perversely annoying form of humility.

The truth was, in all Janis's many years farming her own land, she'd never seen such a perfectly arranged and pristinely tended vegetable patch as the Harveys'. Not a weed seemed to sprout, not a leaf was chomped by beetles, not a root vegetable was pulled up by critters.

What nearly drove her out of her mind was that the Harveys claimed not to have set a single trap. "There hasn't been a need," Brad had told her with a shrug, blinking those innocent, Brooklyn-bred eyes from beneath the green brim of the John Deere baseball cap she'd given him to replace his utterly impractical fedora. For some mysterious reason, the wild critters left his garden alone.

Meanwhile, Janis was having the single worst infestation of chipmunks, voles, raccoons, and gophers that she could remember. Nearly every day, she'd plant a new row of hand-raised seedlings from her hoop house. By the next morning, they'd be dug up and eaten. She reinforced her fences and sprinkled the dirt with all the old remedies she could think of: coffee grounds, and human hair cadged from the local barber shop (in farming towns, barbers are used to this request). She tried corncobs marinated in vinegar, hot pepper flakes, dried bloodmeal, even cotton balls soaked in coyote urine she'd special-ordered from a garden supply store out west. Nothing worked.

There was only one option left to consider, and she didn't care for it one bit. Traps were a depressing nuisance; a sad job if they worked and a sadder one if they didn't. Still, this year she might have no choice.

She thought about all this as she added a fourth layer of chicken wire to the bottom edge of the fence, just a few weeks into the season. So far, she'd grown nothing but bad luck, and she longed for an explanation.

It couldn't be anything as simple as the fact that the Harveys kept a dog and she didn't. She'd seen their dog. That dog was no more of a farm dog than those bright-eyed fluffballs that got paraded around the dog show once a year, preening for the crowd and the TV cameras.

Janis liked dogs fine, but she preferred useful ones. She never kept a dog because she didn't want to upset the chickens. Stress was bad for the eggs, and with the critters waging war on her vegetables, those eggs might be her salvation. What an embarrassment! At this rate, she'd be the last farmer in the county to see a ripe tomato. Usually she was among the first, offering rare heirloom varieties that made tomatoes her specialty. She was the only farmer around who still grew Lester's Perfected, and she was deeply proud of the fact. Now *that* was a tasty tomato.

Janis leaned on her shovel and gazed down the hill, where the Harvey's tomato-red farmhouse perched in the distance. Could it be the dog? It couldn't be. That pampered pooch was a house dog, one hundred percent. Why, if it ever met a rabbit it'd probably make friends with it! There had to be another explanation.

Then again, she'd clearly underestimated the Harveys. Maybe she'd underestimated their dog, too.

⁂

The two-legged farmers of Prune Street Farm may have fallen down a rabbit hole of inexperience, but what about Alice? Did *she* ever consider what the farmer-people might think about a vegetable garden that planted itself, sprouted by itself, and went on to mind itself better than most gardens get minded, even by the most skilled and devoted garden-minders?

In a word, nope. It never occurred to her, and you can chalk that up to a lack of experience, too. Like any cottontail, Alice had gotten an earful about farmers since the day she left the nest, but she'd never heard one word about how farmers themselves felt about things. Farmers were just an idea to her, not complex individuals who might be full of feelings and thoughts of their own, the way animals were.

Alice had no more insight into the mind of a farmer than the average human had into the mind of a rabbit. Yet now that she was a farmer herself, a quiet change had begun. Her thoughts just naturally started to take on new, more farmer-like opinions and preoccupations. She began to care about the things that farmers care about, and to worry about them the way farmers were inclined to worry.

First and foremost, she worried about the weather. She worried about unexpected freezes, sudden hailstorms, wild winds, or too-heavy rains that might batter tender young plants to the ground. Or else she worried there might be too little rain, which could cause her precious crops to wither and dry up.

After weather came insects. She'd struck deals with all kinds of animals, even the birds, but you couldn't negotiate with insects; their brains were just too different. It was the farmer-rabbits' nightly task to pick the aphids and beetles and leaf-cutters off the seedlings. Much as they preferred greens, Alice and Thistle agreed that eating the bugs was the simplest way to get rid of them.

She had her own special worries about "critters," as Janis called them (although Alice simply thought of them as her neighbors). Sometimes Alice worried that the deals she'd struck might go sour in one way or another. Perhaps her fellow creatures would lose patience, or change their minds, and she and Thistle would show up at the garden to find that all their hard work had been lost.

And when harvesttime came, what then? Would there be enough crops to go around for all the creatures who'd been promised a share? It was possible she'd promised too much to too many—rabbits are whizzes at multiplying, but not nearly so skilled at division.

Like farmers everywhere, Alice's biggest worry was financial. Lester had said that successful farmers turn their crops into money. Alice knew she'd have to do the same, and she wondered exactly how that was going to happen.

She wished she understood money better, where it came from and where it went, for she suspected that growing all the tender spinach in the world wouldn't matter if she couldn't manage to turn her crops into cash for the Harveys.

That's what would protect them from the egg-headed man's trap. That's what would keep the Mauler away, in the end.

⁂

There was one animal in the valley with whom Alice hadn't made a deal. His name was Worm. He was a long-tailed weasel, as slim and gray-bodied as his name suggested. During the snowy winter, he shed his gray fur and grew a thick white coat. Only the black tip of his tail never changed color.

His long, straight body and dark eyes would put any human observer in mind of a sock puppet, with one important difference. Sock puppets are cute. The lithe and deadly weasels could be beautiful to watch, but no creature in the valley would call them cute; no, sir.

Alice, being so young, had never met a weasel, and she surely wasn't expecting to meet one on a fine May morning. She'd slept through the sunrise and missed coming out for the breakfast graze, due to another long, late night of farming. Even Thistle had eaten and gone. The watchful, rabbit-brained part of her knew it was too late to graze alone; the day predators would be out and about, and she had no Foxy or Doggo to guard her. A sensible rabbit would go nap in safety and wait until dinnertime to eat.

But her hardworking and hungry farmer brain wanted breakfast, and that's the part that prevailed. Worm was waiting for her. He'd found his way to Split Rock and lay there, his long body wrapped around the base of the cool stone, hidden in the shadows until he slithered out to present himself. Soft-furred as a rabbit, long like a snake, dark-eyed as a doe, clever and vicious as a crow. There was no other animal in the valley quite like him, and the moment he appeared, Alice knew exactly who and what he was.

There was a split second in which she could have bolted, but her reflexes were slowed from fatigue, and she missed her chance. Worm circled her, and her heart filled with relief that Thistle hadn't waited, and that he knew enough about farming by now to carry on without her.

"Are you Alice, little cottontail?" the weasel said. "If so, it's you I've come to speak with."

"Yes, of course I'm Alice," she said rudely, out of fear. "And you're a weasel. Ho, hum! I expect you've come to hunt rabbits? If so, you've missed your chance. I'm having my breakfast now, and in the mood to eat, not to be eaten. Come back later."

He snickered. "How brave you are! So unrabbitlike. I find it interesting, and strange. Well, I have heard something else strange, brave rabbit Alice. The jays have whispered it to me, but I find it hard to believe, and wanted to find out for myself."

He circled closer to her. "They say you have made arrangements with the animals to go against their natures—you have even convinced my fellow hunter, my carnivorous cousin, the fox, to leave you in peace while you play in the farmer's vegetable garden, across the meadow. Is it true?"

Alice's whiskers twitched with pride, that news of her accomplishment had made its way to the mysterious Worm's lair. "It may be strange," she said, "but it is also true."

"How did you manage such an unlikely feat?"

The weasel seemed to be in a talking mood, not a hunting one, but that might be a trick. "I asked them," she said. "When I told them the reasons why, they agreed."

"And what did you promise them in exchange?"

"Various things."

This seemed to anger the weasel, and his eyes took on a reddish glow. "But no one has asked *me* to leave you in peace! No one has told *me* the reasons why! No one has promised *me* various things in exchange! Why? Are you afraid of me?"

"All rabbits are afraid of weasels, so don't give yourself airs," she said. "I would have told you about it myself, but I've been rather busy. Anyway, this is the first time you and I have met."

"True, rabbit, true! And if we had met before, that would have been the first and last time." His voice was hypnotic like the eyes of a cat; listen too long and you might well go dark. Alice decided to listen to the chirping of the birds instead.

Worm waited, but she didn't freeze, or bolt. "Tell me about this garden of yours," he said, sounding interested, the way a friend would. Truly, he was a dangerous creature.

"Pish-posh!" Alice retorted, to keep herself angry and awake. "Since when do you care about vegetable gardens?" Weasels were true-blue carnivores and vicious hunters. In lean times they'd dine on frogs, insects, and birds' eggs, but they much preferred meat, and all the smaller animals feared them.

"I care about what my prey cares about, for that's where I will find you. For that reason, I make it my business to know what's going on in the valley between the hills." Worm stopped circling. "Perhaps I, too, will leave you and your friends alone, for now. But you'll pay me my price. And you're right; I don't want any of your vegetables," he said, in his musical voice.

"What do you want?" Alice asked.

"Rabbit." He stretched his neck long, and a thin smile curved from one side of his head to the other. "I want rabbit."

"Well," Alice said, after a moment, "you may have some; it's only fair. For you to eat rabbit is as natural as me eating grass. But you'll have to wait."

"Why must I wait, sweet Alice?"

"Because of the Mauler," she said earnestly.

Worm feared little, but even he flinched at the word. Alice saw this and went on. "We rabbitfolk are working hard to stop the Mauler from coming.

Other animals are doing their part, too, either by helping us or by leaving us alone to work in peace. Those are the reasons why."

"Hmmm," said Worm, sounding unconvinced.

"If the Mauler comes, we'll all be sorry. You too must wait until the rabbitfolk's work is done. What's good for the bee is good for the hive," she added, for all the animals of the valley knew that saying.

"Bees dine on flowers. I prefer rabbit," Worm said, after a moment. "*Brave* rabbit. How long must I wait?"

"Until winter is near," Alice replied, holding firm. It was so hard not to bolt, with his face so close to hers! His teeth were sharply pointed, like a mouthful of thorns. "Until the harvest is done, and our work is complete."

"Winter, you say! Months away. A lifetime for some. Yet the seasons pass quickly. All right," he said. "I too will do my part, by hunting elsewhere, for now. I will wait. When the days grow shorter and winter is in the air, my gray fur changes to white—all except the tip of my tail."

The weasel turned, and his tail tip flicked like a splatter of ink along the grass. "When I have turned the color of snow, I will come back for my reward. Does that sound fair, tender rabbit? Do you and I now have a deal?"

"It does. And we do," she said. Finally, Worm slithered away.

Alice was relieved to see him go, and pleased that she'd been able to strike any kind of bargain with the hypnotic creature.

Anyway, winter was a long way off.

CHAPTER FOURTEEN

Carl gets a real education.

Carl's refusal to try a new school had persisted. His reluctance surprised him as much as anyone. He'd always liked school before. He just couldn't bear the thought of all the scrutiny he'd get, strolling in as "the new kid" practically at the end of fifth grade. All those people looking at him, asking dumb questions like "What's your name?" and "Where'd you live before?" and "Why'd you move?" and "How do you like it here?"

He didn't want to talk about it, that's all. Best to keep a low profile, at least until he knew what the kids around here were like. Imagine growing up on a farm, with your parents home doing farm stuff all day! All that peace and quiet and supervision was bound to warp a person's outlook.

Anyway, his parents had their own misgivings about the local elementary school, which they conferred about in Marie's room without always remembering that the baby monitor was on. Carl could hear every word just by sitting in the kitchen. Brad thought it might be too "by the book" for their sensitive son, while Sally wondered whether a more "results-oriented" environment would "do Carl some good."

Well, that sounded terrible. He wasn't setting foot in any school that was on a mission to "do him some good," and that was that. But it was the only school in town, and since he'd made his feelings plain about not going, his parents had moved on to plan B.

"Lots of farm kids homeschool," Sally said, by way of encouragement. The Harveys had gathered in the living room to decide his fate. Carl liked the living room. It felt old and cozy, with dark wooden beams across the ceiling and a big stone fireplace that was almost as tall as he was. A Christmas tree would look good in here, he thought. But Christmas was many months away.

Marie rolled and crawled on the carpet, pummeling Foxy's side with her tiny fists. The dog snored peacefully throughout the friendly beating.

"Your mom and I are excited, champ. We hope you are, too."

Homeschooling, of course! He should have seen this coming. Emmanuel homeschooled, so it wasn't an unfamiliar or unappealing idea. Carl had even asked to try it once, after realizing that Emmanuel did his schoolwork in pajamas and sometimes got pancakes for breakfast on a weekday, but Carl's parents had nixed it, saying "it wasn't a good time for the family." This was before the golden parachute, when Brad was at work all the time, and Sally was newly pregnant with Marie and needed to rest a lot.

Times sure had changed. Now you'd think they'd invented the idea themselves, the way they went on about it.

"Hey," Brad said, "remember when you went on that field trip to the farm?"

"That was second grade, Dad."

"Your whole life is a field trip now! Homeschooling will be awesome."

Sally, who was teaching herself to knit from a book, waved a needle in the air, trailing yarn. "It'll be fun. Don't you think so?"

"Ehhh," Carl replied. Not a ringing endorsement by any means, but not a flat no, either. Did they mean it about homeschooling, or was it the old parental switcheroo trick? That's when they pretended to go along with *your* plan, but only so you could "learn for yourself" that *their* plan was the better plan in the first place.

"Remember, it's your decision, champ."

"That's right, honey. School or homeschooling; it's up to you."

Life would be a lot easier if his parents just told him what to do every now and then. Maybe that's what "results-oriented" meant. Maybe his parents were the ones who were trying to "do him some good." They were being awfully sneaky about it, if so.

"Ehhh, okay," he said. "We could try it, I guess."

Within days, boxes of books began arriving at the house. Sally called it "curriculum," but Carl knew a book when he saw one. There were math books and history books and penmanship books. There were books about reading other books. There was even a book called *Nature Study*, which didn't seem like you should need a book to do it, but it had plenty of pages and the pictures were good.

A week passed. The skyscraper of "curriculum" tottered on the wooden desk Brad had set up in a corner of the kitchen. Nobody said a word about doing schoolwork. Basically they just left Carl alone.

Carl began to wonder. The old, citified Brad and Sally had noticed his every slouch, eye roll, and overdramatic sigh, but these new, rustic versions seemed benignly uninterested in his daily affairs. Had they been secretly swapped for robot versions of themselves? *Attack of the Robot-Farmer Parents Who Mind Their Own Business and Let You Mind Yours?*

There were other signs of change. Brad had already traded his Brooklyn fedora for the John Deere cap, but soon he replaced that with a lightweight, broad-brimmed straw hat that shaded him all the way around. The padded, skateboarding-style sneakers that had been his everyday shoes since the dawn of time had been traded for stiff work boots, to protect his feet from sharp rocks and dropped tools.

Sally had acquired a similar pair of boots for doing outdoor chores, and a whole wardrobe of aprons, oven mitts, and hairnets for her culinary endeavors. Glass jars with metal lids were delivered by the case, along with enough science lab gear to outfit ten homeschools, but Sally said this equipment was for her, not Carl. There was an enormous stainless steel pot called a "water bath canner" (with a built-in thermometer, she noted with pride), funnels, tongs, a "jar lifter," a "sterilizing rack," a "magnetic lid wand," and something called cheesecloth, which had nothing to do with cheese as far as Carl could tell, but would make a terrific mummy costume if you wrapped yourself up in it.

There was no mention of learning, homework, quizzes, or any of that. Sally glanced at the desk now and then, but kept her thoughts to herself. Meanwhile she was studying all day long; apparently there was a lot to know about preserving food in jars, especially if you intended to sell it to people without making them sick.

Brad mostly worked outside, building fences for a sheep paddock, scouting locations for a beehive, pruning and communing with the fruit trees, and a million other things.

By the middle of homeschooling week two, Carl was so bored that he started to play with Marie. She liked it a lot, and Sally appreciated it to no end. He found himself trying to teach the baby stuff she was too young to learn, but it made her laugh, anyway.

Janis dropped by nearly every afternoon to admire Sally's new canning equipment, advise Brad on his fence building and other projects, and grab a neighborly cup of coffee. Sometimes she brought pie, and they were the best pies Carl had ever tasted. She always managed to work in a casual stroll to the vegetable garden. Sometimes she gave Foxy a probing, suspicious look.

By the end of that second week she finally spoke up. "Hey, kid. Were you ever in a spelling bee?" she asked as Sally refilled her cup.

"Nope," said Carl. He was showing Marie how to divide whole numbers by using Sally's homemade sourdough cheddar cheese crackers. The baby kept eating them and yelling "Go fish!" It wasn't clear if she wanted more or was simply demanding the store-bought kind.

"Today's your lucky day, then," Janis said. "How do you spell 'truant'?"

"I don't know what it means."

"In that case you're supposed to say, 'Can you use it in a sentence, please?'"

"Can you use it in a sentence, please?"

Janis thought hard, then said, "Carl Harvey was a notorious truant. He hadn't been to school in weeks."

"What does notorious mean?"

Sally chuckled and sipped her coffee. Janis laid both hands on the table. "Kid! When are you going to school, for Pete's sake?"

"We're homeschooling. See?" Carl gestured proudly to the stack of unopened books on the desk.

Janis raised an eyebrow and looked at Sally, who nodded in confirmation.

"Too cool for regular school, huh? I get that. I liked school well enough myself, got good grades, made friends, but I was glad to be done with the whole scene when the time came. Some of us prefer to gallop to the sound of our own hoofbeats, isn't that right, kid? Hey, seen any pterodactyls lately?"

He hadn't, though he scanned the skies daily. By now, his encounter with the eagle felt like a dream, but the hard evidence of Foxy's severed collar, which sat on his bookshelf right next to Big Robot's battery-free remote control, remained.

"If I were a groovy homeschooled kid like you," Janis said slyly, "my natural curiosity about that white-headed bird would be driving me nuts. I'd do some research. I'd consult some experts."

"What kind of experts?"

"Eagle experts! Consulting eagle experts sounds like an absolute bull's-eye of a homeschooling project. I'm just saying."

Carl naturally glanced at his mother for a reaction, but Sally just gave him a blank look from across the table. Then she found something to pick up with her magnetic lid wand and got deeply interested in it. His own mother! You'd think she didn't care whether he ever got an education at all.

Carl kicked his feet back and forth a few times. "Eagle experts, huh. Do you know any?" he finally asked.

"No, but I bet I know someone who does," Janis said. "Sally, can I borrow the kid for a while?"

"Absolutely," Sally said.

"Hop in the tractor, kid. We're going on a field trip."

⁂

Finally, a ride in a tractor! There wasn't a passenger seat, so Carl had to squeeze in next to Janis. It was also incredibly loud, and Carl and Janis could only grin at each other as the machine rumbled along the road into town. Janis drove on the shoulder of the highway with the flashers on, but around here it wasn't unusual to see farm equipment on the road. Other drivers slowed down and waved and shouted "Hey, Janis! Hey, Tin Can! Hey, kid!" as they passed, and Carl waved back. It was like being on a parade float.

The one-tractor parade ended at the library. The librarian seemed to be a friend of Janis's. Then again, Janis seemed to know everyone in town.

"Just returning a few titles, Orin." Janis dumped out her canvas tote bag, which had a picture of an antique red tractor above the words I LOVE TRACTORS on the front, and spilled twenty dog-eared paperbacks on the desk.

Orin showed no surprise at the quantity of books and scooped them onto a waiting cart. He had a pleasing appearance, with wide eyes, a roundish face, and not much hair. His glasses were perfectly round, with metal frames. Over his button-down shirt and tie he wore a sweater vest, a fashion item Carl had never seen before but found quite compelling.

"Well, thank goodness you brought these back, Janis," he said, deadpan. "I was going to have to close the murder mystery section until you did."

"I like murder stories," Janis confided to Carl. "But just for fun. Not, you know—research."

It hadn't previously occurred to Carl that Janis might be planning a murder. Now there was no way not to consider it.

"My friend Carl here is the one doing research today," she went on, to Orin. "Maybe you can help him while I choose my murder books. If you need me, I'll be in the how-to section. I'm kidding, kid! I'll see you fellas in a bit." She left.

Orin turned his owlish face to Carl, bright-eyed with friendliness. "So how can I help you, Carl? I don't think I've seen you in here before. Are you a homeschooler?" Carl's startled expression made the librarian laugh. "No, I'm not psychic. Or a great detective, like Sherlock Holmes. But it's lunchtime on a school day and here you are at the library doing research.

Doesn't take a genius. Hey, there's a group of homeschooled kids in the multipurpose room right now. They're building geodesic domes out of toothpicks and gumdrops, I think. Do you want me to introduce you?"

"Maybe next time," Carl said, though he wouldn't have minded a gumdrop. This library visit was his first real attempt at homeschooling and he wanted to keep it low-key. Sally had tucked the copy of *Nature Study* into his backpack, in case the eagle experts needed proof of his educational motives. He took it out to show Orin.

"I wanted to do some . . . uh . . ."

"Nature study?" Orin helpfully suggested.

"Right. About eagles. I saw one in my backyard," he added.

Orin's eyes grew rounder. "Really? Was it wearing a tracker?" Carl looked confused, and Orin explained, "It's like a tiny backpack. There's a GPS tracker in it that lets the scientists collect data on the bird's movements."

"I don't know about a tracker," Carl said. "But it did have something around its leg. Like a piece of tape."

"An ankle band. Yup, that's a tracked bird. How cool! You're so lucky to have seen one. There are only four at the moment, I think. Come with me, I'll show you."

Orin walked to the computers and sat down. Carl followed, but remained standing. He could just glimpse the homeschooled kids through the glass, shoving toothpicks into gumdrops and making a big mess. It looked like it might possibly be fun.

"Do you have a computer at home?" Orin asked as he logged in.

"Yes, but we don't have internet. There's no cell phone signal, either."

"A satellite dish will fix that. You can use the computers at the library as much as you like. If you go to this site"—he wrote down the name and website address on a notepad with the words KEEP CALM AND ASK A

LIBRARIAN printed across the top of each page—"you can see what all the tracked eagles are up to."

Carl looked at the paper Orin handed him, and his heart swelled. Finally, the golden ticket that would make his parents see reason about putting a satellite dish on top of the house! That eagle was bringing him good luck after all, even if it had scared him half to death.

"The Eagle Restoration Project," he read, curious. "Is it like an eagle cam?"

"They used to have an eaglet cam, when the babies were in the nesting box. The eaglets slept a lot, but you got to watch the scientists feed them. Now the birds are all grown up. They're out there, free." Orin gestured with one hand and moved the computer mouse with the other. "Look at all the data the scientists collect with those GPS trackers. You can see where the birds fly, how high they go, how fast, typical flight paths, all kinds of neat stuff. See, I was right; they're tracking four birds. Each one shows up as a different color line on the graph. Neil Armstrong, Buzz Aldrin, Sally Ride, John Glenn."

Carl let his backpack slip off his shoulders. "I feel like I've heard those names before."

"These eagles are named after famous astronauts." Orin smiled. "Space exploration! That's another research project for you."

"Eagles are enough for now." Carl grabbed a chair and sat down in front of the computer, next to Orin. "Can you show me how to read the data?"

⁂

That night at dinner, Carl was full of facts. "Did you know that baby eagles are called eaglets? Did you know that bald eagles can fly ten thousand feet in the air and go fifty miles an hour? They can swim, too."

"That's amazing. Pass the potatoes, champ?"

Carl speared a potato for himself as he handed the serving platter to his dad. "Sure. Hey, Mom. Did you know there was an astronaut named Sally?"

Sally dabbed her lips. "I'd forgotten that. Were you researching that, too, today?"

"No, just eagles. Oh, I almost forgot," he said, his mouth half full. "We need a satellite dish. Right away."

Brad and Sally exchanged a look. "Because?" Sally said.

"Because I need the internet. To do nature study."

"What about doing nature study in nature?"

Carl spoke reasonably as he ladled gravy onto his plate. "Mom. Dad. Conservation scientists rescued four baby American bald eagles from Westcondon—"

"I'm guessing you mean Wisconsin?" Brad asked.

"I do mean Wisconsin," Carl said, brimming with confidence. "They raised the baby eagles by hand. In a box! When the birds grew up, the scientists set them free wearing tiny backpacks with GPS thingies in them, so the scientists can learn stuff. There's new data every day, and it's all on the internet. Therefore, I can't do nature study without a satellite dish."

"I'd say this homeschooling thing is going well," Sally said, amused. "Eagles, conservation, astronauts, 'data,' names of the states, sort of . . ."

"I smell a whiff of debate club in there, too." Brad was smiling. "All right, champ. We were planning to get a dish anyway. I was going to surprise you. I can't build a website for the farm without high-speed internet, and it turns out we need to have a website to be in business properly as farmers. It's the twenty-first century, after all! I'll get on it tomorrow."

"Thanks, Dad," Carl said, keeping his demeanor calm. Inside he was whooping with joy. Satellite dish! High-speed internet! Could premium TV channels be far behind?

"Big ba! Jan Glaa! Fa ma mint!" Marie yelled, pounding her fists on her high chair tray with excitement. Clearly she was delighted to hear mention of that big bird, the majestic John Glenn, whom she sometimes wondered if she would ever see again.

She liked the idea of a tiny backpack, too. She owned one herself, with a picture of a happy Japanese cartoon kitty on it. She wondered what John Glenn's backpack looked like. Perhaps they could share!

"Woof, woof," Foxy remarked, briefly alert. She too hoped they would see the noble raptor again, and by the way, she would be *ever* so grateful if Marie would rub between her shoulder blades with one of those firm, pudgy feet of hers, once she was unbuckled from her special eating chair and down on the floor once more, where all the truly interesting things happened. And perhaps a tiny taste of that minced roast chicken might find its way down as well? Stealing table scraps was a far cry from hunting prey, but at least the chicken hadn't come out of a can.

Marie was happy to oblige.

CHAPTER FIFTEEN

A friend in need.

Several thousand feet above the roof of Prune Street Farm, upon which a shiny new satellite dish had recently been installed, John Glenn was struggling against a minor headwind. Something wasn't right. He was off-balance, and the flight feathers on his right wing had a snagged feeling on the downstroke.

The source of the difficulty seemed to be situated high on his back, dead center, below the base of the neck. On a human, or even a dog, you'd say it was right between the shoulder blades, but birds don't have much in the way of shoulders. Frustratingly, it was the only part of his own body he couldn't closely examine.

John Glenn needed help. It was a rare thought for an eagle to entertain, proud and independent creatures that they are. But help from whom? If he was older he'd have likely found a mate to spend the breeding seasons with. Not yet, though. Eagles mate for life, and John Glenn was still too young for that kind of commitment.

He had no friends to call upon, either. Bald eagles are true loners.

Even after they choose their mates, they hunt and migrate alone for most of the year.

If he dropped in on the scientists, they would be glad to see him, and surprised—usually they were the ones who tracked him down, by use of a quick stinging bite that came from nowhere and made him sleepy enough for even a human to catch—but John Glenn knew from experience that they'd give him way more attention than he liked. Much like young Carl Harvey, John preferred to keep a low profile.

Still, life is full of unexpected swoops, and it appeared that even an eagle might need another set of eyes to help sort things out now and then. John Glenn could only think of one creature who might be inclined to do him such a service. Banking sharply, he began his descent.

⁂

It was Foxy's first sunny afternoon as a free Shiba in six weeks, and it felt like heaven. That she'd had regained her off-leash privileges at all was thanks to Janis, who'd suggested that the dog get trained to herd the sheep that Janis was still urging Brad to acquire.

"She can't. She's locked inside all the time," Carl had replied.

"Locked inside? That's no life for a farm dog. She should be running around the property, guarding the place and earning her keep." Janis rubbed the back of her head. "Wait—kid—you mean to tell me that dog of yours hasn't been outside scaring off the critters?"

"She's been grounded." Carl explained it the best way he knew how. "Leash walks only. It's because she ran away."

"Well, I'll be." Flummoxed, she turned to Sally. "And you still have no voles? No chipmunks? No rabbits? You haven't set any traps?"

"Traps! Heavens, no," Sally said, laughing at Marie, who shook her head *no no no* with a profoundly serious expression on her face.

"No traps. No dog. No critters in the garden . . ." Janis looked like she might say something sharp, but she didn't. "Well, it's hard to believe, I'll say that much."

"Beginner's luck is still with us, I guess," Sally said brightly, waving it off.

Foxy had approached Janis with an inscrutable gaze, and gave a plaintive *woof*. Janis patted the dog's head.

"Sick of being out of work, huh, pup?" She turned to Carl. "I say let the dog loose. Let her do her job."

"But she ran away—"

"Leaving and coming back isn't the same as running away. Look at her. She wants to work, don't you, bright eyes?"

"Woof, woof!" said Foxy, right on cue, which made them all laugh. The dog looked so eager that the Harveys decided to let freedom ring once more. No yellow vest was needed until hunting season, Janis assured them, but the dog should wear her collar with ID tags at all times.

Foxy thought this was a fair deal, as long as Carl opened the door for her whenever she scratched at it, which he did, well-trained lad that he was.

What a relief to be free! The grass was lush, the sun was warm, the air was full of smells. Foxy was anxious for news of Alice and Thistle, but her particular concern was Doggo. Had the fox found the stash of Glitter-Tooth treats she'd put aside as payment for chaperoning? Had the rabbits been escorted properly during her time in lockdown? Were Foxy and her doppelgänger still friends? Would she like him better if his breath weren't so foul?

To answer these questions properly, she'd have to be out after dark, when the rabbits and their vulpine escort arrived, yet she knew it would sizzle Carl's nerves for her to stay out late on her first day of untethered bliss.

What to do? She'd mulled it over until her brain hurt and her eyes grew heavy. She dozed on a sunny patch of grass near the barn, where her overanxious humans could at least see her.

All at once a cool shadow fell over her, followed by a graceless *thud*.

"John Glenn!" she exclaimed, springing to her feet. "What a delightful surprise!"

"It pleases me to see you as well, dog named Foxy. I came because I need your help," John Glenn confessed, his white head bowed.

"At your service, friend bird! But I ought to tell you: My humans made an absurd fuss about your previous visit. Perhaps we ought to speak somewhere out of sight of the house? Follow me, if you please."

They reconvened behind the barn, Foxy trotting silently, John Glenn lurching along in awkward, gliding hops. His balance seemed to be getting worse.

"That's better," Foxy said, when they'd found a private spot. "Now we can speak about whatever's troubling you. But first, John Glenn, tell me: How did you ever manage to find me again from the great wide sky above?"

There was vanity in the question, and no doubt Foxy would have liked an answer like "Oh, you're such a distinctive creature!" but eagles don't flatter.

"This house is easy to spot," John Glenn replied. "Like a single red poppy in a wide green field." He swiveled his neck, and his magnificent profile was something to behold. "It's changed since last time. There's something shiny on the roof."

Foxy's ears drooped. "Oh, that! When Brad said they were getting a new dish, everyone was so thrilled that naturally I assumed it was for me. But then they stuck it on the roof, where no one can eat out of it. I don't see the point."

"I could eat out of it," John Glenn said mildly.

"Well, yes, of course *you* could. Maybe it's meant for you, then? Was there food in it, perchance?"

"There was not," said the bird.

Foxy snorted. "I will never fully understand my humans. They mean well, though."

"I feel that way about my scientists," John Glenn said. "They mean well. But their behavior defies explanation." He paused. "Foxy, do you remember when I took off your vest and collar?"

Foxy's tail was up and waggling. "Do I! That was marvelous."

"I need you to do the same for me. My tracker is askew. It pulls on my secondaries, and now I'm off-kilter. See?"

The eagle bowed low and spread its great right wing along the ground. The wing was bigger than Foxy, who examined it as best she could.

"I think I see what you mean," she said. "The strap is twisted, and the whole thing has slipped to the side. Did you want me to try to slide it back?"

"I want you to take it off. I'm done wearing it."

Foxy sat and gazed up at the hopeful bird. "John Glenn. I can sit, stay, roll over, and shake hands with the best of them, but my paws are not suited for fine work, and my teeth are nowhere near sharp enough for quick and accurate slicing. I'm more of a destructive chewer. You should see what I did to a chair leg once! What you propose is a delicate operation. I'd hate to make things worse by damaging your feathers."

"Dexterity is needed," John Glenn agreed, and turned his noble head to the side in disappointment.

Foxy grinned until her back teeth showed. "Don't be glum, Glenn! Your problem is easily solved; we just need the right personnel. I have some very small and lightweight friends who could scamper onto your back and make short work of this. They've got deft little paws and teeth like tiny wood chippers, and they're nimble as can be. They can help you for sure. You'll have to come back after dark, though. That's when they'll be here. Can you manage that?"

"Certainly," John Glenn said. "I'm no owl, but I can see in the dark well enough to get around."

"Wonderful! Just so you know: They're rabbits. Alice and Thistle." Foxy's tail paused in its waggling. "You don't eat rabbits, do you?"

"Everybody eats rabbits," said the eagle. "I'd eat them if I were hungry and had nothing else. But I prefer fish. There are plenty of those in the river."

"Well, if you eat them, they won't be able to help you, so please bear that in mind." Foxy glanced at the house. "If I happen to get locked inside later and can't be here to introduce you, just tell them you're a friend of Foxy's."

"Even though you're not a fox." There was a hint of mischief in the bird's usually somber aspect.

Foxy's ears twitched forward, amused. "Well, you're not an astronaut, either, John Glenn! Yes, I know who John Glenn is. Carl has a book about him on the shelf. How did you come to have such a name? I bet it has to do with those scientists you mentioned."

"It's a long story. Perhaps I'll tell you another time." John Glenn preened the feathers on his good wing. "I do fly extremely high, though, all on my own, no spaceship required. Just me, my wings, the thermals. It's beautiful up there. It's very quiet, when you're up high." He ruffled all his feathers. The twisted backpack hampered his right wing noticeably. "I miss being up high, but I can't do it with my tracker like this."

The eagle sighed. His hooked beak gave him a stern expression by nature, but now his golden eyes just looked sad.

Foxy wagged her tail and nudged the big bird with her nose. "Cheer up, John. You'll be up there again in no time. My friends are small but terrifically clever. They'll fix you right up."

⁂

Janis asked Carl to walk her to the street so she could show him something interesting that had to do with Tin Can. When they got to the green machine, she strolled to the far side of it, shielding them from view of the house, and turned to him.

"Look, kid. I haven't read all those murder books for nothing. I love a good mystery, and I'm pretty good at cracking them. But the mystery of what's going on at your house is better than any I've ever read in a book."

Only now did Carl understand that the tractor was a ruse, and Farmer Janis just wanted to talk to him in private. It was exciting when grown-ups lied, and his attention was sharply piqued.

"What mystery?" he asked.

"The garden, you city kid, you. The vegetable garden!"

Carl shrugged. "I thought it was growing fine. Isn't it?"

"That's what I'm talking about." Janis removed her hat to smooth her hair, then put it on again. The gesture seemed to calm her. "The mystery is: Who's the farmer? Someone is weeding, fertilizing, keeping the bugs and critters away. Someone even staked the pea vines, for Pete's sake! Did you notice that? But your dad spends all day building the world's most architecturally innovative, energy-efficient, and biodegradable sheep pen, never mind that he's still working up the nerve to put actual sheep in it, and your mom's a full-time mad scientist in the kitchen. They're doing bupkes out there in the garden. And don't tell me it's Applesauce doing all the work." She'd taken to calling Marie Applesauce, for obvious reasons. "That kid can't even walk across a room without holding on."

"What's bupkes?" Carl asked, lost. "Can you use it in a sentence, please?"

"I just did. It means nada. Zippo. Diddly squat. Have you ever heard of Sherlock Holmes?"

"Sure."

"For a made-up fictional guy he said some smart things. My favorite is this: 'When you have eliminated the impossible, whatever remains, however improbable, must be the truth.' Well, I've figured out the truth, kid. And it's you. You're the farmer."

Carl almost looked over his shoulder to make sure she meant him. "But—I'm not," he protested weakly.

"Oh, yes, you are. No point in denying it. I know it's you, kid. What I don't know is why you're keeping it a secret. Maybe you're embarrassed about being a farmer—no, hear me out. A lot of people with educations think that farming is dumb folks' work, or that country people are all rubes who don't have the brains or sense to become lawyers and podiatrists and financial planners. They're wrong. Farming is the greatest profession, and I'll prove it. How many days in your life do you need a lawyer?"

"Um, I don't know?" he answered. He'd never needed one yet.

"Or a podiatrist? Very rarely, if you're lucky. But how many days of the year do you need a farmer?"

Carl thought of the milk on his cereal, the eggs in his egg salad sandwich, the garlicky mashed potatoes, beef stew, and fresh green salad they'd enjoyed last night at dinner.

"Every day," he said. "Every day of your whole life."

"That is one hundred percent correct. And that is why farming is the greatest profession there is."

She put a hand on his shoulder. "Kid, you're doing an amazing job with that garden. You should take credit it for it. You've got the greenest thumb I've ever seen. You could win a blue ribbon at the county fair, if you set your mind to it." She seemed to take Carl's lack of response as something other than the utter confoundedness that it was. "No interest, huh? Don't you like being a farmer?"

Carl thought about it. "I do like being a farmer. I didn't know what it meant, at first. But I like it now. I think." He looked up at Janis. "But I'm *really* not the one taking care of the vegetables. I'm not lying, I swear!"

She dropped her hand and climbed into the tractor, clearly annoyed. "Look. I've eliminated the impossible and you're what's left. I just wish you'd own up to it! Farmers need to help each other, not keep secrets. Here's an example of what I mean: I'm getting killed by critters this year. Slaughtered! You guys, not at all. It breaks my heart to set traps, but I'm gonna be forced to do it in self-defense. If only you'd show me your methods, maybe I wouldn't have to."

There, in the driver's seat of the John Deere, Janis's profile was momentarily backlit by the sun. It made her look noble, like an advertisement for farm machinery. "Kid, I think of you as a friend, a neighbor, and a fellow farmer above all. I hope you'll consider what I've said to you today." She turned on the mighty machine and shouted over the roar. "Come clean. Stand proud. Tell me how you're handling the critters. Is that asking so much?"

He didn't know what to say.

"Ich bin ein Farmer!" she called as she drove away. "We're in this together! You, me—all of us! Think about it!"

⁂

That night Carl couldn't fall asleep. The more he thought about what Janis had said, the more agitated he felt.

She was wrong about one thing, obviously—it wasn't him doing the gardening—but could she be right about the other?

Was there a big mystery going on at Prune Street Farm, right under the Harveys' collective noses?

He desperately wanted to know the answer, but he didn't want to ask his parents or get any helpful librarians involved. For a mystery of this scope and complexity, Carl preferred the old-school detective model of investigation, amply documented in any number of paperbacks that had a kid holding a flashlight on the cover. Basically, he wanted to solve it himself. It was more fun that way.

But where to begin? Perhaps the internet could help.

He slipped out of bed and sock-shuffled to his computer, dragging his blanket behind him, as the house got cold at night. The new satellite dish on the roof had opened up a world of possibilities, and Carl's nature study was going like gangbusters.

He'd watched a ton of cute kitten videos.

He'd rated dogs.

He'd played a game about a family of mutant frogs trying to cross a radioactive pond by hopping from lily pad to lily pad without falling in. If they landed in the water, they started to glow and mutated into something else (what they turned into was always a fun surprise), before bursting into fireworks of glittering ash.

The point of the game was to save the frogs, but it was more entertaining to watch them fall in than save them, he'd realized. There was a sad truth about human nature embedded in this discovery, but Carl was just a kid having fun, and he wasn't inclined to think it through that deeply. Luckily, it was only a game.

He'd looked at the Eagle Restoration Project site a few times, but the graphs of data had quickly lost their appeal. The best feature on the site was a real-time eagle tracker. It reminded him of the site that tracked Santa Claus at Christmastime, only more scientific-looking. The map view showed where all four tracked eagles were. They showed up as four differently colored points of light: Neil Armstrong was red, Buzz Aldrin was green, Sally Ride was blue, and John Glenn was bright yellow.

If one of the eagles happened to be flying, that was the best; it looked like a shooting star blipping along the screen. The birds traveled separately but tended to stay in the mountains farther north, where the river was twisty and narrow.

He tried typing "gardens that grow by themselves" in the search bar, but it just delivered general gardening tips and advice about growing something called "perennials." That didn't seem pertinent, and like many an online investigator before him, Carl soon got distracted from what he'd meant to look up and started checking his favorite sites instead.

Kittens, check. Dogs, check. Frogs, check. What were the eagles up to?

Tonight he found Neil, Buzz, and Sally, all stationary, up in the mountains. Neil and Buzz were on the west side of the river, while Sally was on the eastern shore. He had to scroll farther south to find John Glenn. The bird was in the air, a golden blip moving across the screen.

Curious, Carl zoomed in.

"Holy cow," he whispered. The aerial map view was full of familiar shapes. There was the exit ramp from the interstate that looked like a check mark, the snaking road that led to Prune Street.

The yellow blip hovered in one spot. Carl zoomed all the way in and switched to street view. The big red house was unmissable; a bright red poppy in a green field. The yellow blip was directly above, making ever smaller circles, zeroing in.

The bird was coming to his house.

CHAPTER SIXTEEN

Nothing short of a miracle.

The feeling of slipping on one's coat over pajamas is the feeling of adventure. Binoculars slung around his neck, sneakers hastily put on and left untied, full of stealth and strategically avoiding every squeaky floorboard in an old farmhouse that was full of them, Carl padded downstairs and crept outside.

The moon was one of those strange, bloated moons, not full but getting there, with a shape like a balloon that had started to deflate. It had a name he couldn't remember, something like gibbon, but a gibbon was an ape, not a moon. Later he'd look it up. Now that he was homeschooling, he guessed he'd be looking up a lot of things.

It was pitch-dark in the country, no streetlights or house lights to be seen, but the balloon-moon was extra bright. It was plenty of light to see by, once his eyes adjusted.

He made his way to the garden, and hid himself behind an old lilac bush not too far from the garden gate. The lilac was still in bloom and the rich perfume masked his scent nicely, though Carl didn't know that. He was cold, but willed himself not to shiver.

He scanned the skies, then the ground. What he saw almost made him cry out. Foxy! But it couldn't be. Foxy was curled up on her cozy bed in the kitchen. He'd just tiptoed past her. She'd been deeply asleep, paws twitching, as if chasing something in a dream.

This Foxy lookalike—Carl quickly guessed it must be a fox—padded confidently across the moonlit yard and went straight to the garden. Two rabbits, one smaller than the other, hopped along behind. The sheer unlikelihood of this trio was lost on Carl, who was more used to the behavior of cartoon animals than real ones. Roadrunners and coyotes, moose and flying squirrels, rabbits and foxes—it was all the same to him. Still, he wondered: What were they up to? They looked as if they knew exactly where they were headed.

The fox yawned and sat down. The rabbits wriggled easily beneath the gate and popped up on the other side, inside the garden.

Rabbits in the garden! Farmer Janis had it all wrong. There was no mystery here. The Harveys had just been lucky so far, and now the critters were coming for their vegetables at last, just as nature decreed. Carl knew he ought to chase the rabbits away, but he desperately wanted to see the eagle again, and that meant holding still.

Thinking fast, he pocketed a few pebbles, to toss when the rabbits began their destructive work. Maybe it would be enough to scatter them. For now, he'd watch. He lifted his binoculars to get a close-up view.

As the fox waited outside the gate, the rabbits methodically hopped up and down each planted row. They nibbled the weeds—but not the plants—to the ground. They inspected each leaf carefully, and when they found a bug, they ate it.

They turned tailward and made poo pellets by each plant, then scratched the pellets into the soil near the roots.

Next, they gnawed long twigs into sharp-ended stakes. When they used these stakes to prop up the ever-expanding pea vines, the boy had to put down his binoculars and rub his eyes. Agriculture was still a relatively new vocation for young Carl Harvey, but he recognized farming when he saw it. Those rabbits were taking the most dedicated and tender care of the vegetable garden that any farmer could have. Farmer Janis had been wrong in the particulars, but she was one hundred percent right about the mystery.

She'd never believe this, though. No one would. Carl wasn't sure he believed it himself. He thought of Sherlock Holmes and wanted to laugh. Eliminating the impossible sounded easy, until the impossible was hopping along, right in front of your eyes!

It was a strange sensation, to know that you'd seen the most mind-boggling thing imaginable before you'd even reached the end of fifth grade. If he lived to be a hundred and two, nothing in his life was ever going to top this.

Flap. Flap. Flap.

He looked up. The beat of broad wings was heavy and slow. Something sizeable plunged through the moonlight, casting long blue shadows on the ground. Then, *thud.*

The eagle had landed.

⁂

John Glenn, formidable as a German shepherd and awe-inspiring as the Rocky Mountains, shook off the hard landing by spreading his wings and folding them up again to make sure all his parts were working properly.

Doggo was already on his feet, fiercely holding his ground. "Identify yourself, giant bird," he barked. "We don't see your kind here much."

"I apologize for my clumsy descent into your territory," John Glenn replied meekly. "I'm John Glenn, a friend of Foxy's. She told me to say so."

Doggo's bristled stance softened. "Oh, Foxy! I'm not surprised. That Shiba makes friends wherever she goes. We foxes tend to be more solitary."

"Eagles are solitary, too," John Glenn said. "But at least we're not going extinct anymore. There's nothing more solitary than that."

"No doubt," Doggo agreed. "All right, friend of Foxy's. What brings you here?"

"I would like to speak to the rabbits."

Doggo tensed once more, and his lips curled into a snarl. "Easy now, bird! No one's bothering those rabbits on my watch. If I can't eat them, no one can."

"I won't eat them. In fact, I've come to ask for their help." John Glenn sounded sad and humble. "My tracking device is askew and causing me no end of discomfort. Foxy thought the rabbits could remove it. Unless you'd rather do it yourself?"

John Glenn turned around and showed the fox what he meant. Doggo was forced to agree; it was a delicate job far more suited to the rabbits, if the eagle didn't mind waiting a bit. "They have important work to do," Doggo explained. "When they're finished, I'll bring them over to you. Just don't frighten them."

"I would never," John Glenn said gravely. "I come in peace."

"I certainly hope so," the fox replied, "but you *look* like you might want to eat them, and they frighten easily."

The eagle blinked. "That's odd. Foxy said they were brave."

"Well, I suppose they are!" Doggo exclaimed. "Imagine having so much to be frightened of, and yet they carry on. They're the bravest little creatures I know. Wait right here, and in a while I'll introduce you."

⁂

The rabbits paused to stretch and flex their paws. Frankly, they were exhausted. Their farming chores seemed to be growing faster than the plants. Staking the pea vines was an ongoing puzzle. As the cottontails couldn't reach very high, they'd trained the vines to grow sideways, but peas were fast growers and the sprawling plants had already run out of room. Should they find a way to add taller stakes and train the tendrils upward instead? Or should they admit defeat, trim back the vines at both ends, and lose pea production as a result?

Meanwhile, the tomatoes had barely survived an attack of cutworms. It was pure luck that they had. Cutworms feed at night, so the rabbits had caught them in the act and put a quick end to it. Alas, the victory was short-lived. A population of small striped beetles had come out of dormancy to lay their eggs on the underside of every leaf they could find. The nibbling of the hungry newborn larvae promised to be fast and brutal, and Alice wasn't sure what to do.

"Thistle, I'm starting to think that coming here every night is not enough," she said, flicking yet another cluster of the tiny orange eggs into the dirt. "What if those baby beetles hatch at dawn? By the time we arrive to stop them, the damage will be done."

"Do you mean we ought to come during the day, too?" Thistle combed his whiskers as he pondered it. "It would be pleasant to work in the sunlight. But what would happen if the farmer-people saw us? And, not to sound lazy—but when will we sleep?"

Alice had wondered the same thing. "I honestly don't know," she said.

Too tired to zigzag, their ears limp with worry, the farmer-rabbits hopped wearily to the gate. Doggo was waiting for them.

"Buck up, you two. The night's not over yet. There's someone here to see you, and I don't want you to get so frightened you fall over," he said, before adding, "It's a bird."

"Doggo, honestly! Do you think we're afraid of sparrows?" Thistle rallied enough energy to give his friend a playful nudge. "We're not as bad as all that."

"He's no sparrow, but don't say I didn't warn you. He's a friend of Foxy's, and he's given me his solemn word he won't eat you. He wanted me to tell you that before you saw him. To avoid—you know." Doggo mimed playing dead.

"It can't be an owl, can it?" Alice exclaimed. For a cottontail to speak peaceably with an owl was nearly unthinkable. If it were an owl, she'd be half dark in a second, no matter how many solemn promises were made beforehand.

Doggo climbed back onto his feet. "Not an owl!"

"It's a hawk, then," Thistle declared, full of dread.

"He's bigger than a hawk, so get a grip on yourselves," Doggo said. "All right, bird! Might as well show yourself, or they'll worry themselves to death with guessing."

John Glenn appeared from the shadows and spread his wings wide. "Hello, rabbits," he said.

Three things happened in rapid succession, then.

First, the rabbits bolted for cover into the nearest shrub, which happened to be the old lilac bush.

Second, there was a yelp, a crash, a suspiciously human-sounding sneeze, followed by a scramble and a rush of lilac-perfumed, boy-people-scented air.

Third, the rabbits flew out of the lilac bush even faster than they went in.

The fox, the eagle, and the incredulous cottontails turned toward the quaking shrub.

"What," Alice panted, too astonished to even be afraid, "was that?"

⁂

Foxy couldn't stand it another minute. Those darling rabbits were outside, Doggo was outside, even John Glenn was outside—Foxy couldn't see the garden from the kitchen windows, but she could see the sky, and the great swoop of wings descending across the face of the moon couldn't be missed.

Most maddening of all: Carl was outside! What was *her* boy doing outdoors in the middle of the night? It had been all she could do to feign sleep when he'd tiptoed through the kitchen. She assumed he'd come downstairs for a glass of milk and a cookie, as he did far more often than his parents realized. If she'd had the slightest expectation that Carl possessed the moxie to sneak out for a late-night adventure, she would have bounded right after him!

Alas, it had all happened so quickly, too quickly even for her alert Shiba reflexes to anticipate. Now she was inside, and he was out. The rabbits and other animals could take care of themselves, but Carl? That child hadn't a clue how to manage things. He was completely reliant on Foxy, even though he didn't know it.

Foxy paced and panted. The situation was unbearable. Unbearable! She had no way of knowing precisely what was happening out there, in the dark, away from her direct supervision. It's a dog's powerful inclination to bark at such times, but Foxy couldn't let herself bark. Barking would wake up the Harvey parents for sure, and the less they knew about the outdoor shenanigans of her boy, the better.

Foxy panted harder, as if her hot, anxious breath could somehow force the door to open. No such luck. What to do? Turning a doorknob required hands that gripped, a type of appendage that Foxy did not possess.

Then she thought of it.

Marie.

Marie was reasonable. A dog could talk to Marie. Best of all, Marie had two chubby fists with a small but functional set of opposable thumbs.

Careful not to let her toenails click on the steps, Foxy made her way upstairs to Marie's room. The baby was asleep in her crib, and the baby monitor was on, as shown by a small green indicator light on the front. Using her teeth as gently as she would to lift a pup by its neck scruff, Foxy tugged the cord from the wall outlet until it came free. The monitor light flickered and dimmed. Poor humans, with their practically useless ears! They had to use little robots to do their listening for them.

She tipped her head upward, toward the crib. "Marie, Marie! Wake up," she whined, softly.

Being what her parents called "a good sleeper," the baby snored.

"Marie!" Foxy stood on her hind legs with her front paws on the crib railing. She snuffled near the baby's face. "Marie! Smell my breath, wee thing. Wake up to a blast of minty freshness!"

Marie stirred. "Ahhhh," she cooed, dreaming.

Foxy wedged her snout through the bars of the crib and stuck out her long pink tongue as far as it could reach, until the very tip of it flicked Marie's nose.

The baby's face scrunched as she inhaled deeply to cry. Then her eyes flew open. There was Foxy, inches away. The incipient wail blossomed into a laugh.

"Quiet, you cutie-pie baby, you," Foxy scolded, though she couldn't help being charmed. "It's nighttime, and we don't want to wake your parents, as they're getting on in years and need their sleep. Otherwise they'll be cranky all day tomorrow, and you know how stubborn they can be about taking naps, even when they clearly ought to. Understood?"

"Nite! No ma, no pa," the baby agreed.

"Clever girl! Now, Marie, I need you to come downstairs with me. Adventure calls! Are you willing?"

"Vencha, ya!"

Foxy proceeded to toss stuffed animals from the toy bin into the crib until there was a big pile, enough for Marie climb up on and slip over the railing. Foxy stood underneath to catch her, and Marie chortled as she clung to the dog's back, her fingers and toes gripping the thick fur like the little primate she was.

Foxy grunted and made for the top of the stairs. This was no lightweight rabbit on her back. Marie weighed more than the dog herself. Still, Shibas are a sturdy breed, strong for their size, and Marie could crawl downstairs on her own by going backward, a recently mastered skill of which she was justifiably proud.

They reached the kitchen without incident. The doorknob was too high for Marie to get a proper grip, so together they pushed one of the chairs across the floor, slowly, so it wouldn't squeak on the "vintage linoleum," as Sally liked to call what was clearly just an old kitchen floor.

The chair solved it. The baby clambered onto the seat and reached, reached, *reached,* until she got both chubby hands around the knob and gave it a mighty twist. With a well-oiled click, the door opened.

"Such a brilliant child," Foxy praised, helping the baby down again and nudging the chair out of the way. Thoughtfully, she grabbed a fleece blanket from her own dog bed and gave it to Marie. "Wrap yourself in this, you sweet furless creature. It's chilly outside. Now, let's go—but quietly!"

"Go!" Marie whispered. "Ahh, vencha!"

⁂

What happened then was not something Carl could ever fully explain. Even years later, when it was a story he told his own children and grandchildren, it had the feeling of a fairy tale about it, or a magical fable from an old storybook with yellowed pages and a faded ribbon sewn right in.

But it wasn't so hard to understand, really. What happened was simply this: In a moment's time, and much to their mutual surprise, a few well-intentioned creatures came to discover that they'd woefully underestimated one another.

The two cottontails had bolted into the lilac bush and landed in Carl's lap. They looked at him; he looked at them. Now doubly startled, they bolted out again at top speed. Carl scrambled to his feet, lost his balance, and toppled into the shrub. Lilacs have no thorns but they sure do smell nice, and the strong wash of perfume made the boy sneeze and started his eyes watering. He stumbled away from the fragrant shrub in self-defense and found himself face-to-face with an enormous bald eagle, a small fox, and two tiny rabbits, all of whom held still as statues and stared at him as if he'd just dropped in from another planet.

And before any one of these furred or feathered or pajama-clad beings could move or make a sound, good old Foxy came trotting unsteadily through the darkness from the house. Marie rode belly-down on the dog's back, gurgling with joy.

"Oh my, oh my!" Foxy said as she arrived, breathless. "It looks like we've made it *just* in time. John Glenn! Alice and Thistle, my dear rabbit friends! And faithful Doggo, too! Oh, how I've missed you all. Being under house arrest is no picnic, I must say. It's good to breathe the wild night air. How it stirs the blood, and kindles ancient canine fires!"

Marie grinned as she slipped from Foxy's back and onto her feet. If she kept one hand firmly on the dog's head, she could stand up with only a tiny bit of wobbling.

"Hi, cham," she said to Carl. It was her way of saying champ.

"Marie!" Carl kept his voice low, but he was gobsmacked. "What are you doing outside?"

The baby pointed at the animals. "Ja Glan! Bun bun! Doggo!" By Doggo she meant Foxy. When she got to the fox she stopped. "Who?"

"That's Doggo, too," Foxy explained. "I know it's confusing."

"*Doggo* Doggo!" the baby said in delight.

Foxy sniffed. "Doggo, something around here smells minty fresh, and I do believe it's your breath! I heartily approve. But what am I saying; first things first. John Glenn, have my friends been able to help you with your tangled thingamabob?"

"My tracker? No, not yet. We're all just getting acquainted." The bird looked wary. "I wasn't expecting a human to be here. He's not"—the eagle paused, and his voice dropped—"a scientist, is he?"

Foxy laughed. "Hardly. Carl is more the comic-book type. He's a good boy, though. Clever, in his way."

Remember that Carl could understand none of this, except for Marie's baby talk. But it seemed to him that the animals were conferring with one another. He thought he ought to try to say something.

"Um, hi," he ventured. "I'm Carl. You're John Glenn, right?"

The eagle stared at him with those fearsome yellow eyes, and blinked.

"I know your name from the website," Carl explained, trying not to feel foolish. "And you two rabbits—I watched you through my binoculars. I saw you taking care of the garden."

The cottontails' whiskers quivered, but they stared at him bravely, and didn't bolt or freeze.

Foxy's tail waggled with pride. "I told you he was clever," she said.

Carl turned to his sister. "Marie," he said, his voice shaky, "do *you* understand what's going on here?"

"Sa vee dent," she burbled.

"It's self-evident to everyone but him," Doggo scoffed.

Thistle leaned close to Alice and whispered, "Do you suppose the boy-farmer will figure it out?"

"I don't know," Alice whispered back, "but if he does, maybe he'll be able to help with the pea-vine stakes. Look what a giant he is!"

"Okay," Carl said softly. "Maybe I'm crazy, but I think you rabbits planted this garden, and now you're taking care of it. I think the fox stands guard while you work. I saw how he jumped up to protect you when the eagle arrived. I'm not sure what John Glenn is doing here"—he turned to the bird—"but it's not the first time you've come, so it's probably not an accident. Foxy, I bet you know everything. You dumb dog! If only you could talk."

Foxy whimpered and nuzzled the boy's hand. The other animals held still, quiet and expectant. Carl felt like he was dreaming, but he also felt suddenly spacious inside, like a parachute near his heart had bloomed wide open and was longing to rise.

"Don't worry," he said. "I'm not going to tell anybody what you're doing. They're already suspicious. At least, Farmer Janis is. I think I can keep her from finding out the truth. But it means I'm going to have to come down here every day and pretend to do stuff in the garden. Don't be scared of me, okay? I promise I won't mess it up."

The animals gazed at him calmly, as if they understood.

On impulse, Carl dropped to the ground, to his knees. He held his hand out to the rabbits. The smaller one shrank back, but the larger one hopped once, twice, three times. She touched her tiny nose to the boy's fingertips.

Foxy woofed quietly to Marie.

"Alice," Marie said clearly. "Alice bun bun!"

"Alice? Is that your name, little farmer?" he said. The rabbit looked up at him, her white tail wriggling. "Okay, Farmer Alice. I'll do my best to help you. But you're in charge."

CHAPTER SEVENTEEN

Tend your garden well.

The morning after a miracle is a rare and curious thing.

A person's liable to wake up extra early, with a powerful appetite and a fresh outlook on life. All things seem possible on such a morning, even things that aren't. Or weren't. Or shouldn't be, but nevertheless. It made you want to laugh and cry and yell "Merry Christmas!" out the window, like that reformed old miser did in the Christmas story Carl's parents liked to read aloud at holiday time, about the three ghosts and Tiny Tim.

That's how it was for Carl, anyway. He bounded out of bed to bid "howd'ya do" to that wonderful, bright yellow sun the moment it peeked above the treetops, shining its happy beams through his bedroom window and right onto his pillow. He dressed in a hurry and made a beeline for Marie's room. This wasn't his usual routine, as he'd always tended to think of Marie as his parents' job. However, he'd acquired a whole new respect for his baby sister now that he knew she, too, was capable of daring escapes and late-night adventures. A kid who couldn't yet use the bathroom! It was impressive, to say the least.

Even her knack with the animals made sense to Carl, once you considered that she was still a four-legged creature herself half the time. It was a shame she was so bad at conversation. He would have liked to talk over the previous night's events with someone, and she was the only human witness he had. But when Marie saw her big brother was the one to come in her room and take her out of the crib, her face lit up like a small, chubby-cheeked version of that morning sun. She started babbling "bun-bun" and "Ja Glan" and "Cham, Alice, yay!" and that's when Carl knew for sure it hadn't been a dream.

By the time Sally came downstairs, a good three-quarters of an hour later than usual, Carl was feeding Marie her breakfast applesauce. The high chair buckles were too childproof for Carl to figure out, so they'd made a picnic in Foxy's dog bed. Marie sat on the little sofa, a perfect size for her, and Foxy curled around the baby's bare pudgy feet to warm them, as Carl hadn't thought to bring a pair of her absurdly small baby socks downstairs.

Sally was stunned. "Well, would you look at that," she said, when the power of speech returned. "Good morning, early birds! What brought this on?"

Carl squirmed and avoided eye contact. "I got up early because . . . it was morning, I guess? And Marie was already awake, so . . ."

"So you got her up and made breakfast. And you even unplugged the baby monitor to let me and Daddy sleep in? It's—I don't know what to say, honey. It's like a miracle!" She felt her own forehead, as if checking for fever. "I can't believe you thought to do all that."

Carl frowned. "I didn't unplug the baby monitor."

"Woof." Foxy gazed inscrutably at Carl. "Woof, woof."

"I mean, yeah, I did," he went on, smooth as milk. "I unplugged it. The monitor. Like you just said." Carl spooned more applesauce into his sister.

"I didn't want the noise to wake up you and Dad, since I was already taking care of Marie. You two deserve to sleep in for a change."

Sally looked ready to weep with joy. "A miracle. There's no other word for it."

"Di di di di di," Marie growled, yanking at the seat of her pajamas.

"Wait; was I supposed to change her diaper?" Carl asked innocently. Feeding Marie breakfast was one thing, but diaper chores were a whole other category of big brotherdom.

"No worries, I'll do it." Sally smiled and reached down for the malodorous Marie. "I'm glad you two had a fun morning of brother-sister time. Although part of me thinks I must still be dreaming! Come on, baby girl." Child in her arms, Sally practically skipped upstairs for the diaper change, a real spring in her step. Amazing what a little extra sleep can do for a hardworking mother!

⁂

The miracles kept piling up. The next came a short while later, after Brad, too, appeared downstairs, and he and Sally had enjoyed their morning coffee. This marked the official start of the Harvey household day.

That's when Carl, with the clear-eyed sincerity of a vacuum cleaner salesman working on commission, stood before his unusually well-rested parents and announced that he had a request. "Not for a new video game," he said quickly. "It's educational. Homeschooling-related."

"Go on," Brad said, amused.

Carl proceeded to explain that he wanted their permission to take care of the vegetable garden, alone, without help or interference, and that he would even be willing to write a nature study report about it if necessary, but the main thing was that he wanted to do it by himself. Independently and unobserved. Flying solo, as it were.

Sally sipped her coffee. "That's a lot of responsibility."

"Ponsiboo," Marie declared, vouching for her brother's readiness for such a weighty role in the family economy. Brad mistook her character reference for an invitation to play. "Peek-a-boo!' he said, in his falsetto talking-to-Marie voice. "Peek-a-boo!"

"And it's a lot of work," Sally added.

"I know it is," said Carl. "But the garden's been growing pretty well so far, right? So, I just need not to mess it up. Which I won't."

Done clowning for Marie, Brad tented his fingers and leaned back in his chair, earnest and solemn. "It's not just a school thing, champ. That garden, the orchard, all the preserving and canning your mom's doing, the sheep—"

"The imaginary sheep, you mean," Sally teased. Brad's reluctance to put actual sheep in his state-of-the-art paddock had become a family joke.

"Real sheep will come in the fullness of time. Let me finish, this is important—everything about this farm is the family business now. It's our livelihood, our home, our way of life."

Carl kept every trace of sass out of his voice. "I understand, Dad. That's why I want to do it."

"Okay, but that was me saying why. Put it in your own words," Brad urged.

It felt like a test. Marie gurgled encouragingly (to her parents it sounded like a burp), and Carl took a deep breath. "Because of—just what you said," he fumbled, and then recovered. "It's not some science fair project that ends up in the basement when you're done. It's real. It matters. It's *food*. I mean, I'm a farmer now, too, right?"

Marie burbled, very pleased. Sally had to dab at her eyes with the hem of her shirt, and Brad put a newly calloused hand on Carl's thin shoulder.

"Right you are, son. The garden's all yours. Tend it well."

⁂

It was a dewy-eyed morning in the farmhouse, but the cottontails' eventual triumph over John Glenn's tracker during the preceding night had been no miracle. On the contrary: It had taken guts, preparation, and strong teeth. After Foxy and her humans had gone back to their farm-burrow, Doggo attempted a calm introduction between the tender rabbits and the great winged predator. The eagle cooed like a fledgling dove, but it didn't matter. Alice and Thistle couldn't help but be terrified.

They worked on this by sitting quietly near him for a while, until the pure survival reflex subsided and he didn't seem quite so strange and deadly. When the last drops of fear had melted, the rabbits carefully climbed atop the eagle's back and nibbled at the straps. He praised their lightness and gentleness the whole time, and soon the annoying gadget slipped right off.

John Glenn spread his wings in unencumbered bliss. "Let freedom ring!" he said. "Rabbits, you are sharp-toothed indeed, and brave of heart. How can I repay you?"

"You've already promised not to eat us. That's a pretty good trade," Thistle said gaily. Not many cottontails have climbed the back of a fox and the back of an eagle in one lifetime, but Thistle had. The straps had tasted awful (he'd never been near a synthetic polymer before, otherwise known as nylon), but on balance, he felt himself to be a lucky bunny indeed.

"Still, I would like to help in some way. And I will never eat you," John Glenn said earnestly. "Not unless you ask me to."

Both rabbits' tails had a good shimmy over that one.

Once her fear was gone, Alice liked John Glenn right away. She was impressed by his qualities: his size, his plumage, his noble temperament, and the fierce grandeur of his profile. He wanted to help them, and help was something they desperately needed. She wasn't going to let him go without asking for something. But what should it be?

"There is an item we need for the garden," she said, after a moment. "It's called a scarecrow. Our friend Lester told us about them. They can be in the shape of a human, or an owl, or any other creature that will frighten away the crows."

"I have seen these scarecrows," John Glenn said. "Many farms have them."

"Well, we need one, too. The crows have been coming around lately, watching us. I expect they'll be a problem once the peppers and tomatoes are fruiting."

The crows had been gathering for a week already. First they came singly, then in twos and threes. Most birds could be trusted to stick to an agreement, but crows weren't like other birds. They were brilliantly clever, with long memories and complicated brains. They were fiercely loyal, but only to each other. The rest of the earth's creatures were the Others, the Not-Crows, the Lesser Birds, the Lowly Wingless—the crows had many names for those to whom they felt superior, but they all meant the same thing.

Crows were scavengers who ate anything they could find or steal, from insects to human garbage. They'd eat animals crushed by cars on the smooth, black roads the people built. They'd eat the eggs of other birds, and sometimes they ate the newly hatched babies, too. They loved crops they could peck at, like corn and sunflower seeds, and they ate all kinds of fruits and vegetables.

Human farmers loathed them, for crows were destroyers. Alice was forming her own opinion about the matter. She didn't loathe them—they were her fellow creatures, after all—but she surely didn't want them ruining her garden.

"Crows are interesting," John Glenn observed. "Genus *Corvus*, species *brachyrhynchos*. What sort of scarecrow would you prefer?"

"It doesn't matter. It just needs to keep them away from the garden," Alice said.

"Anything crows hate," Thistle added.

"*Hate* is a strong word," John Glenn said mildly. "Crows and eagles are not friends, but we respect each other, bird to bird. The crows won't bother you if I'm here. I will be your scarecrow."

"You will?" Alice couldn't believe their luck. "You'll be here every day?"

"Not every day. I have to be free, to hunt, and mate, and soar. I need my time in the sky, alone. That gift has been returned to me, thanks to you, my rabbit friends." His wings twitched, eager to go. "But I will return here often, often enough that the crows will understand. They are intelligent birds. They will not trouble your garden."

To say the rabbits were grateful would be an understatement. They thanked John Glenn so many times the grand bird grew uncomfortable. In his view, the rabbits had more than earned this consideration, and he was only doing what was right.

Doggo finally put an end to it. He was tired after a long night of rabbit-minding and unexpected encounters with giant raptors and human cubs. Seeing Foxy had been rewarding—he'd especially liked that nice compliment about his breath—but he longed to be back in his den, curled tail to nose, deep in the dreams of a fox. If the rabbits wanted an escort home, it was now or never.

Alice and Thistle conceded, for they, too, were exhausted.

John Glenn bid them all good night and took to the skies, free and unobserved for the first time since he was a fledgling seized from the nest in Wisconsin.

Before the rabbits left with Doggo, they hid the tracker in the barn, buried deep in a pile of useless metal pieces, broken tools, and such. That seemed to be where it belonged.

⁂

Carl hadn't seen his mom dressed like this since they'd moved from Brooklyn. There she stood in the kitchen, in a skirt and blouse with her hair pinned up, reddened lips, and shoes that made her stand on her toes. She was packing up a gift box, like the kind you'd give someone full of fancy chocolates on Valentine's Day, except this box was full of prunes and other samples of her dehydrated wares. It was a rotten trick if you were expecting chocolate, but the dried fruit seemed to be the point. Farmer Janis was there, watching and advising.

"I keep wanting to say Shoo-bert." Sally's hands fluttered like anxious birds as she tied a wide ribbon around the box. "But it's Shoo-bear, right?"

"Chef Armando Shoo-bear. Shoo, bear! Go away, bear!" Janis acted it out. "That's how to remember it. Though I'd bet my favorite tractor it's not his real name."

Sally closed her eyes to concentrate. "Go away, bear! Shoo-bear. Got it. Ugh! I don't know why I'm so nervous."

"He's a character, but they say eccentricity is common in the restaurant business." At Janis's prompting, Sally had scheduled a meeting with Armando Shubert, owner and head chef at Loco for Locavore, the new "farm-to-table" restaurant in the next town. Strictly speaking, all restaurants are farm to table, as where else could the food come from? At Loco for Locavore it meant that the menu changed daily and Chef Shubert only used ingredients that were grown or raised within a ten-mile radius of his kitchen.

As luck would have it, Janis's farm was nine miles from the restaurant, and Prune Street Farm was nine and one-half miles exactly. All the neighboring farmers were wooing Shubert as a customer. Janis felt Sally should do the same. Loco for Locavore had already become one of her main egg buyers, and the place seemed on a path for success. There'd been several magazine articles written about Shubert already. Folks were saying he'd be publishing a cookbook that would make the town famous. Could a TV show be far behind? That's what Janis had heard, anyway.

"You know about the no-fork rule, right?" Janis asked. This was the place she'd been talking about when she was practicing with chopsticks.

Sally stood tall to recite: "'No mere fork may pierce these 'bespoke culinary preparations.' Only teeth! Thus, every molecule of flavor is released within the mouth.' I saw it on the website." She put both hands on her heart and took a breath. "I think I'm ready. Janis, thanks so much for taking care of Marie."

Carl hadn't realized Janis was here to babysit. "Where's Dad?" he asked.

"He has jury duty, remember? I won't be long. Wish me luck."

"You'll do great, Sal. Knock 'em dead! Not literally," she added, making her crazed murderer face for Carl's amusement.

Carl rolled his eyes. "Good luck, Mom," he said, and gave the old gal a hug for good measure. She always liked that.

"Thank you, honey," she said, hugging him back tightly. "Now I'm not nervous anymore." Purse over one shoulder, box of rubberized fruit under her arm, car keys dangling from her hand, Sally made her exit. She looked scared but also excited, like she was off to have an adventure of her own.

Carl liked seeing his mother that way, plus he was relieved she was going out so he could pretend-garden in peace. But now there was Janis to contend with. She yawned and stretched. "Okeydokes, kid. Technically I'm the babysitter, but you're no baby and I've got stuff to do. I'm taking Applesauce with me to price rototillers. I don't need one; I just like to drive Phil Shirley crazy by looking and not buying. Come or don't come, it's up to you."

"Can't. Too many chores." Carl scuffed his feet and gave Janis a side-long look of remorse. "Farmer Janis, I owe you an apology."

"You do?" Janis pulled up a chair, eager to hear.

He put a quiver of emotion in his voice, for effect. "What I said to you about the vegetable garden a while back . . . well, it wasn't exactly true. I *have* been taking care of it. I mean, you were right. I planted it and everything. It was me."

Farmer Janis smacked her own thigh and grinned. "You rascal! And here you had me doubting my own sanity. Why did you lie?"

That he was lying now about lying then was ironic, but the tractor of truth had already left the barn, so to speak. "For the reasons you said," he confessed. "I wasn't ready to admit I was a farmer. It felt weird. But after we talked . . . it doesn't feel weird anymore."

Janis looked smug. "And your parents know?"

"They know now. But they don't know I've been doing it all along. I didn't want to embarrass them for not noticing," he added.

Farmer Janis nodded. "Gotcha. I'll back you up on that. Your parents are on a learning curve; mistakes will be made and we don't have to rub it in. Now, let's you and me talk business, farmer to farmer: Any chance you'll give me a tour of your handiwork? There's stuff I can learn from you, and I'm not proud. I take my schooling where I can get it."

Carl stammered, "Eh—maybe? Soon? But not today. I really have a lot to do."

She looked at him appraisingly. "Holding on to your competitive advantage, huh? Fine. All's fair in love, war, and farming. You owe me your anti-critter secrets at least. I'm serious." Janis stood and began to unbuckle Marie from her seat.

"I will, I promise. It's complicated to explain, I guess."

"Whenever you're ready, Farmer Kid. But remember: There's a regular chipmunk invasion going on at my place, and if it doesn't stop soon I'm declaring war. If you're too squeamish to feed a chicken just because it's fated for the rotisserie, I don't think you'd want the chipmunk apocalypse on your conscience, either." Janis grabbed the diaper bag and slung the baby under her arm like she was a bag of topsoil. "Come on, Applesauce. We're going to go look at farm machinery. Fun, right?"

"Whee! Bye-bye." Marie waved to Carl. "Bye-bye!"

CHAPTER EIGHTEEN

A taste of radish.

Carl got that this chipmunk situation was serious, but the brain has a mind of its own, you might say. His first reaction to the words *chipmunk apocalypse* was to imagine a new video game, in which an army of zombie chipmunks confront an opposing force of, say, robot squirrels. The squirrels would be armed with tiny explosive acorns made of Rodentium, the only substance in the universe able to demolish zombie chipmunk armies while still being stable enough to store in your cheeks.

But Janis wasn't playing games, and traps meant bloodshed. Carl didn't know why the chipmunks plagued Janis's garden and not his, but he was a clever boy, as Foxy liked to say. Alice and her bunny friend had to be behind it. If he could warn them of Janis's ire, perhaps the animals would be able to settle the matter among themselves before it was too late.

He wasn't sure how much of what he said the rabbits understood, but Foxy was a different story. So was Marie. To do this right, he'd need their help.

First, Carl asked Brad to add a doggy door in the kitchen, so the dog could go outside at will. Brad nixed the idea, as he thought a doggy door made it too easy for critters like raccoons and skunks to get in the house. Instead, after watching a morning's worth of YouTube videos and making two separate trips to the hardware store, Brad rigged the back door with a new latch that Foxy could operate herself, simply by hitting it with her paw.

"Now you have to train her how to use it. Good luck with that!" Brad joked when he was done. He was still thinking of Foxy as a dumb dog. Carl knew better. He only had to show the dog once, no treats required (although he gave her one anyway, because she was so good and so cute). Foxy had her own strong motivations for knowing how to work the latch, and that makes learning anything easy.

Let freedom ring! Finally, Foxy was a true farm dog, able to come and go as needed and ready to be put to work.

With phase one of his plan accomplished, Carl sat down privately with the dog and Marie. He explained that the chipmunks had gone too far at Farmer Janis's place, that consequently she was planning to set traps, and that someone needed to let the chipmunks know they ought to lay off, and that they should also be careful, as Janis was pretty riled up.

Foxy held still and listened, sporting her usual sleepy, regal stare. Marie threw in her two cents by chortling "munks, twaps, boo-boo, bad!" An answering *woo-woo-woo* from the dog seemed to conclude the negotiation between them. Carl didn't know what would happen next, but he fervently hoped nobody got hurt.

There was only one more angle to cover. The next time Carl saw Janis, he confessed that his anti-critter "secret" was Shiba Inu pee, a little-known but powerful chipmunk repellent. If she'd like, he could bring Foxy over now and then to anoint her property, just as the dog had done to such good effect at Prune Street Farm.

Janis still had her doubts about Foxy, but anything was worth a try. Imagine her amazement when, within a week or so of Foxy's first ceremonial tinkling, her chipmunk problem seemed to have vanished!

⁂

Foxy's freedom meant more freedom for the rabbits, who could now come to the garden whenever they liked. During the day, Foxy served as their bunny-guard; at night, Doggo remained on duty. Any last-minute requests or schedule changes were arranged by blue jay. Those chattering jays were always glad to have other creatures' business to stick their beaks into, but it was the birds' way of helping, too. They hadn't forgotten why the rabbits were working so hard. Nor had the other animals in the valley. Every rumble of summer thunder reminded them of the Mauler, and made them appreciate their days in the meadow even more than they already did.

Alice and Thistle never forgot about the Mauler, either, and often worked until they were tired to the bone, but that didn't mean they weren't having fun. The switch to farming in the daylight hours was a pure sunlit pleasure, and they no longer had to worry about being seen by the farmer-people, since Foxy's boy was the only human who ever came to the garden. Bit by bit they got used to the huge, clumsy, two-legged creature, until they were hardly afraid of him at all.

A boy-farmer, imagine! He didn't do any of the things they'd been raised to think farmers did. He didn't yell and chase after them, or set traps, or raise a shotgun to his shoulder and point it in their direction. It was just the opposite. He never made any fast moves in their direction and always seemed pleased when they arrived. Foxy assured them that Carl was a good boy, as befitted being the boy of such a good dog as she herself was, and the rabbits came to see that it was true.

Over time, they even learned to communicate with him directly, without Foxy's help, or Marie's. If they wanted him to reach something that was too high for them, they stood up and batted their paws in the air. If they wanted him to water the plants, they lolled their tongues and panted. Most of the garden chores they could demonstrate slowly, until he figured them out. Soon he was picking beetles off leaves as if he'd been doing it all his life. He even restaked the pea vines to his own astonishing height, which would quadruple the amount of peas the plants could produce. The rabbits were thrilled about that. He couldn't always tell a weed from seedling, and he was no use at all at making pellets, but overall he was turning out to be a big help.

The boy even started bringing them carrots! He wasn't digging them from the garden. It was too soon for that; the carrots Alice and Thistle had planted still had weeks of growing to do. But he'd gotten hold of carrots nevertheless, and he started to leave a few small ones out, where the rabbits could help themselves.

At first Alice and Thistle refused on principle, as eating garden-grown vegetables was the very thing they'd made the other animals swear not to do. Then Foxy explained that these were not so much carrots as they were something called crudités, and that they came not from the earth, but from the bottom drawer of the Harveys' refrigerator, and that made it all right. They were the sweetest thing Alice had ever tasted.

Thistle loved them, too, and together they implored Foxy to carry one back to Burrow for Lester. If they'd expected gratitude from the old rabbit, they would have been awfully disappointed. Lester bemoaned the tragedy of such a magnificent vegetable being manhandled by a human farmer—the enemy!—and then slobbered with dog drool—the other enemy! The crudité argument also failed to impress. "It's a ruined carrot, and that's that," he said. Stubbornly he refused to eat it.

"Well, that's too bad," Alice said mildly, as Thistle nibbled the tip, right in front of the cranky old flop-ears.

"Tastes awfully good to me," said Thistle, his busily grinding teeth threatening to make short work of it.

"Ah, that carroty smell!" Lester's nose twitched madly. It was too much for the old fool to bear, and Alice and Thistle gladly turned the rest of the carrot over to him. "Who'd believe it?" he grumbled, even as he devoured this most special of treats. "My first carrot in years; probably it'll be my last. And I have a farmer and a dog to thank for it."

"And us, too," Thistle reminded him, but Lester just keep nibbling and muttering, "A farmer and a dog, a dog and a farmer! Will wonders never cease?"

⁂

Before long, the fast-growing radishes were ready to be picked. Alice was beyond excited. She dug up the first row herself, and Thistle came over to assist. Together they marveled at the bright red bulbs hiding underground, like a secret, ruby-colored treasure.

The boy-farmer noticed and tried to help. Alice slowed down, to teach him, and soon he was as excited as the rabbits were to see what their efforts had produced. They even showed him how to leave a few radish plants in the ground, to flower and make seeds for the next planting.

Carl worked quickly and filled a whole basket. Alice and Thistle followed behind him, restoring the dug-up soil to order and enriching it with fresh rabbit pellets. Later, they'd replant these rows with the seeds they had left.

"Now we're *really* farmers," Thistle said merrily. "Our first harvest!"

Alice was glad, too, but her mind raced ahead. What came next for that overflowing basket of radishes? Would the boy-farmer know how to turn them into money? Would one basket of radishes, or a hundred, be enough to make a difference?

Maybe the boy noticed her longing looks. Moving slowly as ever, he went to the basket, chose two good-sized radishes, and offered them to his hardworking fellow farmers.

The rabbits froze. Was it a trick? Crudités were one thing, but could the boy-farmer *truly* want them to eat vegetables fresh-picked from the garden? It flew in the face of everything they'd been taught. Farmers and rabbits! Rabbits and farmers! Sworn enemies, as old as time!

Now the boy was the one who slowed down to demonstrate. He chose a small radish, rubbed it on his pants leg to clean it, and popped it in his mouth.

"It's good," he pronounced, crunching away. "Try it. You'll see."

He rolled one toward Alice. She caught it between her paws. There was no mistaking his meaning. The boy really did want her to eat it.

Should she, despite all the promises made and extracted from others? Could she? Just this once? The other animals would get a share of the harvest in exchange for their self-control; surely she was entitled to the same. She glanced at Thistle, who'd already seized his rolled radish from the boy and was looking at her for guidance. His shining, eager eyes showed which way he'd vote, if asked. She could hardly deny *him* the experience, could she?

And so, her decision was made. Never again would she be a silly, naive cottontail who'd never so much as tasted a radish! She felt lighter than air and full of joy, just as she had on her very first trip to the meadow's middle.

Now she crossed that same meadow twice a day and scarcely thought about it. Would radishes, too, come to seem ordinary in time? Perhaps they would, but at that moment, Alice would have sworn: no, never. The radish she cradled before her was too fresh-smelling, too thrillingly cherry red, too perfectly sized for a little rabbit's paws and appetite.

And she'd grown it herself! What could be more wonderful than that?

These were her thoughts as she summoned her keen senses to the task of eating. She brought the radish to her lips and sank her incisors into the flesh.

"Yuck!" she exclaimed, spitting it out. "Too spicy! Like biting a thorn."

She made a funny face and sneezed. The boy-farmer laughed out loud. Radishes can be quite strong-tasting, and this one was fresh and pungent as they come, the earth still clinging to its roots.

"Let me try," Thistle said. He took a bite and his eyes grew wide, but he chewed and swallowed with determined enthusiasm. "I like it," he said. "It burns my tongue, but in a good way. I'll finish yours, too, please!"

In time, Alice came to find radishes edible, at least, but their overall appeal remained one topic upon which she and Thistle held firmly opposing views. Thistle declared radishes his favorite; he loved the juicy crunch, the tart flavor burst of the bulb and the peppery taste of the greens, but carrots were sweet from the orange root tip to the tops of their gloriously frilly leaves, and Alice much preferred them.

⁂

Doggo and Carl only occasionally crossed paths, but they too developed a relationship of sorts. Carl had noticed that Foxy was leaving a fair proportion of her GlitterTooth Chew-Bones outside. It made him suspicious, so he'd done a little pajama-clad spying and discovered that the fox he'd seen on that first night would sometimes show up after dark and take them. From then on he always kept one in his pocket, in case the fox ever came close enough for him to offer it.

That never happened, of course. The fox looked so much like Foxy that Carl naturally longed for it to become tame, but Doggo was a wild creature, and he wouldn't dream of letting Carl get too close or, heaven forbid, pet him.

And what of Doggo's longings? His guard-fox services weren't as urgently needed as before now that Foxy was free, but he still held to his side of the bargain. Whenever asked, he'd bring the rabbits across the meadow safely, even if he had to use teeth and claws to do it.

To his own surprise, the fox had begun to look forward to these trips, and he missed them when they became less frequent. A fox is not a pack animal like a dog. For genus *Vulpes*, species *vulpes*, friendship does not come naturally. Yet Doggo found he liked spending time with creatures who depended on him and trusted him, and who thought of him kindly and with gratitude, as a protector, as strange as that idea was to him. The job of keeping the rabbits safe made him feel fierce and strong and useful, and it was a good feeling.

Certainly, there were times he looked at Alice and Thistle and thought about how nice it would be to eat them. His mouth ran with saliva, and he'd get that twitchy, ready-to-hunt feeling in his nose, eager to lead him to his next meal.

But the more he heard the rabbits talking about the Mauler and how they hoped to keep it away, the more he began to have ideas that were new to him: like the difference between short-term satisfaction and long-term planning. Short-term, eating his new friends would provide a satisfying snack. Long-term—well, if these brave cottontails didn't finish the job they started, there'd be no hunting grounds left at all, for foxes or anyone else.

That's what the rabbits seemed to believe, anyway. It wasn't the first time he'd heard of the Mauler—foxes had their own stories about the earth-eating monster, just as all the animals did—but it was the first time he'd seen any creature try to do something about it. These rabbits weren't just telling tales; they were putting their paws in the dirt about it, every day. He found he wanted to help them. He wanted to make a difference, too.

And of course, there was Foxy's good opinion to think about. What a mysterious creature she was! They could never be mates, as foxes and dogs are different species and don't mix that way, but Doggo's fascination with this glamorous canine went beyond such concerns.

On the outside, they were close to identical, yet she was his opposite in nearly every way—cheerful and friendly where he was vicious, sweet-smelling where he was rank. The strangeness of their bond made him marvel at what a random thing it was, to be born a fox or a dog, a rabbit or a chipmunk, a chattering jay or a prattling baby human like the one who lived on the farm, the one who kept yelling "Doggo, Doggo!" when she actually wanted Foxy.

Each of these creatures was so different to the eye and ear and nose, and yet they were all bound together by their shared valley home. It was a good place to nest and hunt and raise one's young. It was their common ground, he thought, from the top of the food chain all the way down to the bottom.

The GlitterTooth treats weren't bad, either. He didn't like them nearly as much as Foxy did, although he didn't tell her that. Doggo was used to gnawing on real, crackling bones full of marrow and blood, not factory-made rods of rice starch and artificial spearmint flavor. But having fresh minty breath was useful. It gave him a real advantage when hunting. The overwhelming spearmint smell sowed olfactory confusion on the breeze, enough to distract his prey from the approaching fox scent until it was too late, and he was close enough to pounce.

CHAPTER NINETEEN

The learning curve.

The shy tendrils of April and May had transfigured to the exuberant blossoming of June, and still Sally and Brad Harvey often asked themselves: Had they done the right thing, leaving Brooklyn behind and moving to the farm?

Judging solely from the changes in Carl, they'd have to say yes. Their firstborn's newfound work ethic and obvious green thumb were a wonder. He was fixed on that garden in a way they'd never seen him fix on anything before, except for the Christmas when Big Robot came on the scene and he wouldn't go anywhere without it for months.

But you couldn't compare a child's love for a toy to a young man's staunch dedication to real responsibility. This was honest, moneymaking labor their son was performing, and outdoors, no less!

It made the elder Harveys feel pretty dang successful as parents, which was important, as they weren't feeling that successful about anything else. Brad's latest calculations forecast that the golden parachute bank account would be empty by Thanksgiving. Spring may have turned to summer, which would inexorably turn into fall, yet the strange alchemy that turned farming into money remained maddeningly out of reach.

It wasn't for lack of trying. Sally's juicy hopes for becoming Loco for Locavore's chief supplier of dehydrated delicacies had yet to pan out. She never did get to meet with Armando Shubert. When she'd arrived, the chef was having a supersized tantrum about a problem no bigger than a mustard seed. In fact, it was precisely the size of a mustard seed, one of which had mistakenly found its way into a sesame seed paste, thus "ruining" the flavor with its minuscule tang. Chef Shubert couldn't stop yelling about it long enough to say hello, never mind taste the samples Sally had so lovingly prepared.

The restaurant's manager had been wearily apologetic; one got the impression this happened a lot. She suggested that Sally try again in a month or so, as the current pressures of meeting his cookbook deadline and doing media appearances while running a restaurant kitchen had kept Chef Shubert at a rolling boil for months. Sally was unlikely to catch him in a tolerable mood until things simmered down a bit.

The manager softened the blow with two consolation prizes: a set of Loco for Locavore chopsticks, and a glossy magazine with Armando Shubert's face on the cover. Sally kept the chopsticks but tossed the magazine into the wastepaper box in the corner of the kitchen as soon as she got home. Discouraged but not defeated, she changed her clothes, pulled on her apron and hairnet, and got back to chopping, drying, and preserving.

Brad worked hard on the orchards, replanting dead trees and making overdue and costly repairs to the irrigation system. There was no money there yet, either, as most of the orchard was planted with apples, a late summer and fall crop.

He'd finally acquired a few sheep, though, three ewes and two lambs. No rams for now, he'd decided. That meant no new lambs, either, but wrestling with a big-horned, bad-tempered ram seemed like a challenge best saved for future Brad, a Brad who'd acquired more sheep-wrangling experience. For now, the sheep were mostly decorative. Shearing might yield some cash, but that was next spring, ten months away. Beekeeping was also on Brad's mind, but a decent hive would take some investment to set up and wouldn't produce honey until the second year. At least he already owned the suit.

The farmer's zigzag path to cash was as clear as rabbit tracks in the snow: labor and expenses now, money (maybe) later. Thankfully, the vegetable garden was starting to produce. They sold Carl's first harvest of radishes at the cooperative farm stand the town sponsored in the library parking lot every Sunday. The radishes sold for two dollars a bunch; the co-op kept half and Prune Street Farm got the rest. It was just enough to buy gas for the round trip to town, but radishes were only the beginning. By the end of June, Carl was hauling baskets of delicious fresh peas, crisp lettuce heads, and other early crops into the house.

For a while it seemed like things were looking up. The orchard's small harvest of stone fruits was ripening, firm dark plums and sweet yellow peaches. Sally's inventive dehydrating (dried radish coins, anyone?) and passion for pickling, canning, and preserving were filling jar after jar. It was time to open a farm stand of their own.

They set it up in front of the house, on their own land. First they opened on Saturdays, so as not to compete with the town market, but as business picked up they opened on Wednesdays, too. They posted signs everywhere they could think of that read: "The Prune Street Farm market stand is open! Family-owned. Fruits & vegetables raised with love." Carl struck a deal with Janis to sell that morning's eggs at a premium, warm from the chicken's bottom. Sally got her sourdough starter alive and bubbling again, and added fragrant loaves of fresh bread to the table.

Throw in some cute sheep to pet, and the Prune Street Farm market stand soon had a stream of regular customers. The superb vegetables were always the biggest draw. In two mornings a week, the stand sold out everything a boy and two rabbits could grow, usually by eleven o'clock.

Success! Or was it? The Harveys were working as hard as they could and selling everything they made or grew, but the numbers still didn't add up. The money flowing in was nowhere near enough to keep the farm afloat. Sally began to panic and wanted to get a job in town (ironically, the only place hiring was one of those fast-food restaurants with the drive-thru windows), but Brad insisted it was merely a "cash-flow problem," which was somehow different from going broke.

Apple-picking season would fix everything, he said, for this was a farm where the money literally did grow on trees. The apple harvest would peak right around the time the golden parachute was due to run out, and those profits would be enough to cover expenses for the season and carry them through the winter, when things were quieter and they could plan new ventures. By this time next year, they'd be selling homespun yarn and apple blossom potpourri and whatever else they could think of, and everything would be dandy.

That's the old farmers' tale that Brad told, anyway. Sally dearly hoped he was right.

Ruth Shirley never did stop by for coffee, though she beamed and cooed and promised every time they ran into her in town. The Harveys saw Tom Rowes now and then, too. He was always presiding at ribbon cuttings of new businesses, speaking at town council meetings and the like. He'd nod hello before strolling on with a superior, knowing smirk on his face.

There was one time he and Brad spoke. They'd bumped into each other at the Pee Wee Softball League opening day parade. Rowes was the grand marshal, and the players' team shirts had THE ROWES RATTLESNAKES printed on the back.

"Why rattlesnakes?" Brad had asked, to make conversation.

Rowes shrugged. "They wanted a name that started with R to go with Rowes. And 'reticulated python' was too long to fit on the shirt. Joke!" He slapped Brad on the back, laughing. Then he turned serious. "How's the farming going? Are you ruing the day yet, Harvey?"

"Nope, not yet," Brad answered, more bravely than he felt. "Not yet."

⁂

The Fourth of July came and went. It was fun for the Harveys, but not for Foxy; she hated the noise and hid under Carl's bed while the family went to see the fireworks. Marie pressed her hands against her ears but squealed with joy at the brilliant, many-colored lights in the sky.

"There is nothing like a small-town fireworks display," Brad said warmly on the drive home. Sally squeezed his hand. It had been a good night. There were maybe two hundred people in the town square, most of whom seemed to know one another. The owners of the local car dealership set up a tailgate BBQ on the back of four brand-new pickup trucks, free of charge, and there were enough hot dogs and hamburgers for everyone. Carl swore it was the best hamburger he'd ever eaten. Marie had her first taste of cotton candy and was sticky as a spiderweb from head to toe, despite the liberal and frequent application of a moist towel. Nothing but a bath would do.

A few miles away, past where farmland turned to meadow and then forest, the animals of the valley had cowered from the deafening booms and bright lights in the sky. The older creatures assured the younger ones that it was all right, just another inexplicable piece of human tomfoolery that happened once a year, at the peak of summer. It made smoke, but it wasn't a fire; it smelled like gunpowder, but it wasn't a shotgun; it cracked lightning across the sky, but it wasn't a storm.

It wasn't the Mauler, either. Lester had said so and Alice believed him, despite the noise and fright. She'd seen the farm stand in action a few times, watching from within a clump of hydrangea near the foot of the driveway. Those dry, tough slips of paper the humans handed to the boy seemed like an awfully meager trade for all the work, sun, rain, rich soil, and time it took to produce the bags full of wholesome food the customer-people received in return. How could such a modest exchange have the power to keep the Mauler away?

Yes, sir; being a farmer meant a wheelbarrow-full of worry, and that was true no matter how many legs you had. The sweet ignorance of youth provided the only exception to this rule, and of all the farmers on Prune Street, young Carl Harvey was the most carefree. After all, he had parents to do his worrying for him, while he spent his day in a pretty garden with friendly rabbits and his own faithful dog for company.

Homeschooling was proving to be a breeze, too: Running the farm stand took care of math and public speaking, and the garden provided all the nature study he could want. Helpfully, Marie had recently decided that being read to was her favorite activity and she wasn't particular about subject matter, so that covered everything else. Currently he was reading to her about Greek and Latin roots, the life of Sir Isaac Newton (an apple orchard figured prominently in that story, which seemed fitting), and European history during the Dark Ages. For some reason the phrase "bubonic plague" made Marie laugh, so he'd read that chapter of his history book aloud several times. It gave him a healthy respect for fleas, and he finally understood why his parents were so obsessed with throwing Foxy in the tub.

As for science: He'd checked quite a few times, but the Eagle Restoration Project website was no longer being updated. "DUE TO AN INTERRUPTION IN GOVERNMENT FUNDING, OUR WORK HAS BEEN SUSPENDED UNTIL FURTHER NOTICE," the home page read. It was a shame, as John Glenn had begun stopping by the farm regularly, and it would have been fun to see his yellow blip coming and going. The eagle would pose in a particularly frightening manner on the roof ridge of the barn, wings ominously spread and that sharp, flesh-tearing beak half open, until the crows that were always hanging around squawked and flew off.

It was almost as if the big bird was trying to scare them away.

⁂

If Carl did have a problem—and he wouldn't have said that he did—it would be that he needed friends. Kid friends.

Carl didn't think so. But his parents did.

"Honey, get your shoes on. We're leaving for the meeting in five minutes," his mom said after dinner one night, before adding, "There will be kids there."

He ignored that last bit and slowly located his shoes. "What kind of meeting?"

"The Valley Farmers Association. Janis told us about it, don't you remember? We'll learn a lot. We'll meet new people, too. Including kids."

"Is Farmer Janis going to be there?"

"Yes. She's the one who told me there would be other kids."

Kids! New kids! Other kids! Tempting or terrifying? Carl couldn't decide which. He'd grown used to being on his own with Foxy and the rabbits and the vegetables and Marie, who was neither animal nor vegetable but had elements of both, as she still occasionally traveled on all fours and always smelled like fruit.

He dropped his shoelaces. "Can't I just stay home?"

Brad bounded down the stairs, beard freshly trimmed, dressed in his skinny jeans and his most rustic flannel shirt, although on him it just looked like he was a bass player in a band. "That's not an option, champ. You're coming with us. Didn't you hear your mom say there'd be kids there? Maybe you'll make some friends."

"That's why I don't want to go," Carl blurted. But it was the wrong answer, as it put a concerned, "let's talk about that, son" look on Brad's face. He grabbed a kitchen chair, spun it around, and sat down, facing Carl.

"Let's talk about that, son. What's so terrible about making friends?"

Carl shrugged. "I didn't say it was terrible. I'm just busy, and I don't feel lonely. I mean, I talk to you and Mom and Foxy and Marie and . . ." He couldn't very well say that he spent all day with two rabbits who felt like friends, could he? "And I talk to Farmer Janis, and Orin at the library, and all the customers at the farm stand. I mean, that's a lot of talking right there."

The truth was, Carl was not missing other kids much at all, not even Emmanuel. There was too much going on in the garden for him to ever be bored, and he wasn't prepared to spill the unbelievable—one might even say, magic—beans about how and with whom he spent his days, anyway. It just felt right to keep to himself.

You might say Carl was discovering the rewards of solitude in nature, which, having grown up in the city, he'd hardly experienced before. He found that he liked it, a lot. Farmers and poets know all about a healthy love of solitude and being outdoors, but grown-ups don't always recognize the need for it in children, or in themselves.

Brad grabbed his dress hat, meaning, his fedora. "Yes, there will be kids there. You might talk to them; you might not; that's up to you. But that's not the main reason we're going. In the city, it's called networking; I don't know what it's called here. It means we need to meet other farmers. People with experience, who I can ask for advice."

"You have Farmer Janis."

"Janis is a wonderful, wise, and generous friend, but her way might not always be the right way for us. I need a multiplicity of perspectives."

"Whuuuu."

"I need to hear more than one opinion."

Carl nodded. "You're in a learning curve."

Brad looked at him, impressed and somewhat startled. "Yes. Yes, I am."

"We all are," Sally said, hoisting Marie to her hip. "Oh, did I mention? There will be pie."

This changed everything. "What kind?" Carl scrambled to get his shoes tied.

Brad adjusted his hat and grabbed his keys. "There's only one way to find out."

Pie may have lured Carl to the station wagon, but Foxy flatly refused to be left home. She jumped in the car and wouldn't budge, until Brad grew impatient and said, "Let the dog come, it's fine." Sally wondered if dogs would be allowed in, but Brad pointed out that the meeting was in a barn. "There'll probably be all kinds of animals there," he said. To Carl he added, "Keep an eye on her, champ. Make sure she doesn't bother anyone."

But Carl was more worried about people bothering Foxy, and insisted on running back in the house to get her new yellow reflective vest, which he buckled onto her as they drove.

CHAPTER TWENTY

The farmers call a meeting.

Stuart Gilroy's Bustin' Barn of Antiques was an enormous red barn that was either packed with junk or overflowing with vintage treasures, depending on your taste. Every month or so, when the barn was "full to bustin'," Gilroy held an auction to clear the place out, just so he could fill it up again.

"Why haven't we been here before?" Sally murmured, both hands hovering over the old glassware and sets of dishes. There were tables full of mixing bowls in candy-bright colors, hand-cranked mixers, wooden rolling pins, old typewriters. Stacked and leaning along the walls were deep farmhouse sinks, sweetly painted furniture, potbellied woodstoves, old shop tools, you name it. Sally was in the vintage treasure camp for sure, and her eyes grew bright with longing for just about everything she saw.

"It's all junk," Brad said, moving away from the tables. Marie straddled his hip and grabbed at the air with her chubby digits, a disaster waiting to happen. "Let's find some chairs before it gets too crowded."

But Stuart Gilroy had spotted a live one. He sidled over to Sally, sporting an enormous smile.

"Hey there, neighbor! I'm Stuart Gilroy, and the barn is full to bustin'! Next auction is a week from Thursday, but if you see something you like, we'll strike a deal right now." He had long gray hair that tumbled loosely to his shoulders, and a thick mustache that nearly hid his mouth. "Make me an offer, ma'am! I can practically promise I'll say yes."

"I'm just looking," Sally said, charmed. "We're here for the meeting."

Stuart's bushy gray eyebrows shot up. "You are? Funny, I wouldn't have taken you for farmers. Thinking about getting into it, are you? A lot of folks are, these days. Well, it's good to do your research. Farming's harder than it looks. I wouldn't last a week at it, personally!" He picked up a teacup Sally had been admiring and held it to the light. "Ever thought about getting into the antiques business? I can see you have excellent taste."

Brad scowled in irritation, but maybe it was from Marie's vigorous squirming to get down. Luckily, Janis had already made her way over. "You've lost your eye for value, Gilroy," she interjected, slurping the last pie crumbs off a paper plate. "These aren't future farmers, these are here-and-now farmers. Meet my friends, the Harveys. They bought the old Crenshaw place. They're doing well with it, too. This is Brad, this is Sally, and this wiggly person is Applesauce."

Stuart tugged at his mustache. "The old Crenshaw place; well, well! Nice to meet you all. Hey, Applesauce! Aren't you a cutie."

Marie went *brrrrrrr* with her lips and spit flew everywhere. Janis offered Brad her paper napkin, which he used to wipe the baby's face and his own. To Stuart, he said, "We call it Prune Street Farm now."

"Prune Street Farm, sure, that's the name. I've heard good things about it. Got your own farm stand, selling quality goods. My apologies. Please, grab some coffee and a slice of pie and take your seat. We'll get started in a few minutes." He winked at Sally. "Farmers always get ten percent off at the Bustin' Barn of Antiques! If you see something you like—and you will!—don't be shy."

Carl had missed this exchange, as he and Foxy were hunting pie. Together they'd sniffed their way to the back of the barn. What a spread! Two long tables full of homemade heaven. He got in line and held Foxy's leash short and tight, so she stayed right at his feet.

There were kids milling about near the food. He counted about a half dozen, all gorging themselves and teasing each other like they'd known each other all their lives. Two boys, very alike and about his own age, approached him as he inched forward in the line.

"Hey. Who are you?" one of the boys asked. He wasn't rude, exactly, but he did seem to think he was entitled to an answer.

"Is that a dog or a fox?" The other boy dropped to the ground. "Is it friendly? Can I pet it?"

"She's not that friendly," Carl said. Foxy looked unhappy, trapped in a sea of legs with a strange boy trying to pet her. Her tail drooped until the line moved again. The two boys stuck close, wanting to know more. Where did he go to school? Why hadn't they seen him around before? Why was his dog wearing a yellow coat?

Carl answered their questions as best he could until he reached the front of the line. The pie lady wore a hairnet; she looked pleasant but frazzled. "You want pumpkin, apple, or a little of both?" she said, breathless. "It's a dollar either way."

Carl dug in his pocket for a dollar. "Both, please."

She put two good-sized slices on a paper plate, then frowned when she saw Foxy. "You can't bring your dog back here by the food; it's a board of health rule." Then she noticed Foxy's yellow vest. "Oh, I'm *so* sorry, honey!

I didn't realize he was a guide dog." Carefully she seized Carl's hand and guided it to the paper plate. "You got that? Here, I'm putting a fork on the plate for you, too."

Carl looked at her with intensity, so she could see he didn't need that kind of help. "I'm good, thanks. Thanks for the pie. Here's my dollar."

She nodded and smiled, overflowing with kindness. "No charge, sweetheart. Your dog is so cute! He looks just like a fox." But then she gasped and her hands flew to her throat at the heart-tugging irony of a boy not being able to see how cute and foxlike his own dog was. Life was truly a mystery, wasn't it? Bitter and sweet by turns.

⁂

Eager to dig into his pie, Carl took a seat against the wall, near the other kids. Finally, the two boys introduced themselves. They were the Fleischman twins, Billy and Greg, eleven years old, not identical but a great deal alike. They struck Carl as rough and tumble but not necessarily mean, just blunt and lacking all shyness. They weren't homeschooled but didn't blink when Carl said he was.

Mostly they thought it was hilarious that the pie lady thought Carl was blind. Their laughter made Carl uneasy, as the pie lady was just mistaken and trying to be nice. Nor did he think it would be funny to be blind, although bringing your dog everywhere would be pretty great.

"Is your dog even smart enough to be a guide dog?" Billy asked, scratching Foxy's head. "She doesn't look that smart."

"Woof," said Foxy.

"She's very smart," Carl said. "But she's not, you know. Trained."

"Can she herd sheep?"

Carl shrugged. "I don't know. Our herd is kind of small."

"How many?"

"Five."

Greg laughed. "That's not a herd. A herd is, like, five hundred. That's what my aunt and uncle have."

Billy started issuing commands to the dog. "Sit! Fetch! Roll over!" Foxy gazed implacably into space, ignoring him. To Carl, Billy said, "You're not blind, but I think your dog is deaf!"

Billy and his brother guffawed until Greg looked up. "Oh man, look at the dude with the hat! What a hipster. I bet there's a man bun underneath."

It was Brad, looking for Carl. He grinned when he spotted him. "There you are, champ! Should have guessed you'd find the food. Come on. Mom's saving our seats. Hey, who are your friends?"

The Fleischman boys jumped up and introduced themselves. They had a whole different way of talking to grown-ups: they stood up straight, offered firm handshakes, and said sir a lot. Brad seemed very taken with them. Carl felt a little sick. Maybe he'd eaten his pie too fast.

"Our dad is Larry Fleischman. He's the biggest farmer in the county," Greg explained.

"We grow onions," said Billy proudly. "Just onions."

"Well, he's lucky to have two kids like you to help him out," Brad said. "Carl is a huge help on our farm."

The boys snickered. "Our dad hires people to do the work," said Greg.

Still smiling, Brad steered Carl away. "Bye, *champ*!" Greg teased as they left, and Billy repeated it. "So long, *champ*!" They were doubled over in laughter, and Carl was glad to leave them behind.

Meanwhile, on the other side of the barn, Sally had draped her sweater and Brad's jacket over four folding chairs, to save them, and was walking a fussy Marie up and down the aisle.

"No, she's my youngest," she was saying to an older couple with kind, weather-beaten faces. "My son Carl is nearly eleven. He's here, too, someplace."

The man chuckled. "Interested in farming, is he? A lot of the young 'uns aren't."

"He is interested, very much. He does a fantastic job caring for our vegetable garden."

"Does he, now." The woman leaned forward. "I've heard your produce is nice and early. Where'd you get your seeds?"

"Bun bun seed," Marie confessed, irresistibly.

Sally smiled as she and Marie pivoted for another lap. "The plants in our vegetable garden came up by themselves. I guess we have Mr. Crenshaw to thank for that."

The woman's expression stayed blank. "The plants came up by themselves?"

"Sure. Why? Is that unusual?" Sally asked, all innocence.

"Oh, no," the woman replied, deadpan. "It happens all the time. They're called weeds!"

Everybody within earshot laughed, and Sally wondered if she'd been made the butt of a joke she didn't understand. Janis came to the rescue by throwing her own coat down on a chair next to the Harveys'. Then she spirited Sally and Marie off to look at a vintage gas engine she had her eye on.

Janis whistled. "What a beauty. That's an Emerson-Brantingham Type H, from 1918 or so. One and a half horsepower. Sweet."

"It's adorable." Marie's grabby hands headed for the engine, but Sally stopped her. "Hey, what was that all about? What that woman said, about the weeds?"

Janis waved it off. "They're just jealous because your vegetables are bigger and earlier and tastier than everyone else's."

"Are they really?" Sally was dumbfounded. "Why do you think that is?"

Janis paused. "Ask the kid," she said lightly. "Maybe he knows."

"Bun bun bun bun bun," Marie sang in explanation, but no one paid her any mind. It was time for the meeting to begin.

⁂

This was no cottontail meeting, that's for sure. It was noisy, with plenty of crosstalk and not one moment of quiet contemplation. There were as many kinds of farmers in the room as there were slices of pie on the table in back. There were large-scale farmers with thousands of acres, and small family farms with five. There were dairy farmers and meat farmers. There were "monocrop" farmers who grew a single crop, year after year: corn, say, or wheat, or onions, or Christmas trees; and "specialty crop" farmers, which meant everything else, including fruits, vegetables, nuts, and flowers.

There were organic farmers who used no chemicals at all and grew heirloom seeds that had been saved from season to season, going back generations. They composted and used cover crops, and they chatted knowledgeably about the health of the soil, moisture retention, and "regenerative agriculture."

There were chemical farmers who relied on artificially produced fertilizers, insecticides, and weed killers, and used seeds that had been genetically modified to withstand those very same chemicals. Naturally, the only place to buy these seeds was from the same company that sold you the chemicals, and you had to buy new seeds every year because you weren't allowed to save any. These farmers talked about the cost of "inputs," meaning, all the things they had to buy from the company every year to stay in business.

Some of the other farmers called this "a racket" and being put "over a barrel." Many of the chemical farmers didn't disagree, but it was a system that worked for now and would be difficult and time-consuming to change, and in the meanwhile they had families to support.

When the conversation got heated, they talked about the weather. Every farmer had something to say about the weather. They also found unity by naming a common enemy: in this case, stinkbugs. Carl found this part of the meeting quite engrossing. Apparently, stinkbugs were a big problem, and it wasn't just the smell. They were an invasive species that literally sucked the juice out of all kinds of fruits and vegetables and caused enormous damage.

Interestingly, one way to manage the stinkbug problem was to sic a different invasive species on them: an army of tiny wasps that liked to lay their own eggs inside the stinkbugs' eggs, thus killing them. These were called samurai wasps, and if *Samurai Wasps vs. Stinkbugs* wasn't the most weirdly appealing idea for a video game since Zombie Chipmunks vs. Robot Squirrels, Carl didn't know what was.

This conversation led to a serious discussion of bees that kept Brad on the edge of his seat. Bees were the all-important business partners of farmers—no pollination meant no fruit—and everyone was worried about them, as there had been major bee die-offs in recent years. Some of the organic farmers blamed the chemical farmers for contributing to the bees' decline. Others blamed different causes, or a combination of things, or noted that scientists still didn't know exactly why the bees were dying.

It seemed like everybody had a lot to say. Sally got a headache from all the loud voices and strong opinions. Brad took notes like crazy. After the first hour, there was a break for more pie and coffee, and immediately the farmers were all friends again, asking after one another's health, kids, livestock, elderly relatives, and so on.

In short order the meeting reconvened, now with Farmer Janis presiding. She tapped on the microphone to make sure it was on. "Settle down, everyone. Time for thank-yous: First, to Dorothy and Phyllis, for the great coffee and the spectacular pies." Everyone clapped. "And thanks as ever to Stuart, for hosting us here in the barn."

"My pleasure. Remember, farmers get ten percent off!" Stuart called from the side.

"We appreciate the consideration. Before I introduce our guest speaker, I have two announcements—what is it, Ruth?"

Ruth Shirley was in the front row, waving her hand wildly and bouncing in her seat as if trying to get picked for a game show. At the sound of her name, she jumped on stage and took hold of the microphone.

"I just need a second, Janis." She smiled at crowd. "Hey there, everybody! I'm Ruth Shirley? Of Ruth Shirley Realty?"

"We know, Ruth!" someone called out, to laughter. "Just don't mention your billboard!"

"Not *everyone* knows who I am, Claire. Yet!" More laughter. "Seriously, if you're buying or selling houses, farms, or land, I'm your gal. Call me, my number's on the billboard—gotcha!" Ruth's smile was pure sugar. "I just wanted to remind everyone about the raffle." She waved a roll of tickets. "Only a dollar a ticket, ten dollars for twelve. Phil's raffling off a new rototiller. All proceeds go to the public library. I told him he's nuts, but you know Phil."

Phil waved from the side of the room, where he leaned against a wall.

"I'm nuts, all right. Look who I married!" More laughter. "Seriously, it's a beautiful machine and there's plenty more in my showroom. Hey, Janis! Why don't you get rid of that Tin Can of yours and buy a real tractor? I'll pay for your raffle ticket myself."

Janis smirked. "Funny you say so, Phil. I've been thinking of upgrading. To a horse!" That cracked everyone up. It was a running gag, Phil's endless attempts to sell the latest equipment to Janis, who just kept rebuilding a fifty-year-old tractor engine and carrying on. She dug some cash out of her overalls. "Ruth, here's ten bucks for a dozen. You fill 'em out for me." With a sly look to the audience, she added, "I'm in the egg business, what can I say? The rest of you should do the same. It's a worthy cause."

Ruth beamed and waved as she took her seat, and Janis continued. "As I was saying: two announcements. First, as chair of the hospitality committee, I want to make sure you've all met our new family. Stand up and take a bow, Harveys! That's Brad, Sally, Carlsbad—you thought I forgot, huh, kid?—and that's little Applesauce right there. They farm the old Crenshaw place. Be nice to 'em; they're good folks."

"The boy is blind, poor thing," Dorothy the pie lady whispered to her friend, Phyllis. Only those in the back row (and one sharp-eared Shiba Inu) could hear. Foxy woofed in displeasure. Carl thought she was bored, so he let her lick the pie crumbs from his fingers.

"Speaking of apples," Janis said, "it's time to start planning the Harvest Festival. How's the second Saturday in October look for everyone? Show of hands?"

The second Saturday of October seemed fine with most.

"Done. Put it on your calendars. That was my second announcement. Harvest Festival subcommittee, come see me before you leave. Now, let's give a warm valley welcome to our guest speaker, Theodore Collins."

Janis handed the microphone to their guest, who'd set up a small projector and portable screen during the break. He pulled a sleek tablet computer out of his mud-stained knapsack and began his talk.

Farmer Ted was a fourth-generation farmer from Pennsylvania Dutch country. His talk was about branding, website design, e-commerce, digital marketing, mail-order fulfillment, and other topics of the sort that used to occupy Brad Harvey full-time at his old job. Some folks' eyes glazed over; others listened hard and asked questions. Brad couldn't help leaping in at one point, to clarify a technological issue that Farmer Ted was fuzzy about. That let the cat out of the bag, and now everyone wanted to talk to Brad.

Later, as the chairs were folded and stacked, and the leftover pies were packed up for the food bank at the church, one of the older farmers, Larry Fleischman Senior—he was the twins' grandfather—approached. His son, Larry Junior, and a few others were in tow. They all introduced themselves.

"What's your story, Brad?" Larry Senior said, gruff but friendly. "You used to work for an ad agency, sounds like? Selling cornflakes to the masses and whatnot?"

Brad held his fedora; now he tucked it behind his back. "Not exactly. It was a branding agency." That drew blank looks, so he explained. "It's what comes before advertising. We develop the brand's conceptual and visual messaging and strategize how to communicate it to a precisely targeted customer avatar, through a range of media outlets, direct marketing, special events . . ." The words poured out with practiced ease, but Brad would have liked it better if they'd wanted to discuss beekeeping instead.

Larry Senior crossed his arms. "Are you talking about selling? I give you my wares, you give me your money?"

"Indirectly, yes. Increased sales are the whole point."

"It sounds like you're an expert."

Brad shrugged. "I worked in the field for quite a few years. It wasn't much fun, actually. I moved up here to get away from all that."

The old farmer guffawed. "Unless you want your farm to go bankrupt, you can't get away from selling, Brad. That's a fact."

CHAPTER TWENTY-ONE

Marie's brilliant idea.

"So, according to the alpha human," Foxy concluded, "by which I mean, the human who was the strongest and smartest and clearly deserved to be in charge, which was obvious since he was the only one who could make pictures appear on a screen: Farms make money by doing something called branding."

"Branding," Alice repeated, ears adroop in confusion. Like Larry Fleischman Senior, she didn't know what branding meant, although, unlike Larry Fleischman Senior, she didn't reflexively think of it as being a painful stamp inflicted by a red-hot iron that some cattle farmers still applied to the flanks of cows, to mark them as their own.

"Yes, branding. And marketing. They are absolutely necessary, and they must include a website," Foxy said firmly. "That's what the alpha human said, and he certainly smelled like an expert."

It was a hot August afternoon in the garden, a Wednesday, a few days after the meeting. Carl had gotten up early to run the farm stand. Afterward he'd eaten lunch, and now he was napping in a pile of soft hay in the shade behind the barn. Such naps are always a farmer's prerogative, which explains why farms tend to have so much hay lying around.

Carl was supposed to be watching Marie while his parents walked the orchard and strategized about the apple harvest, but Foxy was right there and a highly competent babysitter. The animals decided to let the boy sleep for a while. It was the perfect opportunity to hear Foxy's detailed report on the farmers' meeting. Marie had heard it all firsthand, but Alice and Thistle hung on the dog's every woof.

Foxy accepted their rapt attention as her due. Yes, she'd made a fuss about going to the meeting, but it wasn't just because she hated being left home alone (although she did). Her pert ears missed nothing; from Brad and Sally's private parental chatter she'd gleaned that the meeting had to do with how to properly run a farm and turn vegetables into money, a subject much too vital to leave to her humans to figure out.

Ah, those well-intended, slow-paced, blunt-nosed, practically earless humans! How could they be expected to understand important things?

And so, the dog had boldly seized her spot in the Subaru, endured the interest of the Fleischman twins, accepted her meager taste of pie crumbs without begging for more, and snoozed in discomfort on the cold wooden floor beneath Carl's chair—all to hear Farmer Ted's presentation. She'd listened hard and now felt completely confident in her general understanding of his message. That Foxy was prone to overconfidence was beside the point: She knew what the man had said as well as anyone there. Better, probably, given her superior hearing.

"Branding is simple," she assured the others. "It has to do with letting people know how wonderful you are. I do it all the time. Marketing is the same, but at a market, obviously."

"It sounds straightforward," Thistle agreed. "But what's a website? Can we get the spiders to make one? Sounds like something they'd be good at."

"We could ask the spiders," said Alice, who wasn't yet convinced it was as simple as Foxy had described. "But it seems that the main thing is making sure a lot of humans know about the farm, and how tasty all the vegetables are."

"That's a job for the blue jays, then," Thistle said wisely.

Foxy nuzzled the little cottontail. "It would be, my young friend, except for one fact: Only the Marie-sized people can understand the blue jays, and the Marie-sized people have a terrible time getting the Sally- and Brad-sized people to understand anything."

"Yahhh," said Marie, who knew the truth of this firsthand.

Foxy licked the baby's face consolingly before concluding, "Alas, it's the big, uncomprehending grown-up humans who have all the moolah."

"What's moolah?" Thistle asked.

"Cash. Dough. Simoleons. Scratch. It all means money. Humans have as many words for money as you rabbits have for—well, whatever it is you think about most."

What *did* rabbits think about most? The answer depended on which rabbit you asked. Some thought mostly about eating, and some thought mostly about getting eaten. In people, that's the difference between being an optimist and a pessimist. In rabbits, too, it was a question of temperament, but also choice: Being part of the food chain was unavoidable, but how you felt about it was up to you. Thistle wanted to debate the point. Alice preferred to stick to the subject at hand.

"On this we all agree: There's a wide range," she said diplomatically. She'd begun using that phrase in honor of Violet, who'd been taken by a predator a few weeks back; an owl, probably, but it might have been a hawk, and everyone hoped that it was. "Foxy, please finish your point about the simoleons."

Foxy scratched herself vigorously with a hind leg. The Harveys were so frantically busy these days it had been weeks since her last bath, and she was beginning to feel unkempt. "My point is, the blue jays would be useful if all humans were as clever as Marie. But they're not."

"Nope nope nope," Marie said, in passionate agreement. Her own frustration about this was keen, and for obvious reasons: Her speech improved slowly, while the list of truly fascinating topics she wanted to discuss grew longer by the day. It's well known that toddlers are prone to tantrums, but think how it must feel to be so thoroughly misheard and underestimated! Anyone, of any age or size, would be likely to have at least a few tantrums about that.

Alice gazed up at the clever baby, who had learned to stroke those soft rabbit ears with great delicacy, and thus earned the privilege of having the bun-buns sit in her lap when Carl wasn't looking (much as they liked the boy, sitting in a human farmer's lap was still too much for any wild rabbit to contemplate, and they didn't want to put the idea in his head). "We'll have to find another way to spread the news, then. Marie, how do the big humans learn things?"

The baby pursed her rosy lips. "Cham, book," she answered, after a moment's consideration. "Bubonic plague!"

What Marie meant, of course, was that Carl had learned a great deal about the bubonic plague from books, which suggested that putting information in written form was an excellent way to get humans to learn things.

Her logic was correct, and so was her conclusion, the rabbits realized at once, for how many times had Lester bragged about all he'd learned from consuming literature? All they needed to do was put the news of Prune Street Farm's spectacularly good vegetables in written, readable form, someplace where as many humans as possible would see it.

If the spiders knew how to weave a website, that might be worth a try, too, but they certainly couldn't help with the writing part, as everyone knows spiders can't write, any more than rabbits or dogs or foxes can. Only humans could do that.

Alice licked Marie's grubby hand, which could barely hold a crayon. The animals had done all they could.

The rest was up to Marie.

⁂

Any parent will tell you: it's dizzying how fast a baby changes. The littlest young 'uns grow nearly as fast as radishes. At eighteen months of age, Marie still wore diapers and talked nonsense, but every day her lovely babbling sounded a smidgen more like the kinds of words that, someday, even a grown-up human could understand.

She could walk on her own now, and grew teeth at an alarming rate. Interestingly, she'd found that the GlitterTooth Chew-Bones were the only thing that really hit the spot when she had teething pain. Sally kept snatching the Chew-Bones away and replacing them with teething biscuits meant for babies, but Foxy would generously bring Marie new GlitterTooth treats from her own private reserves. The baby's newly erupted teeth were white as snow and sparkled like dewdrops; minty applesauce was her aroma, and an appealing one it was, too.

The dog days of summer were rolling by, and Marie gave serious thought to that conversation in the garden, in her own baby-brained way. She thought about how much she liked petting the bun-buns, and how pleasant it was when Foxy licked her face, and how nice it was to be able to put dirt in her mouth when Cham fell asleep and only the animals were watching her.

Now she had an important job to do, just like Cham did. What a big girl she was! But as she herself couldn't read or write just yet, she'd have to be strategic about it. Cham, she felt, was going to be the key. That boy was scribbling all the time, lately.

It was getting toward the end of August. Marie had been toddling around the kitchen, looking for things to chew on, and got herself busy dumping out the box of old paper. What a fine mess she made! The Harveys kept a tidy house, mind you, but neither Brad nor Sally liked to throw things in the trash if it could be helped. Items purchased at the store were bought in bulk, without packaging if possible, and stored in glass jars at home. Kitchen scraps were composted and returned to the soil. Most kinds of paper—newspapers, magazines, brown bags, plain cardboard—were saved in a box in the corner of the kitchen. These would be used to start fires in the fireplace when the cold weather came, or shredded to use as packing material.

"Shoo bear!" Marie crowed in victory, bits of damp paper spraying from her mouth. "Shoo bear! Cham, *look!*" She pointed, a new skill.

"What's up, Applesauce?" Carl said. They'd all taken to calling her that. He was at his desk, pencil in hand. Sally had just gone downstairs to check on the dehydrating operation, which now took up half the cellar and was poised to destroy every fruit on the Eastern Seaboard. Carl was figuring the week's earnings from the farm stand. He'd learned to make spreadsheets on his computer, but it was more fun to do it by hand, drawing columns for all the different kinds of products, the prices per bunch or per pound, quantities sold, and so forth. It was the most interesting math he'd ever done, as he knew exactly what all the numbers meant and cared deeply about the outcome.

Marie toddled over to him and put a half-chewed piece of paper on his leg.

"Faam," she said, and fixed him with her unblinking stare. "Bwanding."

"Do you need a Band-Aid?" he asked. She shook her no, no, *no*, perilously close to a tantrum, and waved the paper in his face. Eventually Carl figured out that he was supposed to look at it. It was the torn-off cover of a magazine featuring a photograph of Chef Armando Shubert, who grinned charmingly into the camera. Sally always shut off the television when the ad for Loco for Locavore came on the local news channel! "Shoo-bear!" she would mutter, clearly unhappy. Yet here he was on the cover of a magazine, holding a bunch of fresh spinach in one hand and a fistful of cash in the other. If only she could make Cham understand!

"*Hipster Farmer* magazine," he read. "Huh. I wonder where this came from?"

"Read!" Marie demanded.

"Okay, okay." Carl started from the top. "*Hipster Farmer*. Volume three, issue one. 'Will Armando Shubert reinvent farm-to-table?' Hey, this guy must be Chef Shubert," he explained to Marie, as if she hadn't just told him the same thing. "He's the one who doesn't believe in forks."

"Poon," Marie concurred, for she preferred using a spoon herself.

"He was rude to Mom. I guess he must be famous, to be on the cover of a magazine." Carl continued reading. "'Got cheese? All it takes is a little culture.'" He looked up. "Culture! Like yogurt. It's a pun."

"Bun-bun," Marie crooned longingly, for this would all be so much easier if Alice were here snuggled in her lap, soft and warm and able to understand everything she said.

"Not bun. Pun," Carl corrected her. "When you can say real words you'll learn about puns, trust me. Dad makes them all the time." He turned back to the magazine and read, 'Are *you* our next Hipster Farmer of the Year? Tell us your story! Details and application inside; see page seventy-three.'"

"Hip hip." Marie pounded both fists on Carl's thigh. "Bwanding! Market! Faam!"

Carl looked at the cover. Then he went to the box in the corner and found the rest of the magazine. He turned to page seventy-three. He read.

"Applesauce," he said, after a while, "I think you might be onto something."

CHAPTER TWENTY-TWO

Visions of the future.

As Labor Day approached, Sally wanted to know all about this Harvest Festival idea, especially since it sounded like an opportunity to make a few simoleons.

"It's a local tradition," Janis explained, peeling an apple. The days were getting shorter and ripe apples were dropping from the trees. It was what Brad called an "all hands on deck" situation. He'd hired a few part-timers to help him pick, and anyone old enough to hold a peeler was put to work the minute they stepped inside, coring and peeling and slicing, to ready the fruit for applesauce, fruit leathers, and the like. "All the farms participate. We pool money and put ads in the paper. Folks park at the MegaMart lot in town, and we hire a school bus to shuttle visitors from one farm to the next, to pick fruit, eat pie, pet the cows, and so on. Some years we'll do a hay maze, or a pumpkin-carving contest. Depends on who's got time to do what."

Janis turned to Carl. "It's mostly people from the city who come. You should invite your friends from Brooklyn for a day in the fresh air and sheep dung. Maybe you'd like to introduce *them* to my chickens?"

Carl had visited Janis's farm numerous times by now with Foxy in tow, to continue her regular application of Shiba-made chipmunk repellent. It was all an act, of course. Alice had simply told the greedy chipmunks to lay off or risk getting smooshed in a trap.

The chipmunks nattered and complained, but they were grateful for the warning. Since then, they'd been strategically marauding over a broader territory, taking care not to provoke any particular farmer to declare all-out war against them. When a farmer plants crops in a different field each season so as not to exhaust the soil, it's called crop rotation. The chipmunks were doing something similar. Sustainable garden thievery, you might say.

But Carl still hadn't worked up the nerve to meet those dang chickens. There was a guilty stain on his conscience the exact color of barbecue sauce straight from the packet. The chickens might forgive him, but could he ever forgive himself?

"Maybe," Carl replied. "I think my city friends might be allergic to chickens."

"I'm not the one laying the eggs, kid," Janis said, reasonably. "Might as well meet your business partners, say thanks and howd'ya do. It's only polite."

In a similar spirit of neighborly cooperation, some of the local farmers had taken Brad under their collective wing. The group included Larry Senior, Larry Junior, and a few other farmers who'd been at the Bustin' Barn of Antiques the night of the meeting. All through August they'd convened weekly for breakfast at Cindy's Diner, six a.m. sharp, last one to arrive picked up the tab.

Cindy's was nothing fancy—it was no Loco for Locavore—but it opened early and the breakfast was cooked to order, often by Cindy herself, in portions big enough to fuel a hard day's work.

Over plates of rich yellow eggs and mugs of strong coffee, the farmers gave Brad advice whether he asked for it or not. They urged him to buy his apple bushels early, before the suppliers ran out. They lectured him about "the economies of scale," which meant that if you were going to go to the trouble of building a sheep paddock, you better raise enough sheep to turn a profit from it. Likewise, two beehives did not a honey business make, but twenty would be a start, and you still only needed one beekeeping suit.

They didn't waste words encouraging him; they just told him what to do. This plainspoken guidance was of great use to Brad once he got over feeling yelled at. In return, he did his best to answer the farmers' questions about the most up-to-date ways to promote their farms and products to potential customers.

Interestingly to Brad, none of these farmers saw one another as competition. Being a farmer was tough enough. They just wanted to do what it took for all of them to survive. As Larry Senior sourly remarked, "The powers-that-be think us farmers are a dying breed. Sometimes they offer to help us die more slowly. The joke's on them, though. Know why?" He slurped his coffee and chuckled. "Because everybody's got to eat, that's why! Even those dang politicians."

⁂

"But I don't *want* a playdate with the twins!" Carl was adamant. "First of all, 'playdate' is a kindergarten word. Second of all, I'm busy. I have stuff to do."

Carl hadn't seen the Fleischman boys since the meeting with the pie. He hadn't missed them, either. And he did have stuff to do. He'd been struggling to fill out his application for the Hipster Farmer of the Year contest for almost a week now. So many questions to answer! Some were easy and short—Where do you farm? How long have you been farming? What do you grow and sell?—but others were more complicated, in dreaded essay-question form. What's the hardest lesson you've learned since becoming a farmer? What's been the biggest surprise? What's your vision of the farm of the future?

Carl had ruled out getting his parents involved, as he thought his dad especially might take offense at the "hipster farmer" designation. However: If the fedora fits, wear it. Sometimes it takes an outside eye to see things clearly, and right now that eye was Carl's. If they won and got Prune Street Farm on the cover of a magazine, it would be worth any indignity suffered. If they didn't win, his parents would never need to know about it.

He'd been working on the application privately, in spare moments, sitting on his hay pile behind the barn, pencil and paper in hand. But the days had flown. Now it was Labor Day, the third of September. The contest deadline was midnight. Carl hadn't finished writing his answers, and he still had to type them into his computer to email to the contest.

His thoughts kept arranging themselves into essay form, and therefore, in conclusion: It was the worst possible day for entertaining the Fleischman twins, not to mention he wasn't sure he liked those boys. He hadn't forgotten how they'd teased him.

Brad wiped his brow. "Okay. You're right, I used the wrong word. It's not a playdate. Look, champ"—his tone shifted from sensitive dad to pleading coconspirator—"I didn't even know they were coming. Larry Junior offered to help me fix one of the irrigation sprinklers and he brought the boys along. They're sitting outside in his truck. It'd be rude not to invite them in. Can't you be a good host, for a little while? Their dad is doing me a big favor, and on a holiday, too. It won't take long, I promise."

"I guess so," Carl said, defeated. He didn't see what was so bad about sitting in a truck, but clearly he had to get this over with so he could finish the application. "But *please* don't call me champ in front of them. Okay?"

Brad gave him a funny look. "Okay, it's a deal. Thanks a bunch—Carl," he said, stiffly, and left.

⁂

In the kitchen, Billy and Greg Fleischman were the parent-approved version of themselves. They politely accepted glasses of lemonade from Sally and made funny faces at Marie. They took pieces of dried fruit and ate them without complaint, and asked if they might pet the dog before reaching out their sticky hands to do so. They even offered to peel apples, but Sally would hear none of it. Soon they ended up in Carl's room. Billy closed the door behind them. Greg immediately started going through Carl's shelves.

"So," Billy said, "do you belong to a gang?"

"What? No," Carl blurted. He sat on the edge of his bed, his leg twitching. "Why would you even ask that?"

Billy shrugged. "My dad said you were from the city. Is it true?"

"I used to live in Brooklyn," Carl said. "So, yeah, I guess."

"Cool," said Greg. He'd found the comic book section of Carl's bookshelves and seemed interested, judging from how he kept pulling issues off the shelves, glancing at them, and dropping them on the floor. "Did you ever get murdered?"

Carl used his robot voice, to be funny: "Your question does not compute."

Greg shrugged. "My parents always say we can't go to the city or we'll all get murdered."

"Well, that's dumb," said Carl. "I lived in the city my whole life and I was never murdered once."

"Are you calling our parents dumb?" Greg said, suddenly heated. Carl's face flushed, but Greg had already gone back to wrecking the shelves.

"Maybe you were just lucky," Billy said. "Our sister watches this crime show on TV and people get murdered all the time."

Carl had sincerely had every intention of being a good host, but this conversation was getting on his nerves. "That's because it's a crime show," he snapped. "It shows crimes. If it were a farming show it would show farming."

"And no one would watch it!" Greg said, cracking himself up.

That broke the tension, and they all agreed that Greg had made a pretty funny remark. He'd also managed to get all the comic books in messed-up piles on the floor before moving on to the next shelf. "Hey, can we play with your robot?" he asked.

"The robot's not really for playing with anymore. He's more of a . . ." Memento was the word Carl was looking for, from the Latin verb that means "to remember." A memento was like a souvenir, an object you keep to remind you of a place you once visited, or of a person you used to be.

Big Robot was a memento of his former life, his younger self. But he couldn't remember his Latin roots just then, as he anxiously watched those clumsy boys manhandle what was left of his favorite possessions. Instead, he thought of Old Man Crenshaw. "He's retired," he explained.

The Fleischman twins had already taken Big Robot off the shelf.

"What do you mean, retired? Is he busted?" Billy asked.

"He doesn't look busted. I bet he just needs new batteries." Greg looked up at Carl. "Do you have any?"

"I guess."

"Do you know where they are?"

"I think so."

"So go get some, derp!"

Carl hesitated. Big Robot hadn't had batteries in him in a while. Maybe it would be fun, to see him walking and talking again, like old times. Or maybe it would feel weird, like a zombie version of the big guy come back to life that wasn't really Big Robot at all.

"Okay." Filled with trepidation, Carl padded down to the basement to get batteries.

When he returned to his room, Big Robot was missing an arm.

"Oops," said Billy, holding the severed limb. "It's busted. You were right. We were trying to get the battery compartment open and his arm came off."

Carl stared at them with dead eyes. "The battery compartment is on his back," he said. "Not on his arm. Your story doesn't make sense."

"It was an accident, okay? Sorry."

"So why are you lying about it?" Carl said, his voice rising. "Why not just admit that you broke it?"

Billy looked like he was going to say something, but Greg stepped forward. "Did you just call us liars?" he said, his chest puffed out.

Carl was too angry to be scared. "I dunno. Did you just lie?" he retorted.

Greg took another step.

"Greg, leave it," Billy said quickly. "He's a city kid. He's probably got razor blades and murder stuff hidden all over him."

To Carl's enormous surprise, Greg froze. Both boys looked at Carl. They were, remarkably, afraid.

"That's right," said Carl, standing tall. "Razor blades, and, uh, murder stuff. That's how we roll in my gang. Now, why don't you farm boys go home? Scat!"

The Fleischman twins didn't have to hear it twice.

⁂

That night, the light in the upstairs bedroom of the big red house stayed on much later than usual. As midnight approached, the truly sharp-eared might have heard the quick soft clacking of fingers on a keyboard, some anxious canine whining, a boy whispering, "Shush, girl! I'm pressing send right now." Then, silence. Minutes later, the lights went out.

Yes, it was midnight, and all the animals of the valley were asleep or awake, hunting or digesting, soaring, burrowing, alone in a den or pressed together for warmth as they slept, each according to the natural order of their kind.

The boy and his dog would be extra tired the next day, as humans are naturally diurnal, awake during the day and asleep at night. Wild dogs are crepuscular, like rabbits and deer, but domesticated dogs tend to do as their humans do.

For the nocturnal creatures of the valley, midnight was rush hour. The owls were on the hunt, and the bats flitted here and there, gobbling insects. The coyotes loped after their prey, which was pretty much anything they could catch, and the porcupines waddled in pursuit of their favorite food, which was tree bark (there's no accounting for taste, but porcupines do have the teeth for it). Doggo and his fellow foxes were likely to be up and hunting, as were the bobcats.

Quite close to the farmhouse, near the garden gate, a long, slim creature prowled in the moonlight. He was a nocturnal hunter, too; all weasels are.

Weasels must eat frequently to keep their long bodies fed. They're one of the few animals who hunt for sport as well as nourishment, but tonight, Worm was simply hungry.

He didn't expect to find rabbits on the farm at that hour, although he would have liked it if he had. He would have gladly eaten a chipmunk, or a field mouse. Oddly, the small rodents all steered clear of this garden. Worm usually steered clear as well. It was too close to the farmhouse, and humans were the real creatures to fear in the valley; every predator knew that.

He sniffed, and caught bird scent. Weasels are expert climbers; he was up a tree in no time and seized an egg from a jay's nest, which he cracked and ate. The squawking of the mother jay was terrible. He ignored her cries and easily slipped out of reach of her frantic, dive-bombing attack.

After a few minutes, she left him alone. Jays are intelligent birds; no doubt she realized she was better off guarding her remaining eggs than being upset about one that was already lost.

The weasel stretched his gray-furred body, so long and lithe he could see most of himself just by turning his head. The fur of a weasel is luxuriously soft. When the pelts are used to make human garments, the fur is called ermine. People have paid a great deal of money for pure white ermine coats over the centuries; they still do.

Worm examined himself thoroughly. The change always started at the belly, where the thick winter fur started to grow in. He could see it happening, the streak of white growing along the midline, spreading upward like tendrils along his sides.

Four or five weeks from now, nearly all his fur would be pure white, from his nose to the jet-black tip of his tail. He would be ready for winter then, and the snow.

⁂

"You'll never guess who won the raffle," Janis said over the phone. "Me! Proud owner of a new rototiller. I'm on my way to pick it up. Ask the kid if he wants to take a ride to Phil's showroom with me in Tin Can. I'll be there in twenty minutes."

Naturally, Janis had jovially accused Ruth and Phil of cheating to make her win. Wasn't this their way of getting her to finally own a piece of farm machinery built after World War II? Absolutely not; Ruth swore it. The raffle was fair and square and Janis was just lucky.

"You did buy a dozen tickets," Sally observed. "That's pretty good odds. Isn't it, Carl? You're good at math, I bet you can figure it out."

"It depends"—he stopped, overcome by a yawn—"how many tickets they sold in total." Janis's phone call had come at eight a.m., which was late in the morning if you lived by the farmer's rule: Never let the sun catch you in bed. But it was awfully early for a kid who'd been up until midnight penning his vision of the farm of the future.

Still, a ride in Tin Can was too fun to turn down, and he'd never been inside Phil Shirley's showroom. Janis took a special pleasure in parking the old tractor right in front. "Gives the place some class, don't you think?" she said to Carl.

He knew it was a joke. The showroom was sleek and modern as a new car dealership, and the farm equipment wasn't at all what he'd expected. The tractors had touchpad computer screens on the dashboards. The irrigation systems ("what we used to call hoses and sprinklers," Janis remarked) featured "soil moisture sensor kits, with a digital controller interface," as Phil was proud to explain.

Was this what the future of farming looked like? If so, he'd gotten the question all wrong in his essay. Too late to change it now.

Janis walked around with her hands in her pockets, guardedly curious about the equipment on display. Phil brought out her prize and insisted on taking her picture with it, despite her objections.

The rototiller was a high-tech beauty, state-of-the-art and environmentally friendly, according to Phil. It came with a rechargeable electric battery and a solar panel mounted on the handles. It was a sweet piece of equipment, bright green and very slick. Once they'd strapped it to the back of Tin Can it looked positively futuristic, like they were machines from different centuries—but of course, that's exactly what they were.

The tractor rumbled and sputtered, and Carl steeled himself for the bone-shaking ride home. Janis looked thoughtful.

"You know what makes this tractor go?" she called over the roar.

Carl thought. "The engine?"

"Kid, sometimes I think you just might be a genius. Yes, the engine! Without an engine, Tin Can is just, well, a tin can. It's got an internal combustion engine that runs on diesel. That's a kind of fuel. You know what that fuel is made of?"

Carl did not know, and shook his head.

"Dinosaurs!" Janis said.

He laughed. Janis was always pulling his leg. "Dinosaurs are extinct!" he said.

"That's what I'm talking about. Dead dinosaurs. You know what a fossil is, right?"

"Sure."

"Gasoline and diesel are made from oil. Crude oil is what's left over from dead dinosaurs and other dead stuff from way long ago. That's why they call them fossil fuels. It took millions, maybe billions of years for the earth to make all that crude oil, and we're using it up pretty quick, thanks to the internal combustion engine."

Carl forced his sleep-deprived brain into gear. How many times had he seen his parents put gas in the car? Multiply that by all the cars, buses, trucks, motorcycles, lawn mowers, airplanes, trains, boats . . . "What happens when it runs out?" he asked.

"That last tank of gas is gonna be mighty expensive, that's for sure." She paused. "People get attached to the past, kid. I've been too attached to this tractor. I'm gonna see Phil Shirley again next week. Look into something more modern. Fuel efficient, low emissions. Maybe I'll try one of those electric models. A quiet tractor! Who'd've thunk?"

Carl had a whole different appreciation for riding in Tin Can now that he knew it might be the last time. The spluttering engine, the bone-rattling ride, the stink of the exhaust. Goodbye to all that, and good riddance, too. But it still felt sad, the way goodbyes can.

Janis seemed to feel similarly, and didn't speak again until she made it up Prune Street and turned off the engine. She patted the steering wheel like it was the neck of a favorite elderly horse. "She's a hardworking thing, this tractor. I'll always like old ways of doing things. It's my nature. But looking back over your shoulder is no way to drive, if you want to go forward." She laughed. "You're likely to crash into a tree!"

Carl thought about it. "That's progress, I guess."

"Yup. New doesn't always mean better," she agreed. "But sometimes it does."

CHAPTER TWENTY-THREE

The farm has many visitors.

At the end of the second week of September, the scientists arrived. There were two of them, one taller, one shorter. That was the main difference between them at a glance. Sally was too busy to pay closer attention.

She'd been in the midst of several different projects when the doorbell rang. The abundance of apples and the bounty of the autumn garden had her preserving, drying, and simmering nonstop. At the moment, she had applesauce going into jars, compote simmering on the stove, string beans being prepped for pickling. Critical temperatures were about to be reached, and multiple timers had been set. It was a bad time to be interrupted.

Hurriedly, she ushered them into the kitchen. "Sorry, you'll have to talk while I work," she said. The kitchen was full of steam and Sally wore an apron and hairnet, elbow-length rubber gloves, and held a large pair of tongs. One could argue she looked more scientific than the two men in cargo shorts and polo shirts, hiking socks and cork-soled sandals who nervously stood before her.

The taller man sniffed. "Smells good in here, ma'am! I wish my wife liked to cook."

"Do you! I wonder what she wishes." Sally smiled flatly and brandished her tongs in a way that was not entirely friendly. "Who are you gentlemen, and how can I help you?" She glanced at one of her timers. "Quick as you can, please."

They each handed her a business card, which she couldn't take because of the gloves and tongs and so on. Awkwardly they dropped the cards on the table.

"We're from ERP," the shorter one explained.

"Go on," Sally urged, about to lose her mind.

The tall one cleared his throat as if preparing to make a speech. "Ma'am, ERP is the Eagle Restoration Project. It's a government-funded scientific research project based in Harriton, across the river from here. We currently have several American bald eagles under observation, generating valuable data—"

One of the timers beeped. "Sorry to cut you off," Sally said, silencing it with one hand and turning down one of the stovetop burners with the other, "but I'm in the middle of something potentially explosive and the baby will wake up any minute. I know about your project. My son took an interest after he saw a bald eagle in the yard. I don't know when it was. April, maybe?"

"April, yes! That was the first data point we registered." The two men exchanged a look, and the taller one went on, "As you might have read in the newspapers, our funding was interrupted for some months while the folks in Washington sorted themselves out." He heh-heh-

hehed sheepishly, as grown-ups did when unsure of each other's political opinions; it was a less efficient form of the sniffing that dogs did before deciding whether the other was friend or foe. "We've only recently been able to resume our work and sift through a summer's worth of data. What we've discovered is . . . worrisome."

The shorter scientist cut in. "Ma'am, have you seen any bald eagles on your property recently? Since April, I mean?"

"Nope," she said, and turned to adjust her pressure valves.

Sally was telling the truth. She hadn't personally seen John Glenn, but he was a frequent visitor to Prune Street Farm nevertheless; the scientists had asked the wrong question and she had no time to explain. True to his word, the noble bird continued to come by a few times a week, usually quite early. If the crows were so brazen as to be perched on the roof, the eagle would swoop over them like a strafing warplane, barely grazing their heads as he landed on top of the barn. There he'd perform his scarecrow duties until the point was well made and take to the skies once more.

The scientists exchanged another look. The shorter one said, "The thing is, ma'am—"

"I'm Sally Harvey," she said. "No ma'ams allowed. House rule."

Both men seemed unsure if she was joking. The shorter one forged on anyway. "Mrs. Harvey, the data suggests that one of our birds is in trouble. We're still getting a locator signal from his tracker, but . . . it's not moving." He looked down, chin to chest, and shook his head.

"We're afraid something has happened to the bird," his colleague said, very grave. "You might not know this, but it's a federal crime to injure a bald eagle."

"I did know that, and if you're implying that some harm has come to the bird on purpose, you've got the wrong farmhouse, buddy." Sally had gotten way more tough-talking since leaving Brooklyn. Probably some of Janis's bluntness had rubbed off on her, but mostly it was because she was much busier and spoke to far fewer people during the day, outside the family. She'd become more used to silence than talk, and when she did speak, she liked to get to the point and preferred others did the same. Some would say this is a trait many farmers acquire, but not all farmers are alike, either, just as not all rabbits are alike, or real estate salespeople, or librarians or scientists or dogs or kids or babies, for that matter. Generalities can be made, but scientifically speaking, the actual data points are all over the map.

"We're not implying anything, ma'am," the shorter man replied, less friendly. "Mrs. Harvey, I mean. But the tracker signal is definitely here. On your farm."

The taller scientist was consulting some sort of gadget he'd produced from the capacious pockets of his cargo shorts. "Hey, Chuck," he said, his voice low. "The GPS locator says it's within five hundred feet of the house."

Now all three grown-ups looked at one another. A kitchen timer went off, and the pressure cooker valve started to squeal, rising in pitch with the urgency of a siren.

"No need to disturb your activities in the kitchen, Mrs. Harvey," the shorter scientist, apparently named Chuck, called over the din. "The tracker is federal property; we're just here to retrieve it. May we poke around outside for a bit? I think we'll be able to find what we're looking for."

By now the other scientist was at the back door. He consulted his gadget, then pushed the curtains aside to look out the window, toward the garden and the barn.

"Thataway," he said to his partner.

From the baby monitor, a tinny robot Marie voice began to wail. Naptime was over. Sally sighed and peeled off her gloves.

"Go ahead," she said, already on her way upstairs. "My son, Carl, is out there. He'll help you."

⁂

The scientists showed no interest in Carl, in the vegetable garden, or in anything to do with the farm. They just stared at their GPS locator gadgets, checking coordinates. It was like a game the kids at Carl's old school used to play, where you caught imaginary creatures in real places by staring at your phone. The third time a kid walked into the street without checking for traffic was the end of that game, at his school, anyway.

Carl watched them, vaguely worried. He wasn't sure what he was worried about, but these were authority figures of some sort, and an important piece of government-owned equipment was missing, or so he'd gleaned. It was the kind of situation that made him feel like he'd done something wrong even when he hadn't.

Also, he didn't want them to step on the plants. The garden was at peak production and there was hardly room to walk between the rows. The rabbits had bolted behind the barn at the men's arrival. Foxy was nearby but pretending to be asleep, an ancient Shiba strategy that allowed her enemies to underestimate her while she conserved energy for the battle ahead.

The scientists remained fixed on their gadgets. They hadn't asked Carl much, except, "Are you the one who saw an eagle in April?" to which he said yes. He'd seen John Glenn many times since then, of course, but they didn't ask about that, and Carl didn't volunteer any information. Really, he just wanted them to find the thing and leave, so he and his cottontail colleagues could get back to picking string beans.

Carl's face must have betrayed his unease. The tall scientist looked at him consolingly. "No one's in trouble. We just want to see if the bird's all right."

"What bird?" Carl asked. "I thought you were looking for some equipment?"

The man tapped the patch on his backpack. "We're from the ERP," he said, with evident pride. "My name's Enrique."

"I'm Chuck," said Chuck. He had an ERP patch on his backpack, too.

Carl hadn't noticed the patches before; right away he felt more at ease, and excited, too. Finally, here were some real bird scientists who could answer his nature study questions! "The Eagle Restoration Project! Cool," he said. "Hey, can I ask you a question? Do eagles have predators?"

You might remember that Carl had no idea about all the fuss regarding John Glenn's tracker. The rabbits had been the ones to remove it and dispose of it. Of course, a metal device like that doesn't just compost nourishingly into the soil like leaves do, or apple peels or bunny poo. Possibly the rabbits hadn't realized this, although if they'd thought about that old wheelbarrow rusting in the woods they might have figured it out.

The scientist named Enrique shook his head. "Eagles don't have predators. They're apex predators themselves. Top of the food chain. Nothing messes with them."

"So how did they almost go extinct?" Carl tried to remember what Janis had said. "Was it something to do with the water?"

"Loss of habitat was a factor, but pesticides were the main culprit. One called DDT, in particular." Enrique smiled ruefully. "The disadvantage of being at the top of the food chain is that when you eat other animals, you get a dose of everything they've eaten, too. In the case of the eagles, the rivers and waterways got contaminated with DDT runoff. The fish were full of it, and the eagles ate the fish."

"And—it killed them?" That was sad to think about, even though Carl knew the story didn't end there.

"Indirectly, yes. It messed up their eggs. The shells were too thin to survive. No eggs, no baby eagles, and that's how you go from a hundred thousand birds to—what was it, Chuck?"

Chuck answered without looking up from his gadget. "Eight hundred and change. By the early 1960s, there were four hundred and some-odd nesting pairs left in the whole United States, not counting Alaska and Hawaii."

Carl's eyes grew wide. Only eight hundred eagles left! There'd been more kids than that at his old school.

"It's better now, of course," said Enrique. "Laws were passed protecting the wild birds, and in 1972 they banned the use of DDT. That was the main thing. Last count, I think we're up to ten thousand eagles in the lower forty-eight."

Enrique rocked back on his heels. No doubt he'd given this talk many times. "Nowadays, a dead eagle usually means the bird got into some poison somebody set out for vermin."

"Or was shot by mistake," Chuck added. He was at the barn door.

"Or on purpose, but illegally. You'd be amazed what some people will do." Enrique tapped his gadget. "Carl—it's Carl, right?—is it okay with you if we look in the barn?"

"Sure, go ahead."

Carl waited, more curious than anxious. When the scientists came out of the barn, they looked grim.

"Found the tracker, but no bird. The straps look—nibbled." Chuck looked like he might cry. "By rats, maybe? Most barns get rats, or field mice. Do you ever see rats back here?"

Carl shook his head. "I haven't seen any rats since I lived in Brooklyn."

Referring to Foxy, Enrique said, "Well, you've got a dog. Maybe they stay away when she's around."

"Woof." Foxy barked with her eyes half-closed. Rats, indeed! As if she would waste her time chasing rats!

Chuck looked mournfully at the tracker's remains. "If rats took this off John Glenn—well, they wouldn't have been able to do it while he was alive." He paused, overcome with feeling, and looked pleadingly at Carl. "Is there any chance—I mean, have you seen any eagles more recently? Since April, I mean?"

"Woof, woof." Foxy stood and panted at Carl, her brown eyes full of meaning. The more time Carl spent with animals, the more his intuition about what they were thinking had improved. He felt quite sure Foxy was telling him something. What was it, exactly?

Stalling, he scratched his head. "I mean, there are a lot of birds who come by. Black ones, and blue ones, and red ones . . ."

Chuck looked impatient. "He's an American bald eagle. Genus *Haliaeetus,* species *leucocephalus*. Seven-foot wingspan, sharp yellow beak, white head?"

Tik tik tik tik tik!

"You mean, like that?" Carl pointed. John Glenn was perched in splendor on the roof ridge of the barn, backlit by the sun. The great bird spread his wings wide, then turned his head in profile for maximum iconic effect.

Tik tik tik tik tik! John Glenn chirped again. His whistling, high-pitched squeaks were what you'd expect from a baby seagull. Nothing was wrong with him; that's just what bald eagles sound like. Their voices are not nearly as intimidating as their looks, which is but one example of why you shouldn't go making assumptions based on appearances.

"Well, I'll be. There he is!" Chuck exclaimed, dumbfounded. "He's alive! But how on earth . . ."

Enrique was already unbuttoning the cargo pockets of his shorts. "Wait, I have a dart with me—everybody just hold still—"

"Grrrr, woof!" Foxy leapt at the scientist, quivering with rage. Her very sharp, very white teeth were fully bared and hovered about an inch from his leg. She growled and drooled as if it took every fiber of self-control not to tear into the meat of Enrique's exposed calf.

Carl got the message, finally. He spoke in a calm voice, so as not to frighten the scientists any more than they already were. "You know," he said, "now that I'm thinking about it, I'd prefer that you left the bird alone."

"Okay. Okay! Call off your dog, please!"

Carl obliged. "Foxy, sit."

Foxy sat.

Enrique rubbed his leg, though the dog hadn't touched him. Chuck looked stern. "Carl, I don't think you realize how serious this is. Maybe we should talk to your parents."

"We're on the eagles' side, remember?" Enrique said, still flushed with adrenaline. "We're the good guys. You get that, right?"

Carl gazed at them both kindly. "I understand. Just like you understand that this farm is my family's property, and I'm in charge of the garden. No one else. My parents will tell you it's true. I can't let you harm an animal out here. It's against the rules."

Tik tik tik tik tik, said John Glenn, from above.

The two men looked at Carl, flabbergasted.

"I'll make you a deal," Carl went on. "That eagle likes to hang out here. You can visit whenever you like, to watch him. You can even take pictures. You'll have to help out with the garden, though. It's really busy right now and everybody has to pitch in. All hands on deck, that's what my dad says." Carl crossed his arms, meaning business. "Just don't mess with the bird. Or try to shoot him with one of those darts."

Foxy stared at Enrique's leg with a fierce, drooling longing. Red in the face, the man spluttered, "This eagle is the property—I mean, he's a participant—in a government-funded research program—"

"He *was* a participant. Now he's a wild animal." Carl blinked, an innocent child. "Hey, aren't wild eagles protected or something? By law? I think you just said so. Or maybe I read it on your website. Homeschooling, you know. Anyway," he went on, "it's just a feeling I have, but I don't think that eagle wants to get shot with a dart. I mean, I wouldn't. Would you?"

The scientists looked up at the bird.

Tik tik tik tik tik! John Glenn spread his wings all the way. *Tik tik tik tik tik!*

"Okay," said Chuck, full of wonder. "It's a deal."

CHAPTER TWENTY-FOUR

Lester makes a request.

Some rabbits considered fall-born kits unlucky, as they have cold and snow and lack of fresh greens to contend with soon after they leave the nest.

Not Lester. He insisted all rabbitfolk were lucky, cottontails doubly so, and he worked just as hard to train the fall-born kits in the ways of rabbithood as he did for the others.

"Zigzag, you rascals, that's it! Put a little speed in those legs!" He flattened his ears in frustration and turned to Alice. "I must be getting old. Each litter seems lazier than the last. Where's that old-fashioned cottontail verve?"

"You said the same thing when we were fresh out of the nest," she replied, amused. She and Thistle were enjoying an evening graze near Burrow for a change. The garden was in its glory as autumn neared; the boy filled basket after basket, and now he had two assistant farmers who came to help him every other day or so. They were two man-people in short pants with big pockets on the side.

No doubt about it: Foxy's boy Carl had gotten pretty dang good at this farming business. Alice trusted him to handle things, and the rabbits were finally able to relax a bit.

"It was true then, too. Now it's worse." Lester tipped his nose upward and sniffed. "The whole place smells like canine, that's the problem. These young 'uns are so used to that predator smell, they don't have the sense to bolt when they should."

Alice was used to Lester's complaints by now, but this one struck her as unfair. "Maybe not everything that smells canine is worth bolting over," she began. "Not all dogs are alike, you know."

Lester silenced her with a look. "I'm not arguing with you, sweet Alice; I'm merely making an observation. The old are supposed to be befuddled by the ways of the young. It's the natural order of things. Come on, you foolish babies, this isn't nap time! Show me some survival instinct!" The kits were understandably confused by Lester's instruction and had frozen in place. Each baby bunny was no bigger than a pine cone, and they were as cute as you could possibly imagine.

Lester exhorted the infants once more. "Hop, you short-whiskered blaggards! You nub-tailed scoundrels! Hop, hop for your lives!" To Alice he continued, "Cute, aren't they? I'll teach 'em how to get by, don't worry. At least a few of these layabouts will see springtime, if I have anything to say about it. It's more than I can promise for myself."

Thistle's ears popped up. "I don't believe you, Lester. You're good for another few seasons in the meadow, at least."

"Oh, no, I'm not," the old rabbit replied, perfectly cheerful. "I'm older than I should be, and there's not much zig nor zag left in these worn-out legs. I've had a good life, and a long one. I've no complaints and nothing left to wish for. Except for one thing."

Alice pretended not to hear that last remark, and nudged Thistle to do the same. They knew how to tease the old flop-ears!

Lester waited a moment, and sighed. "Yes, indeedy. My cottontail heart has only one ambition left; just one small, final dream . . ."

Alice yawned. Thistle scratched his flank.

". . . and I've already made my peace that it can never, ever come to pass."

"All right, what is it?" Thistle asked, unable to control himself.

"Oh, it's nothing," Lester said modestly. "It's just that . . . well, I'd like to see this vegetable garden of yours for myself. Set foot in it, if I may. A vegetable garden, my, my! Wouldn't it be fine to outwit the farmer, dodge the dog, slip under the fence, and feel like a clever, crafty young rabbit once more!"

He closed his eyes in bliss at the thought.

Alice and Thistle pawed at the ground. It was no small request Lester was making. The old fellow seemed to anticipate their objections.

"I know you've brought me scraps of this and a taste of that. It's been dang nice of you both. But where's the cottontail pride in being fed by farmers? No, sir! I'm no tame rabbit! I'm no farmer's pet!"

"All right, Lester, that's enough." Alice still felt guilty about the treats that Carl continued to give them, and of course they never, ever nibbled on the crops that were growing. That would be a foolish transgression. But she hardly thought of herself as a tame rabbit!

Thistle also took offense. "Farmer's pet! That's low, Lester. We're farmers, too, you know. We work hard. It's not what you think."

"Sure, I know you work hard. Apologies! I'm getting too old, Thorny—Bristle? Thistle!—and my thoughts are zigzagging one way and then another." A heartbeat later Lester went glassy-eyed and utterly blank. The two younger rabbits held their respective breaths, for they thought he might have gone dark right there in front of them. But it was only a momentary lapse, or maybe Lester was just playing with them the way he used to, telling old rabbits' tales to make them shiver.

Sly as a snake, he blinked his eyes open as if nothing at all had happened. "Do me a favor, young 'uns," he said in a weary voice. "Tell that litter of fall-borns it's time to go in. The days are so short now, the darkness comes quick. Sneaks right up on you, like an owl. I wouldn't want to lose one before the frost, if it can be helped."

He hobbled off, singsonging to himself. "No fence can stop a one of us, and no trap can catch us all. Ah, to be clever and crafty, as a cottontail should! Ah, to sneak under the fence once more!"

⁂

Just when they were enjoying a day off! Now Alice and Thistle had something to think about. In his current condition, it would be a few hours' work for Lester to shamble all the way across the meadow to the farm. Once there, he'd be vulnerable as a newborn mouse, and there was no chance of getting him back to Burrow again. The return trip was all uphill.

It was certainly too much to ask of Foxy or Doggo to escort him, even if Lester would accept help from a dog—or a fox! "Which he certainly wouldn't," Alice said, as close to angry as she ever got. "The old shouldn't be so foolish! What does he imagine we can do?"

"I don't know, sister," Thistle said thoughtfully. "It would be nice to give him what he wants. I'd want the same thing, in his place. Personally, I don't mind riding on a dog's back, but I'm rather small and Foxy's my friend. So's Doggo."

"Don't let Lester hear you say that," she retorted. "Stubborn old rabbit! Well, we may not be able to do it. Some dreams are only for sleeping time. He's had a long, full life. I wish him a peaceful end."

"Longer and fuller than most, that's for sure. May a hawk take him, in good time," Thistle said kindly, offering the traditional cottontail blessing.

"Yes; may a hawk take him . . . ," Alice began in answer. Then she stopped. Her eyes went half-glazed, just for a second.

Thistle's whiskers twitched in curiosity. "Alice! You're having an idea, aren't you?"

Alice nuzzled her brother, who knew her so well. "Possibly. Thistle, do as Lester said. Go mind that litter of fall-borns and get them back to Burrow, would you? They're dozing off in the grass, and the sun's already sunk past the treetops!"

⁂

Alice had come up with many a rabbit-brained idea in her young life, but this new notion of hers was surely the most unlikely of them all. She knew she couldn't say a word about it to anyone, not even Thistle, until she'd had time to gnaw on it a bit herself and see if it was worth the attempt.

Alas, her planned evening of quiet rumination beneath the great tree near Burrow was soon interrupted. It was the chipmunks, overfed and overanxious, as they always were in autumn.

They arrayed themselves before her, along the ridge of an exposed tree root. There were more of them, nearly twenty, and they were plumper than the last time she'd seen them, thanks to a whole season of good eating.

"Good evening, friends," she said, although she had a bad feeling already. "You're looking so well. Soon you'll be too plump for your own stripes, ha ha!"

Her tail practically shook itself off with hilarity, to let them know she was joking. The chipmunks did not seem amused.

"We are well, but not as well as we might be," their leader intoned.

"And we're not as plump as we intend to be, either!" another exclaimed. "Winter is on its way. Can't you feel it? Can't you hear it in the cricket's song, and smell it in the evening breeze?"

All of the chipmunks shouted seasonal poetry of their own devising, about falling leaves and long cold nights, and the need for seeds, seeds, and more seeds to keep them full-bellied once the snow fell. To Alice it was a bit much, but that was the chipmunk way. She expected they would get to the point eventually.

Finally, the leader spoke again. "Rabbit Alice! We have something to say to you." His buckteeth pushed forward over his lip, a very serious expression indeed. "We have heard rumors we do not like. We hope they are not true, but we fear that they are. We are very, very, very, *very* upset!"

"About what?" she asked.

The little fellow drew himself up to his full height, perhaps six inches tall. "We were told you've been nibbling vegetables from the garden, after making us promise not to!"

"Did a blue jay tell you that?" It was Thistle, furious. He'd seen the chipmunks arrive and had the sense to follow them.

"What if one did?" a chipmunk threw back at him. "Is it true or not true?"

Thistle towered over the rodent. "They were crudités! From the bottom drawer of the refrigerator!"

Alice's ears drooped with shame. "No, don't argue, Thistle. It's true. It's part of a farmer's job to make sure the vegetables are suitable for eating. We hadn't known that at first, but the boy-farmer insisted . . ." She gave up. There was no real way to make an excuse. They'd been caught, and that was that.

The chipmunks lined up before the two cottontails like a well-dressed firing squad.

"The jays told us something else, too." The chipmunk folded his tiny paws, praying-mantis-style, which made him look exceedingly stern. "You promised us a share of the harvest, if we kept our end of the bargain."

"Which you have," Alice said quickly. "And you'll get your share, too."

"And did you promise all the other animals a share of the harvest, too?"

"Not all of them," she said, thinking of Worm. "But most."

"Will there be enough to go around?"

"Oh, yes," she said quickly. Was that what they were worried about? "The garden is overflowing with vegetables. There will be so many seeds for you!"

This got a positive response, at least, with many satisfied *chip-chuck, chip-chucks*.

"And when do we get our share?" the leader asked.

"After the Harvest Festival," Alice declared. "After that, the people-farmers will be done taking what they need, and we can share what's left with all of you."

"It's the second Saturday of October," Thistle said knowingly. They'd heard Foxy say it a dozen times.

"When's that?" one of the chipmunks demanded.

It was not an easy question to answer. Animals understood the passage of the year by the length of the days, the wheeling of the stars, the cooling of the nights, and the phases of the moon.

Alice had learned to think in farmer time. She counted the days to winter by the bushels of tomatoes left to pick, the number of autumn squash fattening on the vine, the amount of work left to do and the decreasing hours of daylight left to do it.

But she honestly had no idea when the second Saturday of October was, or how long to tell the chipmunks to wait.

"Harvest Festival is soon," she answered, full of hope. "Very soon."

⁂

"How about a haunted hayride?" Carl suggested. "We'd need a hay wagon, and a horse to pull it, and hay . . ."

Team Harvey had assembled for a brainstorming session about how to make the most of the Harvest Festival. Brad was running it like a work meeting, and he was serious about it. There were sticky notes and markers on the table. Everyone had a yellow pad. Marie was chewing on the package of index cards.

"How about a haunted something that we already have?" Sally suggested. "A haunted sheep paddock? A haunted apple orchard?"

"Haunted applesauce?" Carl suggested, chucking Marie under the chin.

"Boooooo," the baby crooned, and went back to chewing.

Carl was full of ideas. "A corn maze would be fun, if we had a cornfield," he said.

"Let's think inside the box, people. Inside, not outside." Brad tapped his pencil to his forehead. "What can we actually get done with the resources we have? In two weeks?"

"I had a crazy idea," Sally confessed. "Not for now, but for spring: What if we offered farm-themed weddings?"

"Weddings?" Carl made a sick face. "Gross!"

"Destination weddings on a farm? Hmm." Brad closed his eyes, imagining. "'The bride wore overalls in pale blush denim; the groom carried a rake. After the ceremony, the guests spent the afternoon shelling peas and churning butter before sitting down to a wedding feast they'd picked and prepared themselves . . .' I like it. Work that idea up. In spring. Not now."

Sally, pleased, scribbled notes on her yellow pad.

"How about a rock concert?" Carl suggested. "Like Woodstock. That was on a farm, wasn't it?"

Brad looked up. "It was, and how did you know that?"

"You've told me a million times, Dad. On Yazgoo's farm or something, right?"

"Yasgur."

Brad and Sally starting singing a song together that Carl didn't know.

"Gurrrrr," Foxy added from beneath the table. "Gurrrrrr!"

Marie burst out laughing at what the dog had said about Brad and Sally's singing, and tossed her a piece of the cut-up GlitterTooth Chew-Bone that Sally had reluctantly given her to get the cellophane package out of her mouth.

"What about glamping?" Sally asked, when the song was over. The others looked at her like she was speaking gibberish. "It's like camping, but comfortable. Farm glamping could be a thing."

Brad frowned. "Where would the people glamp?"

"In that meadow, out back?" Her enthusiasm waned. "But we'd have to feed them and let them come inside to use the bathroom, I suppose."

To Carl's relief, Brad nixed all of that; no strange glampers traipsing around the house. "Back to the Harvest Festival, guys. Time is short, the budget is tight. Let's work with what we have. The sheep are okay being petted, right? How about a 'pet a sheep' corner?"

"I'm writing it down," Sally said.

There was a tapping at the door, and an energetic scraping of shoes on the mat. "Halloo!" sang a voice. "It's me? Ruth Shirley? Anybody home? Must be, I just heard you all singing a song!"

There was no choice but to let her in. "Door's open," Brad called.

Ruth Shirley entered, chirping away. "Looks like everybody's home, how nice. *So* sorry for stopping by uninvited, but I was in the neighborhood . . ."

"We've invited you many times, Ruth," Sally said, pushing her chair back. "Can I get you some coffee?"

"I might as well." Ruth slung her purse over the back of a chair and sat right down. "What are you all doing around the table? Playing cards, I bet! Go Fish, that's a good one."

"We're having a planning session," Brad said brusquely.

"Planning what?" Ruth Shirley asked, all charm. "Or is it a secret?"

"No secret. We're planning for the Harvest Festival, just like everybody else around here." Sally placed a mug of coffee on the table. "Cream? Sugar?"

"Black's fine for me. Well, I bet you've come up with something new and fresh! That's what our community needs. New ideas!" Ruth Shirley made a funny face at Marie.

"Glamp," Marie replied. She'd found her mother's suggestion about glamping to be the most appealing proposal so far.

"Gurrrrr," countered Foxy, who preferred Carl's rock concert idea. "Woo, woo, gurrrr," she added, noting that people were still talking about Woodstock and Yasgur's farm despite it being extremely old news, judging from the musical style of Brad and Sally's duet.

"Your dog doesn't bite, does it?" Ruth asked, sipping her coffee. "It just growled something awful."

"Foxy's pretty nice to most people." Carl stood. "Mom, Dad, are we done? I'll take the dog outside."

Brad nodded his permission.

"What a good idea!" Ruth beamed at Carl. "And I've heard *so* much about your garden. Would a tour be all right? I can meet you outside in a minute. I just want to talk to your folks a tiny bit. One minute!"

"I guess so," Carl said, uneasy. "Come on, girl."

With a worried, backward glance at Marie, Foxy trotted after him.

Once boy and dog were gone, Ruth Shirley turned to Brad and Sally. "Look, I didn't want to say this in front of your son. I remember how upset he got that one time . . ."

"We're not selling the farm, Ruth," Brad said flatly.

Ruth Shirley didn't seem to hear him. "Brad, Sally, I *like* your family! Everybody around here likes you folks. I hear nothing but good things, so don't take this the wrong way."

"We're not selling," Sally said, not even attempting a smile.

Ruth went on as if no one had said a word. "I happen to know, and I really shouldn't say this—but I happen to know that Tom Rowes made an offer a few weeks ago on a piece of property he liked *almost* as much as he likes this one—and the deal *just* fell through. He's back looking, and I am almost one hundred percent sure his offer on *this* property would still stand. Now, I know what you said in the spring. You've gotten a whole growing season under your belts since then, right?" She smiled indulgently. "Maybe you can make a more *informed* decision now, hmm?"

"We appreciate your concern," Brad said firmly. "We're doing just fine."

"Well, that's good to hear." She looked at them with sympathy shining in her eyes. "Are you folks making any money, though? I don't mean to pry, but . . . are you?"

Something about the ensuing silence emboldened Ruth Shirley to switch gears. "I grew up on a farm myself, you know. I spent my childhood summers sitting behind a roadside table, getting sunburned and selling apples by the pound, while the other kids were playing sports and fishing in the lake. I knew I wasn't ever going to do that to a child of mine."

"I didn't know you had kids, Ruth." Sally looked ready to growl herself.

"I don't. I'm just speaking symbolically."

"I think you mean hypothetically," Brad said.

"I'm speaking from experience, is what I mean. Your kid is not going thank you for this someday. He's not. I'm telling you."

"This is really none of your business." Brad stood up.

Ruth stood, too, still talking. "The truth is, there's not that many people interested in buying a small farm these days. Tom Rowes happens to be interested, and unless you've struck oil on this land, you won't be able to do better than what he'll give you." Her voice dropped. "You haven't struck oil, have you?"

"Not yet." Brad crossed his arms tightly against his chest, as if trying to restrain himself. "Maybe we ought to start digging."

"I'm just saying: Think of your family. Tom's offer is a unique opportunity to do the right thing for your family."

"It's always such a pleasure to see you, Ruth," Sally said, moving to the door. "I wish you could stay longer. Here, take some of these for the road."

Ruth took Sally's offering. "What's that?"

"Part of the Prune Street Farm product line of dehydrated snacks. I'm still refining this one, but I'll be presenting the finished version at Loco for Locavore *very* soon." She tried not to look at Brad, who was cracking up and fake coughing to cover it. "They're *very* interested. I expect we'll have a distribution deal in the works imminently."

Ruth trilled a laugh, but she looked concerned. "You mean Chef Shubert and that funny little restaurant of his? Chopsticks only and they don't even serve Chinese food, isn't that something? The portions are so small you don't have time to miss the fork, ha ha!"

She put the tidbits in her mouth. "That's . . . minty!" she said. She chewed, and chewed, and chewed. "Well," she said, after a moment, "some things are just meant to have a little juice in them, I guess. Oh, I have *got* to skedaddle. Tell your son I'll come back another time for that tour of the vegetable patch. I'm sure he's doing a bang-up job. It's so much responsibility for a child. Too much, really. I know."

Sally held the door wide open. "Such a pleasure, Ruth."

Brad added, "Come by the Harvest Festival. We've got some fun stuff planned."

"Booo, go way," said Marie, meaning it.

Ruth Shirley backed out, smiling and chewing. "Harvest Festival, you bet! I will pop in for sure."

CHAPTER TWENTY-FIVE

Trouble in the henhouse.

Ruth Shirley had been just plain rude, and perhaps Sally shouldn't have fed her the GlitterTooth Chew-Bones, although Marie had eaten plenty with no ill effects—but the visit weighed heavily upon Brad and Sally, despite their bravado. It shone a bright and unforgiving light on their true circumstances.

Glamping and rock concerts, seriously? What kind of vision for the farm of their future was that? Clearly, they were desperate. The golden parachute had fluttered to the ground and now lay in a crumpled heap at the bottom of their empty bank account. The First Annual Prune Street Farm Harvest Festival was a week away, and it was highly unlikely there would ever be a second.

In front of their children, Brad and Sally joked and sang duets. To each other, they spoke bravely and exuded hope. Privately, they worried and prepared for the worst.

Without telling Sally, Brad put out feelers to some old clients to see if he could get any freelance work. Without telling Brad, Sally sat in the car in the parking lot outside the fast-food restaurant and tried to will herself to go in and apply for a job. But it was a small town, and people she knew kept pulling up in their cars and trucks and rolling down their windows to make conversation.

Finally, she got out of the car and walked inside. There, beneath the blinding fluorescent lights, with the stink of burned grease eagerly knitting itself into the fibers of her clothes and hair, she ordered herself a supersized chocolate milkshake. Back in the car, she slurped it down too fast and had to spend ten minutes massaging the brain freeze out of her temples. Then she drove straight to Loco for Locavore.

The ice cream headache of truth was this: Sally had never been able to get a follow-up appointment with Armando Shubert. Her weekly phone messages had gone unanswered, and on the few occasions the restaurant manager happened to pick up, the woman had been evasive. She almost sounded nervous, and hustled Sally off the phone fast.

Sally knew when she was getting the brush-off. There was no point in courting humiliation by pestering Loco for Locavore any further. But desperate people do desperate things, and her overwhelming impulse was to barge into Armando Shubert's legendary kitchen and find out just how big a fool she could make of herself.

Supersized, was the answer.

"It's so much worse than I thought," Sally wailed when she got home. "They've been dodging my calls for a reason. They were *told* not to buy from us. *Told.*"

"By who?"

She let her purse drop to the floor. "Rhymes with crows."

Brad put down his apple peeler and looked up. "Tom Rowes told Loco for Locavore not to buy from us? Why? And why would they listen to Rowes?"

Sally's headache was coming back. She slumped into a chair and grabbed a peeler. "I took the manager outside and begged her to tell me the truth. I showed her pictures of the kids on my phone. When she saw Foxy she burst into tears and told me everything; apparently she had a Shiba of her own once who ran off, and she's never gotten over it."

Sally peeled manically as she spoke, the little curled bits of apple skin flying everywhere. "Shubert leases the restaurant space—from Rowes! He owns the building and sets the rent. He's their landlord, and he told them not to buy anything from us, not so much as a raisin. Tom Rowes wants us to fail, but it's worse than that. The man's a saboteur."

"Saba saba saba," Marie said. She was helping with the apples by taking bites out of each one, to test them for sweetness. Her baby teeth were only able to make tiny vampire punctures in the skin, which Brad was peeling anyway, so no harm done.

Brad picked up a fresh apple and handed it to Marie. "That's pretty unscrupulous."

"Janis says he's greedy and can't take no for an answer, and he just wants to gloat over Old Man Crenshaw by getting hold of the place in the end." Sally grabbed another apple. "Is that the whole reason, though? I wonder."

⁂

Carl checked his email every day, first thing. He hadn't lost hope, but he wasn't expecting much, either. It was October, for Pete's sake. Surely they'd read all the applications by now?

He ran to the mailbox every morning, too, just in case the people at

Hipster Farmer magazine were too hip to send emails. He timed out the postal worker's routine so he could be the first one there. He still hadn't told anyone about his application to the contest, and now he was glad he hadn't, as the odds against Prune Street Farm winning were sky-high. But he didn't want to risk his parents throwing away a letter from the magazine. They might think it was a subscription offer and toss it in the recycling bin. Best if he was the one to take in the mail.

His mother noticed, of course. Sally noticed everything. "Why such an interest in the mail? You didn't apply to college, did you?"

"Mommmmm!" He drew out the word with maximum sarcasm and eye roll. He'd be a teenager soon enough. It was time to start practicing.

Sally chuckled. "I'm teasing. Never mind. I don't want to think about it."

"Why not?"

"Because college means my little chick is ready to leave the nest."

"I'm not a bird," he said, flapping his arms like wings. Marie flapped hers, too.

"Stop being so cute, you two." Sally kissed the baby on the head. "Birds aren't the only ones who grow up and leave the nest."

Carl stopped flapping and thought about it. "Do I have to leave? Can't I homeschool for college?"

Sally's face changed. "Oh, honey, so many things are bound to happen between now and then . . . who knows what our life will be like?" She paused, and when she spoke again, she sounded more like her normal, upbeat self. "When the time comes, you'll know what you want to do. Anyway, after a certain point, all of life is homeschool. It's just you going through the years, deciding what you want to do next and learning what you need to know in order to do it."

"Does that mean yes?"

"Cham, go *mail*," Marie ordered. She was not so easily distracted as her brother. Didn't he realize how much was riding on this contest? "Bwanding!" she said sternly, in case he'd forgotten.

Carl ran to the mailbox, but there was nothing but advertisements and bills.

⁂

The day before the second Saturday of October was a busy one. From county line to county line, the farmers went all out. Pies were baked, paths were swept, jugs of fresh lemonade were prepared. Farms with orchards braced themselves for a pick-your-own stampede, with folded stacks of custom-printed canvas bags ready to be filled. Those with reasonably docile farm animals set up petting areas and "selfie stands."

The farms that were less visitor-friendly had to be more inventive, but even the Fleischmans had come up with a few things. Larry Senior has been persuaded to wear a crown that said THE ONION KING and walk around with a scepter (it looked a lot like a garden spade that'd been spray-painted gold). They'd made jars of onion soup and onion jam to put on sale, and there'd be barrels of pickled onions, too. They even had a cook-while-you-watch onion ring stand all set up and ready to fry. Larry Junior and his wife would take turns dunking wire baskets of fresh-battered onion rings in the deep fryer and serve them in cardboard baskets lined with paper. The entire family spent Friday slicing the onions. The smell of their farm was stupendous and wafted quite a distance.

By the end of the day, every farmer in the valley was exhausted. Those downwind of the Fleischmans couldn't stop crying because of the fumes, but one farmer was downright furious.

"Of all the days to be under attack!" It was Janis, and she stood at the back door of the Harveys' place with a shotgun in her hands.

"What's the matter?" Sally cried, alarmed. "Are you all right? Is that thing loaded?"

"Nope. Shells are close at hand, though." Janis patted the pockets of her overalls. "You wanna hold it, kid?" She offered the gun to Carl.

"No, not really," he said, backing away.

Janis sat down and laid the gun on the table. "When I was your age I hunted squirrels with a .22."

"Why would you hunt squirrels with a .22?" Carl asked, horrified. He liked squirrels! They were chock-full of personality, and they seemed just as happy in city parks as they did out here in the country, which struck him as wonderfully open-minded.

"Well, now I wouldn't. Now I'd use a shotgun," Janis answered, missing his point. "There's too many people around. A shotgun's good for three hundred yards, max. A .22 bullet will travel over a mile. Hard to know exactly where it'll end up."

Sally wiped her brow with the edge of her apron. She, too, had worked all day preparing for the festival and was feeling spent, maybe too spent to deal with even an unloaded shotgun in her kitchen. "Is it the chipmunks again?"

"I wish it were." Janis sighed heavily. "Something got into the henhouse. Whatever it was killed three of my best laying hens!" She looked like she was about to cry, but it might have been from driving through the onion fog. "I should have followed my instincts and set traps in the summer, when I had the urge. Well, that's what I'm doing now, you bet." Her hand flexed around the gun barrel.

Sally tried to be sympathetic, but she really wanted that gun off the table. "Do you know what it was?"

"Could be a fox. I'll get him, don't worry." Janis scowled. "Dang critters! He got Florence! That's what really stings. She was my favorite. Pretty little hen, fatter than the rest, cream-colored feathers with brown speckles all over her."

Carl looked stricken, and it wasn't from the onions. "Florence?" he said. "So you really give them names?"

"I told you I did. Poor Florence. You should have met her when you had the chance, kid."

"I'm sorry," said Sally, not sure how sorry to be. "I'm sorry for your loss."

Janis shook her head. "Me too. I was saving her for Christmas dinner. She would have been delicious. Now it looks like I've got a real-life murder mystery on my hands. Hey, where are you going?"

"To get Foxy's vest," Carl said in a choked voice, and disappeared upstairs.

⁂

It was the night before the Harvest Festival, and Alice and Thistle had never worked so hard. The rabbits were exhausted. They longed for the morning and dreaded it. Tomorrow would be a big day, indeed.

Doggo had been the one to bring them to the farm, as Foxy had been abruptly locked indoors. The fox was in a curious mood, quiet and secretive. But he seemed in no hurry, and the rabbits tidied, pruned, and nibbled until it was quite late.

Afterward, they sat in silence. Whether animals pray is a question unanswerable, but there was surely something prayerful about the way the two rabbits and their guardian fox sat, grateful for another day in the meadow, another few hops in the grass.

It had been a good day, and they'd done everything they could do.

Would it be enough? That wasn't for two little cottontails to decide. Alice was ready to accept whatever outcome there was. She felt the cool autumn nip in the air. Winter was around the corner, but she didn't expect to see it. After tomorrow's festival, every seed and vegetable that remained would be divided among the animals of the valley, all of whom had sacrificed in ways great and small to help make a good harvest possible. She and Thistle may have done the most, but they surely hadn't done it alone.

And then there would be Worm to settle with.

The weasel had been seen skulking around Burrow only a week or so earlier. According to the jays he looked like a skunk in reverse, pale-bellied and pale-flanked, with a thin dark stripe along his back. That stripe would be the last part of him to change colors. By now it must be gone.

Alice's time had run out. She fully expected Worm to turn up over the next day or so, in his winter-white coat, ready to collect. She still hadn't told Thistle or anyone else about her promise to the weasel, but there was no need. Rabbits come and rabbits go; their lives are brief and prone to end without much notice or fanfare. That's true for all living creatures, but it's extra true for rabbits. They're not squeamish about it the way people are. They don't regret the past, and they don't pin all their hopes on the future. Each season in the meadow is a gift, and one season is as good as the next.

Still, that night both cottontails prayed, in their fashion, that their work had been sufficient, and that the Mauler might never come to wreak havoc on the valley they called home.

It was a modest wish, when you think about it—to sit there, flank pressed against flank, wishing for their world to simply continue, in all its harsh and tender beauty. For the sun to rise again each morning over the meadow and its delicious green grass. For the woods' edge to meander until it gave way to low shrubs and the banks of a nearby stream. For the trees' leaves to blaze color in autumn before falling, one by one and then all at once, drawing a warm blanket over the earth that would shelter the rabbits' dark underground home, the whole winter long.

They could feel each other wishing for it, and it gave each of them strength. When the time felt right, Alice thumped her back foot, the way Violet used to. "May the seasons in all meadows go on and on," she said. "On this we all agree."

Thistle nuzzled her. "We've done our best," he said.

"All right," said Doggo, breaking the spell. "It's time for me to say goodbye." He'd looked preoccupied the whole time they'd been there. Alice had chalked it up to his usual grumpiness about being around rabbits and not eating them, but now she could see there was something restless within him.

Thinking he meant that he was going back to his den, or perhaps even going hunting, Thistle sat up. "All right, Doggo, but you should come by the festival tomorrow. Think how funny it would be for the humans to see you and Foxy together!"

"Humans!" the fox exclaimed. "They're the last creatures I want to see. It's time for me to go away, far from here and all humanfolk. Perhaps I'll come back in springtime. Perhaps I'll find some other place to live." Doggo stretched his limbs. "I'd hoped to say goodbye to Foxy, but it seems she's been locked in by the people tonight."

He was right about that; Carl had made sure of it, after Janis's unsettling visit. "Farewell, rabbits!" Doggo said. "I never thought we'd end up friends, but you're still here and not in my belly, and that's saying something. I wish you luck. I hope you succeed in keeping the Mauler away."

Thistle's ears drooped. "Why do you have to go?"

The fox snorted. "Foolish rabbits. Smell the air. It's cold and crisp, with the scent of wood fires burning in the humans' dens, the smell of fungus growing beneath the fallen leaves. Don't you know what that means?"

Alice and Thistle didn't know. It was their first autumn, after all.

"It's hunting season," the fox explained. "The humans will be looking for me and my kind. Your kind, too."

"Hunting? With shotguns?" Alice asked, remembering Lester's springtime teaching. It seemed like a lifetime ago.

"Shotguns, arrows, traps. From now until the end of winter, it's not safe to be near humans. Any humans," he said pointedly. "That's my opinion, and any fox would feel the same. I won't be coming back here again."

Doggo stood, tensed to go. "Do you want me to bring you back to Burrow? It'll be safer there, and safer still the farther you go from where humans live. Either way, after we part tonight I won't see you anymore."

"No," said Alice, with only the slightest hesitation. "Tomorrow is an important day. We'll sleep here, at the farm, in the hay. Like the boy does," she added.

"The boy, pshaw! Remember what you are," the fox said sharply. "You're not a house pet, like Foxy. You're wild. Like me."

"We'll remember," said Alice. "We'll remember you, too, with thanks."

"Goodbye, Doggo," said Thistle. "I'm proud to have had a fox as a friend."

The fox licked his lips. "Goodbye, then," he said, and loped into the darkness.

⁂

Saying goodbye to Doggo made the rabbits quiet for a long time. It was an autumn feeling, a feeling of things changing, seasons ending, attention turning inward.

As the two cottontails snuggled together, Thistle quietly asked, "Do you think the boy hunts?"

"I don't think so," said Alice, to reassure him, but of course she had no way of knowing. The boy had to eat, after all.

The hay was cozy and sleep was welcome, but they did get awoken once during the night. Thistle was the first to smell it and spread his whiskers wide, on alert. The scent was heavy and hot. It was an animal, big and warm-blooded, but without the bitter tang of a meat eater.

It was a black bear, making a slow exploration of the property. It circled behind the barn and tugged at the lids of the trash bins (Brad had wisely latched them shut, on the advice of his new farmer friends). It dug its massive paws deep in the compost heap, where it found a stash of fat worms. These it ate, one by one.

Neither Alice nor Thistle had seen a bear before, but they knew right away what it was. There was no other creature of that size in the valley. This one was full grown and well nourished, and easily weighed over two hundred pounds. Standing on its hind legs, the bear was taller than a man. Its fur was thick and black except for its deep chocolate-brown muzzle, and it moved like a silent shadow in the dark.

How strong such a creature must be! Bears can tear down tree branches with ease, to get to the fruit and nuts they offer. But despite its size and bulk, the bear moved with grace, loping on four feet and rising to two as the terrain required. When it was done snacking on worms, it clambered over the garden fence and stood upright, looking around.

The bear was quiet and serene. He didn't seem interested in the rabbits. Still, Alice's belly tightened with fear. It wasn't the bear's size that frightened her, though to get stepped on would have made a quick end to her and Thistle both—but the last thing she needed the night before the Harvest Festival was a bear rampaging through the garden! A creature of this size and strength would take minutes to wreck everything they'd accomplished all season long, and there would be no time to put things right again.

Alice's determination not to let the bear ruin their festival preparations overruled any brief panic she might have felt. She shook herself to get the hay off, for dignity's sake, and hopped once, twice, three times, into a pool of moonlight, where the bear could see her plainly. The eyesight of bears is nothing special, but their senses of smell and hearing are astonishingly good.

"Excuse me," she said, her voice so small and piping it might just as well have been a bird's. "May we speak, friend bear? What brings you here, so close to a place where people live?"

The bear towered over her in silence for a full minute. "Curious," he finally replied. His voice started deep in the belly and slowly rumbled up and out, low, like late-summer thunder. "Just. Curious."

"I see," said Alice, who quickly intuited that this conversation would require patience on her part. This is true of all conversations with bears. They don't have to work to get anyone's attention; it just comes with being a bear. As a result, they speak few words and take their time about each one.

"Also." The bear took a long sniff. "Honey."

"Honey! You must be looking for the beehives, then." Thistle appeared next to Alice, an act of astonishing bravery. "According to Carl, there's not much honey just yet. The hives are still too new. Enough for you to smell, certainly, but not to make a meal of."

"The beehives are that way." Alice was desperate for the bear to leave before any damage was done, even accidentally. "At the edge of the orchard."

"I. Know," the bear said, and patted that great stomach with a paw the size of two cottontails put together.

It was hard to tell if the bear was trying to be funny, but Alice thought he just might be. Her belly softened. Her tail gave half a shimmy.

Thistle sniffed again, deeply. "You don't eat much meat, do you?"

The great beast shook his head. "Plants. Nuts. Bugs. Fish."

"Not rabbits, then?" Alice wanted to make sure.

"In a pinch," the bear responded. "Not. Now."

"Well, that's a relief," Alice said. The bear seemed peaceful and well-intentioned and she thought she might as well be truthful. "Friend bear, we're worried about the condition of this garden for reasons too complicated to explain right now. We wonder if you might find someplace else to look for your bugs and nuts and such? And be careful where you step on the way out?"

"Winter. Time to sleep," the bear said, then placed both paws on his belly as if to explain: To be well nourished is a must when preparing for a long winter's nap, and tonight he was just looking for food. Then he yawned. Already, the big fellow was getting sleepy.

Earlier that night, Thistle had dug up a whole basket full of potatoes as a surprise for Carl, who'd forgotten about them (it wasn't hard to overlook potatoes, as they grow underground without much fuss, and these had been rather casually planted beneath a pile of rotting leaves at the garden's edge). On impulse, Thistle fetched the biggest one and nosed it toward the bear.

"Here, take this. You'll sleep better on a full stomach," he said.

The bear took the potato with great tenderness. One might imagine that it was the first gift he had ever gotten from a rabbit. Possibly it would be the last. Such moments are full of grace, always.

"Thank. You," said the bear, sounding deeply, slowly sincere.

"You're welcome," said Alice. Gently she added, "Now, shoo, bear! Shoo!"

"And sweet winter dreams to you," said Thistle. "Enjoy your potato!"

"I. Will."

The cottontails watched the great creature shamble away.

CHAPTER TWENTY-SIX

One wonderful day.

The first yellow school bus of visitors arrived right at nine o'clock in the morning, and the first person to climb down the steps was grinning from one ear to the other.

"Emmanuel!" Carl yelled, jumping up and down. His friend was taller than the last time they'd been together. Carl was taller, too, but you tend not to notice things like that about yourself in quite the same way, at least until your pants don't fit anymore.

They ran at each other like two knights jousting and stopped just short of a hug. They bumped fists and shoved their hands in their pockets, smiling and looking shyly but happily at their feet. Emmanuel wore clean skateboarding sneakers with a logo on the side. Carl had on the mud-crusted, high-topped hiking boots he'd taken to wearing every day. Regular sneakers were no good for farm work; they just got filled up with dirt and burrs and were too slippery when the ground was wet.

"My parents wanted to come early and beat the traffic going home, so we drove upstate yesterday and stayed in a hotel. It had a pool and a hot tub and, get this: a climbing wall! For dinner, they had a buffet with *so* much food. Like, literally all you could eat. I filled my plate three times. I couldn't even finish it." Emmanuel looked around. "So, wow! Do you live in that red house? It looks like a postcard or something."

"It's nice," Carl said. A climbing wall sounded fun. He was also imagining that buffet. Part of him liked the all-you-could-eat idea, and part of him was thinking of how much work it would be to grow all those limitless heaps of food that people would take too much of and then toss in the garbage.

Emmanuel gave him a bashful look. "I was going to bring you a Captain Skeeter's Crunch Nuggets bar, but I forgot. Sorry!"

Carl laughed. "Crunch Nuggets! I haven't thought about those in a while."

Foxy, decked out in her bright yellow vest, trotted toward the boys, then broke into a full-on run.

"Woof!" She jumped up on Emmanuel, front paws on his thighs, grinning and panting. Dogs never forget their friends, and Foxy had known Emmanuel since she was a puppy.

"Foxy, no jumping," Carl said automatically, but Emmanuel didn't care.

"Foxy! Foxy, you old pupper, you. How do you like living in the country?"

"Woof," the dog said, tail waggling hard.

"She likes it," Carl said, nudging her down. "I like it, too."

"It's cute to see her running around loose. Why is she wearing a coat? Is it going to rain?"

The sky was a cloudless autumn blue. Carl shrugged. "It's hunting season. It's safer that way."

Emmanuel grew wide-eyed. "Hunting season, wow. Hey, can I see your room?"

"First, let me show you the farm," Carl said. He was just about bursting with pride.

⁂

Carl was right to be proud, for Prune Street Farm had never looked quite like it did that glorious October morning.

The garden itself was tidy as a pin, with not a single stray weedling to be found. It was the end of the season but the harvest was still abundant: There was acorn squash and butternut squash, hardy greens like kale and spinach, and root vegetables like beets (and a basket of potatoes, Carl was delighted to discover). The second plantings of lettuce and broccoli were at their peak. The *Farmer's Almanac* said mid-October was past the first frost date for the region, but so far they'd been lucky and hadn't been nipped yet. The garden was radiant in the golden light of autumn, a cornucopia of nature's bounty.

But weeding and tidying was not all the rabbits had done; no, sir! Foxy had said branding meant letting everyone know how wonderful you were, and the farmer-rabbits had taken that instruction to heart. Lester had offered suggestions as well, based on his somewhat patchy knowledge of what humans found pleasing.

By the morning of the festival, everything had been made as wonderful as two cottontails could manage. They'd nibbled faces on the pumpkins (they were rabbit faces, as those were the kind of faces they knew best). They'd grazed surprising zigzag patterns in the grass, which now ruffled invitingly in the breeze. They'd used their cottontail nesting techniques to line the garden paths with hay. This was to keep the dirt off people's shoes, as Lester had assured them that being clean and sweet-smelling was something people valued a great deal.

They even left piles of autumn leaves here and there for the small people to play in, a kind of game that Lester told them human young'uns enjoyed.

Their crowning achievement was the simplest and most wonderful of all. It had been Marie's idea, and in terms of *bwanding* it was going to be hard to beat. It was the bun-bun factor. Alice and Thistle were, well, rabbits. They were irresistible. The cuteness of rabbits made humans happy, as sure as the sun rose each day. Rabbits were the main thing that made this farm different from any other farm in the valley, or anywhere else for that matter, and rabbits were what they should be showing off. "Bun bun," Marie had insisted. "Bun bun bun bun bun!"

Alice and Thistle had done so much work already without complaint, but the notion of putting themselves on public display with flocks of humans wandering about—well, that was something else altogether. It flew in the face of every cottontail instinct. They'd grown used to being in Carl's vicinity, but would they be able to hop around calmly in a crowd and accept crudités from the hands of strangers? Their experience being around dogs and foxes and eagles and so on suggested that it was possible, once the initial discomfort wore off. They were willing to try, anyway.

But would two rabbits be enough to get the full bun-bun-bun-bun-bun effect? It was a lot to ask, but if two rabbits were good, surely more would be better. "Of course, I wouldn't expect that even the bravest cottontails from Burrow could endure a day of human company," Alice had said, when she strategically let slip to Marigold and Berry what she and Thistle had planned.

"Well, if you two can manage it, we certainly can," Marigold had answered, haughty as a cat. "What do we have to do once we're there?"

Among people, this kind of maneuver is called "reverse psychology." Cottontails aren't burdened with much in the way of psychology, but they've no shortage of pride. Marigold's response was exactly what Alice had hoped for.

"Oh, not much," she'd replied, ever so casual. "Just hop around and graze and don't bolt when the people come near."

"They might want to feed you vegetables, though. Is that all right?" Thistle had slyly added.

That did it. "Sold!" Stuart Gilroy would have cried, with a strike of the auctioneer's hammer. Marigold and Berry were on board.

Of course, Lester had dearly wanted to come as well, and mourned once again that he was too old to travel that far. "We'll be your eyes and ears and tell you all about it," Thistle had said to the old fellow, trying to be kind. Alice still held hope, though, for unlikely as she knew it was, she did want the old rabbit's wish to come true.

And where was John Glenn, anyway? The festival had already begun, with big humans wandering the straw-covered paths and little humans jumping in the leaves. Everywhere you looked, people were eating apples as if they'd never tasted anything so wonderful. That's what comes of picking fruit off the tree yourself, of course. It bestows virtues that can be appreciated in no other way.

Alice looked up at the barn's roof ridge, and at the sky, but there was no sign of the great bird, yet.

※

Every hour or so the yellow bus returned, to drop folks off and pick them up. It was a smart idea to have the bus making a circuit of the local farms. This way people could visit several farms in one day without creating traffic jams in the towns, and the farms wouldn't have to worry about providing parking on their precious land.

The sheep petting proved popular, and the sheep didn't seem to mind it, but Foxy thought the whole thing needed more pizazz. Despite her lack of experience, she decided to herd the sheep. This wasn't difficult, as the sheep were tied up anyway. The elegant Shiba raced around the placid group like a yellow streak, first in one direction, then the other. Every now and then she'd plant her feet and *yap, yap, yap* to the sky. Then she'd grin and pose for pictures.

The five sheep just stood there chewing, but it made for a thrilling display. "Imagine," the visitors remarked, as they snapped countless photos with their phones. "A tame fox that herds sheep! None of the other farms have anything like that."

None of the other farms had bun-buns, either, as Marie so brilliantly foretold. Foxy had delivered Marigold and Berry to the farm shortly after dawn. Their nervousness subsided quickly after they'd tasted their very first carrots. They were dee-lectable! And made more so by a hint of maple syrup, as some of the early-arriving families had enjoyed a pancake breakfast at Cindy's Diner prior to getting on the bus, and the children's hands were sticky with flavor.

Alice and Thistle joined in the bun-bun action now and then, when Berry and Marigold needed a break from all the love and crudités, but they kept working, too, tidying the hay and picking up stray candy wrappers the humans dropped. It might not make a difference in terms of keeping the Mauler away, but they were so very proud of the garden for its own sake. After today, everything would change. The growing season would be over. Debts would be paid and the garden put to bed until springtime, to rest and gather strength through the winter, just as their new friend the black bear was doing. It was a big day, a special day. For reasons of her own, Alice wanted to enjoy every minute of it.

Thistle made a few remarks about what they ought to grow next season, but Alice wasn't thinking about springtime. For her, there was no need.

Now and then she thought she saw a flash of white, sneaking around the barn, flicking a black-tipped tail as it curved its sinewy way along the garden fence. But Worm would come when he came. Today was what mattered. She'd give it her all, until the day was done and she could do no more. She hoped that would be enough.

⁂

Emmanuel's family stayed at Prune Street Farm for the whole morning, and they were helpful as can be. His dad Andrew poured apple cider into paper cups for visitors, and his dad Joe collected the money for the pick-your-own bags. Emmanuel praised Carl's enormous light-filled room and played peekaboo with Marie, which pleased her a lot.

But they'd planned to leave early, and as lunchtime approached, they decided to head over to Fleischman's Farm to get some of those amazing onion rings the people on the latest bus were both raving about and reeking of. They'd head back to the city from there.

"Will you come to Brooklyn soon, to visit?" Emmanuel asked, before he left. Carl said he'd try; maybe in a month or so. There'd be more time for visiting when the growing season was done, but he wondered how he'd feel in his old neighborhood. All that concrete, all those apartments stacked one on top of the other like shoeboxes in a shoe store, all those people rushing to get here and there. Funny how he hadn't thought any of that strange when he lived there. It was just the way life was.

He had a brief urge to tell Emmanuel about what the Fleischman twins had said to him, about being in a gang and being murdered—but he let it pass. Just as Carl was when he lived in Brooklyn, the twins were steeped in a particular way of life. What they thought they knew about how other people lived and thought and behaved came from sideways sources, television and movies and things repeated secondhand. It was like a big game of telephone, so no wonder there were some oddball opinions at the far ends of the line. Carl hadn't known what to think about farmers when he lived in Brooklyn, either.

Anyway, the Fleischman twins weren't so bad. They'd told their dad about Big Robot right away and he'd fixed the metal guy himself; he'd even let Carl try on the welding mask. They'd spent a few days helping with the apple harvest, too, when it became clear that Brad was in way over his head.

Best not to form opinions about people too quickly, Carl had decided. And there was no need to repeat stories that were simply unkind.

Carl bid his friend from the city goodbye, and this time they hugged long and hard. "Thank you for coming, Emmanuel," he said. "Next time, I'll come visit you."

Now, wasn't that something? A few months of digging in the earth beneath a wide-open sky, and young Carl Harvey had grown wise as the Great Rabbit himself!

⁂

It was one o'clock, halfway through the festival. The day was going well—as well as it could go, really. The only wrinkle was when Brad gave the first orchard tour of the day and discovered that something both big and strong had knocked over his beehives in an apparent attempt to extract the honey. Luckily the damage was minor. The bees would be fine.

At the top of the hour the bus honked to let folks know it was time to board and go to the next stop, but many chose to stay at Prune Street Farm for one more shift. The bun-bun factor remained the number-one draw, the sheep were placid and pettable, and the orchard practically threw its remaining apples into the prepaid canvas bags. Happy visitors filled their shopping baskets with jars of applesauce and homemade relishes, sourdough crackers and the last tomatoes of the season, bundles of fresh herbs and purple kale, and those adorably carved pumpkins, too.

"Make sure you tag your photos!" Brad said many times as he wandered around shaking hands. He'd had a T-shirt made that said FARMER BRAD with #PRUNESTREETFARM written underneath. Sally had one that said FARMER SALLY. Marie had a romper that said BABY FARMER, but by midday she was overwhelmed by all the visitors and had become too cranky to stay outside. A panicked phone call was made; in a heartbeat, Margie Fleischman (the twins' mother) had dispatched her sister Phoebe to babysit for the afternoon. Baby Farmer Marie and Aunt Phoebe were holed up in Carl's room watching *Finding Nemo* on the computer while eating the store-bought Goldfish crackers that Phoebe never went to a babysitting job without, and all was well.

Carl thought the T-shirts were weird and politely declined to wear the Farmer Carl shirt his parents got for him, but they didn't mind, truly. Brad and Sally were in a strange mood, a mellow, bittersweet mix of joy and loss, gratitude and dread. This was a special day for them, too, maybe the best day of their whole farming career. Years from now, when they looked back at their brief, foolish stint at working the land, this was the day they'd remember and smile about. If the First Annual Harvest Festival had to be their last, at least let it be fun, they thought.

It's not that they'd given up hope. But they'd been up half the night doing the math, and the truth was plain as the tail on a cottontail's rump. Even if they sold everything they had by day's end, every jar of applesauce and tomato relish and pickled string beans, every fresh-picked bag of apples, every little ribbon-tied packet of dried fruit and spicy radish coins, every last scrap of gorgeous produce—the money wasn't going to be enough.

The numbers just didn't add up.

Brad would be the one to make the phone call when the time came—Sally was much too angry at Rowes; she'd never be able to get through it without losing her temper—but not yet. First they would enjoy this day.

This was not a day to rue, not one bit. It was a wonderful, special day, and like all days, it would never come again.

⁂

By midafternoon, all the visitors smelled of onions; it was obvious where they'd already been. Some carried small baskets of hard-boiled eggs decorated in colorful tie-dye patterns, as if it were Easter and Woodstock at the same time. Those were from Janis's place. There were families with kids and couples without, casual groups of friends and solo travelers, old and young and in between. It was a joyous day for the visitors, many of whom were from the city and seemed to think of farms as scenic nature preserves full of friendly animals and effortless bounty, a cross between a petting zoo and an all-you-can-eat buffet. It was Camp Cityfolk in the Woods, and the cityfolk were happy campers indeed.

Among the late crop of visitors were two people Carl couldn't help noticing. They were so hip you could spot them a mile away. The man was dressed in skinny black jeans that looked dipped in wax and a floral-print vest under a tightly fitted blazer. He wore dark-rimmed glasses, a thick walrus mustache, and a derby hat. The woman was in a maroon velvet jumpsuit that revealed a T-shirt underneath, with a picture of the earth and the words THERE IS NO PLANET B written across it. She wore a wide-brimmed straw hat and huge sunglasses with yellow plastic frames that made her look like a bug.

Were they work friends of his dad's, art-school friends of his mom's, or just some random people? They didn't have kids with them, but they did have old-fashioned film cameras slung around their necks.

"We're looking for Carl Harvey," the woman said. "I'm Tallulah, coeditor of *Hipster Farmer* magazine. This is my coeditor, Zane Banks."

"Hipster?" Carl blurted. "*Hipster Farmer*? Is this about the contest?"

The man grinned and checked his phone. "It sure is. Are you—Carl?" Carl nodded. "We thought you might be a kid; that's awesome! Well, Carl, you applied to be Hipster Farmer of the Year, and guess what? You're a finalist, dude!"

Tallulah smiled, which made the delicate ring that pierced her lower lip twitch upward. "Zane and I are here for the site visit."

"What's a site visit?" To Carl it sounded like an eye exam.

"It was in the application," Tallulah said. "In the fine print, I guess. All finalists will be subject to an unannounced site visit before we choose a winner. Prune Street Farm is the last one on our list. We'll be making our decision imminently, so you won't be in suspense for long."

Zane bopped his head as if listening to some private music. "We would have come sooner, but when we heard about this festival of yours, it just seemed like the perfect day to drop in."

"Wow." Carl didn't know what else to say. He'd been half asleep when he submitted his application, and if there was fine print, he'd missed it. "This is good news, I guess. But how'd you know about the Harvest Festival?"

Zane's head was really bopping now. "It's on your website, dude. Cool website, by the way! Love the pop-up animations. Really clever."

"My dad made it."

Brad was already on his way over, a look of curiosity mixed with caution on his face.

Carl stepped aside. "Here's my dad. Um, may I introduce Brad Harvey?"

"Mr. Harvey"—Tallulah spotted the T-shirt—"Farmer Brad, I mean. Such a pleasure to meet you."

"Congratulations, dude!" Zane seemed to call people *dude* in general.

Brad looked puzzled. "Thanks. Carl, do you know these people?"

"Not really," Carl said. "This is Zane Banks, and this is Tallulah."

The woman extended a hand. "Just Tallulah," she explained. "We're from the magazine." At Brad's evident confusion, she added, "*Hipster Farmer? Hipster Farmer* magazine."

"Wait—did you say *Hipster Farmer* magazine?" The word magazine made Brad stand up straight. As for hipster farmer: His journey from confusion to comprehension, from mild offense to openhearted acceptance of the label took all of two seconds. "Sweet!" he exclaimed, full of newfound hipster farmer pride. "Welcome! Welcome to Prune Street Farm."

Brad quickly flagged down Sally, who was over at the sheep-petting area, and gestured for her to come, here, quick. She made the connection right away. "*Hipster Farmer*—oh! Aren't you the magazine that had Armando Shubert on the cover?"

Zane flashed a thumbs-up. "Right-o. That was way back in January. Poor Armando."

"Armando Shubert, what a shame." Tallulah clucked her tongue, *tsk, tsk*. "We had high hopes for him, but . . ."

"He's kind of on the way out," Zane confided. "*So* inventive. But still . . ."

"*So* creative," Tallulah agreed. "And yet . . ."

Sally tried to look sad. "Do you mean his restaurant is not doing so well?"

Zane interlaced his fingers like an undertaker and dropped his voice. "Loco for Locavores is . . . struggling."

"The food is too, what you'd call . . . experimental," Tallulah elaborated. "Tiny portions, and it's hard to eat. Not what people crave when they go out for a meal. You know what I'm saying?"

"But hey!" said Zane, now a happy preschool teacher, clapping his hands together. "We had an awesome meal this morning. At Cindy's Diner! Pure Americana. Delicious food, huge portions, everything homemade."

"That's what our readers love. Authenticity. Real small-town cooking," Tallulah agreed.

Brad nodded. "What about being locally sourced? Is that not a thing?"

Tallulah grinned. "Cindy buys all her eggs and produce locally because, duh, all her neighbors and customers are farmers. She's always done it that way. She didn't realize it was something to brag about. Now, *that's* a thing!"

Zane nodded. "Cindy is awesome. I think we should put her on the cover. Do you concur, Tallulah?"

"Totally." She beamed at the Harveys. "Anyway, finalists: We're stuffed, but not too stuffed taste some of *your* products. Official site visit begins now. Are you ready?"

The look on Sally's face was nothing short of angelic. "Of course. Can I interest you in some dried fruit?"

"Yummy, dude! Bring it on!" said Zane.

Tallulah looked just as thrilled. "Oh, yeah! I *love* dried fruit!"

Throwing a backward "can you believe this?" look at her husband and son, Sally led them away.

CHAPTER TWENTY-SEVEN

The golden hour.

The scientists had come to the festival, too. They didn't seriously expect John Glenn to show his noble face on such a noisy, crowded day, although it would be a real showstopper if he did. Still, bird or no bird, it was a perfect opportunity for "public outreach and education," which was one of the things the Eagle Restoration Project's precarious funding depended upon.

With Carl's permission, they'd set up a table not far from the sheep pen. They gave out ERP brochures and ERP buttons and ERP ballpoint pens, and they talked about the plight of endangered species. To keep things interesting, they offered several slimy and goopy science activities. The best one was how to compost with worms in a bucket. It was irresistibly gross, and all the kids in attendance gathered around, groaning in mock-disgust and begging to hold the worms.

"Great job with the educational component," Tallulah remarked, as she, Zane, and Sally speed-walked past the science table on their way to the farmhouse. "You're really serving the community."

"Well, we do what we can," Sally replied. She had no idea what the scientists were up to; it was all Carl's doing. "As I was saying, I've been experimenting with drying all kinds of fruits and vegetables. It's fascinating to see how differently they respond to the process . . ."

"Good afternoon, Mrs. Harvey." It was Chuck, calling from the table. The scientists had been extra respectful toward Sally since that first awkward meeting. "Nice festival. Just checking: You haven't seen John Glenn today, have you?"

"No, not that I've noticed," she called over her shoulder, still walking. "Anyway, dried apples were my first attempt—"

"John Glenn, the astronaut?" Zane asked. "What an awesome dude. Is he coming to the festival?"

"He's dead, Zane," Tallulah replied. "But an awesome dude for sure."

Zane quickly course-corrected. "Bummer. I loved that movie he was in. About the Apollo space program. *The Stuff*, right?"

"*The Right Stuff*. You were close!" Sally knew her movies, even the ones Meryl Streep wasn't in. "That was an actor playing John Glenn, and it was about the Mercury space program, not Apollo. But I agree, it was an awesome movie." The word was contagious. Sally took a breath and turned to Tallulah. "There's an American bald eagle the scientists have named John Glenn. For some reason, the bird likes to hang out here."

Tallulah peeked over her sunglasses. "Here? At the farm?"

"Funny, right? That's why the scientists come, I don't know, a few times a week. They're observing John Glenn. The eagle," she added, for Zane's benefit.

Sally was matter-of-fact about it. Tallulah nodded, deep in thought, and Zane took rapid and copious notes. He finished scribbling and motioned for Sally and Tallulah to wait while he jogged back to take a photo of the science table. "Mind if we chat with you dudes later?" he asked the scientists. "Pose a few questions about science and eagles and whatnot?"

Enrique handed him a flyer about the ERP. "We'd be delighted. It's why we're here."

"The dried radish coins are what I'm most excited about," Sally went on, to Tallulah. "Radishes get extra spicy when they're dehydrated. I'm playing around with different flavor profiles. Sweet, savory . . ."

"Are those rabbits yours?" Tallulah interrupted. They were in sight of the bunny-petting area.

"Nope," said Sally. "They're wild rabbits. I guess they live around here."

"People are petting them," Tallulah said, a note of wonder in her voice. "Those wild rabbits are playing fetch with your dog."

Indeed they were. Much to the delight of the crowd, Foxy was tossing crudités by flinging them with her mouth. Marigold and Berry found them and zigzagged all the way back, to drop them at Foxy's feet.

"That is your dog, right?" Tallulah asked.

Sally didn't know what to say about the dog playing fetch with rabbits, so she chose the easier question. "Yes, Foxy is ours. A city dog in the country. She's adapting well."

By now Zane had torn himself away from the awesome worms and caught up with Tallulah and Sally. "Question for you, Sally: How did a city dog learn to herd sheep?"

Sally laughed. "Foxy, herd sheep? No way. That dog is lazy, if you ask me."

He tapped his camera. "She was herding the sheep earlier. I saw it when we arrived. Captured it on film, right here."

The conversation had slipped far out of Sally's control. Weakly she replied, "Well, I guess it's a new trick Carl taught her."

"This farm is pretty unusual," Zane said.

Sally didn't want to disagree, but she wasn't going to make the mistake of talking about how the plants had come up by themselves, either. "Yes, it is," she said, forcing a smile. "And just wait until you taste the applesauce!"

⁂

Carl was wiped out, with another two hours of festival to go. They'd sold out of the pickled string beans and sourdough bread; the produce was nearly gone. The rabbit-face pumpkins were a huge hit, but he felt strange every time he sold one. The customer always said something like, "Adorable! Did you carve these yourself, young man?" to which Carl felt obligated to say yes, because if not him, then who? The lie felt heavy in his belly, though.

Seeing Emmanuel had been fun but too quick, so that was also kind of heavy-feeling, and added to the tiredness for sure.

And then there was the surprise arrival of the magazine people! Being a finalist was positive news, but now Carl had supersized anxiety about what kind of impression the farm was making on Tallulah and Zane. Would they want to talk to him again? If they did, would he say or do something to mess everything up? He could barely remember what he'd put on the application, other than that stuff Janis had said about farming being the most important profession, and his own observation that maybe if plants and people and animals could all stop underestimating one another and cooperate, things might go better for everyone.

Anxiety was exhausting, and so was talking to strangers, so when his dad showed up with a hummus sandwich and a thermos full of cold and extremely fizzy cola after a summer of no soda in the house whatsoever, Carl was one hundred percent ready for it. Father and son retired to the farthest, most private side of the barn, where a pair of upended apple bushels provided seating, and a wooden crate that had once held plums for Sally's prune-making experiments served as a picnic table.

"I've given two farm tours an hour since ten o'clock. I think I'm losing my voice." Brad took a slug of cola before handing it back to Carl. "Ahhh," he said, and burped the way only a dad can. "Don't tell your mom about the soda."

Carl drank and burped, too. "I thought it was bad to keep secrets."

"Okay, you're right. I'll tell her. I think she'll support our choice on an emotional level, even thought she might not agree with it from a nutritional standpoint. But speaking of secrets—there's something I want to ask you, champ."

Aha! Carl knew it was too good to be true. This sandwich break wasn't just about sneaking soda and bonding over man-burps. There was going to be a Talk.

Brad gave him that sensitive dad look, half smiling and gentle-voiced. "Why didn't you tell us that you applied to this contest?"

Carl's face grew hot. He never should have entered that dumb, dumb contest in the first place. "Are you mad? Did I do something wrong?"

"No! Not at all. It was a good idea, a smart idea. Thanks to you, we now have a chance at some serious media coverage in a national magazine. That's initiative, son! I'm proud of you, and I'm grateful." Brad smiled warmly at his boy. "You're looking out for the family in a really grown-up way. I'm just curious why you didn't tell us."

"You and Mom have been so worried lately," he said with a shrug. "I didn't want you to have another thing to worry about."

Brad exhaled and rubbed his face. "You kids don't miss a thing, do you?"

Carl thought about this. "I miss Grandma, since she moved to Arizona. But I know we'll see her at Christmas."

"It was a rhetorical question. Let me ask you a real one: Do you know why we're worried?"

Carl gestured around. "It's about the farm, right? It's not making money or something? But maybe if we got on the cover of the magazine it would be good marketing. Or is that branding? Sorry, I get those words mixed up." He looked earnestly at his father. "If we win the contest, will that fix everything?"

Brad exhaled hard and tugged at his beard. "Carl, you're a farmer, too. We wouldn't be here today without your efforts. You deserve an honest answer about where things stand. But I don't want *you* to worry. Promise me you won't, okay?"

"I promise," Carl said, but it was a promise no one could be expected to keep. When people tell you not to worry is when you know things are bad.

Brad pulled his bushel closer to Carl's. "First: You're right. Being on the cover of the magazine would be excellent marketing for Prune Street Farm. It would help more people know about us and what we do. But that alone is not enough to 'fix everything.'"

Carl took a big bite of hummus sandwich, which just proved how very hungry he was. "Mmmmf?" he asked, his mouth full.

For once, his dad understood his meaning. "I'll tell you what would be enough. We need something to sell to all those people. Something that makes a profit."

Carl tried to ask more but the hummus was too smooshy in his mouth. His dad held up a hand. "Don't choke. I know what you're going to say. We have plenty of stuff to sell. The vegetables are practically gone. The bread sold out an hour ago. We ran out of bags for apples. Purely from a sales point of view, the day has been an incredible success." He leaned forward, elbows on knees. "Sales are not the whole story. What we need is a product to sell that we can charge more money for than it cost to make. That's what I mean by 'profit.'"

Carl swallowed, finally. "I don't get it."

"It's just math. If you sell an apple for fifty cents, but it costs you sixty cents to grow each apple, selling more apples doesn't fix the problem. Can you tell me why?"

"Because you lose a dime on each apple—and the more apples you sell, the more money you lose." Carl looked up. "That doesn't make sense, though."

Brad nodded. "I know. It's a challenge a lot of small farmers face, for a whole bunch of reasons. Your mom and I have been trying to figure it out. It was harder than we thought, and like I said—I want to be honest with you. We've just about run out of time."

Carl's face quivered. He looked down and kicked at the dirt. "Sorry," he mumbled. "I didn't know about the profit part. I thought winning the contest would be enough."

"It's fantastic, champ. I really hope we win," Brad said. His voice was ragged, and not from giving tours. "You're a great kid, you know that?"

Carl endured the hair-ruffling that ensued. "Dad, what happens when we run out of time?"

"Those are next steps, champ. We'll figure it out." Brad gazed westward, into the sun, and shielded his eyes. "Those rabbits are something, aren't they? So friendly. I always thought wild rabbits were skittish."

"There's a wide range, I guess." Carl stood up, deeply preoccupied. "I'm gonna go play with the animals, okay? Thanks for the soda."

"You're welcome."

Brad let Carl go.

That had not been an easy conversation; no, sir.

On impulse, Brad walked to the end of the barn and leaned against the corner, where he could watch Carl approach the wild cottontails. There'd been two rabbits earlier, but now there were four.

Well, that's rabbits for you, thought Brad.

Two of them hopped right up to the boy, almost as if they knew him, and he fed them from his pockets. The afternoon sun cut through the trees and caught them all up in a golden haze of autumn light.

It was a perfect moment, and one that would end far too soon. All perfect moments did, of course, and the imperfect ones, too, for that matter—but it still felt deeply unfair.

Brad didn't know whether to cry or put his fist through the side of the barn.

⁂

Meanwhile, Sally had given the magazine people a grand tour of the farmhouse operations. She walked them through her well-stocked shelves, the dehydration equipment in the basement, her gleaming kitchen laboratory for canning and preserving. They showed a respectful interest in the dried fruits and veggies operation, and Zane took diligent notes, but she didn't get the feeling they were knocked out by it.

Then Tallulah spotted a basket of vegetables in their fresh-picked, pre-dried state, waiting on the kitchen counter. That made her very interested, and she oohed and aahed over the generous size, the vivid color, the utter lack of blemishes.

"Talk to Carl," Sally said for what felt like the twentieth time that day, as she offered them what they each immediately declared to be the best broccoli florets they'd ever tasted. "He'll be able to tell you all about it."

Tallulah and Zane tracked down the young farmer by the rain barrel, where he was filling a jug with water to bring to the animals. Being petted all day was thirsty work.

"Okay, Farmer Carl," Tallulah said, with the bright-eyed energy of someone who's ready to wrap things up and go home. "We've learned a *ton* from your mom and dad, and we've toured the entire farm. Which is beautiful!"

"Does this mean we're going to win?" he blurted. Even after what his dad had said about running out of time, he still did want to win. It would make his parents happy. Or at least, less unhappy.

Tallulah laughed. "I promise, we'll decide very soon. We're going to conclude our site visit by asking you a few questions." Zane poised his pen to take notes. Tallulah continued. "Can you share some of your farming techniques with our readers? In your application, you said you don't use any chemical fertilizers, pesticides, or sprays. Yet the produce is flawless."

"Well," said Carl, "the fertilizer is rabbit poo."

Zane wrote it down as Tallulah nodded. "Completely natural, excellent. Do you buy it, or gather it, or . . . ?"

Carl squirmed. Now that it didn't matter, he might as well tell the truth. But how much would they be able to believe? "The rabbits come and do it," he explained. "They make poo. In the garden. By the plants."

"They don't eat your crops, though?"

"No, never. They're pretty helpful, actually."

Tallulah nodded slowly. "Helpful rabbits, wow. Why do you suppose that is?"

"I have no idea," said Carl. "My sister might know. I'm not sure."

"Your sister?" Zane said quickly. "Can we talk to her?"

"You could try. She's not that great at talking, though." Carl glanced at the house. "She's mostly still a baby."

"A baby, okay." Zane wrote it down. Tallulah's face was blank. It was only a matter of time before she decided he was pulling her leg. Still, he resolved to be as truthful as possible. He was too worn out with hard work and strong feelings to make anything up, anyway.

"Let's talk about insect damage, then," Tallulah said. "You don't seem to have any. How'd you manage that?"

"The rabbits pick the bugs off the plants and eat them. I do it, too—but I don't eat the bugs! That would be gross," he quickly added. "When it gets to be too much work, the birds help."

Tallulah was looking at him strangely. He slowed down, to help her understand. "So, for example: One time the tomato plants got swarmed with beetles. A zillion of them showed up all at the same time. They'd hatched, or molted, or something, I don't really know. Alice—she's one of the rabbits—hopped over to that big tree over there to talk to the birds, and, like, maybe fifteen minutes later, all these blue jays came over and ate the beetles. The tomatoes were saved, yay!" he added, with a half-hearted cheer. It was a story with a happy ending, but Tallulah still didn't seem to be getting the point.

"So the rabbits are helpful, and the birds are helpful, too." Her voice was calm, but a deep frown line had formed between her eyebrows.

"That's so Disney," Zane joked, jotting away. "Animals and plants, working together. It's biodynamic, dude!"

"Only some of the birds are helpful," Carl clarified. "The crows aren't."

Tallulah leaned forward. "Cool. Tell me about the damage done by crows. That's something our readers can relate to."

The water bucket was full. Carl turned off the spigot. "Well, they haven't done any damage, but that's only because we have a really good scarecrow."

"Can we see it?"

"Um. He's not here right now." Carl didn't want them to think he was nuts. Still, he'd gone this far. "You know about John Glenn, right?"

Zane lowered his pen. "The astronaut, or the eagle?"

Tallulah peered over her glasses. "He means the eagle, Zane."

Carl nodded. "Right, the eagle. The crows don't like him. So, when he's around . . ."

"No crows. Got it." Tallulah removed her sunglasses completely and sat back. "Do your parents know about all of your . . . animal helpers, I guess we could call them?"

Carl hung his head and shook it, nope, nope, nope.

She was trying to be nice about it, you could tell. "I'm not accusing you of lying, Carl. But what you're describing doesn't seem normal. It's hard to believe."

"I know, but it's all true." Carl looked downcast. "I guess that means we won't win the contest, huh?"

"I'd like to see some evidence, is what I'm saying."

Carl thought about it. "Okay," he said, "I'll introduce you. But don't make any fast moves. Rabbits get scared easily."

⁂

It was the end of the afternoon, what the photographers at Brad's old job used to call "the golden hour," when the daylight grew soft and rosy and everything just naturally seemed to glow. The last of the visitors were boarding the very last bus. Aunt Phoebe had brought a freshly awakened

Marie outside, and the child was sweet as an angel now that she'd had her nap.

Everyone who remained was playing with the bunnies. Carl was there, and so were the people from the magazine. Marie seemed to have a special knack with the rabbits, who climbed all over her until she squealed with laughter and prattled nonstop. Zane kept snapping pictures and taking notes. Even the scientists had wandered over.

They all seemed very interested in what Carl had to say.

Sally and Brad stood next to each other on the steps outside the kitchen door, soaking it in. The First Annual Prune Street Farm Harvest Festival was winding to a close.

This was the end, and they knew it. They held hands like people on a ship going down.

"It's beautiful, though, isn't it?" Brad said. "Look at this place. Look at the kids. Look at Carl, talking to those magazine editors and scientists! Look at Marie eating dirt! Look at those rabbits! Look how tame they are. It's ridiculous."

"It's been an adventure. I'm glad we tried," Sally answered, a catch in her voice.

He squeezed her oven-mitted hand. "Me too."

Neither one mentioned the Brooklyn apartment they'd impulsively left behind and to which they could never return. Nor did they mention the vast sum of money they'd plowed into the farm, like so much compost dissolving into the dirt.

Sally even chose not to mention how she'd already checked eBay to see what, if any, resale value there was on all the fancy kitchen equipment she'd purchased, and which it was now too late to return.

There was no need to say any of it. They both knew what had to happen next. Brad would call Tom Rowes's office Monday morning and eat as much humble pie as he could stomach. Now that they were desperate, they'd be lucky to get half of what Rowes had offered in the spring, but it was better than letting the bank foreclose.

Neither of them talked about looking for jobs, finding daycare for Marie, and sending Carl back to regular school. They didn't say a word about what it would feel like to work indoors all day under fluorescent lights and head home as the sun was going down, during that dim, crepuscular time when the day problems (traffic, deadlines, bosses) are changing shifts with the night problems (dinner, homework, cranky kids vying for attention, and tired parents longing for sleep).

They were both being very brave.

The last departing bus of the day honked, and honked again, but the honking was in harmony this time, high-pitched and low-pitched, as if a choir of geese had burst into song.

It wasn't birds, though. It was an argument between a cherry-red sports car that was heading up the street toward the farm, and the crayon-yellow school bus that was trying to leave.

Honk! HONK!

Hoonnnnnnk!

"Tom Rowes!" Sally blurted. Inside her oven mitts, her hands curled into fists. That was his cherry-red sports car. He left insolent tire marks on the front lawn as he swerved around the Harveys' station wagon and stopped in a careless diagonal across the driveway.

The yellow bus lurched downhill. The departing onion-scented passengers craned their necks out the windows and pointed. Some pointed at the sports car. Most pointed upward, toward the sky.

A series of squeaky baby seagull chirps pierced the air—

Tik tik tik tik tik!

—followed by an awestruck cottontail exclamation that only the animals and Marie could understand.

"Hey there, young 'uns! Look at me, whee!"

Alice dropped the crudité that the tall red woman with yellow-rimmed bug eyes had given her, and looked up. "It's John Glenn!" she cried. "And Lester!"

CHAPTER TWENTY-EIGHT

May a hawk take you!

Now everybody looked up. The great bird was descending, with something small and ecstatic clutched to his chest.

It was Lester, and the old cottontail was full of joy.

"Well, isn't this something!" the airborne rabbit cried. There was no fear in him at all. Why should there be? As far as he knew, he'd finally gone dark; a supersized hawk had swooped him up and carried him skyward, on a short and scenic journey to paradise. "It's just as I dreamed it would be. A garden overflowing with vegetables! May a hawk take you, in good time, ha ha! And they say those old proverbs are just words. In my case, it seems like an eagle took me, but close enough. And look where I've landed. My, my!"

"Should we tell him he's still alive?" Thistle asked Alice. His tail wriggled so hard it took his hind end with it.

"You can try, but I don't think he'll believe you." Alice's tail was wriggling, too. This was what she'd been hoping for ever since Lester made his wish to visit the garden, but she knew the odds were against it happening. Not because of John Glenn—when she'd privately asked him to offer Lester a ride, the mighty bird agreed at once—but because of Lester himself. That stubborn old rabbit-brain! Would he have the patience and sense to hear the eagle's offer without fear or suspicion? Would he find it in himself to trust a creature so strange and forbidding, with the scent of a flesh-eater rising from his feathers? If Alice had suggested it outright, she knew Lester would have rejected the idea with a "No, sir; no, ma'am; there'll be no eagle's claws on me!" Instead, she'd decided to let nature take its course, so to speak. But she never imagined that Lester would interpret the big bird's arrival as his ride to cottontail heaven! That was a pure delight, the merriest rabbit prank imaginable.

John Glenn floated to the gentlest of landings not ten feet away from where the other rabbits cavorted, releasing Lester when there was no more than a hop's distance to the earth. The old rabbit sat up on the grass and looked around, and John Glenn towered next to him, blinking and preening. He turned his incredible profile first one way, and then another.

The lighting was, admittedly, excellent. The people watching gasped. Eyes filled with tears; hands flew to hearts; and the journalists reached for their cameras. That this highly symbolic apex predator could cradle and care for a soft-bodied rabbit, that defenseless prey from the hard rock-bottom of the carnivore food chain—well, you'd have to have a heart of stone to be unmoved by such a sight.

"Hey hey hey; good afternoon, Brad! Hey, Sally." Tom Rowes was nattily dressed as ever, and strode up to the Harveys like an old friend. "Doesn't this festival of yours look sweet! And this is only the aftermath.

I bet you sold a lot of apples today, didn't you? Why, I expect you've got at least three hundred dollars burning a hole in your pocket right now! That'll get you through the winter in style." He laughed. "Sorry! I know it's not funny. Yet. Someday maybe you'll see it that way."

Sally glued her lips together and eloquently refused to speak. Brad picked up the slack. "Look, Tom: You've made your point. I'll call you Monday. We need to talk."

"Sure, Brad. About what, pray tell?"

Brad's voice dropped. "We need to talk about selling the farm."

Rowes rocked back and forth on his heels. "Well, don't say I didn't warn you. But there's no need to drag it out. I'm here right now. You wanna talk, let's go in the kitchen and talk."

"Can we just enjoy this day?" Sally said, her jaw tense. "Please?"

"What's not to enjoy? Oh, I know it took a while to see your way clear about things, but you and your hubby are about to make the best decision possible, given your current situation. That's cause for celebration right there." Rowes sounded kind, even concerned. "I'm just glad I can be of assistance in your time of need."

Brad's voice was steely. "If you came here to gloat, don't bother. We feel bad enough as it is."

"Now, don't feel bad, Brad!" Rowes looked around, shielding his eyes from the late-day sun. "I never miss the Harvest Festival. I've been by most of the farms, except for the Fleischmans' place. I can't take that smell. Anyway, I saved the best for last. I mean, look at this place. It's the prettiest little failure in town." He gestured expansively. "I do appreciate what you folks have done. For your sake, I wish you hadn't done it, don't get me wrong. You wasted time and money. You swung for the fences and struck out, one two three. But you took a hard swing. I respect that."

"You're so certain that we've failed. Why?" Sally asked pointedly. "Do you think maybe someone sabotaged our efforts?"

Rowes spread his arms wide, a nothing-to-hide gesture. "It's a small town. I have friends on the board of the bank. Let's just say I know who makes their mortgage payments and who doesn't."

"We're not behind on the mortgage." She turned to Brad. "Are we?"

Brad hung his head. "I used the mortgage money to buy that extension ladder we need for picking fruit, and then I had to pay the guys I hired . . . I was going to pay it right back out of the first apple sales, but the irrigation system broke . . ."

"Well, how do you like them apples? Sorry, I know I shouldn't joke." But Tom Rowes kept chuckling nevertheless.

⁂

Lester wasn't a bit surprised to see Alice, Thistle, Marigold, and Berry here in his own personal heaven. He liked these young 'uns, so why wouldn't they be there? Now that he was stripped of all fear, everything was just dandy. The whole world seemed arranged for his delight. He even allowed himself to be petted and coddled by the humans. The people-young 'uns fed him vegetables and stroked his ears. He posed for pictures like a practiced celebrity.

"You're what they call a cherub, aren't you?" he said to Marie. "There were a bunch like you on some pretty little holiday cards I ate once. Say, did you know that I myself am named after a particularly fine strain of tomato? Lester's Perfected! That's me. I'm just about as perfected now as a rabbit can be."

"Perfect," Marie agreed. She took his little rabbit face in her hands and kissed him on the nose. "Perfect bun-bun!"

Meanwhile, Foxy was outraged; her keen pert ears had caught every word of the terrible conversation between the Harveys and Tom Rowes. "Can you believe this bald man! The mockery! The coldheartedness! A cat with a mouse would toy with it less than this Rowes person is toying with my poor humans." She trotted to Marie, who now had Lester in her lap. "Marie, please alert your brother! Your parents are outmatched. We need to do something about it, quick."

Alas, Marie's urgent cries of "Rowes, Rowes, Rowes!" simply made Aunt Phoebe sing "Row, Row, Row Your Boat" to the baby, which didn't help at all. Fortunately, Foxy's herding skills had developed swiftly over the course of the day. Zane, Tallulah, Chuck, and Enrique were deeply engrossed in conversation with Carl, in a tight, sheeplike formation. John Glenn's arrival with Lester had made believers of them all, and now they wanted to hear everything again: "Are these the *exact* rabbits who helped with the farm? How long has the eagle been serving as a scarecrow?" and so on.

Methodically, Foxy ran circles around them, nudging and yapping until they moved nearer and nearer still to where Tom Rowes was obnoxiously chuckling over the Harveys' bad fortune.

Zane leaned closer to Carl. "Hey, who's the rich guy hassling your parents? He sounds like a real jerk."

Carl rolled his eyes. "His name is Tom Rowes. He wants to buy the farm, and he's been really mean about it."

Tallulah's lips curled in distaste. "Let me guess: He's going to build himself a country home? Or maybe a shopping mall?"

Carl shrugged. "I don't know. But not farming. My parents said he'd tear it all down."

"Would your parents sell to him?" Zane asked.

"Never!" Then he thought of his conversation with his dad. Was this what "next steps" meant? "I mean, not unless they had to," he added, suddenly ashamed.

"Zane, see if you can get any of this," Tallulah whispered, and Zane took out his phone.

⁂

Carl's parents were visibly unhappy. "You've made your point, Tom," Brad said, sounding firm. Sally was sniffing back tears. "We'll talk about it Monday."

Rowes reached inside his blazer and took out a sheaf of papers. "No offense, but I'm calling the shots now. Finish up your festival and we'll sit in the kitchen and do business. I hope you don't mind; I brought a few documents over to get the ball rolling. My lawyer drew 'em up. He's a real eager beaver, that guy. Also, he knows I always get my way."

"Stop right there, mister!" It was Chuck, closely followed by Enrique. "It sounds like you're pressuring these people to sell this beautiful farmland. Is that right?"

Rowes took them in slowly. "Who are you two? And why are you sticking your noses in my business?"

The scientists stood their ground.

"I'm Chuck. From ERP."

"I'm Enrique. Also from ERP."

"I see." Rowes folded his arms. "You got a digestive problem or something?"

"I did eat a few too many apples," said Chuck. "But that's not the point. The point is, you should leave these people alone. Leave this farm alone. It's of no use to you."

"Hey, fellas—I know you're trying to help." Brad stepped forward. He sounded nervous. "But this is between us and Tom—"

"Hold on a minute, Brad," Rowes interjected. "I want to hear what these two gentlemen have to say. Explain yourselves. Why is this land of no use to me?"

Chuck looked very smug. "Because even if you did take possession, you could never, ever develop this land."

Rowes cocked his head to one side. "Sorry to contradict you, but the zoning says otherwise. In fact, the zoning is what makes this delightful property so uniquely attractive to me."

Enrique handed Sally a tissue so she wouldn't have to wipe her nose with the oven mitts. "The zoning doesn't matter," he said.

"Is that what you think?" Rowes's jaw started to twitch. "I've been developing land in this area for thirty-five years. The Fern Creek Fashion Outlet Mall? I built that. The Springdale Luxury Homes gated community? I built all of those homes. The ClutterKeepers Mini Storage, over by exit sixty? That's mine, too. I know the zoning in this region like the back of my hand, and thanks to a quirk of the surveyor's pen, this particular piece of land is fully zoned for commercial development with no restrictions. That's a rare find in these parts. Land like this is practically extinct! But you two geniuses in cargo pants stand here telling me that the zoning doesn't matter? Why the heck not?"

"Because," said Enrique, with a charming smile, "this land is a designated habitat for the American bald eagle."

Tom Rowes got a look on his face like he'd just swallowed a piece of gum. "That's news to me. Says who?"

"Says him." Enrique pointed at John Glenn, who had returned to his usual spot on the roof ridge of the barn, framed by a glorious sunset. He spread his mighty wings, and the nearby crows took flight, cawing in protest. "And says the Bald Eagle and Golden Eagle Protection Act."

"I thought eagles weren't endangered anymore," Carl blurted.

Chuck gave Carl a thumbs-up. "Correct! They're not endangered, but they're still protected by law. It's a federal statute."

Tom Rowes was turning red. "So what if there's a law? I'm not going to shoot the dang bird. I just want the property."

"According to federal law, you cannot interfere with the substantial lifestyle of a bald eagle, including his natural habitat," Enrique recited. "Prune Street Farm is his habitat."

Rowes paused, then laughed meanly. "Natural habitat! There's nothing natural about what's going on here. Look at the bird! He's playing with the animals he should be eating. He's posing for pictures. He's a scarecrow, for Pete's sake!"

Enrique nodded. "This particular eagle has chosen the substantial lifestyle of a scarecrow, and who are we to argue with that?"

Rowes pointed a finger at Enrique's chest, furious. "I don't care who you are, but you're going to find out who I am, I can promise you that. You'll find out who my friends are, too. I've made some generous contributions to folks in pretty high places, and I get what I pay for—"

"Hey there, Tom, we're from the press." Tallulah pushed forward, flashing her ID so fast he couldn't read the name of the publication. "These scientists are eagle experts and federal employees, and we've got this whole conversation on video. I'm just saying."

Rowes looked around wildly. "You've got to be kidding."

"Dead serious," said Zane, waggling his phone in the air.

"ERP is serious, too," said Enrique. "We have months of recorded data proving that this bird uses this farm as a habitat. We have GPS readings, photographs, personal logbooks."

"And eyewitness testimony," said Chuck, tapping his own temple. There was no question whose eye he meant. "You will never break ground here. ERP will tie it up in court forever or until you lose, whichever comes first."

Rowes held very still, like a cat does when deciding whether it's worth the trouble to pounce. "Old Man Crenshaw told me I'd never get my hands on this land, not in a thousand years. I guess the old geezer was right. I'm outta here," he added abruptly. "Good luck, Harveys. Looks like you're gonna need it. I won't bother you anymore."

Brad threw his hands in the air. "Tom—I don't know what to say."

"Doesn't matter. I've heard enough."

Tom Rowes strode to his car without looking back. He drove away fast, leaving rude tire marks on the grass.

"Well," said Chuck, beaming. "That's settled!" He and Enrique traded high-fives.

Carl's parents looked at each other, frozen.

"Dad!" Carl cried, overjoyed. "Didn't you hear? He said he won't bother us anymore. Now we can be farmers forever! We just need to do that thing you said. Make a profit, or whatever. Isn't that good news?"

Sally smiled and rubbed away a tear. "It's great news, honey."

"It's the best news I ever heard." Brad was so stunned it came out like a robot voice, but he meant it.

"Woof," said Foxy, jumping up on his boy. "Woof, woof!"

Tallulah leaned over to Zane. "I think we've found our Hipster Farmers of the Year, don't you?"

CHAPTER TWENTY-NINE

The totting up.

"We won, we won!" Carl did a happy dance, spinning in place with his arms in the air. He hoisted Marie onto his back and gave her a ride, with Foxy yapping at his heels. "We won, Applesauce, we won!"

"Won, won!" she echoed, her arms around his neck. "Bun, bun!"

Marie was right. The cottontails deserved to be part of this celebration, for hadn't they done the lion's—that is to say, the rabbits'—share of the work?

Leaving his parents to sort out the administrative details of victory—already Tallulah and Zane were talking about photo releases, a video crew, media appearances on local news and even public radio if they could swing it (and Brad was already throwing in a few marketing suggestions of his own)—Carl hightailed it with Marie on his back to the grassy plot by the sheep pen, where they'd been feeding and coddling all five rabbits just a short while earlier, before Foxy had herded all the humans away.

"Alice! Little Guy!" he said, breathless. Little Guy is what he called Thistle, whose real name he didn't know. (Marie had done her best to tell him, but Thistle was not a word she could pronounce; it just sprayed spit everywhere and Carl had gotten tired of getting wet.) "We won the contest! We did it! Hey! Where are you?"

A few crudité remnants were scattered on the grass, which the sheep were quickly cleaning up.

"Where'd they all go?" Carl said to the sheep. By now it just seemed normal to ask them.

"Baaaaaaaaaa," the big ewe said, tossing her head.

"Woof," said Foxy with urgency, and bolted toward the meadow.

"Hey, Foxy, wait up! Hey! You don't have your vest on!" Someone had taken it off during all the photos, as Foxy was just so much more attractively foxlike without it.

"Foxy! Foxy! Come back!" Carl yelled, but he couldn't chase her very well because of Marie on his back.

"Ja Glenn!" the baby said, pointing.

He looked up at the barn.

John Glenn was gone, too.

⁂

Alice had known this moment would come. All spring she'd known, as the days grew longer. All summer she'd known, as the days contracted again, and into the fall, when the nights spread like pools of darkness, stealing daylight at both ends.

And so it had, at twilight, on a day the humans called the second Saturday of October. The animals knew it in their bones. The growing season had come to an end. It was time for winter burrows to be dug and winter larders filled. Bears went to find their winter dens, geese began their migrations, and dappled summer coats were exchanged for winter whites.

It was dusk, and Alice was summoned, as she knew she would be, to the middle of the meadow, a place out in the open and with room to gather, to make good on the promises she had made to so many. The chipmunks, the deer, the raccoons, the possums, the voles, the birds, and so many more—all of them waited for her to take her place on the low stump, so she could be seen and heard.

She found herself wishing Doggo were here, or even John Glenn. But Doggo was long gone, and John Glenn had disappeared after carrying Lester to the meadow. The time for fierce bodyguards was over. Alice would have to settle this business herself.

"We've come for our share," the chipmunks said.

"And we for ours," the voles said.

"And we, and we, and we!" All the animals chimed in, even the other cottontails of Burrow. They wanted their share. Everyone had sacrificed; everyone had agreed to wait, and now they expected to be paid.

"And don't tell us there's none left!" the impatient creatures said. "We can smell carrots on your breath."

"Not carrots," Thistle protested. "Crudités!"

There was a general outcry at that, for the animals were not so simpleminded as to believe that a carrot stick was so vastly different from a carrot.

Marigold was the first of the rabbits to make herself heard over the din. "Who cares about a carrot or two, or a celery stick?" she cried, for she had been stuffed all day with them, and although they were tasty and made for a change, she thought them no better than the sweet grass and clover that grew wild. "That's nothing to be upset about. I want to hear Alice tell us what really matters." Her whiskers flared. "Did you do it, sister? Did you do what you said? Did you stop the Mauler?"

"I don't know," said Alice, and it was the truth. "The Harvest Festival was today, and I think it went well. But you'll have to come back to find out about the Mauler, and to collect your share. I simply don't know yet." She tried to remember what Carl had once said. "The farmer-people have to add it all up first. I don't think it will take long. Let's meet again tomorrow, behind the barn. That's where your shares will be."

"Ah, but tomorrow will never come, I fear. For I'm here now, little rabbit." There was a ripple of white in the meadow. It was Worm.

Everyone drew back. They were all afraid of Worm. Weasels were vicious hunters and fighters, and so stealthy. Just look how he'd snuck in among them, unseen!

"Tomorrow is too late," he cooed. "I, too, have come for my share, and I will not wait one more day."

"Didn't you hear her?" Thistle bleated in terror. "No vegetables until tomorrow! Come back then!"

"I've not come for vegetables, young fellow. I've come for rabbit. That is what we agreed, was it not?"

"It was," said Alice calmly. "I haven't forgotten."

Lester hopped forward. "You want rabbit? Well, then. Here I am!"

Alice's ears shot up. "Lester, no!"

Lester's tail shimmied—shimmied! He thought it was hilarious. "Don't be silly, young 'un. What difference does it make to me now?"

Thistle came forward, too. "Lester, I don't know how to tell you this. You're not dark yet. You're still alive!"

The old cottontail laughed, silently of course, but his tail was a blur of comedy. "I know that, young 'un! Do you think I've lost all my wits? Now, listen to me, you weasel. Leave the little cottontail alone. She's still young, and she's worked hard, for the sake of all of us. She needs more time in the meadow to enjoy herself. I'll go with you right now. I'm ready for you."

But Worm would not be persuaded. "You are not nearly as young and tender as what I had in mind. Besides, this one and I have an agreement."

"We have an agreement with her, too!" the high voice of the chipmunk leader piped up. "If you eat her now, we'll never get our seeds for winter. And that will not do! *Chip-CHUNK!*" At his command, the chipmunks formed a phalanx. There were hundreds there, in battle formation. It was a whole chipmunk army!

Worm sneered. "Since when has a weasel been afraid of a chipmunk?"

"There's safety in numbers!" one brave chipmunk cried.

"Is there, though?" Worm bared his teeth. The front lines flinched.

Alice took a forward hop, to the edge of the stump. "I will keep to our bargain, Worm. But first, these animals must receive what they've been promised. I ask for one more day!"

"One more day!" the chipmunks cried. "One more day, to get our share!"

"What on *earth* is going on here?" It was Foxy, tearing into their midst at a gallop—the sheep had told her the situation was baaaad; dire, in fact. She spotted Worm. "My goodness, that is a *handsome* coat you have! Even more striking than fox fur, and I say that with full admiration for foxes." There was a method to her chattiness, for it gave her a moment to get the scent of the situation. "Handsome, and yet—it seems no one here is glad to see you. Alice, are you all right?"

Before Alice could reply, Berry jumped in to explain. "The weasel wants to eat her right, right now," he said. "And we'd all rather he didn't."

"Well, that's absurd. Of course he won't," Foxy scoffed, but her fur was bristling.

"Get out of my way, dog," Worm hissed at Foxy.

"Foxy! Be careful. He's a good fighter," Thistle warned, with a yelp of fear.

That Worm was a better fighter than Foxy was a given. Weasels were sharp-toothed, experienced killers. Foxy was no match for this. What she had, of course, was confidence.

"Is this *rodent* bothering you, Alice?" the dog asked, oozing authority.

"We did make a deal," Alice confessed.

"Nonsense," Foxy said. "Weasels and rabbits making deals is not a fair exchange at all. You can't possibly negotiate with a ferocious creature who's threatening to eat you. Who could think properly in such a situation? The agreement is null and void," she declared, using a phrase she'd once heard Brad use on the phone with a client. To Alice, she said, "He should never have asked you to agree to such rubbish, and he's not going to eat you now or later. I won't have it."

"A deal is a deal! You know nothing of how we *real* animals live," Worm said, full of contempt. "Now get out of my way and let me take what's mine," he hissed, before hurling the ultimate insult: "You . . . perfumed house pet!"

Foxy's lips drew back in fury. "I may be well-mannered and relatively clean," she snarled, "but I am no house pet! I am a farm dog! I work! I herd! Above all, I protect!"

The Shiba growled as fiercely as any canine before her ever had. She snarled like an animal so wild that no human could dream of taming her. Carl would have been shocked.

Worm got the message. Even as the dog lunged, the weasel bolted, with Foxy in single-minded pursuit.

It had all happened so quickly. Alice was beside herself. She trembled and shook. No one had ever seen her so distraught. Lester, whose vigor had been renewed by his day's adventure, offered to hop with her slowly back to Burrow, so she could rest and settle herself. Otherwise, she was going to make herself go dark with upset, and then what was the point of Foxy saving her from Worm in the first place? Together they zigzagged into the fading twilight, toward home.

All the animals were shaken by Worm's appearance. That Alice had made such a deal with the weasel for the sake of the farm's success also gave them something to think about. With not much pleading required, and the support of Marigold and Berry, Thistle convinced them all to come back tomorrow; and to meet behind the barn to collect their shares, as Alice had asked them to do.

Exactly how he and Alice would provide enough seeds and vegetables to satisfy all these animals was still a mystery to Thistle. But rabbits do have a knack for multiplying, and all animals have the advantage of being inclined to take life one day at a time.

"As the Great Rabbit said: Tomorrow isn't until tomorrow," Thistle reminded himself, "and a lot can happen in a day."

⁂

Tallulah and Zane had finally gone back to their hotel. As soon as they left, Marie was put to bed, yawning, but she'd been happy all evening, prattling in her semi-coherent way to the newcomers and tugging on Zane's mustache as hard and as often as he'd let her.

"Hey, Applesauce! You're a cool little dude, aren't you. Ouch! Strong, too." Zane closed his eyes. "Isn't it cool to imagine all the stuff that goes on in a baby's head? If only they could tell us. Like animals. Don't you wish you knew what they were thinking?"

"Baa baa baa," Marie said, tugging.

"I think she thinks you look like a sheep," Tallulah teased.

As it turns out, that was exactly what Marie was thinking, and she laughed uproariously that somebody finally got it right.

Brad and Sally kept their brave faces on until the magazine people left. They expressed *so* much gratitude for the contest win, *so* much excitement, they couldn't wait, this would be a game changer. They said all the right things in all the right ways. Then the door closed.

Brad counted to ten and turned to his wife. "Hey! Did you hear the one about the farmers that were going out of business? There's good news and bad news . . ."

"Brad, don't."

"The good news is, they're still in business. And the bad news is . . ."

"What's the bad news?" asked Carl, who'd just come in from yet another anxious trip outside. He liked a good joke, but his dad's jokes were mostly not that good.

Brad sighed. "Never mind, champ."

Sally looked annoyed. "It's not funny, Brad."

Carl hadn't come in for the jokes anyway. He was worried. "Mom. Dad. Foxy hasn't come back yet."

"This again." Brad looked to be on his last nerve about the dog's wandering habits. "She knows how to find her way home. She's used to being outside."

"Not during hunting season she's not," Sally said darkly.

Brad looked at Sally. "What about the vest?"

"You mean this?" Sally held up the yellow vest.

"I'm really worried, Dad," said Carl.

"I'm worried too," Sally confessed.

Brad frowned. "Okay. Maybe I should go look for her."

"I'm coming with you," said Carl.

Brad considered it. "Fine, champ. We'll both go. Let's grab a couple of flashlights from the basement, it's already pretty dark out . . ."

BANG!

BANG BANG!

The shots rang out through the valley.

"Dad!" Carl cried, his eyes welling up. "Was that a gunshot?"

"It was three shots," Sally said, white as a sheet.

Brad tried to comfort them both, though he, too, felt sick with dread. "It's hunting season, remember? It's okay. We're going to hear shots now and then . . ."

Marie started wailing upstairs, and Brad brought her down.

They waited.

There were no more shots.

Ring! Ring! Ring!

It was the telephone in the kitchen. Sally grabbed it. "Hello?" she said, her voice quivering. "It's Janis," she mouthed to Brad as she listened. "Okay," she said. "Okay. Okay."

She hung up the phone. "Foxy's fine."

Carl started to cry.

"Who got shot, then?" Brad asked.

Sally shook her head. "She's coming right over."

⁂

The animals heard the gunshots, too.

The rabbits didn't worry about Foxy being mistaken for a fox by hunters. That dog seemed to have total control over humans, and the difference between a dog and a fox was obvious to anyone with a working nose. Perhaps they weren't taking into account how dull people's noses were, but still.

Doggo, on the other hand. Doggo was the one in real danger.

"He knew enough to leave. I bet he's far away by now," Alice said to her brother. She'd finally calmed down, but Thistle had started trembling at the first *BANG!* and couldn't seem to stop.

"If it's the fox's time, it's his time," Lester said consolingly. "But you're right to be ill at ease about it, young 'un. It's not a nice way to go."

⁂

It took Janis a while to get there, but the rumble and groan of the tractor gave plenty of notice of her arrival. "My car's in the shop," she explained. "But look who's riding shotgun!"

At the word *shotgun*, Carl let out a little moan, like he'd been hit in the stomach. There was Foxy in the tractor, panting and wide-eyed. She was unharmed, but her tail was not what you'd call furled.

Janis climbed out. There was a bloodstain on the top of her dungareed thigh. She didn't seem to know it was there. "This brave pup of yours needed a ride home. I can't believe she made it all the way to my place. She's got more stamina than I gave her credit for. More spunk, too." She gave the dog a rough tousle, which made Foxy's ears flatten in distaste.

"What was she doing at your place?" Sally asked.

"Chasing this guy."

Janis reached into the cab and held up a dead animal. Long-bodied, with a black nose and a black tail tip. The rest of him was pure plush white, except for a dark spot where the bullet had entered. "The chicken killer. That dog of yours flushed him out and chased him right into my sights, like a good hunting dog should."

Brad gave the dog a half-hearted "Atta girl," but none of them liked looking at the dead weasel. Sally kept trying to cover Marie's eyes. "First sheep herding, now hunting," Brad went on. "What next, huh, Foxy?"

In answer, Foxy climbed down off the high seat of the tractor and jumped to the ground. She trotted directly over to Carl and leaned against his legs, eyes closed.

Sally's eyes were shining all over again, this time from pure relief. "She's giving you a dog hug, honey. What a good girl. Extra treats for you, Foxy."

"Woof," Foxy said, but it was little more than a whimper.

Janis looked at Foxy with new respect. "That's a good dog you've got there. Pound for pound, weasels are the meanest fighters in the valley. If your dog had been raised here, she'd have learned long ago to leave weasels alone. Poor thing didn't know any better. Just goes to show, one brave heart can outgun a whole regiment."

"Stop saying gun!" Carl said. A moment later he was crying. Marie started crying, too. Sally wasn't far behind.

Brad didn't know what to do. "What's the matter, champ? Foxy's okay. Everything's okay."

Carl sank to the ground and hugged his dog. He turned his furious, tearstained face to Janis. He pointed at the dead weasel, lying across the seat of the tractor.

"You *shot* him!"

Janis kept a level way about her. "You're dang right I did. He's been killing my chickens."

"He was just trying to eat," Carl returned heatedly.

"I don't blame the weasel for wanting to eat chickens. I like to eat 'em, too. But those were my chickens. Not his."

"That doesn't mean you had to shoot him!"

"Hey, hey," Brad said, still trying to comfort the boy, but Carl shook him off.

Janis spoke gently. "He was already caught in a trap, kid. Believe me, it was the kind thing to do."

At the word *trap* Marie howled, "Doggooooooo!"

Sally consoled the baby. "Foxy's fine, sweetie, see? She's right here." But of course, Marie was worried about Doggo.

Brad turned to Janis. "You set traps, finally?"

"Once the critter figured out how to get into the chicken coop, it was him or me." She shrugged. "I owed it to Florence."

Carl began to cry all over again. He was sad about Florence, but he was heartbroken about the weasel. It was so cute, like a sock puppet, its thick fur pure white except for a dark button nose and the tail tip that looked like it'd been dipped in ink.

Why did life have to be so hard? Why did cute things have to die? Why did chickens have to taste so good? Why did everything have to eat and be eaten? It all just seemed so mean-spirited.

Janis gazed at Carl. She didn't seem mad at all. "I'm sorry, kid. The food chain's no picnic. See what I did there? Food? Picnic? It's a pun."

"It's not funny!" Carl wailed.

"I know it's not funny. But it's not a tragedy, either. Trust me, a weasel's nothing to get sentimental about. Neither is Florence, really. Remember, I was planning to eat her myself, come Christmastime."

"You are so gross!" he yelled, and ran off. He was angry, but also confused, and sad, and guilt-ridden, and a few other feelings mixed in.

After all, Carl had eaten plenty of chicken in his day, too.

He just didn't know whose side to be on.

CHAPTER THIRTY

The taste of victory.

The Harvest Festival had been a day of victories at Prune Street Farm, and a day of some other things, too.

First and foremost was the victory of science and the rule of law, as Tom Rowes was made to row, row, row his little red sports car gently down the street for good.

There was the victory of the Harvey family, now anointed as *Hipster Farmer* magazine's Hipster Farmers of the Year. Their photo would grace the cover of the December issue and make them the most well-known farmers in the valley, for a while, at least. What they'd do with all that free publicity was yet to be determined, but winning was winning, and nothing to scoff at.

Most victorious of all was the triumphant return of Foxy, the bravest Shiba around! Foxy, the weasel chaser! Foxy, defender of rabbits and protector of chickens!

Every elegant bone in her body ached from that long-distance chase across the meadows and through the trees to Janis's farm. She'd even had to cross a two-lane road, with actual cars zooming by! That was the most terrifying part of her ordeal. She knew she was supposed to "look both ways" (she'd heard Sally say it a million times), but there was no time for looking while in the fever of the hunt, racing pell-mell after your prey.

Not once did Foxy consider what would happen if she actually caught the dang weasel. That's a species-wide quirk of the canine brain, and if you've ever seen a dog chasing a garbage truck, you know all about it. If at any point during the chase the weasel had turned to fight, he'd have had his teeth in her throat before she could utter a single charming remark.

So why did he bolt? Instinct, probably. He might have meant to lure her to familiar ground before turning. Or perhaps he wanted to tire her out with a difficult chase before the fight. Or perhaps, somewhere deep in his weasel heart, he truly had a split second of doubt, when faced with Foxy's unassailable self-regard and noble defense of her friends.

Whatever his motive, in his careless rush, he ran right into one of Janis's traps. The mortally injured weasel let out a harrowing cry that would have drawn every carrion eater in the valley, had Janis not heard him and put a quick end to his suffering.

By the time the panting and disoriented Shiba scratched fearfully at Janis's door, whining for a bowl of water and a ride home, the victory over Worm was complete. But whose victory was it? Foxy's? Janis's? The shotgun's? You could argue it was justice itself that had prevailed by letting the clever, selfless, and brave outwit the vicious. Or maybe it was simply a matter of firepower. As the saying goes, if you bring a weasel to a gunfight, the odds are pretty much stacked against you.

Once back in her own home, Foxy endured the excessive attentions of her relieved family, but she was too tired and full of sadness even for a treat. She curled up in her dog bed and didn't budge till morning.

⁂

Upstairs in his room, Carl slept in fits and starts. His dreams made him restless; all of them ended with a *BANG!* and a whimper. By morning he'd done a wheelbarrow full of thinking. He came downstairs, ate the pancakes his mother had made but politely declined the scrambled eggs, and then asked his parents if one of them could drive him over to Janis's place.

Janis didn't seem one bit surprised to find Carl standing at her door. Then again, Janis had a pretty good poker face in general.

"Good morning, kid," she said, ushering him in. "Want some coffee? Never mind, you're too young. What can I do for you?"

Carl stood up straight, hands by his sides. "I have three reasons for coming," he said clearly, as if he'd practiced the speech, which he had. "First, I want to apologize for being so rude yesterday."

Janis nodded in a thoughtful way. "No need, but I deeply appreciate the good manners. When emotions run high, the mouth runs after. I get it, believe me. I've lost my filter often enough myself. I accept your apology. Let's shake on it."

They shook hands with gusto. Carl resumed his straight-backed position.

"Second," he continued, "I wanted to ask you if you could please get rid of your traps. There are a lot of animals around here who might get into them by mistake."

"Are you worried about your dog?"

"Yes, but other animals, too. Like rabbits," he said. "The harvest season is pretty much over, and rabbits are no threat to your chickens. I just think we should try to live and let live, you know? As much as seems reasonable, anyway."

"That's a fair point." It seemed like Janis was trying not to smile. "I agree to your request. I'll take the traps in today. I'm no big fan of traps myself. I had to be pushed to my limit to set 'em. But I was pretty riled up about Florence."

"I know. That's the third thing." He cleared his throat. "If it's all right with you, I'd like to go talk to the chickens."

⁂

The exact details of what was said in the chicken coop that day was a private matter, known only to birds and boy. Janis had offered to go in with him, but he said no. He wanted to do it alone.

"I keep a clean coop, but it's still gonna smell," she warned.

Carl didn't care. He went in by himself, and he came out by himself. In between he said everything he'd planned to say, and more.

Not that it was easy. He'd been raised to give thanks before a meal, but he'd never had to face a whole chicken coop full of potential extra-crispy drumsticks before, all looking at him the way chickens do, shifting their plumed heads first one way, then another. They reminded him of the pigeons in Brooklyn: the beady bird eyes, the comical jerky motion when they walked, the way they had wings but didn't seem like they'd be that good at flying.

Like many a eulogist before him, Carl stuck only partly to his prepared speech and improvised as the spirit moved him. It was too late to thank Florence for her eggs, but at least he could offer his condolences to the rest of the flock.

Janis had given him a small pail of feed to bring as a peace offering, and that went over well. Whether the birds were as moved as Carl was by this exercise in saying grace while the meal was still alive and clucking is something only the chickens knew. But they didn't seem to hold a grudge, even after he'd shakily confessed his best estimate of how many chicken fingers he'd eaten in his young life. He'd done the math, and it was a lot.

⁂

While Carl was with the chickens, Brad drove to town and bought the Sunday papers. Then he drove aimlessly, killing time and wasting gas as he waited to pick up his boy. Brad liked to drive while thinking; it calmed him somehow. Today he was thinking about how to save his family from the catastrophic victory they'd just been handed.

Sally had a more fuel-efficient approach to managing stress: When in doubt, wash the dog. Consequently, she and Marie were in the midst of giving their returning hero the most lavender-scented bubble bath imaginable when a far less delicate aroma began to pervade the premises. Moments later, there was a knock at the door.

Farmers are early risers, remember, and news travels lightning quick in a small town. The neighbors had already gotten wind of what had happened with Tom Rowes. None of them particularly liked Rowes. He'd long been in the business of buying farmland from struggling farmers and turning it into parking lots, shopping malls, and homes no farmer could afford. They considered Rowes a scavenger with a nose for blood, who waited until a farmer was caught in a financial trap so he could swoop in for a meal. To see the vulture Rowes get beat by a big bird and a couple of true eggheads was a source of merriment in more than one farmhouse that morning.

Rowes's predatory interest wasn't the only clue the neighboring farmers had that the Harveys must be in trouble. The early years of running a farm are always a learning curve. First season harvest blues? They'd all been there. They knew that Brad and Sally probably were out of cash and out of hope.

The neighbors had problems of their own, of course. Many of them weren't much better off than Brad and Sally when it came to totting up the numbers at the end of the season, but that didn't matter. Farmers are a little like cottontails in that way. They'll mind their own business out of respect, but they know when to lend a helping hand, too. Now that time had come. Larry Fleischman Junior had transported it all himself, and the truck was loaded with baskets, baskets, and more baskets.

Sally couldn't believe it. It was a welcome wagon deluxe. Nearly every farm found a way to pitch in. They'd all picked and washed and cooked to excess in preparation for the festival, and there was plenty left over. Some of it could be frozen, some was already put up in jars and would keep. Those who could tucked a few bills in their baskets, too, whether it was five dollars or fifty.

The farmers shared what they had, and what the Fleischmans had was onions. Ten large bushels, to be precise, along with a big paper bag of the best deep-fried onion rings imaginable. Foxy sneezed repeatedly at the smell, or maybe it was from having been rushed out of her bath without a proper toweling-off.

That Sally's eyes filled with tears at the sight of this offering goes without saying.

"I know it's a lot of onions," said Larry Junior sheepishly. The twins were with him, and lugged all ten bushels into the root cellar in the back of the barn. They did it gladly, as they liked to show off how strong they were. "But you folks are into all that dehydration stuff. Maybe you'll be able to find a use for them."

⁂

When twilight came, the animals of the valley gathered once more, as near to the back of the barn as the meadow reached. They were in a less argumentative frame of mind than they'd been the previous day. Every creature within a mile of the nearest blue jay's squawk—which is to say, all of them—knew what had happened to Worm.

They weren't upset about it the way Carl was, or as righteously pleased as Janis, but they did feel something. A trap *and* a shotgun! It was not the best way to go; on that they all agreed.

Alice sat up on her hind legs, the better to be heard. Rabbits don't have tear ducts, but she sniffed hard, the way a person might if she were crying. "I know you've come for your share of the harvest," she began. "You'll get it, I promise. But first I want to say a few words of farewell . . ."

"For the weasel?" one of the voles asked. "Why? He wouldn't have done the same for you!" The other voles squeaked in agreement. Their eyes, too, had grown shiny. Of course, they weren't used to being in the light. Even this dim time of day was a bit much for them.

"I suppose it's only fair that we include him," Alice said quietly to Thistle, who nodded without enthusiasm. "All right. Farewell to Worm, a wild creature living according to his nature. As are we all."

"As are we all," the animals repeated.

One of the possums rubbed his eyes with his paw. A few of the chipmunks started to have sneezing fits. Alice waited for the worst of it to subside, and went on. "I would also like to express my gratitude—"

"Hey," said one of the raccoons. "Why does it smell like onions?" The raccoons knew all about onions. They were garbage eaters, which meant they'd tasted everything that any person had ever dumped in the trash.

Alice and Thistle conferred again. "Better skip the speech," Thistle advised. "We ought to get to the main event."

Alice knew her brother was right, but she was disappointed, as she'd prepared a few remarks for the occasion. Sitting up tall, she addressed the crowd. "You've come here to get your share of the harvest. Good news! There's more than enough for all of you. Fresh onions for everyone! Take as many as you like."

The discovery of this windfall could have been counted as a miracle by Alice and Thistle, if animals believed in miracles. But animals don't tend to think of things that way. Seeds sprout, the sun rises and sets, the rain falls, new litters come. That's just nature's glorious business-as-usual, and if winter can change to spring, and spring to summer, and summer to fall, surely a heap of onions could show up in an unlocked root cellar just when you needed it.

Most of the animals dug right in. Many had grazed on wild onion grass in the meadow, so this wasn't so very different; the farmed onions were just way more flavorful and juicy. However, the chipmunks had never tasted anything like onions, and the smell was so strong they were hesitant to try. Their leader went first, as befitted his role.

"Pungent," he observed. Then he took a bite. His eyes filled with chipmunk tears. "And delicious!" That was all his many followers needed to hear.

"But what about our seeds?" one of the chipmunks cried, when his belly could hold no more. "For the winter?"

Providence seemed to have taken care of this, too. "Any seeds you find in the garden are yours to gather," Alice said, "and Thistle will show you a special surprise, too."

Thistle led them to the nearby compost heap, where an abundant layer of Sally's dehydration experiments had been tossed in a fit of pique, after that last terrible visit to Loco for Locavore. The dried fruits and vegetables were tasty and nourishing and would keep all winter long. "It'll be a nice change from seeds," he said, as the chipmunks ransacked this remarkable find.

The dried apples were universally liked, while the radish coins appealed to those with spicier tastes. But the chipmunks came to love the onions best of all, so much so that Foxy donated a few of her GlitterTooth Chew-Bones for their winter stores. She was in her yellow vest again, but there was no need to keep her tied up or remind her to be careful. She'd seen firsthand what the world could be like, the best of it and the worst, and all that lay between.

"Take these, you wee little rodents!" she said, generously nosing her gift toward them. "It's bound to get stuffy underground. There may come a day when you might appreciate fresh minty breath." To her delicate dog's nose, the chipmunks' aroma was already unbearable.

⁂

Many of the animals were newly deferential to Alice as they took their leave. They treated her more like an apex predator than a hardworking cottontail. She didn't understand why until later that night, when she and Thistle were back in Burrow, full-bellied and sleepy, and smelling an awful lot like onions themselves.

"We did it, Alice. We became farmers," said Thistle. "We paid back all the animals, just the way we promised. And we stopped the Mauler from coming!" Foxy had assured them they'd stopped it. In fact, she'd reenacted the scientists' magnificent takedown of Tom Rowes several times. The dog had witnessed the momentous occasion with her own eyes, nose, and ears, which made her all the more eager to tell and retell the tale, with new embellishments each time, of course.

"Well, I think John Glenn mostly stopped it, with Foxy's help," Alice replied. "Foxy said those man-people with the pockets on their legs had something to do with it, too."

"But we helped, too, didn't we?" Thistle snuggled close for warmth. "None of it would have happened without us!"

"Absolutely. We were in-dis-pensable!" she said, imitating Lester. They were still feeling sentimental about the old rabbit, who'd been so utterly satisfied with his high-flying garden adventure that he'd quietly and peacefully gone dark early that morning, hunkered under his favorite tree at the wood's edge, not too far from Split Rock. They'd found him at the morning graze, already covered by the autumn leaves. The rabbits of Burrow were deeply grateful that any of their kind could enjoy a life so full and so long and come to such a peaceful end. It was a rare thing, and if any cottontail deserved it, it was Lester.

That's what Alice had planned to say to the animals of the valley earlier, behind the barn, but there really was no need to say it. There hadn't been a kit born for years who hadn't learned the ways of cottontail life from Lester. His wisdom and his old rabbits' tales would live on and on, until there were no more rabbits left to remember them, may that day never come.

There was a sniffing in the dark. A tiny doe, maybe four weeks old, had crept through tunnels to the den where Alice and Thistle were resting.

"Are you Alice, the brave cottontail that everyone talks about?" the kit asked, in her wee piping voice.

"I am," Alice said, amused. "And who are you?"

"My name is Radish," the kit said.

This made Thistle chuckle. "Careful, young 'un!" he said. "My sister Alice doesn't like radishes much."

"I can't see your tail so I can't be sure," Radish answered, "but I think you might be joking."

"This one is well named. She has a nice bold flavor," Thistle remarked to Alice.

Radish may have been young, but all rabbits are born to joke and tease, and she understood that Thistle meant to be funny. Her tail shimmied politely, and she went on, "Alice, the kits in my litter want to know: Is it true that you had one of your humans kill the weasel?"

"Silly kits! Of course not," Alice exclaimed. "In the first place, I don't have humans of my own. Only tame animals keep humans. But even if I were tame, I would never have done what you just said. The weasel met his own fate, in his own time, as we all must. I had nothing to do with it."

Skeptical, Radish flicked her whiskers. "Some of the kits are saying that you did, though."

"It's not true, and you oughtn't go repeating it. Now, it's late and getting cold. Come in here and cuddle up. We're tired and ready to sleep."

The little kit did as Alice said and fell asleep at once, as babies do.

"And that's how old rabbits' tales get started," Thistle murmured drowsily.

"Don't you go repeating it, either," she whispered, so as not to wake up Radish.

It was only a few more breaths before Thistle and Alice were asleep as well. They were warm and safe and their work was done. They slept the deep, restful sleep of farmers in the off-season.

CHAPTER THIRTY-ONE

A plum idea.

A few days later, as his family was sitting down to dinner, Carl announced that he would henceforth be a vegetarian.

"No more chicken fingers for you, huh?" If Brad was amused, he was doing a good job of hiding it. "What prompted this decision?"

Carl unfolded his napkin and put it in his lap. "I like vegetables now," he said. "More than I used to. Now that I've gotten to know them better, I mean."

His mother delivered a platter of baked butternut squash to the table and took her seat. The roast chicken was already there; it had always been one of Carl's favorite dishes. "So, this has nothing at all to do with visiting Janis's chickens?" she gently asked.

"It sort of does. They had more . . . personality than I was expecting. But I don't think I was *wrong* to eat them, before." Carl had given the matter quite a bit of rumination since his visit to the chicken coop. "Like

Janis said: The food chain is no picnic. But I could have thought about it more. About the birds, and what their lives were like. I guess I could have been more grateful."

"Now that's what I call saying grace," Brad said, picking up his fork. "Let's eat."

It was a lovely dinner, all things considered. Now that selling the farm to Tom Rowes wasn't an option, the Harveys were taking a moment to breathe and give thanks for having made it this far. Mostly, they had to figure out what to do next. Winning the *Hipster Farmer* contest felt like an opportunity, if they could only find a way to take advantage of it. The golden parachute was gone, the bank account nearly empty, but there was food in the house and the mortgage had been brought up to date, thanks to the neighborly gifts of moolah found in all those baskets.

Sally and Brad had called and thanked every one of the folks who'd sent over a contribution. In typical farmer style, their benefactors all said the same thing: No thanks necessary, any neighbor would do the same. As Dorothy the pie lady told Sally, "Don't worry about it, honey! No one gets a ticker-tape parade for bringing a pie to a potluck; it's just the right thing to do. Now, tend to your family's business, and you'll be able to help the next person who needs it."

Dorothy's friend Phyllis had long ago corrected her mistaken assumption about Carl's vision. When she realized her error, she laughed so hard she nearly dropped her rolling pin. Her farm was little more than a big backyard, but she grew cut flowers year-round in a greenhouse. She'd sent the Harveys a beautiful wildflower bouquet with a ten-dollar bill stuck in it—and, to Carl's great satisfaction, a homemade apple pie.

⁂

Like Alice, Carl was being treated a little differently these days. Tallulah and Zane had privately assured the Harvey parents that their article about Prune Street Farm was not going to mention Carl's wild tale about his secret animal helpers. Instead, they'd focus on the photogenic John Glenn. Zane had snapped some great pictures of the bird, and the "cover concept" was coming right along. "We know you're gonna love it," Tallulah assured them. "Carl's an imaginative kid, and a talented young farmer. His way with those wild rabbits was nothing short of miraculous! But we like to offer our readers stories that inspire. Tips and tricks they can put into practice. We want to help them find their own way to be better farmers."

"We don't want to freak them out, basically," Zane added. "Carl's an awesome dude, though!"

On that the Harveys all agreed, Marie and Foxy included: Carl *was* an awesome dude. His parents didn't question his version of events, but they didn't prod him to say much more about it, either. Carl soon grew weary of how nice they were being, and how careful, like maybe they thought there was something wrong with him.

Finally, one night when they'd invited Janis over for a friendly game of Monopoly, he asked them outright: "Mom. Dad. Do you believe the stuff I told Tallulah and Zane? About the rabbits?"

"I bleev," said Marie, who was sitting in her mother's lap. She was in charge of the bank.

"I bleev, too," said Sally, rolling the dice. "Why wouldn't I?"

"You're just saying that because you're my mom." He turned to Brad. "What about you, Dad?"

Brad stroked his chin. "Champ, I neither believe nor disbelieve. That's called being agnostic."

Sally moved her token along the board. She was the wheelbarrow. Brad was the boat, Janis was the horse, and Carl was the dog.

"Pay up, Applesauce! Your mom passed Go." Janis assisted by removing two hundred-dollar bills from Marie's mouth.

"Thank you." Sally took the damp moolah and poked Brad with her foot. "How can you be agnostic in the face of a miracle?"

"Wait. You think the rabbits were a miracle?" Carl was dumbfounded. He'd spent plenty of time with Alice and Little Guy. They were just nice, ordinary cottontails who liked to farm. It was unusual, maybe, but nothing more than that.

Brad leaned back. "I think your mom is speaking poetically, champ. Everything in nature is a miracle. This farm is a miracle. You and your sister, both miracles!"

"I'm not being poetic, and I'm not talking about the rabbits." Sally traded in some houses for a hotel. "I'm talking about the way those onions disappeared overnight." So far, about half the onions the Fleischmans had given them had been carted away with no sign of human activity to explain it, just a great many paw prints of various sizes and shapes, leading to and from the root cellar. She looked at Carl meaningfully. "Whoever took them is welcome to take the rest."

"That would be a real miracle," Brad remarked. "This farm is making my eyes water!"

"This farm is weird," Janis said, taking the dice from Sally. "Weird, but nice. Oh, I almost forgot. I have a message for you. Here, hold these dice, Applesauce. You can blow on them for luck but no drool, got it?" She fiddled with her phone. "It's a voicemail; hang on."

She put the phone on the middle of the board and they all leaned forward to listen. A tinny voice emerged, gruff and creaky, like a robot version of a very old man. "Uh, hello there. Brad, Sally, Kid, Applesauce—I hope I got your names right, I'm just going by what Janis told me. My name's Art Crenshaw."

Carl scooted back and nearly knocked over the game board. "It's Old Man Crenshaw!"

"Let's listen," Brad said, and put his arm around Sally.

The old man cleared his robot throat. "Janis told me that you folks have done a bang-up job with the farm. Especially you, Kid." His voice grew muffled. "That can't be his real name."

"Just talk, Pops," a woman's voice replied from the background.

Art Crenshaw's voice returned to a normal volume. "All right. Kid, Janis says you've got the knack. That's good. It takes time to get to know your land, so it's good to start young. Okay, now I don't know what else to say."

"Tell them how you're doing," the woman suggested.

"That's Sarah, my daughter," Art Crenshaw said. "Well, I'm doing fine. Florida's humid and there's too many skeeters. I like being with my daughter and her family. My golf game has improved but I'm using the cart more than I should. Still can't keep my hands out of the dirt. I turned part of the yard into a vegetable garden, so the grandkids can learn a few things about how food gets on the table. That's enough about me."

The woman's voice was full of mischief. "Tell them what you said to Tom Rowes."

"Oh, for Pete's sake—okay. When I heard what happened I couldn't stop myself. I called Tom Rowes. I just meant to leave a message but the dang salesman picked up. Well, I gave him a piece of my mind. 'Back off, Art, I'm a businessman,' he says. I tell him, 'Oh, you're a businessman, all right. How's this one for you: Mankind is your business!'"

Sally turned to Brad and whispered, "Isn't that from *A Christmas Carol?*"

"What's *A Christmas Carol?*" Carl asked. "It sounds familiar."

"It's the one about the mean old miser and the three ghosts and Tiny Tim," Brad whispered back.

Art Crenshaw was on a roll now. "Tom Rowes thinks we need more places to buy stuff we don't need and more mini storage to hold the stuff folks shouldn't have bought in the first place. I say we need clean food and clean air and clean water. 'Get yourself in *that* business and I'll be the first to support you,' I said. Then I hung up on him. Ha, hah!"

Art Crenshaw proceeded to have a coughing fit. His daughter's voice got closer to the phone. "Okay, Pops, that's enough. You're getting all worked up. Come in the kitchen where it's cool."

"All right, I'm coming." He took an audible slurp. "My daughter just gave me some lemonade. The lemons grow like crazy down here, it's really something. Anyway, from what Janis says, it sounds like I sold the place to the right family. That's the main thing I wanted to tell you folks. I'd have called you myself, but my daughter got me one of these new 'smartphones' and now I can't find my numbers anymore. Okay, I'm going to take a nap. Naps and prune juice and golf; that's retirement for you. Getting old's not for weaklings. I always liked prunes, though. Guess that's obvious. Bye-bye, now."

That was the end of the voicemail.

"Wow," Brad said, hand on his heart. "That's amazing. Janis, thanks for this, and for giving such a glowing report to Mr. Crenshaw. It means a lot." His face fell. "We can't disappoint him. We have to make this work. I wish I knew what to do . . ."

"Janis, why is it called Prune Street Farm?" Sally interrupted. "It's mostly apples."

"Now it's apples. It used to be plums." Janis took the dice back from Marie and tossed them hand to hand. "Art told me the story years ago. It wasn't long after he bought this place, after he got home from the service. It was all plum orchards, as far as the eye could see. And then, one extra rainy springtime, there was a fungus."

"A plum fungus?" Carl asked, intrigued. *Attack of the Plum Fungus* would truly be the worst horror movie ever. He couldn't wait to tell Emmanuel.

"Yup. It got some of the cherries, too, but the plum trees were hit hard. The Farm Bureau told everyone to replant with apples to put an end to it. Art switched over and never looked back. Never changed the name of the farm, either, since the town never changed the name of the street."

"So that's why we grow apples on Prune Street . . ." Sally had an alert, focused look about her; she was on the scent of something for sure. She turned to Carl. "You used to hate prunes. Remember?"

"Yes, I do," he said, making a grossed-out face.

"What changed your mind?"

Carl shrugged. "I started pretending they were gummy bears."

"That's it." Sally sat up on her knees. "Pruney Bears. Farmer Sally's Pruney Bears! A tasty, healthy treat for all ages."

"Don't say healthy," Carl suggested. "Say, chewy and sweet."

Brad sat up, too. "The kid's right. Farmer Sally's Pruney Bears. A chewy, sweet treat. Made with care on Prune Street Farm."

"Made with love," Sally amended.

Janis chuckled. "I thought they were made with prunes?"

"Made with prunes *and* love." All at once Sally was full of pep, like it was her first day on the farm and everything was a seed of pure possibility. "I like it. Let's do it."

"It's worth a try," said Brad, only slightly less excited. "We'll need a logo. And a website."

"And a lot of prunes," Carl noted.

"And bears!" Marie threw all the Monopoly money in the air. "Yay, bears!"

Sally stood up and went straight for her apron. "Game over. Okay, people. Let's get to work."

⁂

By now Sally was a whiz at that dehydrator. It didn't take her long to figure out how to make prunes into tiny, chewy, bearlike treats. They weren't *exactly* bear-shaped, but that's the power of branding for you. Call a prune a Pruney Bear and you'd swear the thing looked just like a bear.

But what should they put on the label? A bear? A prune? How about John Glenn? Sally noted that the big bird's picture would soon be on the cover of *Hipster Farmer* magazine and they might benefit from the connection, but Brad nixed the idea. The Eagle Tractor company might be defunct, but images of eagles were still used to advertise everything from chewing tobacco to sports teams. An American bald eagle just didn't suggest dried fruit to the average person, and dried fruit was what they were selling, after all.

Sally didn't disagree, but noted that a prune wasn't very photogenic.

Carl was the one who settled it, by insisting they use a picture of a rabbit on the labels. As he pointed out, there's nothing cuter than a bunny rabbit. Everybody loved them. And they did have rabbits on Prune Street Farm, so why not?

Brad grabbed his pencil. It only took him a few minutes to sketch it.

"Rabbits don't really wear overalls, Dad," Carl commented.

"Well, farmers often do," said Brad. "They're practical."

"A farmer-rabbit!" Sally teased. "So you're not agnostic anymore?"

Brad put a few finishing touches on the straw hat the little rabbit wore, and added a neckerchief and a tractor in the background, too. It looked like Janis, if Janis had long ears and a fluffy tail. "All I'm saying is that, as far as we know, no rabbit in history has ever been a farmer."

"Until now," Sally said, smiling at Carl.

"Until now, possibly." Brad smiled, too. "But there's a lot we humans don't know about rabbits, either."

When the December issue of *Hipster Farmer* magazine came out, with a spectacular photo of the Harveys and John Glenn on the cover, Farmer Sally's Pruney Bears were ready to launch. They got a big batch of orders from the publicity, and the rest was chewy, sweet history. People liked Pruney Bears a lot. By the time the family gathered in front of the fire for their annual reading of *A Christmas Carol* (it was the first annual reading in the big red farmhouse, but it wouldn't be the last), Prune Street Farm was actually turning a profit.

Boxes of plums arrived weekly—they were shipped east from California and other, warmer places with a year-round growing season—and the cartons of packaged Pruney Bears went out twice a week to stores and distributors nationwide. The Harveys got to know the truck drivers by name. Sally often packed them bag lunches of coffee and fresh hummus-on-sourdough sandwiches, which were deeply appreciated.

To the rare naysayers who opined that bears and prunes had nothing to do with each other, Brad merely scoffed, "So what? Neither do goldfish and crackers. Would you like to know how many Goldfish crackers are sold and consumed every year?" He pointed skyward. "It's a number greater than all the stars in the firmament, figuratively speaking."

"If Pruney Bears get one-tenth as popular as Goldfish crackers, we're going to do just fine," Sally would observe, whenever Brad made the comparison. "Now, somebody help me with these plums!"

Janis liked dried fruit to begin with, and was a fan of Pruney Bears from the start. "I know that's supposed to be me," she said to Carl, the first time she saw the finished label. "I'm flattered to pieces about it, kid. I wouldn't be offended if you decided to name that rabbit Janis. I'm just saying."

"Thanks," Carl replied, "but she already has a name."

※

The trucks that now came and went with regularity caused a minor commotion at Burrow. Alice and Thistle hadn't seen the trucks for themselves, as the barren winter landscape was too wide-open for the cottontails to venture that far into the meadow. Grayish-brown rabbits were easily spotted against the snow, never mind the footprints they left everywhere.

But the blue jays told them all about it. Trucks in the driveway three days out of the week! Boxes going in the house and boxes coming out!

"You don't suppose the boy and his humans are leaving, do you?" Thistle asked, quite concerned. "How awful! It was so much work to teach one boy how to farm. Imagine if we had to do it all over again."

"Well, if we have to, we have to," Alice replied, although she, too, hoped the boy was staying. It was a special and unusual thing for a wild animal to have a human know her real name, and naturally it made her feel quite attached to Carl, never mind all that they'd been through together. "The blue jays haven't seen an Arm Waahr come out of the house, so I think they must be staying," she added. "If only we could ask Foxy!"

Asking Foxy anything was not easy at present. Between the weather and the fact that hunting season would continue for months yet, Foxy was confined to the leash and house once more.

Foxy didn't mind, though. Her big personality didn't change the fact that she was a smallish dog, and these unplowed country snowdrifts were way above her head. She'd discovered that the hard way, by bounding into one and sinking so deep into the powdery fluff that only the tips of her pert orange ears were visible.

Carl had lifted her right out, but she got chilled to the bone and had to spend a few cozy hours recovering in her fancy dog bed near the fire. Marie tended to her sweetly the whole time, offering spoonfuls of warm chicken broth in between bites of Foxy's usual prescription food.

"Personally, I wouldn't think less of you if you became a vegetarian, too, Marie," Foxy had remarked. "It's not for me, though, obviously. Give me another taste of that fantastic soup, would you?"

"Obveeslee," she agreed, and dribbled more soup into Foxy's mouth. "Yum, soup!"

"You're quite right; chicken is my absolute favorite. I suppose that poor weasel and I had that in common. I do think of him sometimes. He couldn't help his nature and I can't help mine, but that's just the way of us wild creatures. Semi-wild in my case, I suppose! Humans are different. You get to make up your own minds about so many things. It must be"—the dog yawned—"*very* tiring, having to do so much thinking all the time."

"Sheepy Shiba," Marie said, and laughed, for she was trying to say *sleepy*. But "sleepy Shiba" would be a tongue twister even for a highly experienced talker, and Marie was still spreading her wings in that arena, so to speak.

She rubbed Foxy's belly. "Sheepy, sheepy Shiba," the girl repeated, on purpose this time. It was as if to say, "Now rest and enjoy your soup, dear Foxy, and never mind the cold. Come springtime you'll be herding sheep once more, like the noble and hardworking farm dog you are. The snow will melt and the meadow grass will turn green, and the tender new leaves will rustle on the trees. We'll see the bun-buns again and plant the garden and care for it, and watch it sprout and blossom and grow until harvest time comes—and then it happens all over again; the seasons will keep changing and the earth will go 'round and 'round, forever and ever, amen."

"You cute thing." Foxy was enjoying the belly rub immensely. "I'll miss these conversations, Applesauce."

"Why miss?" asked Marie, who didn't yet know that seasons change for children, too.

"You'll see," said Foxy. "Now, a little to the left, if you don't mind. Ahhh!"

CHAPTER THIRTY-TWO

Plenty of credit to go around.

Prune Street Farm became a pretty well-known farm after all that. It wasn't a household name around the globe, like a chain of fast-food restaurants, or a temperamental chef with his own television cooking show, but there was always a steady stream of customers. The Harveys ran a bustling farm stand at a few different markets, all season long (for this they had to hire full-time help, as they couldn't be everywhere at once). And the annual Harvest Festival grew to a two-day, then three-day affair, and became a much-looked-forward-to celebration in the valley that all the local farmers benefited from.

When it came to giving credit for this wonderful success, most would have ballparked about twenty-five percent as being due to the popularity and wide distribution of Farmer Sally's Pruney Bears. Brad's spiderlike way with a website meant that the farm could market and sell the chewy sweet treats to people and stores all over the country.

Another twenty percent would have to go to *Hipster Farmer* magazine for providing free and eye-catching publicity at just the right time. But to most onlookers (the human onlookers, anyway), the lion's share—that is to say, the apex predator's share—of the credit obviously belonged to John Glenn, genus *Haliaeetus*, species *leucocephalus*, who'd kept the crows and Tom Rowes away, just by being a faithful and honorable friend, and by being both symbolic and photogenic enough to make a good story great.

"Eagle Saves the Farm" was the angle taken by *Hipster Farmer* magazine, and the story got picked up far and wide. Headline writers had a field day: "Keeping an Eagle Eye on Small Farmers," "Are Farmers America's New Endangered Species?" and so on. It wasn't anything like the whole story of what happened at Prune Street Farm, but it helped sell Pruney Bears, so nobody complained.

Here's a sweet thought to chew on: If Tom Rowes hadn't been mean-spirited enough to suggest a hunter might mistake Foxy for a fox, Sally never would have insisted on making the dog wear a yellow vest, and eagle-eyed John Glenn never would have spotted the golden Shiba from afar and visited Prune Street Farm in the first place.

Some folks might call that irony, or even poetic justice. Others might shrug and say, what goes around, comes around. That's the scientific explanation. After all, the world is always spinning, so what goes around is always coming back around, and sometimes it doesn't take long at all. When John Glenn the astronaut became the first American to orbit Earth, he flew around this pretty planet so fast, he saw the sun rise and set four times in one day!

Now, that's going around and coming around in style.

⁂

Tom Rowes had been right about one thing: Farming was a lot of work. Hiring help had freed up some time for Brad, and he started writing a regular column for *Hipster Farmer* magazine. He'd hoped to share his thoughts about beekeeping and his unabashedly poetic vision of how small family farms might teach all of us something about how to live in harmony with nature and one another. Yet once again, his marketing and branding expertise was what the readers wanted. At first, he was disappointed, but he quickly saw the value of it. Most folks tend to have a better appetite for poetry once there's food on the table.

Winters on the farm were quieter but far from idle. Sally's dehydrator was replaced with a bigger model, and when she wasn't ruining perfectly good fruit she was fulfilling orders at the kitchen table, answering the cute letters that kids sent to "Alice," as Carl had dubbed the farm's bunny-in-overalls mascot, and inventing new, healthy, and delicious ways of turning farming into money, just as Lester had long ago explained.

By summer, Brad finally got his beehives working right and mostly bear-proofed. Farmer Brad's Apple Honey started appearing on the shelves right next to Farmer Sally's Pruney Bears, along with baby-sized jars of Farmer Marie's Applesauce.

Carl didn't want any of the farm's goods named after him—he felt funny taking credit when he knew he'd had so much help—but when carrots were in season at the farm stand, he liked to put a sign on them that read RABBIT TREATS. The customers got a real kick out of that.

Speaking of signs: The billboard the Harveys rented on the Thruway was just a little bit bigger then Ruth Shirley Realty's billboard. It had a picture of the whole Harvey family on it, including Foxy. Foxy just loved driving past it. How many dogs get their picture on a billboard? Not many, but Foxy just waggled her doughnut tail and took it as her due.

⁂

Carl homeschooled and worked on the farm all through the following spring and summer, and chose to go to school in the fall. That worked out fine, and he found that friends were easy to make now that he was feeling more friendly toward himself, and more at home in his life in general.

He always stayed friends with Emmanuel. They visited back and forth when they could, and Emmanuel's family even spent part of their winter holiday on the farm. Lying under the Christmas tree, the boys talked about going to camp together. They were too old for Camp Kids in the Woods, but Orin at the library had told Carl about some science camp options that might be interesting. One camp was about dinosaurs and one was about birds. This made it hard to choose since, thanks to Meryl Streep, both boys knew that birds were living dinosaurs anyway.

Thinking about Emmanuel and how different their lives had become led Carl to a shocking realization, which he confided to Janis late one January afternoon, over at her place. It was a cold day and short on daylight. Carl's parents had taken Marie to check out a ballet class in town, and Carl and Foxy opted to have dinner at Janis's house. She had a nice fire going, and there was a big pot of vegetable soup on the stove, almost ready to eat.

They sat and gazed at the upward-leaping flames.

"I thought of something weird," he said. "Marie is going to grow up a country girl."

"So?"

"She doesn't even remember living in the city."

"She was a baby then, kid. Babies don't remember being babies anyway."

"I know. But she won't know about subways and skyscrapers and stuff."

He rubbed his feet on the dog, who was curled underfoot on the rug near the fire. "Foxy, do *you* remember Brooklyn? Remember the pigeons? And the dog park?"

Foxy made a grumbly noise in her sleep, as if to say that urban dog parks were cramped and vastly overrated, full of rude canines who didn't know how to share their toys, and *please* don't get her started about pigeons and their interminable, pointless cooing! She'd rather listen to a blue jay squawk any day.

"Riding the subway seems like a big thing not to know about," Carl said, after a bit. "But I guess city kids don't know a lot of stuff, either." He sighed at his own threadbare observation. It was the kind of thing you'd write in an essay at school: "In conclusion, being a city kid isn't better or worse than being a kid from the country. They're just different. The end." Such teacher-pleasing platitudes hardly caught the complexity of the feeling he had inside him.

The fire crackled and leapt. "You don't have to be just one thing, you know," Janis said. "You can be a cosmopolite."

"What's that?"

"A cosmopolite is a cosmopolitan person. Comfortable everywhere and anywhere, with all kinds of people and all kinds of ideas." She leaned back in her chair. "A citizen of the cosmos."

Carl knew what *cosmos* meant; it was one of the Greek roots he'd studied in his homeschool days. "You mean like outer space? A citizen of other planets?"

She chuckled. "Well, I don't know about that. This planet's good enough for me."

"Me too." Carl's stomach made a noise. "Is the soup ready yet? I'm hungry."

"In a minute, kid." Janis stretched her feet toward the fire. She was wearing her favorite pair of slippers, which she'd made for herself in a moccasin style. When weasel fur is made into luxury items it's usually called *ermine*, but Janis was nothing if not a straight talker. To her, a weasel was a weasel was a weasel.

No matter what you called it, the fur was thick and white and soft as a cloud, and the slippers kept her feet cozy and warm, now and for winters yet to come.

⁂

Alice lived a few more years, which was more than enough for a cottontail. She had quite a good number of litters, too. All rabbits are clever, but Alice's offspring tended to be cleverer than most—maybe that was just Thistle's opinion, but he voiced it often. She became a wise guide to all the young 'uns. She taught them how to be careful, of course, but also how to be brave. She had plenty of old rabbits' tales of her own to tell! Some of them were true, too.

When her time came, she was ready. She collected on a very special favor John Glenn had promised her years before. This was nothing like the deal she'd made with Worm. The business between Alice and John Glenn was a joyous pact between two good friends, and indeed, they had remained devoted to each other until the end.

"I'm ready for my ride today," she told him, without fanfare. It was a fine spring day in the meadow, and it had rained a little during the night. Now the sky was pure bright blue, and the air was so clean and clear, you'd think it was the first day of the first meadow that ever was.

"All right. Anywhere in particular you'd like to go?" he asked, flexing his wings.

"Up there," she said, tipping her nose up to the sky. The sky, that glorious firmament! So blue and so big, and she was so small in comparison—but there was nothing small about Alice, really. Not when you think of all she'd done, and the difference it made in how things turned out, for all the living creatures in the valley between the hills.

"Up there it shall be, then," he said. "Higher than you can imagine."

"Then let's go. Do I need to hop on?" she asked, thinking of the time she'd climbed on his back to free him from the tracker.

"No more hopping for you," John Glenn said. "I'll carry you."

The eagle cradled the wise old rabbit with a wing and drew her close to his thickly feathered breast.

"Oh, this is soft!" she said, delighted. "I'd like to see the river, I think."

"I can show you where it flows into the sea," John Glenn said. "That will be a view that no rabbit has ever seen before."

Well, it wasn't the first time Alice would do something no rabbit had done before. Her nose twitched with anticipation. "That sounds wonderful. Let's stay up a good long time. And when I've had enough, I'll close my eyes and be gone. You can just put me down anywhere, then. I'll already be dark."

John Glenn's golden eyes softened. "And what would you like to happen next?"

Alice hadn't thought ahead that far, but she remembered something the great bird had said to her, long ago. "John Glenn, you make a meal of rabbit now and then, don't you? Would that be too much to ask? I know you prefer fish. Still, perhaps you'll be hungry after a long flight."

"I could do that, if you so choose," the bird replied. "But you love the soil, too. You could go back to the earth. I'd bury you myself. My claws are more than capable of that much digging. Either way, we'll always be together."

Alice's tail shimmied with pleasure. "These are both such lovely ideas! Can I decide in the air?"

"Of course," the eagle said. "I always do my best thinking up high. Shall we go?"

The eagle gathered her up with his great clawed feet, and spread his broad wings until they shadowed the ground. With a mighty downward stroke, the two friends were in the air, and rising.

⁂

Through the window in the upstairs playroom, Foxy watched the eagle circle the farmhouse, gaining altitude with each beat of its wings, cradling something small to his chest. The dog whimpered, low and long.

"What's the matter, girl?" Carl looked up from his algebra book. "Do you want to go out?"

"She's hungry. I'll get her a treat," Marie said, putting down her crayon. She was practicing for kindergarten, where she'd been told that coloring with crayons was a big deal. She hardly looked like her picture on the billboard anymore; that's how fast children grow.

Foxy kept her front paws on the sill, gazing out and up. "What kind of glutton would beg for food at a time like this!" the dog replied, full of feeling. "What do I care for treats? I just watched a dear friend fly to her final resting place. Farewell, sweet Alice! A bunny among bunnies, indeed. I salute you, oh brave rabbit, and all that you did for us. We will never forget, never!"

But all the two children heard was *woof, woof, woof.*

⁂

Season after season, the new kits of Burrow would listen raptly to the story of a young eastern cottontail who became a farmer herself, and who saved the whole valley from the Mauler for the benefit of all rabbits and their descendants.

It was a wild and improbable story, no question. By the end of it, the kits' teeth would be chattering with disbelief. "Aw, come on, Thistle!" they'd say. "That's just one of your old rabbits' tales! Isn't it?"

And Old Thistle, who by then had lived to be the oldest rabbit in the warren, would shimmy his tail and answer, "Don't be so skeptical, young 'uns! This tale's as true as they come. It's true as the sunrise. I know it is, because I was there."

But you know how young 'uns are. They thought the old bun-bun was pulling their whiskers. Thistle didn't take offense. He'd just take out his most precious possession, an empty glass jar with a label on it that showed a cute little cottontail in overalls. A raccoon had found it in the human trash and brought it to Burrow as a token of respect. Imagine! A raccoon, showing respect to a cottontail! But the other animals of the valley hadn't forgotten, either.

"There's my sister," Thistle would say, showing the picture around. "That's Alice, right there."

That gave the kits something to think about. By the time the next batch of litters were leaving the nest, it was the older kits who were passing on the tale to the younger ones, who did the same when it was their turn.

The warren wasn't running out of rabbits any time soon; no, sir. And where there are rabbits, there are rabbits' tales. That's something that will never change.

By then, the people of the region had taken to calling Prune Street Farm the old Harvey place, even though the Harveys weren't old at all, and wouldn't be for a great many years to come. But to the creatures of the valley between the hills, it was Alice's farm, pure and simple.

–THE END–

AUTHOR'S NOTE

The real John Glenn was the first American astronaut to orbit Earth. That happened the same month I was born, in February of 1962.

His spacecraft was called *Friendship 7*. A fine name, don't you think? It reminds me of one of my favorite books, which I want to mention here because *Alice's Farm* owes a debt of inspiration to it.

Of course, I'm talking about *Charlotte's Web*, written in 1952 by the great E. B. White, and still read and loved today by children and adults all over the world.

Charlotte's Web takes place on a family farm, where animals, humans, and a very special spider share a remarkable adventure over the course of a single growing season, from springtime to harvest. Together, they learn a thing or two about the beauty of life, how precious and sometimes difficult it can be, and how miraculous, too. Above all, it's a book about friendship.

It's been nearly seventy years since *Charlotte's Web* was written. Life on the farm has changed a great deal since then. Much has been written about the challenges facing today's farmers, and the dangers posed by using the wrong kinds of shortcuts to try to grow more crops more cheaply. In answer, more sustainable, soil-replenishing methods that work in cooperation with nature's diverse wisdom are being rediscovered and put into practice.

Even among farmers, there's a wide range of opinions about how to proceed. What sounds far-fetched today may be less so tomorrow. But the job of putting healthy food on the table will always be with us. Finding a way to do this that's good for rabbits and good for farmers—by which I mean, good for the earth and all its inhabitants, the people and animals and insects and birds, the plants and fish and all living things—well, that's going to take some bravery, cleverness, and cooperation. It might mean trying things that have never been tried before, and acting neighborly toward those we see eye to eye with and perhaps especially toward those we don't. It'll surely mean seeking common ground with each other, and putting in plenty of hard work, too.

Everybody's got to eat, after all.

Few of us will ever get to see firsthand what John Glenn saw when he and *Friendship 7* orbited Earth in 1962 and witnessed the sun rise and set four times in one day. Yet even in the sprouting of a single seed, the everyday miracle of life is at work. We too can feel awe and gratitude for it, just as that brave astronaut did when he gazed upon Earth, its shining seas and fertile land, its mountains and deserts and poles capped in ice, all wreathed in clouds like cotton candy; the delicate, beautiful planet we call home.

"Oh," said John Glenn, "that view is tremendous."

Maryrose Wood

ACKNOWLEDGMENTS

It takes a cozy warren full of industrious geniuses to bring a book to life, and my gratitude runs deep and wide. First thanks must go to my editor, Liz Szabla, whose serene confidence in this book, from first scribble to last dotted i, has made all the difference.

The gang at Feiwel and Friends are simply wonderful, as befits being led by Jean Feiwel, whose passion for children's literature is a treasure. Special thanks to the Macmillan dream team: Mallory Grigg, Kim Waymer, Alexei Esikoff, Cynthia Lliguichuzhca, and Mary Van Akin.

I cannot get over the tender beauty of Christopher Denise's cover art and interior illustrations. Thank you, Chris.

As for my own stellar team, deepest thanks to my witty and insightful literary agent, Brooks Sherman, as well as Wendi Gu and Roma Panganiban, all at Janklow & Nesbit. Many thanks to my film rights agent, Mary Pender at UTA, for navigating Hollywood waters with skill and care.

Writers are not always easy to live with, and the family, friends, and loved ones who keep the home fires burning deserve prizes. Love and gratitude to Jason Culp, who is ever steady and true. Thanks to my beloved kids, Beatrix and Harry, animal lovers both, for being so interesting, and interested. Alice has her brother Thistle by her side, and I have Tom and Jim, the best bro team ever; my always inspiring sis, Deb; and my wonderfully supportive uncle, Vito Gassi.

Thanks to my priceless crew of writer buddies for the sanity. I'm grateful to all my clever and committed writing students, past and present, who remind me of what's essential.

I thank the darling fur babies and animal companions of a lifetime, who exemplify presence and love, and remind us how profoundly we can connect across differences, even the difference between two-legged and four. I think especially of my brave Shiba Inu, Lil, to whom this book owes a great debt.

And how can I ever thank my readers? Words fail. This is all for you, all of you; shining lights, every one.

Maryrose Wood

THANK YOU FOR READING THIS
FEIWEL & FRIENDS BOOK. THE FRIENDS WHO MADE

Alice's Farm

A RABBIT'S TALE

POSSIBLE ARE:

JEAN FEIWEL, *Publisher*

LIZ SZABLA, *Associate Publisher*

RICH DEAS, *Senior Creative Director*

MALLORY GRIGG, *Art Director*

HOLLY WEST, *Senior Editor*

ANNA ROBERTO, *Senior Editor*

KAT BRZOZOWSKI, *Senior Editor*

ALEXEI ESIKOFF, *Senior Managing Editor*

KIM WAYMER, *Senior Production Manager*

ERIN SIU, *Assistant Editor*

EMILY SETTLE, *Associate Editor*

RACHEL DIEBEL, *Assistant Editor*

FOYINSI ADEGBONMIRE, *Editorial Assistant*